12|16

CM5

Visit J. Daniels online:

https://www.facebook.com/jdanielsauthor
Twitter: @JDanielsbooks
Instagram: authorjdaniels
www.authorjdaniels.com

ALSO BY J. DANIELS

Four Letter Word

HIT
THE
SPOT

A Dirty Deeds Novel

J. DANIELS

piatkus

PIATKUS

First published in the US in 2016 by Forever, an imprint of
Grand Central Publishing, a division of Hachette Book Group, Inc.
First published in Great Britain in 2016 by Piatkus

1 3 5 7 9 10 8 6 4 2

A CIP catalogue record for this book
is available from the British Library.

ISBN 978-0-349-41174-3

Printed and bound in Great Britain by
Clays Ltd, St Ives plc

Papers used by Piatkus are from well-managed forests
and other responsible sources.

MIX
Paper from
responsible sources
FSC
www.fsc.org FSC® C104740

Piatkus
An imprint of
Little, Brown Book Group
Carmelite House
50 Victoria Embankment
London EC4Y 0DZ

An Hachette UK Company
www.hachette.co.uk

www.piatkus.co.uk

To Mom and Dad

ACKNOWLEDGMENTS

Thank you to Beth Cranford for being my person. For keeping my life running smoothly and for the support you give. Along with Beth, thank you to Kellie Richardson, Lisa Jayne, and Lana Kart for being my amazing beta team. I appreciate you all so much.

To Lisa Wilson, Tiffany Ly, Yvette Trujillo, and Kellie, of course. Thank you for the beautiful teasers you make me. You ladies are so talented, and I am honored to have you as friends.

To Tasha Thomsen, thank you for answering all of my dick-piercing questions. What conversations we've had, girl! To Kristy Jakeway, thank you for sharing your medical knowledge with me. I appreciate all of your help on this project.

To my agent, Kimberly Brower. Thank you for everything! If we haven't eaten peanut butter sundaes together yet, what is wrong with us?

To Leah and the Forever team, thank you! To all of the amazing bloggers who have supported me and this series, I can't express my gratitude enough. You all are so special to me. Special thanks to Give Me Books, Kinky Girls Book Obsessions, Rock Stars of Romance, and The Literary Gossip.

To my wonderful husband—my biggest supporter and my best friend. I love you, B.

And to my readers, hugs and kisses to you all!

HIT
THE
SPOT

Prologue

TORI

"Sheesh. It's like a ghost town in here. I'm bored outta my mind," Shay commented, coming to stand beside me at the counter where I was leaned over, propped on my elbow and doodling hearts on a napkin.

I didn't need to look up and survey the room to know she was right. It *was* like a ghost town in Whitecaps, the hip, ocean-front restaurant where I worked. Not a lot of people were venturing out today in the freezing rain-snow mixture going on outside.

When Nate had hired me a month ago, he said things slowed down in the winter. That made sense. Who hung at the beach in December?

I preferred being busy, as did Shay apparently, but I didn't mind the slow pace today. It gave me time to doodle. I liked to doodle. When I was happy, I doodled a lot.

And holy crap, was I happy.

Shay's shoulder nudged against mine. "Who's Wes?" she asked, pressing close. "He your boyfriend?"

I traced his whimsically scripted name with the dark blue pen and nodded.

"How long have you been together?"

"Few weeks," I answered, looking over at her. "I met him at the market right after I moved here. He was behind me in the checkout line."

Shay smiled.

"Aw, I love tha—"

A loud banging noise coming from behind swung my head around and jolted Shay.

Sean, the cook Nate hired two weeks ago, stalked out of the kitchen holding a rag to his hand, snarling and spitting profanities through gritted teeth while his profile held hard and sharp with irritation.

He was tall and cut out of muscle and bone, no fat or softness to him from what I could tell, covered in tattoos, and either didn't have the ability to smile behind his thick beard or never felt the need.

Intimidating? Absolutely. Scary? A little.

But he seemed cool, stayed quiet and kept to himself, and wasn't bailing on a job that had him surrounded by women seven days a week who never kept to themselves and hardly stayed quiet.

I thought that was saying something.

He crossed the room, lifted his big biker boot, and kicked the men's restroom door open, disappearing behind it.

"I think he cut himself again," Shay guessed, communicating my own speculation. "That's seven times now, right?"

I did a mental count from what I'd either witnessed myself or heard about after the fact. Maybe someone else should be chopping vegetables for him.

"He should change his name to Stitch," I suggested, looking to her. "Fits him."

Shay's mouth twitched. Her dark brown eyes flickered wider.

"I'll call him that if you do," she said a little quieter, as if she was afraid he could hear.

"Deal," I chuckled. I leaned over and began doodling again, darkening in some hearts and heavily outlining the others, my mind on Wes and the date we'd be having this upcoming weekend.

I was really looking forward to it.

He was always working long and late hours during the week. I hardly saw him. Hardly spoke to him either, unless he was calling me back after getting a free minute.

Thank God for texts.

"I'm gonna go see if my one lonely table needs anything, again, even though I just asked them, and until Stitch stops bleeding and gets back to cooking their food, the only thing I have to give is refills and my wit." Shay slapped the counter, twisted away, then stopped frozen on a gasp. "Sweet. He's here," she whispered.

"Who?" I asked, head down and eyes focused on my Wes doodle.

When Shay didn't answer, I lifted my head out of curiosity, followed her gaze across the restaurant, and met the eyes of the man she had to have been referring to.

I blinked and stood a little taller but stayed angled forward, keeping my weight on my elbows.

He blinked back. And somehow, that blink...was...*sexy*.

I had no idea what qualified a blink as being sexy, but whatever it was, this man was hitting all those qualifiers and could easily take home the trophy for sexiest blink.

Ever.

I am not one to exaggerate either. This was an honest observation.

I realized quickly after moving to Dogwood Beach that there wasn't a shortage of good-looking men here. In fact, I was convinced the sand and salty air did miraculous things to the male race, boosting cellular regeneration and gene quality, making even hard-looking men like Stitch beautiful in their own unique way.

I waited on attractive men frequently at work. I saw them around town. Hell, I was currently dating one. This was nothing new. Looks were a dime a dozen in Dogwood.

That being said, I was unprepared for a sexy blink, not to mention the degree of attractiveness belonging to the man responsible for that blink.

The man I was currently staring at, who just so happened to be staring back, directly at *me*.

Tall, with broad shoulders and long, muscled limbs covered in layered Henley thermals and dark faded jeans, dirty blond hair that looked hand-raked messy and a little damp from the rain, causing it to curl at the ends around his ears and where it lay on his neck. Bright eyes. Thick eyebrows. A perfectly straight nose. He looked model perfect and camera ready, except for the five o'clock shadow speckling his jaw. That roughed him up a bit. And if he wasn't already scoring points in the looks department, boom, dimples. He...had...dimples.

And he was giving them to me as he smiled, big and broad, like he was happy to see me.

Like we already knew each other. Or like he wished we did...

And I had a feeling this man wasn't interested in knowing me the way I knew Shay or Stitch, or even Nate, my boss, who I was friendly with on an employee-employer level.

That wasn't the level Tall, Blond, and Stupidly Gorgeous wanted to be on with me. No, sir. Absolutely not.

"Who is that?" I asked Shay, watching her customer from the two-top stand and cross the room to greet Sexy Blink, though I couldn't make out the words from this distance and over the 311 song playing overhead.

"Jamie McCade," Shay answered. "He's a pretty BFD around here."

"A what?" I asked.

"Big fucking deal." Shay turned her head, met my eyes, and shrugged. "Or so they say. I'm not a huge surfing fan. Tried it once and ended up swallowing my weight in ocean water. He's the best, though. Has been for years. Ask any local."

I studied Jamie's hair and decided it looked more wave-tussled than hand-raked messy.

A surfer...Yeah, that fit. That absolutely fit this guy.

Lowering my gaze, I saw he was back to staring at me and back to smiling. I cleared my throat, cut my eyes away, and looked down at my doodle.

Wes. I had a boyfriend. I had a boyfriend who made me happy. I was simply noticing another man's good looks. That's all. I'd have to be blind not to notice.

So why did I feel guilty noticing in the first place?

"I'm gonna go get him seated. Be back."

"'Kay," I muttered, keeping my head down and my hand busy as I darkened Wes's name even further, the blue ink saturating the paper so much that now it appeared nearly black.

Black, like my noticing, treacherous heart.

Unbelievable.

"You're up, T."

I snapped my head up and gaped at Shay, not because of the new nickname she'd just thrown on me—I liked it and hoped it would stick—but because of the two words she'd just used preceding my new, cute nickname.

"Huh?"

Shay giggled, then reached out and took the pen out of my hand while her other slid the napkin away from me.

"He requested your section. Lucky girl. You're in for a treat. He tips like he invented money or something."

Shay began doodling on my napkin.

I looked across the room again and saw that Jamie was indeed sitting in my section, arm draped over the back of the booth, smiling and waiting to be served.

Well, this was just terrific. Now I had no choice *but* to look at him.

Whatever.

I had a job to do. I couldn't just stand around and doodle.

"Right." Straightening up and snapping into professional mode, I smoothed my apron, pulled out my ticket book, and leaning across the counter, snatched my pen away from Shay.

She smirked. "It's cool. I'm gonna make sure Stitch didn't hack off a finger."

Shay moved around the bar to get to the kitchen window, hopped up on the edge of the counter, and sat there, swinging her feet and waiting for Stitch.

I took a deep breath and headed across the room, wetting my cherry-painted lips and stretching them into a friendly smile when I reached my destination.

He liked to tip? Awesome. I liked getting tips. Time to put on the charm.

"Good afternoon. My name is—"

"Fuck me, babe," Jamie muttered through a thick, sex-soaked voice, cutting me off as his eyes skimmed up and down the length of me. "You make that ugly-ass uniform look fuckin' *good*. No shit."

My head jerked back. "Excuse me?" I asked, losing my smile. I glanced down at my uniform, which consisted of a white polo top, khaki pants, and a black apron tied around my waist. "These uniforms aren't ugly," I argued, lifting my head. "They're cute and super comfy. Honestly, I've worn worse."

"Legs, trust me, they're nothin' to look at," he argued back, tipping his head. "But on you, yeah, different story. I'll look all fuckin' day."

I blinked. "Legs? Did you just call me *Legs*?"

What in the . . . *hell*? Who calls someone that?

Half of Jamie's mouth lifted, revealing one killer dimple.

"Fuck yeah, I did," he answered, dropping his eyes to my limbs and lingering there. "Seen a lot of good ones. Had a lot of good ones wrapped around me, but yours? Babe, seriously." He looked to me again. "Yours take the fuckin' cake. I'd give my left nut for a feel. Straight up."

I stared at him.

I was never a woman of few words. Never. Not even when I needed to be. In situations that didn't warrant talking, I was still a talker. I got shushed at movie theaters because I felt the need to comment or ask questions regarding the plot line. I was *that* girl. Words never failed me.

Yet here I was, stripped of my vocabulary for the first time in my twenty-four years of life, all because a man wanted to chop off his left testicle to cop a feel.

Unbelievable.

Jamie laughed, low and rumbly in his throat, and hearing that, I broke out of my speechless haze.

"Do you offer up appendages to all the women you meet?" I asked.

"Why? Curious if anyone's ever taken me up on it?" He gestured at his lap. "Go ahead and check. I'm down for a strip search if you wanna give it, Legs. Just know . . ." He bent his elbow on the table, leaned forward to get closer, held my eyes, and with a lowered voice, promised, "You touch me, and I am definitely putting my hands all over you."

Breath caught in my throat as I quickly sucked in air.

I felt my cheeks warm, knew Jamie could see my reaction to what he'd just said, and further knew I needed to get far away from the topic of him putting his hands anywhere near my personal space.

I shouldn't even be reacting *at all*. What was wrong with me?

Forcing focus, I clicked my pen open, poised it on my ticket book, and asked nonchalantly, "What can I get you started with?" as if Jamie hadn't just painted a very descriptive picture in my head.

His smile was slow and satisfied as it moved across his face.

"I don't know. You offerin' yourself up?" Jamie smirked through his question as he sat tall in the booth, his one arm still stretched behind him and his other relaxed on the table next to the menu. "'Cause if that's the case, I'll take my order to go. Your legs would look unfuckingreal spread wide in my backseat."

I sighed. *Okay. This was getting ridiculous.*

"I am not offering myself up. I have a boyfriend," I told him with a little attitude, watching his face and waiting for the expected surrender and disappointment to shadow his arrogance.

It didn't. I looked harder.

And still, nothing. Not one bit of change.

Jamie didn't flinch. Didn't lose the smirk he was wearing. Hell, it didn't even falter.

I opened my mouth to repeat myself but he shut me up fast when he finally spoke.

"Not sure what that has to do with us," he said, keeping the arrogance, keeping the smirk, and keeping at *me* like what I'd just shared meant *nothing*. He shrugged, then continued. "Affects him more than anything. Handle it now or wait, whatever. Just know, once we get started, you need to drop him, babe. I don't share."

My mouth fell open. I couldn't believe what I was hearing.

"Once we get started?" I echoed, lowering my arms to my sides. "What makes you think—"

He cut me off quick.

"Guessin' you don't know who I am, considering I've never seen you around here, and trust me, I would've seen you, so let me fill you in." Jamie's face grew serious. "I want something? I get it, and I don't fuckin' lose. Ever. No shit. I'm not just blowin' smoke up my own ass, babe. When I say I don't fuckin' lose, I mean, I do not *fuckin' lose*. That applies to a lot of shit, Legs, and it sure as fuck applies to you. I won't back down, boyfriend or not. You gotta know that."

Something sick twisted deep in my stomach as I studied Jamie, at his eyes wild with promise, because I knew then exactly what kind of man he was and it had nothing to do with his surfing record or good looks or the money lining his wallet.

He was a loser. A player. A jerk. He didn't respect me or the relationship I was in.

He didn't respect love.

And that *disgusted* me.

"I am not interested in being *gotten*," I snapped, nostrils flaring. "Like I said, I'm with someone. I'm happy. I'm *taken*. Maybe that doesn't mean anything to you, but it sure as hell means everything to me. In terms of losing, you've already lost. I'm not available. So if that's all you're here for, you can go ahead and take your conceited ass right on back out into the storm. If it's not, you've got five seconds to give me your order before I walk away for good. I like tips, but I don't need yours. It won't be any loss to me."

"You ain't taken, babe. And I did not fuckin' lose," he repeated, a little firmer this time.

Apparently those were the only parts of my speech he'd heard.

I brought my hand clutching the pen up to my hip and fisted it there, knowing if I didn't, I'd probably end up throwing a punch, and if I did that, I'd be out of a job. For sure.

And I really liked this job.

"Three seconds," I hissed.

He smiled, looked at my hand fisted at my hip, studied it for two out of the three seconds he had left, and then met my gaze when he quickly ordered, "BBQ chicken biscuit. Extra sauce."

"You want something to drink with that?"

"Cherry Coke."

"We don't have Cherry Coke."

"You got Coke and grenadine syrup?"

I did a quick mental scan of the bottles we had lined up underneath the counter.

"Yes," I murmured, having remembered spotting the grenadine bottle.

"Then you got Cherry Coke." Jamie slapped his hand down on the menu sitting in front of him and slid it to the edge of the table.

I reached to retrieve it, tugged on the corner with the two fingers not clutching my pen, and met resistance when he refused to lift his hand.

He stared at me, at my eyes, my lips, the line of my neck revealed from my hair being gathered over one shoulder, and lower, my breasts down to my toes and back up again.

I glared at him, watching his eyes do this appraising wander, and the longer it went on, the more irritated I became.

"You finished?" I grated.

"With you?" He met my gaze. His eyes were burning now. "No fuckin' way," he growled.

"I'm taken," I repeated.

"You ain't taken, Legs. Not unless you're with me."

This jerk was mental. "That will never happen," I promised. "And my name is Tori. *Not* Legs."

Jamie grinned. "We'll see about that," he said, lifting his hand and allowing me to take the menu.

I didn't know if he was referring to the taken argument or the nickname and I didn't want to ask. Truth be told, I just wanted to get away from him.

If he grinned at me one more time, I might actually throw that punch.

I spun around, walked to the hostess podium to drop off the menu, ignored the eyes burning into my profile coming from the loser's booth, and marched toward the kitchen, weaving between tables all while jotting down the order on my ticket book.

Shay saw me coming and slid off the counter. "Great news!" she squealed when I reached her. "Stitch doesn't care if we call him Stitch. He's cool with it." She turned her head and asked through the window, "Right, Stitch?"

Stitch was facing the stove so I couldn't see his face, but I didn't miss the slight jerk of his head as he acknowledged Shay.

"That's about all he's been giving me," she whispered. "I took it as a good sign."

Shay stepped away.

I watched her walk over to her two-top, then risked a glance in Jamie's direction and caught him smiling at me.

Squaring off, I reached into my apron pocket like I was searching for something, lifted my hand back out, keeping all but one finger curled under, and flipped him off.

Anytime, Jamie mouthed.

Ugh! Jerk!

Grunting, I spun around, ripped the ticket off my book, and slid the thin paper across the metal lip of the window.

I opened my mouth to alert Stitch of the order when a piece of food flipped off the grill and onto the floor. It went sliding across the tile when he kicked it out of the way with his boot.

Hello, fantastic little lightbulb flashing above my head.

Rolling up onto my toes, I leaned closer to the window and inquired, "Is there any chance you'd be interested in letting a piece of BBQ chicken hang out on the floor for five seconds before sliding it onto a biscuit? I got a loser who needs a lesson in manners."

Stitch turned his head and peered at me behind the pieces of long blond hair hanging in his eyes.

I rocked back onto my heels.

"He deserves it," I quickly added, worried I was pissing off the hard-looking man by requesting this and blowing my shot at payback. "Really. I wouldn't ask if he didn't."

Stitch didn't say anything for several stress-filled seconds, then shook his head and muttered a rough "what-the-fuck-ever" under his breath, turning away and going back to the food he was cooking that hadn't been dropped yet. "You take the fall if this comes back to me," he ordered.

"Deal."

Yes! Eat shit, Loser!

I spun around, nearly doing a twirl I was so happy, looked across the room directly at Jamie, and watched that jerk's smile turn into a full-blown grin that no longer bothered me.

The tile floor back in the kitchen had to be disgusting. He'd get sick from the food. Sick enough he'd never want to eat here again. There was no doubt in my mind.

This would be the last time Jamie McCade ever stepped foot inside Whitecaps.

And knowing that, I couldn't help myself.

I grinned right on back.

Chapter One

TORI

Nine months later

"He's here again," Kali whispered in my ear as I stood at the bar facing the kitchen, filling a mason jar with sweet tea for one of my patrons.

I breathed deep through my nose.

God...*damn it*.

I didn't need to ask who she was talking about. I didn't need to turn around.

There was only one "he" that she could've been referring to. The same "he" that everyone was always referring to when I didn't catch the Loser walking into Whitecaps myself and had to be told about it.

Jamie McCade. Gorgeous dickhead.

Local asshole.

Biggest player on the planet.

And the man who would not catch a hint and leave me the hell alone.

I didn't get it. I was never in the mood to see him, meaning I was never even remotely nice to him when he came in here, giving him nothing but shitty service and killer attitude, and *still* he kept coming back for more.

And he apparently never got sick!

That was seriously annoying.

I was sure he'd have caught something by now with the amount of germs covering the food I was serving him, but nope. Nothing. He always looked bright-eyed and stupidly energetic, which had me convinced: Jamie was either on a constant dose of antibiotics or had the strongest immune system in the entire world.

I was betting on the antibiotics. He was probably a regular at the local clinic for STD treatment. In fact, I was certain he frequented it *so* often he was getting reward points toward one free prescription of choice.

Disgusting.

He...was...disgusting. And he was sitting in my section—this I knew for sure without turning around—because he was always sitting in my section, and for some reason, my girls didn't have my back and were always seating him *in* my section.

Take sweet-faced Kali, for example. Awesome girl with an adorable kid. And currently blushing because she'd been the one to seat Jamie where I'd be responsible for serving him even though I'd asked her and Shay repeatedly not to do such a thing.

It wasn't entirely her fault, or Shay when she let it happen, this I knew. And it was why I couldn't get mad at either one of them for it.

Jamie had proven time and time again that it didn't matter if he was seated in someone else's section or not. After being greeted by whichever waitress he ended up with, he'd tip her for the greeting, stand up, find my section by process of elimination, and move to it.

Every. Single. Time.

Now? Shay and Kali took him to my section on the first go because what was the point?

He wanted me as his waitress and he got me as his waitress. He'd make sure of that.

I was officially stuck.

I could be a bitch. I could give him shitty service. I could grow a new disease on his food and make him eat it.

Jamie McCade was unstoppable.

And the parts of me that didn't mind looking at something so beautiful hated him for it.

Yes, unfortunately on top of being the most irritating man in the history of irritating men, Jamie was beautiful.

He was cocky. He was unashamed. He was over-the-top pigheaded and spoke like a Neanderthal wielding a club.

And he was beautiful.

It sucked.

Seriously.

I'd noticed the first day he walked in here and I'd been noticing ever since. But I would never admit it. No way.

Not to him. Not to Kali or Shay, who I knew would agree with me. Not to Syd, my best girl, who I admitted everything to.

Not to anyone. Not ever.

He'd always be a loser. He'd always be a player. He'd always be the man who disrespected my relationship, even though my previous relationship with Wes turned out to be nothing more than a joke—one I wasn't in on until I was being introduced to his wife and sweet-looking daughter in the middle of a crowded mall—didn't matter, though. Jamie wasn't in on the joke either and so, unknowing, he still disrespected it.

It didn't matter how he looked. His heart was ugly. His soul was ugly. And nothing was going to change my opinion.

"What are the chances he hasn't spotted me yet and I can sneak out the back?" I asked Kali, turning to her after setting down the pitcher of sweet tea. "I get off soon anyway. You could cover for me with Nate if he asks where I am. Say I'm sick. Say I was kidnapped. Whatever. Just make up something."

Today had been a great day. A ten-hour-shift delight. Great tips. Friendly customers. I really didn't want to end my night on a low note and go home grumpy.

So if I could find some way of getting out of serving Jamie, I'd take it. Even if it meant getting shit from Nate.

"He already spotted you," Kali replied without pause.

I pinched my eyes shut and muttered a disappointed "Damn."

"Yeah . . . sorry. It was pretty immediate." I watched Kali look over my shoulder, wince, then look back to me to add, "He's currently spotting you right now."

Of course he was.

I turned my head and saw dimples and brilliant blues.

Then shifting my attention left, I saw a group of teenage girls sitting in the booth next to Jamie, whispering and talking closely with one another while craning their necks around to stare at him.

Perfect. Just feed his ego, why don't you.

"Whatever," I sighed, turning away to pop a slice of lemon into the tea. "Maybe today will be the day he catches something fatal from the food and I'll never have to look at him again."

Fingers crossed Stitch tracked in something deadly back there and coated the tile with it.

"I don't think I want him to die," Kali admitted quietly. She bit her lip when I frowned at her. "Just... maybe he could get sick but with a full recovery? I could support that."

I rolled my eyes.

"You're just as bad as Syd. You know that?" I clipped. "She's so Team Jamie at this point, I'm certain her first child will be named after him. I don't even believe her anymore when she tells me she got Stitch to do something to his food. I think she's faking it."

Syd was the only other person Jamie ever allowed to wait on him, and I swore she loved every second of it.

I think it had everything to do with her being locked down with his best friend.

Brian and Syd were magical. Meeting under the craziest circumstances a few months ago and then building something from that, something beautiful. I was over the moon happy for my best girl and couldn't imagine anyone better suited for her than Brian.

He had all the potential in the world.

Syd was over the moon happy, too, blissed out and fanatically in love, and because of this, she was wanting to pair me up with her boy's closest friend, I just knew she was. The signs were all there.

And they were becoming more obvious with each passing day.

She was constantly bringing Jamie up and bragging about him whenever we were together, throwing his name into conversations he had no business being in but doing it casually so as to not raise suspicions until I later thought back and realized what she'd been doing.

Plus, there was the whole assigned seating arrangement during Sunday dinner—the tradition Syd started a few weeks ago that had everyone, including Jamie, gathering at her and Brian's house and eating together.

Syd was putting out place cards now, and every time, without fail, mine would be directly next to Jamie's.

No way was that coincidental like she was always telling me. I was so onto her.

"I just don't think he's an asshole like *you* think he's an asshole," Kali explained, pointing at her chest. "*I* know assholes. Believe me. I know them all too well." She shifted her eyes away, then lowered them, pulling her lips between her teeth and appearing deep in thought.

She was referring to her son Cameron's father. Although I'd never met him, I'd heard enough to know he was definitely an asshole. Kali didn't deserve his shit, but she still got it dished on her anyway.

And because of this, I decided to drop the asshole debate. Then my eyes caught sight of the cute side braid she was rocking, and I had a perfect subject change.

"Your hair looks really sweet like that, by the way," I said. I'd meant to tell her earlier but kept forgetting when I got caught up in waitress duties.

Seeing as she was getting quiet on me and most likely thinking about the shit her ex was always dishing out, now seemed like the perfect time to boost her spirits with a compliment.

And I was right.

Kali looked up, reached for the braid that was hanging over one shoulder, and wrapped her hand around the end of it. "Thanks," she said, smiling big. "That means a lot."

"Of course, babe."

I gave her a wink before I turned around and walked out from behind the counter with the mason jar.

After checking on all my tables twice, I finally took my time walking over to Jamie's booth. And before I could utter the most impersonal greeting in the history of impersonal greetings, I was forced to witness fangirl flirting on an eye-rolling level.

"You're Jamie McCade, right?" asked one of the girls from the booth next to Jamie.

She stood on her knees, angled forward with her elbows resting on the back of the seat, her head tipped down as she dragged the tip of her finger across her glossed bottom lip and gazed at him from behind her false lashes.

Her friends giggled with their hands to their mouths.

Give me a break.

"The one and only," Jamie replied with a smirk.

"Oh, my God. We are your biggest fans," another girl quickly said. "Like, in the entire world. We love watching you. We think you're so hot."

Squeals and muffled "oh, my Gods" erupted from the other side of the booth.

Jamie laughed quietly under his breath.

I was a giggle away from choking on my own vomit.

The first girl elbowed her friend, shushing her, then turned back to Jamie and, with a voice sounding years older than she most likely was, said to him, "I hear you give private lessons. Do you think you could teach me? I'm a fast learner and very eager to please."

"Wow," I murmured through a chuckle, looking between desperation and head-up-his-own-ass. "How 'bout I give you two a minute to work out your little underage arrangement. I don't need to witness this. I'll be back." I moved to turn and step away when a hand gripped my forearm, halting me. I whipped my head around and glared at Jamie, yanking my arm out of his hold. "Get off."

"I'm ready to order," he told me, his face serious. He turned to the other booth and said, "Call Wax. You can set up your lesson time over the phone."

The girl looked down at my arm as if Jamie was still attached to it, narrowed her eyes, then glanced from my face to Jamie's, waiting until she landed on his before she showed her smile again.

"Great. I'm *really* looking forward to it," she said, her voice lowering to a purr.

"Right on," he replied.

"Totally," she responded.

"God, it's like I can *feel myself* getting dumber just from listening to this," I commented, wincing as I rubbed my temples.

The girl eager for a lesson scoffed, shot me a hard look, then gave a much softer one to Jamie before she spun around and plopped back down in her booth.

Probably for the best. I was certain her kid's meal was getting cold.

"You are so fuckin' cute when you're jealous," Jamie said, his lips curling up. "I dig that, babe."

"What do you want?" I asked, ignoring his comment, which was both absurd and completely untrue—in no way was I jealous—all while pulling out my pen and ticket book. I clicked the pen open and began doodling on the top of the ticket, writing *Loser* in a fancy script and adding devil's horns and a pitchfork.

It was some of my best work.

Jamie chuckled under his breath. "Not bothering with the greeting today, Legs?" he asked.

I kept my gaze focused on my doodle as I continued tracing, and answered, "What's the point? You never use my name anyway, no matter how many times I've asked you to."

"I use your name a lot, babe."

That admission drew my head up and paused my hand. He used my name a lot? No, he didn't. He *never* used my name. I would've absolutely remembered hearing it, marked the occasion on my calendar, and looked back on it as the day hell froze over.

I watched Jamie's eyes flicker wider, appreciating the attention I was now giving him.

"Excuse me?" I questioned.

Then he licked his lips, tilted his head with a smile, and added, "You spend the night with me, you'll see what I'm talking about. 'Cause no joke, and I ain't ashamed to admit this since, deep down, I think you'll like hearin' it, even though you'll stand there looking pissed off and hatin' on me like you always do. I know hard up when I see it and you're wearing it, babe, so I'm gonna give it to you straight. Your name is all I'm saying when I'm in my bed, getting there by myself."

My eyes widened. Holy…*shit*.

Jamie McCade, God's model for perfection, was talking about masturbating. I really did not need that visual.

I pinched my lips together and inhaled sharply through my nose, all while ignoring the warmth spreading low in my belly.

"You're disgusting," I declared, my voice betraying me and sounding thick with want.

Damn it.

"Yeah, you gotta say that, Legs. Otherwise you'd be admittin' shit to me you're not ready to admit yet."

"There is nothing to admit," I argued.

"You liked what I just said."

"I did not."

"Did."

Gripping my pen and ticket book with both hands, I tipped forward until I was leaning over the table, narrowed my eyes, and repeated with emphasis, "Did. Not."

Jamie quickly reached out, wrapped his hand around my elbow now, and held on firm, a lot firmer than before, keeping me at the close proximity I so willingly entered of my own volition.

Shit. The first rule of sparring with Jamie McCade was to keep your distance.

Rookie mistake. I was screwed.

"How long are we gonna keep playin' this little game?" he asked, his voice dropping low.

"What little game?" I asked back, playing dumb because Jamie was gripping me, he was staring deep into my eyes, and my heart was starting to beat so loudly I could feel it vibrating through my bones, and if I said the words clinging to the tip of my tongue—"*I don't know*"—I was afraid of how they would sound and, worse, how he'd react to them.

Breathy. Helpless. Defeated. I couldn't let him hear my weakness. He'd take advantage. He'd grip harder and stare deeper. He'd pull me closer and then . . .

"You know the game, babe," he said, snapping me out of my thoughts.

I blinked him into focus as he kept on at me.

"I push and you push back, giving me your smart-ass mouth—which I dig, Legs, no question there—but I'm just sayin' and this is a heads-up for you, I can only be so patient before I stop waiting around and start takin'. Your playing time is about up."

My lips parted. I blinked again, struggling to wrap my head around what Jamie had just said, or promised, rather.

He'd just promised to take me. Soon. Like...*soon* soon?

"Uh." I tugged on my arm still being held by a hand that was feeling a little too good at the moment.

He had big hands. Strong hands. Hands that could crush my heart if he touched it.

"Can you let go of me, please?" I requested.

Jamie gazed up at me. "You're feelin' it, aren't you?"

"What?"

"This shit between us." His rough fingers moved along my skin, sliding higher and wrapping firmer. "You're feelin' it. Right now. Fuck, babe, look at you."

"I'm feeling like you need to let me go so I can do my job."

"Not happenin'," he growled. "Not when I get moments like this with you when I know it ain't just me. I'm wearin' you down."

"You are not wearing me down. You aren't even *close* to wearing me down." I yanked my arm again and met nothing but resistance. "Do you mind?"

"I'm wearin' you down, Legs," he repeated.

"Nope."

"It's happening, babe."

"No it isn't."

"Straight up, you say 'no' one more time and I'm gonna shut you up real fast in a way you'll really fuckin' like but won't admit to liking. Think about that."

I thought about it, for all of two seconds, because I was still tipped forward, meaning Jamie's hand was still wrapped tight around my arm keeping me tipped forward and that quickly became the only thing I could think about.

"No, Loser, you are *not* wearing me down," I grated. "Now let go of me or I'll—"

My threat slid down the back of my throat as I gasped and pitched forward with a yank, Jamie's one hand staying firm on my arm while his other slid past my cheek, pushing through my hair to grip and hold me at the base of my neck. I was startled, but I didn't have time to react, pull away, scream, cry out. I couldn't do anything before his mouth was colliding with mine and he was kissing me, firm and fast and determined, and since my lips were already parted from the gasp, Jamie took that as an invite and tilted my head, angled our mouths together, and pushed his tongue inside.

That was when the kiss became a *kiss*.

The kind that should be done behind closed doors.

The kind that made your toes curl and your pulse race.

The kind you told your girlfriends about and commemorated with a diary entry.

Jamie tasted good. *Too* good. And he kissed even better. I couldn't deny it.

That was why when I wanted to fight or twist or bite down, I didn't, and the only reaction I gave was a moan that rolled off my tongue and onto his, which was a huge, *huge* mistake because he heard it and felt it, his eyes flashing open a second after mine and his grip on my neck tensing.

He pulled back slightly to stare, then growled a *"Fuck"* I felt roll right up my spine while his gaze held wild with so many things.

Want. Shock. Curiosity. And that unmistakable look someone had when they were right.

Knowing I'd been had, I jerked back abruptly enough that he was caught off guard, freeing myself from his grasp, then I spun around and bolted across the restaurant.

Yep. I was running. I had no other choice.

I weaved between tables, passing the kitchen and the counter, where Kali was still standing, and giving her a "cover me" look she read loud and clear.

I knew she saw the kiss. I was sure everyone in Whitecaps saw the kiss.

And I was still *feeling* that kiss, panicking because I was still feeling it and because I let it happen in the first place.

That wasn't my only problem, because honestly? I more than felt it. I liked it. I *moaned*.

Sweet Jesus Christ. What was I thinking?

Shoving the door open to the employee lounge, I stepped inside, stuffed my ticket book and pen away in my tiny black apron, and began pacing the length of the lockers along the wall while shaking my hands out at my sides.

Jamie coated my mouth. He tasted like watermelon gum and regretful decisions.

And I loved it.

"*Shit.*" I rubbed around my lips, where I knew my lipstick had been smudged.

My heart was pounding. My limbs were shaking.

No way was I going back out there. Kali could handle my tables on top of her own. Besides Jamie, they were all finishing up anyway. Whatever tip they were all planning on leaving me, she could keep.

I'd finish out my shift in here and then I'd duck out. Avoidance was the plan.

Then the door swung open and my plan went straight to shit.

I whirled around and nearly stumbled backward at the sight of Jamie, stalking toward me like a predator closing fast on his next meal.

Oh, God . . .

"You," he growled. "No fuckin' way, babe, are you pullin' that shit with me."

"You can't be in here," I warned him, not that it did any good.

He kept coming like he didn't hear me, with heated eyes and powerful steps, forcing me to move back, again and again, until I was pressed flush against the lockers and Jamie was pressing flush against *me*, legs to legs, breasts to ribs and hard . . . holy *shit*, he was hard.

"Ja—" I started, sounding breathless, and then that breathless start turned into a mindless groan when he dipped lower, slid his hands around my waist, rolled his hips into me, and pressed his erection directly against my clit.

My head fell back. My eyes rolled closed. And I trembled, right there in his arms.

Worst. Mistake. Ever.

"There it is," he murmured, his breath hot against my face as he bent to get closer. "There it fuckin' is. You're feelin' it now."

No no no no no. God...I couldn't let this happen. I *couldn't*.

Not with Jamie. I'd never forgive myself. He was a loser. A player. A jerk. I couldn't do this with him.

"I'm not," I lied, because I *was* feeling it. I was feeling all of it, and I was scared I'd never *stop* feeling it.

His lips grazed my cheek.

"You want this, Legs," he whispered, moving closer and closer to my mouth. "*I* want this. Fuck, you got no idea how bad—"

"No," I interrupted. "I don't want it."

Another lie.

"Yeah, babe. You do."

He kept moving, closer and closer. We were a breath or a lie away from another kiss and I couldn't let that happen.

"Stop," I whispered. My voice shook.

I shook. Head to toe. My entire body was locking up. This was a genuine freak-out. I was way past the realm of panicking and into full-blown terrifying mania.

Jamie froze after hearing me. His reaction was immediate, then his lips left my skin and his hands left my waist, and at the loss of contact I opened my eyes and blinked up at him where he stood, now a foot away.

His brow was knitted tight. He was staring at me, nostrils flaring with his breaths. He looked worked up and confused and maybe a little concerned.

Concerned?

No. No way. Jamie McCade didn't do concern for others, did he? I was certain he only cared about himself.

I blinked, waiting for him to speak. I wanted Jamie to explain why he was looking at me the way he was, but he didn't do that. He just kept staring.

And the longer he stared, the more uncomfortable I became.

My fingers wrapped under the hem of my shorts and tugged while I chewed nervously on my bottom lip.

Jamie followed my restlessness. His gaze lowered to my hands and focused there, and I watched his chest heave with a sharp breath.

"Do not fuckin' touch that uniform, Legs," he growled, meeting my eyes again with heat burning in his. "No joke. I do not need you adjusting your shit right now and showing me more of you. Cool it."

I felt my spine straighten, then I released my shorts and curled my fingers against my palms, not knowing what else to do with them. I kept my hands lowered and my back flush against the lockers.

We went back to staring at each other.

I contemplated making a dash for the door but figured I wouldn't get far before I was being pinned between Jamie and another hard surface, and I couldn't have that. So I stood there, looking at Jamie while thunder rolled under my skin. I was tense and anxious and still . . . *still* feeling that kiss.

Why did it have to be so good? And why did it have to be from *him*?

Then Jamie exhaled forcefully through a shake of his head, breaking the silence between us and causing me to tense further.

I braced and held my breath.

"You don't want this to happen," he said, more as a statement than a question, but I knew Jamie was asking me for confirmation on this. I could hear it in his voice.

Easy. I could give him confirmation. No problem. I *didn't* want this to happen. I was certain I didn't. All I had to do was just say it.

But did I do that? Nope. I hesitated.

Why, I have no idea, but it happened. And Jamie didn't miss it either.

I watched his face soften as he registered my uncertainty, then panicking because once again, I'd been had, I quickly threw out a firm and decisive "*no*."

I was too late.

"Bullshit," Jamie spat, calling me out. "And straight up, babe, that's bullshit I don't fuckin' need. You want this just as bad as I do and last time I checked, you weren't wasting your time on that worthless motherfucker you called a boyfriend anymore, so what the fuck?"

Jamie knew all about what happened with Wes. I put it on him the night I attacked Wes's car with Syd, Shay, and Kali in tow. Jamie made me tell him.

Then he slashed Wes's tires.

I wasn't going to think about that right now, though. No way.

"Wes doesn't have anything to do with this," I hissed, feeling my anger awaken at the mention of that asshole.

"No?" Jamie's eyes narrowed. "Then explain to me, babe, why you're fightin' me instead of lettin' this shit happen."

"Maybe because I don't want it to happen. Did you ever think about that?"

I was on a roll with the lying at this point. All in. There was no turning back.

"Christ, you're fuckin' delusional," he grated, crossing his arms over his chest. "I kissed you. Yeah, I'm owning that shit, but you sure as fuck kissed me back. I felt it. *You* fuckin' felt it. That kiss might've been instigated by me but you were a flick of my tongue away from soakin' that hot-ass uniform of yours and don't even try and deny it. Then I get back here, and the second I let you feel my cock, you're burnin' up for me again. You want this to happen. You want *me*, but guess what? Time's up, Legs. I get enough pussy and I'm done waitin' around for yours."

My mouth fell open.

I didn't believe a word he was saying. No way was he through with agitating me. It was his life's mission. I was sure of it.

"Oh, really?" I asked, gripping my hips and glaring.

"Yeah, babe, really," Jamie shot back.

He looked his fill of me then, letting his eyes skim my body slowly as if he was looking for the last time.

"Shit," he murmured to himself before lifting his gaze. Then he turned away without another look or glance, crossed the small room we were in, and pushed through the door.

I blinked after him, frozen in place as I waited, and waited . . . *and waited* for Jamie to march back in and go at me again because that's what he did.

He was relentless. Committed.

No matter how many times I'd told him over the past nine months that I wasn't interested, he still came at me.

And now he was gone. Done. Over it.

And I was...disappointed?

What? No! No way. Never.

God, it must've been that kiss. It stripped my brain of blood flow and I was no longer thinking straight.

I needed to get out of here. Regroup. Reevaluate. Rethink some things. And I could. According to the clock on the wall, my shift was over.

So I grabbed my stuff out of my locker, punched out, left the employee lounge, and waved to Kali as I walked past where she was standing by a table, telling her to keep the tips she was holding out for me and brushing off her look of concern and the "Jamie" she mouthed.

As usual when it came to that topic, I was a vault. Always and forever.

But just because I wasn't willing to talk about Jamie didn't mean I wasn't replaying everything in my mind that had just happened between us.

That was absolutely what I was doing.

As I reached my car, swung the door open, climbed inside, and tossed my purse onto the passenger seat, gripping my keys and reaching to start it up, my head was swimming with images, my mouth was saturated with Jamie's taste, and my attention was focused solely and completely on the man I never wanted to think about as I shifted into reverse and backed out of my parking space.

Then I heard a deep voice hollering out as my bumper knocked into something.

Hard.

But not *hard* hard. It was more like a jolt. Or a firm shove.

That was my story.

"Shit!" I gripped the wheel with both hands and stomped on the brake with both feet as I whipped around to look out the back window.

At first, I didn't see anything. Then, slowly, a hand came up and slammed down on my trunk, followed by the top of a head coming into view, covered with sandy blond hair that looked more disheveled than usual.

"Oh, shit," I whispered, focusing on his eyes next as he pierced me with them, blue like ice and holding more anger than I'd ever seen in a pair of eyes.

Jamie slowly straightened fully, and when he did finally stand tall, he bellowed a heart-stopping "WHAT THE FUCK?" so loud my windows rattled.

I shrieked and shifted the car into Park, then opened the door and jumped out in a blur of limbs and long hair.

"Are you okay?" I asked immediately with panic tightening my voice as I moved closer to examine Jamie for injuries.

His shorts were covered in dust and dirt, but other than that, he appeared unscathed. He was standing, not hunched over. He wasn't wincing or rubbing any parts of him. And there weren't any cuts or scrapes on his body from what I could tell.

I looked into his eyes as I reached the back of the car.

"I didn't see you at all. Is anything hurt? Are you hurt?" I asked.

"Stay the *fuck* away from me," Jamie growled, holding his hands up and slowly retreating. "You crazy-ass bitch. Do not fuckin' come any closer."

I flinched, halting my steps. "What? Did you just call me a bitch?"

"Yeah, *bitch*, I did. You heard me," he spat, brushing himself off. "You ran me over. What the fuck is wrong with you?"

"I...*what*?" I blinked rapidly. "I didn't do it on purpose!" I shrieked, appalled by his accusation. "I didn't see you! I thought you left!"

Jamie gestured over my shoulder.

"I'm parked right the fuck next to you! Where the fuck was I going without my car?"

My eyes went round.

Slowly turning my head, I registered the vintage Jeep that Jamie was always driving if he wasn't riding his motorcycle, parked right beside my Volvo.

Well, shit.

"My mind was on other things! I wasn't paying attention," I confessed, which was true. Both counts. I looked back at Jamie. "You know it was an accident. I would never intentionally do something like this. Not ever."

"Yeah, right, 'cause you gotta lot of love for me," he argued, heavy on the sarcasm.

"That might not be the case but I wouldn't hit you with my car!" I insisted. "I'm not *crazy*!"

He stared at me for a beat, jaw twitching, eyes flashing, and breathing heavy. Jamie didn't look convinced. Then he pushed a hand through his hair and shook his head, murmuring, "Figures I fall for psycho pussy," under his breath as he reached into his back pocket and tugged out his phone. He looked down at the screen.

My gazed hardened. *Psycho pussy?* Um, no. I don't think so.

"I am *not* psycho pussy, and I know what you're doing." I pointed at him when he lifted his head. "You're mad I shot you down and bruised your precious ego and now you're planning on making up lies about me."

"*Bruised my ego?* Bitch, I think you did more than that when you ran my ass over."

"I did *not* run you over! God! Stop being so dramatic!"

Reaching behind me, I felt for my phone in the back pocket of my shorts, fished it out, dialed Syd's number, and grinned right in Jamie's face when I pressed the phone to my ear a good two seconds before he did.

He flipped me off.

I flipped him off back, then spun around so he couldn't see the tremble in my lip I couldn't figure out or explain.

I was on the verge of tears.

Why? Because I'd tapped him with my car?

"Your girl's bitch of a friend is certifiable, man," Jamie said behind me. "Fuckin' straitjacket shit. No joke."

"Hey, Tori," Syd greeted me in my ear.

"It was an accident," I said quickly, fighting against nerves and nuisance and this weird, unsettling hurt I couldn't shake. "Okay? It was an accident, and if he says differently, he's lying. I would never purposely do something like that."

"What are you talking about?" Syd asked. Her voice was heavy with confusion.

"She ran me over with her fuckin' car. Can you believe that shit?" Jamie spat, each word feeling like a knife sticking into my back. "Tori. Yeah, I'm serious, brother. That bitch is crazy."

I pulled in a breath.

Not because of the crazy. Or the bitch. I was oddly immune to those names at the moment.

No. I pulled in a breath because Jamie called me Tori. He never called me Tori in places I could hear.

Until now.

The hurt I couldn't explain somehow grew denser and spread through my bones, weighing me down. It was the strangest thing. I didn't understand anything I was feeling except for the regret. That I understood.

I really didn't mean for this to happen.

Honest.

So I held on to that emotion and wrapped my heart in it as I glanced over my shoulder, met Jamie's eyes, and confessed my truth to Syd.

"I sort of hit Jamie with my car."

But my other truths involving Jamie? Those stayed locked inside. I was never letting them out.

Chapter Two

JAMIE

I knocked on the front door of the house my best friend shared with his girl. As I waited for someone to let me in, I took a step back on the porch, shoved my hands into my pockets, and turned halfway so I could see the driveway and monitor that shit.

Because if a motherfucking yellow Volvo pulled in behind my bike, I was rolling the fuck out.

It was Sunday night, meaning it was family dinner night at Dash and Syd's place, something I never passed on considering the good food and good company, but I was willing to start skipping them if Legs and her psycho pussy showed up.

Jesus.

Never imagined I'd be thinking that shit. Nine months of wanting had me fucked in the head for this girl. I'd never pass up an opportunity to get an eye and an ear full of Legs and her smart-ass mouth. Hell, I'd go out of my way to get it.

Now I knew she was crazy. Didn't matter how hot she was, I'd be passing up opportunities left and right just to steer clear.

Tori Rivera took bitch to a whole new level.

Dash told me she was working tonight when I called a couple hours ago for a heads-up, but I knew schedules could change, which was why I was turned around and keeping an eye out.

It'd be just like her to show up, knowing I wouldn't want her here but doing it anyway out of spite, shoving her shit in my face like she was always doing and baiting me for a taste, then luring me outside somehow and running my ass over a-fuckin'-gain.

Not happening. Her hot ass wasn't luring me anywhere.

She'd probably do permanent damage this time if she got a second go at it, crushing my junk since she'd most likely be aiming straight for my dick and balls.

I'd never fuck again.

No doubt Tori would be fucking elated, even though we both knew how hard up she was to ride my shit.

Jesus. That fucking moan...

No matter how many times I'd tried, I couldn't get that noise out of my head. She'd wanted that kiss just as bad as me. Fighting it but getting it so good her body was failing her.

Getting it good. Yeah fucking right. That kiss was nothing special.

Only I'm a liar trying to convince myself concrete shit isn't true, like tits aren't God's greatest creation.

That kiss...*fuck*.

Tasting better than I'd imagined. And I'd fucking imagined, plenty of times. More times than I was willing to admit now.

She moaned. She *fucking moaned*.

Then she bolted, and I couldn't let her rip it all away from me without chasing after her and getting more. And I knew once I got her against me, she'd be giving in and letting herself feel that shit like I was feeling it. I was wearing her down. That kiss was proof. Legs couldn't fight it anymore.

It was happening. *We* were fucking happening. Jesus...fucking *finally*.

Only we weren't. Shocking the shit out of me, Legs hit me with a no instead of giving in to this, to *us*, and it didn't matter how much her body was wanting it to happen or how fucking hard I was, I heard her. Loud and clear. She was telling me to stop.

Telling...me...to stop.

I backed off. Had to, but *fuck*. Moaning one second and then giving me that. Hesitating when I asked her straight out if she was feeling this, which meant she *was* feeling it but didn't want to admit that to me. What the fuck? I didn't need that shit. And if Tori Rivera was going to play those fucked-up mind games with me, then maybe she wasn't worth the nine months I'd put in. And no matter how much I'd thought about it, dreamed about it, and damn near obsessed over it, maybe it was a good thing I hadn't done more than just kiss her.

I was fucked enough as it was. And that was before she tried to kill me.

Now I wasn't just through waiting around for her pussy, I was avoiding it altogether. I was over it. Done. Didn't need that kind of crazy and sure as fuck didn't want it.

I could forget about Tori. Should be easy enough.

Only... *Motherfucker*. That kiss didn't suck. Not even a little.

The door opened behind me, turning my head, and Syd, Dash's girl, stood in the doorway wearing an apron and a welcoming smile that cranked up in brightness at the sight of me.

She had looks and easy charm she didn't need to work at—it just flowed. Was a little nutty with some of the honesty pouring from her at times, but like the honesty, she gave that smile to everyone it seemed, not just to people she knew.

Made her a helluva lot nicer than Legs.

I called her Sunshine as a joke, considering how much she was trying to hate on me on account of her friend. The nickname stuck when she stopped hating and started doing anything she could to shine a good light in my direction, hoping Legs would see it.

Syd was a sweet girl. Thought that before I found out she was healing Dash and getting him back to living instead of just merely existing. Now I had mad respect for Syd and a whole lotta love, too.

She earned that.

"What's up, Sunshine?" I greeted her, stepping closer. When she didn't back up or step aside, allowing me room to enter, I halted, tilted my head, and questioned, "You gonna let me in?"

Her eyes did a quick assessment of me as her lips pressed together.

Christ. Here we fucking go.

"I feel the need to point out, even though I'm happy you're okay and understand in times of stress there is cause for exaggeration," she began, one brow lifting as she met my gaze. "Being one to exaggerate in times of stress myself, I get it. But you don't look like you got run over by a car, Jamie."

"Most of my injuries are internal," I explained, flashing a smile. "And the rest are only visible after I strip."

Her eyes got round, and then those same eyes rolled a second later.

"For real, though, she basically tried to kill me," I added.

"That's not what she's saying," Syd shot back, sticking her hand on the hip that wasn't holding open the door. "And do you really think Tori would do something like that on purpose? 'Cause I don't."

I stared at her.

Figured Syd would be siding with her girl on this one, but it wasn't like she was oblivious to the hate Legs was always putting on me. Shit. A good bit of it was put on me during family dinners in this fucking house.

"Yeah, babe. I do. She's had it in for me since day one," I bit out, not in anger but more in exasperation. "Now what the fuck? Am I eatin' outside on the porch or are you gonna let me in?"

Her shoulders pulled back as her brows drew together.

"Okay, first," she began, her voice getting sharp, "I would only make you eat outside if we were having a cookout, which is something that will be happening after Brian and I get deck furniture, not before. I've always believed in hosting properly, and not supplying your guests with a place to sit is not hosting properly. I personally feel very strongly about this and—"

"Babe, no disrespect, but can we skip ahead to point two so I can come in and get a beer and you can get back to cookin'?" I interrupted, crossing my arms over my chest. I ignored the heated look being directed at me and quickly explained, "You know I got love for you, Sunshine, but you're going off on a tangent, and when that happens, it usually takes you a while to get back on track. I'm just looking out for the food you got in the oven. Straight up. You'll thank me when it doesn't burn."

Her eyes flickered wider.

I didn't think she was going to oblige me. I also didn't think she'd let me off the hook for pointing out her tendency to ramble.

Women usually didn't go for men pointing out shit to them.

So when Syd stepped aside without saying another word and freed the doorway for me to enter, hurrying into the kitchen instead of getting up in my face, I was shocked.

But that feeling was short-lived.

After closing the door, I crossed the living room and followed behind, nearly making it into the kitchen before I jerked back, halting to a stop when Syd came flying around the wall separating the two rooms and approached me.

"I do not go off on tangents. I simply feel passionate about things, and when that happens, I get a little wordy," she informed me, coming up onto her toes to get closer to my face. "Going off on a tangent is when you get off topic and that never happens. I stay on topic. I just usually have a lot to say about whichever topic I'm on. And to prove my point, I'll go ahead and share point two of what I was driving at before I ran to check on my casserole, which isn't burning, by the way."

I bit back a smile. "And what's point two?" I probed.

She rocked back onto her heels, blinked up at me, and shared, "The only two people who eat on that porch are myself and Brian. No one else. It's special to us."

I knew that. I technically knew about that porch before Syd did, considering Dash enlisted my dad to help him find the listing when he was house hunting. And since Dash informed me of the reason he was so hell-bent on having a porch, so Syd could eat popsicles on it like she did when she was a kid, a memory he wanted to give back to her, I knew what it meant to both of them.

"Wouldn't ask to sit out there, babe," I shared. "Know that's important to you."

"It is and I know you know it," Syd replied.

"Just hungry and wantin' a beer, maybe several, considering my ass got run over yesterday. I'm a bit sore all over." I might've been playing up my injuries a bit.

Syd studied my face with narrowed eyes for a second before asking, "Are you really?"

I smirked.

She smiled slowly, like she was fighting it, shook her head through a quiet laugh, then brought her hand out from behind her and shoved a bottle at my chest.

"Here. Brian's out back with Sir letting him play. It'll just be us four for dinner," she said.

I took the beer, giving her a wink in appreciation, then walked behind her into the kitchen, making it nearly to the slider before I registered what she'd just said. *Us four?*

"You mean it'll just be us three for dinner. You, me, and Dash. He said everyone else had work or other shit to do."

Syd shut the oven door and quickly stood, spinning around to face me. "Right. Yep. They do. That's what I meant." She anxiously smoothed her hands down the front of her apron. "I was accidentally counting Sir. I do that sometimes."

My brow grew tight as I stared at her. "You were accidentally counting Sir," I echoed back.

She nodded, saying, "He's part of the family, so it's not weird or anything. I like him feeling included." Then she grabbed the bowls sitting on the island in front of her, turned around, and started washing them in the sink.

I watched her do this, and I would've thought the dog thing *was* weird, but this was Syd, and knowing her, she would count that damn dog as one of her dinner guests. Probably give him an assigned seat, too, with the little place cards she was always putting out. She loved Sir like he was her kid.

So I left it alone and headed outside.

It was early September in Dogwood Beach. Hot days. Warm nights. And the water was prime fucking temperature. Perfect Carolina weather.

Perfect surf weather, too. Thanks to hurricane season.

The sun burned low in the sky, streaking the clouds with oranges and yellows and shadowing Dash, who was tipped forward and leaning against the railing, looking out into the yard with his back to me.

His name was Brian, but I called him Dash. Always did. Dude was fucking fast when we were kids.

He turned his head as I made my way across the deck.

"Shit," he mumbled through a smile, peering at me over his shoulder and doing the same evaluation Syd did when she first saw me. "I was expecting you to show up using crutches or with something in a cast. What the hell, man? You look fine."

"I had a small limp yesterday, all right? So get off my fuckin' back about it," I replied, moving to stand beside him. "And just 'cause that bitch didn't break anything doesn't mean that shit didn't happen. I just got lucky."

I twisted off the bottle cap, bent it in half between my finger and thumb, and sat it on the wood, then took a swig of my beer while watching Sir run around the yard.

Dash was staring at me. I could feel his eyes locked on my profile, prompting me to ask an irritated "What?" before I turned my head.

His mouth twitched. "She really run you over?" he questioned.

"Yeah, brother, she did."

"I'm talking got you under the wheels of her car, Jamie, 'cause that's the definition of someone getting run over."

My gaze narrowed.

"Right," he murmured, looking out into the yard. "She didn't. That's what I thought."

"Backed into me and knocked me down," I argued, gaining his attention again. "Made contact, brother. Enough that it put me on my ass. And straight up, she would've kept on reversing and would've put me under the wheels if I didn't have the reflexes I do, so thank fuck for that. She's fuckin' crazy."

"She's sayin' this was an accident, and not to call you out, man, but it sounds like it was."

"What the fuck? Whose side are you on?" I asked, my voice growing louder with edge.

Jesus fucking Christ. Sunshine got to him.

He shot me a hard look.

"No one's. Are you fuckin' serious? You know I don't give a fuck," Dash said, straightening up and turning to face me. "I'm just pointing out what's being said and giving it to you straight. Yeah, that girl's been shootin' you down for months. We've all witnessed it. But I doubt she'd get that sick of your shit she'd try and take you out with her car. She doesn't seem the type."

"You mean, the psycho pussy type?" I asked, lifting my bottle and tipping it at him. "You're wrong, brother. She's the type. Bitch tried to kill me."

"Christ," he mumbled to the sky, tipping his head back.

"She's psycho pussy. I'm just callin' it like I see it."

I took another swig of my beer.

"Word of advice," Dash started, meeting my gaze again. "You might wanna get the psycho pussy shit outta your system before we head inside. Doubt Syd's gonna be down with hearing you call her girl that."

"Figured," I returned, shrugging weakly. "Not tryin' to leave here without getting some of that food she's cookin' so I'll stick with referring to Legs as 'crazy bitch.'"

"That might not fly either."

"Man, whatever. I've been traumatized. I can't be held responsible for shit I say right now. I was run over."

Dash chuckled. Then he bent his elbow on the railing and leaned his weight onto it.

"What?" I probed when he kept staring at me like I should be saying something.

He cocked his head.

"Really? You got nothing to ask me?"

We kept looking at each other, him not giving up any more, then I mumbled an "oh, shit," because it hit me right then what he was getting at and I couldn't believe I hadn't gotten around to asking him about it already. This shit was important. Had been on my mind the entire drive over here.

Dash got out on the water yesterday. He hadn't surfed since his accident.

This shit wasn't just important. It was huge.

"Fuck, man. Sorry. How was it? How'd you do?" I asked, excitement racing through my voice and my mouth twitching.

He shrugged, looking happy.

"Better than I was expecting."

"You eat it?"

"Twice."

Both of us broke into laughter.

I reached out and slapped his shoulder, then held on and gave it a squeeze.

"Proud of you, brother. Straight up. This is fuckin' awesome," I said, feeling all kinds of warm shit spreading through my chest.

Dash let his grin settle into a smile. "Thanks, man. Means a lot," he told me.

And I felt that, too.

"Know a lot of this has to do with your girl and she'll be gettin' my appreciation, but also know you allowed yourself to get to the place you're at now, and that shit wasn't easy," I continued, letting my arm fall. "You should feel good about that, Dash. Let that shit settle inside you. You deserve it."

"I am. Syd's makin' sure of that."

"Good. 'Cause straight up, I don't want to sound selfish and I won't if you stay at the level you're at right now, but gotta say, I wasn't sure you'd ever get here again, and besides being fuckin' ecstatic for you, I'm fuckin' ecstatic for *me*. I hate waitin' for shit. You know that. So heads up, me and you, soon as we get the chance, we're hitting the water. Just like old times."

Laughing, he nodded his head.

"Sounds good. I could use a fuckin' lesson," he replied, gripping the back of his neck and looking down at the wood.

"Got you covered on that," I said, holding out my arms and grinning big. "Lessons from the fuckin' champ. I won't even charge you."

He chuckled again, mumbling an "Appreciate it," before looking toward the house at the sound of the door opening.

"Hey, guys," Syd called out, sticking her head through the opening in the slider. "Dinner's ready. Come on."

"Sunshine. I owe you a fuckin' hug, babe. Come here."

I crossed the deck, making my way to Syd and keeping the grin on my face. I was seriously fuckin' ecstatic and ready to show my appreciation.

Syd, however, was looking confused and a little hesitant, tilting her head cutely and giving me a blank stare.

"Uh, okay, yeah, better give it to me now," she mumbled, sounding a little strange. Then she stepped outside and let me wrap my arms around her. She slid hers around my back and gave me a quick squeeze. "There," she said, trying to pull away.

I held on, knew Dash was coming up behind me, and got out what I wanted to say before he heard it.

"Thanks, babe. For everything you did for him," I whispered against the top of her head.

Didn't feel like much, what I was giving her, but it was.

I heard her quick inhale of breath a second before her arms tightened around me once more.

"You're welcome," she whispered back.

"No one holds Wild but me, asshole. Back the fuck up before you lose an arm," Dash threatened behind me.

I chuckled and released Syd, who was laughing, too.

She smiled up at Dash, then rushed in to give him a quick kiss. "Did you ask him?"

Dash shook his head.

"Was waiting until after dinner," he told her.

"Ask me what?" I looked between the two of them, settling on Dash.

He threw his arm around Syd's shoulders and pulled her close.

"Wanted to talk to you about buying back part of Wax," he informed me.

"You serious?" I questioned, feeling my lips curl up. "Shit. You don't gotta ask, brother. Wax is ours. Always has been." Syd slid out of the way when I stepped in close to Dash, offering my hand, and when he gripped it, pulling him into a hug while throwing my other arm around his back and patting him hard between his shoulder blades.

"Thanks, man," he mumbled, reciprocating the hug.

We dropped our arms and separated, both of us grinning big.

"This is awesome," I commented, shifting my eyes to Syd and seeing her happiness, too. "Only thing that'll make this night better is gettin' some of that good-smellin' food in my stomach."

I turned to head inside, ready to eat, but before I could take a step, Syd was jumping in front of me and planting a firm hand on my chest.

Not that I couldn't plow through her easily, she was tiny, but I halted anyway.

"You got more good news to share?" I asked her, cocking my head. "Not sure you can top what Dash just put on me, but you can try, Sunshine."

I was still wearing my smile, but hers was gone. She looked uneasy.

"The happy you're feeling right now, I'd really like you to keep hold of that through dinner," she requested with soft eyes and a small voice.

I shot her an odd look, turned that look to Dash, and saw he was wearing one similar—he didn't know what she was driving at either—then looked back down at Syd.

"Say again?"

"You're happy. Keep it," she pressed. "Even when you don't want to, which could possibly happen, just focus on this feeling making you happy right now and let it take over."

"Babe, what the fuck are you talking about?" Dash questioned, stealing the words out of my mouth.

"Yeah, and can we head in and talk about this while we fuckin' eat? I'm starvin'," I threw out, just in case she didn't know the urgency here.

Syd briefly glanced at Dash, ignoring his question. Then when Sir ran over to us, she scooped him up and gave him a kiss on the back of his head. "I'd like confirmation you'll be keeping the happy before we step inside," she demanded, tipping her chin up and meeting my eyes.

Again, I looked to Dash.

He was looking at his girl and he was doing it with eyes searching for understanding, so I did the same.

I sighed. "Whatever, Sunshine. If it'll put food in my mouth, fine," I told her, moving past because I was sick of waiting and wasn't lying when I said I was starving. "Consider it confir—"

The word died on my tongue the second I stepped inside the house and got an eyeful of Legs standing at the island.

Fucking Legs. At Sunday dinner.

What. The. Fuck.

I stared at her, looking my fill as Syd and Dash came into the house behind me.

Her long blond hair was pulled up into a messy ponytail, which made my dick hard for some fucking reason. She wasn't wearing much makeup except for that red lip I wanted to bite, and her hot-ass body was decorated in a blue, floral, hippie-looking, ugly-as-shit dress that wasn't ugly one fucking bit 'cause she was wearing it.

To top that off, she was holding a pie. Looking like Miss Fucking America entering a bake-off.

If it looked like shit, I wouldn't care. But it didn't.

It looked good. Real good. And I was starving.

Goddamned motherfucker.

"*What the fuck?*" I bellowed, causing Tori to jerk back and flinch. I gestured at her. "Your schedule changed that last minute? I just verified two fuckin' hours ago that you weren't gonna be here."

"What?" she questioned softly, setting the pie down in front of her and looking between me and Syd. "I wasn't scheduled to work today. What are you talking about?"

I slowly turned my head to look at Sunshine, who was keeping her eyes on the puppy in her arms and obviously avoiding.

"What is she doing here? I thought you told Dash she was workin'?" I questioned.

"She told me you knew I was coming and were okay with it," Tori announced, drawing my head back around.

My eyes narrowed. "*What?*" I grated.

"Babe, really?" Dash said.

He knew nothing about this either. It was all Sunshine. That was clear.

I breathed deep through my nose, searching for calm.

"I just thought this would be a nice way to smooth things over," Syd said quietly, offering up an explanation. "You know, break bread and all."

"Bad idea, Wild," Dash replied.

I looked from Dash to Syd, echoing, "Yeah, bad idea. She ran me over, Sunshine. You forgettin' that? So why the *fuck* would I be okay with sharing a meal with her?"

Tori slapped the counter and gained everyone's attention when she started yelling, "I did *not* run you over! Jesus Christ! Quit spreading lies about me!"

"It ain't lies if it's true!" I yelled back, glaring at her.

Sir barked.

A laugh bubbled in Tori's throat. She tilted her head and stuck her hand on her hip. "Please. I'm sure you're still able to bang everything with a pulse, *as usual*, which means you're fine. Get over it, Jamie, and grow some balls. I cried less when I watched *Bambi* the first time."

"Who's hungry?" Syd asked nonchalantly, moving behind her girl to round the island and stand near the stove.

I ignored her question because, *What the fuck? Grow some balls?*

Fuck her.

"I gotta pair, babe," I told Legs, reaching down and palming my shit. "You should know since you've been all up on 'em the past nine months."

She rolled her eyes, spitting, "You're disgusting."

I felt my mouth twitch.

And that was when, for some fucked-up reason, I reverted back to my old ways with Tori Rivera, forgetting all about how much I fucking hated her and instead going full-on, hell-bent determined to get an admission out of that smart-ass mouth.

"You want it," I countered, tipping my chin up.

She wasn't expecting that. No more than I was. It threw her off.

Her shoulders pulled back and her lips parted.

Then, maybe to cover her tell, or maybe she didn't have control over what was flying out of her mouth either, I didn't know, but she brought her other hand to her hip, glared at me with heat flashing in her eyes, tipped forward, and shot back with attitude, "*You* want it."

Well, shit. This was new. Legs was challenging me and she was doing it flirting. There was no doubt in my mind.

"Sorry, babe," I said, keeping the smirk and letting go of my junk. "Not interested. I told you yesterday, I'm done waitin' around. But you?" I pointed my beer at her. "You'll be beggin' for it before the month is up. Just watch."

"Fat chance," she snapped. "I wouldn't sleep with you if my life depended on it."

"Wanna bet?"

"Bet what?"

"What's going on right now?" Syd called out, but I wasn't pausing to answer her.

I smiled at Tori, then gestured between us, explaining, "First one to break and come crawling to the other person for sex loses."

"Are you serious?" She laughed, not in amusement but in disbelief.

"Fuck this. I'm eating," Dash announced, stepping around me and joining Syd, I guessed. I wasn't watching him.

I was watching *her*.

"Yeah, I'm serious," I answered.

"You want to bet *me* that I'll want to have sex with *you* before *you* try and have sex with *me*?" she questioned, moving her finger between us. "You, the guy who has been hitting on me for nine straight months and has been *rejected* for nine straight months? You seriously think I'll not only want to have sex with you, but I'll *beg* you for it? Is that what I just heard?"

I nodded slowly.

That fucking moan. I had this in the bag.

Tori thought on my offer for a second, keeping her eyes on me and keeping them steady, then when she was finished, she crossed her arms under her chest and huffed, "No way. I'm not betting that."

I smiled bigger.

"Knew you wanted it," I replied.

"*No*," she quickly shot back. "I just know *you*. You'll keep your dick happy by nailing every piece of ass in Dogwood so you don't break and beg me for sex. I'm not stupid."

I shrugged. "Make it a rule then," I offered.

"What?"

"A rule. No fucking anyone unless it's each other."

Her eyes bugged.

"And no masturbating either," I added, raising my beer and using it to gesture. "Since we both know when you do it you're thinkin' about me, and if you're that fuckin' horny, you need to rub one out or you'll fuckin' explode, you can come to me, Legs, *beg*, and I'll put that fire out for you."

Her mouth dropped open.

"This is not at all how I thought this evening would play out," Syd whispered off to the side. "Are you as shocked as I am?"

"Wild, don't," Dash mumbled. "Doesn't involve us. Just eat."

I briefly glanced at Dash and Syd, saw Dash with his head down, eating, eyes focused on his plate, and Syd with her attention focused solely on me and not the plate in front of her. Then I turned back to Tori, crossed my arms over my chest while keeping hold of my beer, and asked, "What do you say, babe? You in?"

Tori regained her steely composure and questioned with a sharp voice, "Do you really think you can beat me on this? Go without masturbating and sex, *with anyone*, and keep yourself away from me?"

"Didn't say that was part of it," I replied. "You'll be seeing a lot of me, Legs, 'cause I know what seeing me does to you, and if I'm gonna win, I'm using every advantage I got. But yeah, babe, that aside, I know I can beat you. Told you before. I don't lose." I leaned forward and finished with emphasis, "*Ever.*"

"Well, you'll be losing on this," she hissed, leaning forward to deliver her own emphasis. "That's for damn sure." Then Tori turned her head, gave Syd a sweet look, and declared, "Thanks for the invite, but I'm no longer hungry. Call me later."

"Okay," Syd replied, lifting her hand in a wave. "Thanks for the pie."

"No problem. See ya, Brian."

"Later," he said around his bite.

Tori's face was wiped clean of that sweet look when she glanced back at me, only to deliver a glare before spinning around and stalking out of the room.

The front door slammed shut behind her.

Dash continued eating. Syd mumbled something about being happy with her plan and the way it turned out.

And I stood there, smiling because I could already taste that victory on my fucking tongue.

Game on, Legs.

Chapter Three

TORI

"Trust me. It makes no sense for him to bet something like that. He wasn't serious," I said into the phone, plopping down on the couch with my bowl of food.

I'd left Syd and Brian's house over an hour ago and was just now sitting down with something to eat, wanting the casserole Syd made but not wanting it bad enough to put up with Jamie's company, which led to me lying about not being hungry and meant I had to come home and make a meal I hadn't intended on making. And just as I was finishing putting my serving into a bowl, my phone rang.

Syd was done eating and was dying to talk to me about what all went down tonight, not bothering with casual banter and instead cutting right to the chase.

Typically, I wouldn't be in the mood to discuss Jamie, ever, but since I was sure everything that went down was all one big joke, I was humoring her.

In fact, I wasn't just sure. I was positive.

There was no way Jamie McCade had seriously roped me into a sex competition.

Propping my feet up on the coffee table, I muted the TV, then held the phone between my ear and my shoulder as I twirled some noodles on my fork.

"He sounded pretty serious to me," Syd argued. "And I honestly don't think he's ever lost at *anything*. I believe him when he says that. I think you need to prepare yourself."

"He was joking, hon. And why are we even talking about that loser? Who cares?"

"He knows your weaknesses."

"Excuse me?" I asked around a mouthful of pasta. "What weaknesses?"

I hadn't told Syd about the kiss Jamie had forced on me before I gently *nudged* him with my car, so she couldn't know how my traitorous body reacted to that.

She wasn't going to know about it either. Nobody was. I was taking that to the grave.

But I refused to be in denial with myself. It wasn't healthy and there was no point. Because my body reacted and I felt that reaction for *hours* afterward, there was no disputing it; I had a weakness when it came to that beautiful loser.

His stupid, obnoxious, fuck-me perfect mouth.

"Well, for one, you don't hate what he looks like," she suggested. "He could use that to his advantage and start testing the 'no shirt, no service' policy at Whitecaps."

I rolled my eyes and swallowed. "He has no idea I find him attractive," I countered, twirling more noodles.

"I'm pretty sure he thinks *everyone* finds him attractive. Even people who have never seen him."

My hand stilled. I really couldn't argue that. "Fine. Next," I prompted.

"Then there's the dahlias," she reminded me.

I breathed in deep through my nose and released it slowly.

Unbelievable. Out of all the flowers that jerk could've brought me, he somehow managed to pick my favorite.

"Dumb luck. What about them?"

"You displayed them in your kitchen after letting Jamie think you didn't want them, meaning you really *did* want them."

"Yeah, but he doesn't know that," I said, letting my fork hover in the air. "He saw me toss them in the trash and I didn't fish them out until after he paid his tab and left. And I didn't keep them because he gave them to me. I kept them because they were beautiful and the vase was classy as shit."

And expensive. It was now the nicest vase I owned.

She sighed. "Still. That was very sweet of him. Just like what he did to Wes's car. He didn't need to do that, and he did. That was for you, Tori."

My heart seized, causing my body to jerk and tense up. I shoveled pasta into my mouth. *Nope. I was not admitting to that, nor was I going to think about it. No way.*

"Next," I encouraged, chewing and swallowing my bite.

Syd chuckled. "Um, I don't think I need to offer up any more examples. Those are pretty concrete," she said, her voice light with triumph. "He knows you find him attractive, he's capable of laying on the sweet and giving you something besides his arrogance, *and* he's seen what it takes to break through and reach your soft. Knowing Jamie, he'll be aiming for it again now that he knows you got one."

"My soft?" I questioned, brow furrowed.

"Your heart, Tori."

Oh, please. My girl was living in lover's land and was apparently drinking the Kool-Aid if she thought Jamie ever hit me that deep.

"This is ridiculous," I murmured.

"It's not. And I think you're underestimating him."

"He was joking, Syd. No way would Jamie make a bet he's guaranteed to lose."

"It's not a guarantee."

"*Yes*, it is," I stressed.

"He hit your soft, Tori. He's capable of hitting it again. I just know he is."

I dropped my fork into the bowl and sat it in my lap, gripped my phone, and braced myself to argue until my tongue grew tired.

"Syd—"

"He *wasn't joking*," she interrupted, nearly hollering at me. "Okay? He was serious and meaning this bet between you two, and I think you need to be prepared for what's coming."

I blinked rapidly, feeling wrinkles gather on my forehead. *What the...*

Speaking of bets, I'd put money on Syd pacing whatever room she was in right now and doing it while twisting a lock of her hair around her finger.

Something was off. Her voice jumped with anxiousness. She sounded edgy and maybe a little *too* sure of herself.

So I started fishing.

"Why do you sound like that?" I questioned.

"Why do I sound like *what*?" she questioned back with no change in her tone.

"Like *that*. Like you know something."

"I don't know anything. I'm just saying, it's not a guarantee he'll lose and you need to be ready."

"Ready for *what*, Syd? What aren't you telling me?"

I was frowning at the tops of my knees when I heard the unmistakable sound of a motorcycle drawing near.

Not strange. I lived next to a busy road that had direct access to the beach, and bikes flew up and down the street all the time. Especially on a nice night like tonight, cloudless with a cool breeze blowing.

But what *was* strange was the sound kept drawing nearer. And nearer. As if this bike wasn't simply passing by.

I lifted my eyes to the bay window, leaned forward, and squinted when the engine cut off.

Right outside my house.

No. No way.

"Syd," I said in warning as I stood from the couch and sat my bowl on the coffee table. "Did you give Jamie my address?"

"Did I mention how good your pie was? Brian had seconds," she quickly informed me.

My best girl was avoiding. She was guilty and she was avoiding.

The entire conversation we just had was making all kinds of sense now. *New* sense. As was her tone.

A knock sounded at the door.

I gasped, my hand squeezing that phone so hard I thought it might break. "Tell me you *did not* tell that loser where I live," I hissed as I marched across the room.

"I can't do that," she responded.

"Syd!"

"Well, I can't! I'd be lying if I said I didn't tell him!"

"You are unbelievable," I scolded her, reaching the door. I stood on my toes and peered through the peephole.

King of all bastards was smirking like an idiot.

Perfect.

"Go away!" I hollered.

His smirk twisted into a smile as his upper body shook with a laugh. He stepped closer while jerking his head to get his wavy hair out of his eyes, looked directly at me through that peephole, and warned, "Open up, Legs. Don't make me pick the lock."

I dropped back onto my heels. My spine straightened.

Pick the lock? He wasn't serious, was he?

"What did he say?" Syd whispered excitedly in my ear. "Put me on speaker so I can hear everything."

I scowled. Seriously? She was terrible. And a traitor if I ever knew one.

"He said thanks for being Team Jamie all this time. He appreciates it," I lied. Then I disconnected the call without saying a good-bye, per usual, set my phone on the console table, pressed my fingertips to the door, and stood on my toes again to glare at blue eyes.

"I am not letting you in," I informed him. "So you might as well get back on your bike and head on down the highway. And when you reach the ocean, do us all a favor and keep going."

He cocked his head. "Babe, don't play with me. I got pie I wanna eat and I don't wanna do it sitting out here on your porch. Open up."

"What?" I looked as low as my eye could see, which reached close to mid-torso on Jamie. "What are you talking about? What pie?"

He lifted his right hand when prompted, and when he did, I saw he was holding my late nana's ceramic pie plate with the ruffled edges and the washed-away floral lace design speckling the side.

It was irreplaceable. It held meaning and memories and was *always* cherished and handled with love.

And it was delivered to me on a motorcycle. By a loser...

Gasping, I stepped back and made quick work of the lock, then I twisted the knob and swung the door open, getting right up in Jamie's face to yell, "Do you have *any* idea what this pie plate means to me? Give me that!"

I reached for it, but Jamie held it out of my grasp.

"Relax before you make me drop it," he cautioned, all calm and smooth while keeping his arm between us to hold me back.

Before *I* make him drop it? I bared my teeth.

"Give it!"

When I stepped closer to try and snatch it again and bring it to safety, he stepped into me, wrapped that arm that was between us around my waist, picked me up, and carried me with him inside, all while balancing my precious pie plate with a hand I didn't trust.

"Let go of me!" I cried, wanting to twist and wiggle free but keeping still so I wouldn't jar the plate.

He did let go of me, but not until after he kicked the door shut, stared deep into my eyes, squeezed me tight with the one arm keeping me off the ground, and said in a low, promising voice, "Know what this means to you, so fuckin' relax. I was careful."

Chest rising and falling rapidly, I blinked up at him after my bare feet touched the hardwood floor.

Syd must've told Jamie about the plate. She also must've trusted him enough to get it to me safely, but that didn't mean *I* trusted him. I wasn't even sure I believed him, even though the evidence was right in front of me.

"How?" I asked. "You need two hands to ride, don't you? How were you careful?"

Jamie slid his hand along my back and settled it on my hip, stared down at me, and held the plate next to my shoulder while explaining, "Just was. Rode one-handed before. I knew what I was doing. And before you give me any more shit, know if I thought I was riskin' dropping this thing, I would've pulled over, dialed up Sunshine, and gotten her to come help me out. Okay?"

"I don't like you risking something of mine that's precious," I replied. "I don't trust you, Jamie."

"No? Could've fooled me. I thought we were tight."

I scowled. Then I shifted my scowl between the plate and his face, asking, "Are you gonna hand that over or do I need to beg?"

Jamie's eyes brightened and his dimples popped out. "Begging already?" he teased. "That was quick. I thought for sure I'd be workin' you up a little before you gave it up, Legs." He slowly shook his head. "Gotta say, you made this too easy. I'm a little disappointed."

I felt his fingers tense on my side, then realizing he was still touching me and remembering what touching led to yesterday, I quickly stepped back and held my hands out, palms up and expecting.

Jamie breathed a laugh, looking between my hands and my face, then he lifted the plate and inhaled, keeping his gaze on me and smiling through it.

"Fuckin' starved for this. Smelled it the whole ride here. Come on."

With wide eyes I watched him walk past me and head for the couch.

My couch. In *my* house.

"What do you think you're doing?" I called out, trailing behind him.

He tossed a pillow out of the way and sat down on the far end. After setting the pie on the coffee table, he gripped the bottom of the dark oak and pulled it closer until the table was almost touching his knees.

"Sit down. Eat with me," Jamie ordered, rubbing his hands together and hovering over the plate after pulling back the Saran Wrap. He tipped his chin at my bowl of noodles. "See I interrupted you, so don't give me shit about not bein' hungry. I know you are. Come on."

I stopped beside the couch and stuck my hands on my hips. "What makes you think I want to eat with you? I don't even want you in my house."

"Too bad."

"Excuse me?" I bent a little at the waist. "*Too bad?* Are you crazy? I could call the cops, you know? You're trespassing. This is private property."

Jamie laughed under his breath. He turned his head to look at me.

"You reach for that phone and I'm gonna give you a repeat of yesterday, which I don't mind doing, babe, considering what your fuckin' mouth tasted like, so go ahead," he warned, letting his gaze settle on the cleavage popping out of my dress, which I realized I was openly displaying for him since I was bending for emphasis.

Shit.

I quickly straightened up. "You can't threaten me like that," I informed him.

His eyes took their time reaching my face, and when they did, they were burning.

"Think I just did," he stated. He cocked his head. "Now, you callin' or what?"

I quickly realized I was in a bind, and under no circumstances did I want *or need* a repeat of yesterday, except for maybe the part where I tapped Jamie with my car. That I wouldn't mind doing daily.

But the other stuff, which led to me making bedroom noises? No. No way. That was never happening again.

Huffing out a breath, I shook my head.

Jamie smirked, then looked back down at the plate he was hovering over and fished out a precut slice with his hand.

"Normal people use forks," I commented, not at all sounding rude, in my opinion, but simply pointing out the facts.

"Good for them," he shot back, sounding every bit of rude. *Bastard.* He glanced over at me before taking a taste. "You gonna stand there and watch me eat or are you gonna sit?" he asked. "'Cause you can do either one, Legs, but I ain't goin' anywhere until I enjoy this pie, and you ain't rushin' me."

"I don't want you here."

"And I already cleared up my views on that when I said too bad," he reminded me. "Warned you already, so I don't know why you're actin' all surprised about this."

"Warned me about what?" I asked, stepping closer.

Jamie exhaled exhaustively as if this conversation was a chore for him, *please*, sat his elbows on his knees, and held the slice above the plate in case of drippings, which I appreciated but I wasn't about to tell him that. Then he looked me in the eyes and went on to explain,

"Said you'd be seeing a lot of me while we both wait for you to cave and come beggin' for my dick, and that's what's goin' on here, babe. You're seeing a lot of me. Got your address from Sunshine, which I'm guessin' you figured out by now, meanin' I don't gotta limit my exposure to the shifts you work at Whitecaps. Anytime I feel like seein' you, I'm gonna see you."

I blinked at him, trying to absorb everything he'd just said but only managing to focus on the very first horrible chunk of information he shared, and while I focused on that shocking admission, my heart started racing.

"You were serious about all of that? You actually want to *bet* me?" I asked.

Jamie lifted his brows. He didn't say anything, but I read that look. He was serious. *Completely* serious. Meaning Syd was right.

I was in a sex competition with Jamie McCade.

Son of a ... *bitch*.

"I'm not playing," I quickly announced, shaking my head. "No way. *No* way."

This was absurd.

Jamie looked back down at his slice. "You're playin'," he said.

"No, I'm not."

"Yeah, babe, you are."

"Don't tell me what I'm doing, Jamie."

His eyes cut to mine again, only now they were filled with heat and a desire to challenge. Then I watched as he placed the slice back in the dish, shoved the coffee table away, sucked the juices off his fingertips while coming to his feet, and once they were clean, reached down with both hands to work at his belt.

My eyes jumped between his hands and his face as my heart went from racing to runaway, threatening to break free from my chest. *Why is he working at his belt? He's supposed to be eating pie and then leaving. What is going on?*

"What are you doing?" I asked. My voice shook with anxiousness.

His belt whipped lose, startling me. Then he popped the button on his shorts while sharing, "Bet already started, Legs, so if you're tellin' me you ain't playin', that means you're throwin' in the towel and admittin' this is what you want. And if that's the case, I'll take my pie after I'm done takin' you."

What?

WHAT?

His eyes darkened. "Time to find out how greedy that pussy really is," he growled, unzipping his shorts.

I inhaled sharply through my nose. The sound from his throat and the slide of his zipper rolled up my spine.

"Wait!" I pleaded, holding up my hand while his reached inside his shorts.

Jamie froze. He cocked an eyebrow. And he waited.

I was on the verge of throwing up. I'd never felt panic like this. Not just because of what I'd prevented, but because of what I knew to be fact; there was only one way I could play this out.

"Fine, okay? I'll play your stupid game," I told him. "Just please don't . . . take out your penis."

I turned my head away and winced.

Good God. What was happening? I almost saw it.

I almost saw Jamie McCade's penis.

That wasn't a risk I was willing to take. I'd seen ugly penises before, but knowing my luck, there would be nothing ugly about what Jamie was packing and no amount of lying on my part would convince that loser of my disinterest.

He'd most likely won trophies for that thing, too.

A chuckle drew my attention back around.

"Why, Legs? What's your problem? Once you see it, you know it's game over for you?" Jamie questioned with all the arrogance in the world while zipping and rebuttoning his shorts.

Probably.

What? No! I pinched my eyes shut.

God, I was going to kill Syd. She was basically dead to me.

"Just sit down and eat your stupid pie," I ordered, stepping between the couch and the coffee table and huffing in annoyance.

I wanted to get back to my food while it was still warm, and maybe if I let Jamie eat, he'd leave sooner rather than later.

Maybe . . .

I was clinging to that hope, as weak as it was. I wanted him gone. No. I *needed* him gone.

So I picked up my bowl of barely touched pasta and resumed my position on the couch, only now I was sitting smashed up against the armrest instead of in the middle of the cushion.

Distance was my friend. I'd given up on comfort.

Laughing under his breath, Jamie took a seat and scooted the coffee table closer again, causing my knees to bend since my bare feet were propped up on the edge.

I twirled noodles around my fork and started eating.

He started eating, too.

Not that I was watching, because I wasn't. I kept my eyes on the muted TV and took up lip-reading a repeat episode of *Law & Order: SVU*.

When Mariska kneed a perp in the balls, I smiled and imagined he had ocean-salty hair and a surfer's build.

He didn't. He was old and bald and looked like a retired bus driver. But in my head, I was watching someone different drop to the floor.

This was the best show ever.

I was on my third bite of pasta and engrossed in the storyline when Jamie finally spoke.

"Damn. What kind of pie is this?" he asked, smacking his lips loudly and humming in delight.

"Strawberry rhubarb," I answered.

"Strawberry what?"

"Rhubarb."

"What the fuck is a rhubarb?"

I slurped some noodles into my mouth before turning my head.

"It's what you're eating," I said around my bite, delivering some sass with my answer. "If you're curious about it, you can go home and google 'what is a rhubarb.'"

He sucked on his index finger while staring back at me.

I watched his lips, fully capable of doing a lot of things, remove the juicy goodness of my pie from his fingertip for a full second before realizing what I was doing and lifting my gaze.

Rookie.

Should've gone with the macaroon recipe. No juice, meaning no sucking on anything.

Live and learn, Tori.

"Ease up on the attitude, babe. You're gettin' me hard," Jamie shared. Then he leaned a little closer and added, "Unless that's your goal, then by all means. Keep throwin' it."

I sucked in a breath, quickly cut my eyes away, pressed my back firm against the couch cushion, and resumed eating my pasta.

My attitude was getting him hard? He wasn't serious, was he?

Do not look for evidence. Do not look for evidence. Do not look for evidence.

"Christ. This is gonna be a cake walk," Jamie chuckled. "I had you pegged to give me a run, but I take that back. I'm doubtin' you know what you're even in for."

I was on the brink of reacting to that comment with more sass when Jamie grabbed the remote from between us and pointed it at the TV, unmuted it, leaned back, kicked his legs out, and propped his sneakers up on the coffee table, crossing his feet at the ankles. Then he dropped the remote, threw one arm behind him over the back of the couch, and draped his other across the armrest, keeping his eyes on the program.

He was relaxing. Jamie was done eating, but he wasn't heading out. He was getting comfortable. In my house. On my couch. With his loser feet up on my coffee table.

No. Absolutely not.

I stood up, sat my bowl down, grabbed the remote he'd dropped between us, and turned the TV off.

"What the hell, babe?"

"It's time for you to go," I told him, knocking his feet off the coffee table and then shoving it back into position. "You ate your pie. Said you'd be leaving after you ate it. It's eaten, so you're set to leave."

I stood there waiting for him to get up, arms crossed over my chest while my foot tapped impatiently.

Jamie smiled and tipped his head back, keeping his arms exactly where they were. "I'm beat. Wanted to watch a little TV before I settled in," he shared.

My brows lifted. "Excuse me?"

"Beat," he repeated.

"I heard that part. Then I heard something about *settling in*."

"Yeah. That'll be happenin' after I watch a show with you."

"Settling in where, exactly?" I questioned, needing clarification more than my next breath.

I had a terrifying feeling I knew exactly where Jamie was planning on getting settled, and that feeling was only confirmed when he cranked that smile up in brightness, stretched his legs out again, crossed his feet at the ankles, and propped them up on the edge of the coffee table as he switched the TV back on.

Panic twisted my stomach into a tight knot. This wasn't just settling in. He was pulling an all-nighter.

Jamie McCade intended to sleep over at my house, and if that wasn't alarming enough, I didn't see an overnight bag, meaning he wasn't packing pajamas.

Suddenly getting an eyeful of Jamie's penis became the least of my worries. I might actually have to share a bed with it.

Oh, God.

I left all rational thought in the living room, and instead of demanding Jamie remove himself from my house or else, like a sane person, I freaked and took off running.

Again. It was becoming a pattern.

I grabbed hold of my dress to make sure I didn't trip on the hem and darted fast up the stairs, getting to my room out of breath and, in my mind, out of options.

He wouldn't leave if I asked, let alone demanded. I was sure of it.

So I did what I had to do.

"Legs!" Jamie hollered out from a floor below.

I shut and locked my bedroom door, then I took three steps backward until my calves hit mattress, scrambled onto the center of the bed, pulled my knees against my chest, and hugged them while keeping an anxious eye out.

My heart was pounding so loud I could hear the blood rushing in my ears.

Jamie was playing the game and he was playing it dirty. And I knew sitting on my bed and staring at that door, waiting for the knob to rattle, that he'd continue playing dirty, and knowing him, this was just the tip of the iceberg.

Things were going to get much, much worse.

So I made a choice that night, and I made that choice after an hour of waiting for him to force himself into my room, then investigating and finding my house empty, the front door locked, his bike gone from my driveway, and my pie rewrapped in cellophane and placed on a shelf in the fridge.

I was done running away and hiding when Jamie got to me, and I was done waiting around to see what else he was going to do.

I affected him. He was hard up. He'd admitted it a hundred times.

Meaning I had all the power and had it in me to take him down. I just needed to yield that power.

And I was ready. I could do this. I could win.

It was time I started playing the game, and if I had any chance at beating Jamie McCade and proving he was the one who wanted me enough to beg for this, not the other way around, there was only one way to play it.

Dirtier.

Chapter Four

JAMIE

Jesus. That fucking body...

Smirk twisting across my mouth, I shook my head and watched as Tori made her way toward me on the beach wearing the smallest goddamned bikini ever, black and bloodshot like the devil herself, with three triangles and some motherfucking dental floss holding shit in place, not concealing much but, instead, enhancing every knockout curve she had.

She was carrying herself like she'd worn it a hundred times before and knew the reaction it got her, meaning she was wearing it now for one reason and to get one reaction.

Mine.

Damn. All that tanned skin showing...

Motherfucker.

This was some strategic, mind-game shit right here. Something I would've done and did do, just last night. Showing up at her house uninvited and planting the idea that I was settling in and staying over got the reaction I was expecting out of Legs.

She didn't want in on this bet. Made that clear more than once. And she was quickly finding out just how far I was willing to take things and freaking out about it in the process.

That was all anticipated. I had her pegged. Knew she'd go running 'cause that was her thing. Wasn't the first time she ran away from me.

But this? No fucking way was I expecting this.

It was Monday afternoon, nearly three o'clock, and up until a minute ago I was standing by my board on the beach, a short walk down from Wax, the surf shop Dash and I owned together, and I was watching out for this chick I was supposed to be giving a lesson to.

Then red caught my eye, and I gave up watching out.

Couldn't believe what I was seeing at first. Legs never came around this spot. I would know. I was down here nearly every day instructing, and if she had been around, I would've noticed.

Then I got a good look at what she was wearing and I knew...

Game fucking on. Legs was here to play.

Her hair was up in a ponytail and blowing in the wind coming off the water, sending stray blond pieces into her face. She had a beach towel tucked under her arm, a bag over her shoulder, and big, red, retro-style sunglasses keeping her eyes hidden as she moved closer, but it didn't matter. I knew where she was looking. I knew *exactly* where she was looking.

And I was looking right on back.

So much for not wanting in on this bet. Now Tori was seeking to plant herself in my line of sight and make sure she had my full attention.

Well, mission accomplished. She was getting it.

Honestly, she could've stopped a mile down and would've had it then.

Fuck. I kept staring. I had to. Chest expanding with a deep breath, I watched her move closer, taking her in.

Taking it all in.

Hips swaying. Tits bouncing. All that smooth skin showing. Perfect legs. Toned stomach. And that bright red lip curving up.

Damn.

That fucking body.

Yeah...Mind-game shit right here.

Looks-to-fucking-kill came to a stop a foot away from where I was standing and pushed her sunglasses on top of her head.

"Huh. Small world," she said, feigning surprise at seeing me as she looked me over from my face to my board shorts and back up, doing it quickly so her gaze didn't linger.

And I knew it wanted to linger. She wasn't fooling anyone.

My smirk expanded. "You're kidding me with this shit, right?" I asked, wanting her to know I was aware of what she was doing.

"With what *shit*?" Tori asked back, tilting her head a little and squinting in the sun. "I'm just here to enjoy this beautiful weather on my day off. I don't see how that classifies as *shit*. Lots of people are enjoying it, if you didn't notice. It's a public beach. I know you probably think you own it, Jamie, but news flash, you don't."

I chuckled. *Christ.* Her fucking mouth was a major turn-on. She didn't even need the damn bikini.

Not that I'd stop her from wearing it. Ever.

"Who'd you call, Legs? Sunshine? She tell you I have a lesson to-day, right fuckin' now after verifying that with Dash? Or did you call Wax yourself and get the info you needed." I stepped closer and bent down, putting my face in hers and bringing my arms across my chest. "You ain't foolin' me, babe. I know exactly the *shit* you're pullin'," I promised.

"Oh? And what exactly am I *pullin'*?"

"The bikini."

"What about it?"

"*What about it?*" I echoed, dipping my eyes for a quick look down the front of her. "The wind picks up even the slightest bit and you're fucked, babe. I'm not even sure that classifies as swimwear."

Her blue eyes flashed bigger, filling with triumph.

"And what do you care what I'm wearing? You're done waitin' around for me, right? You're not interested anymore. Isn't that what you said?"

I straightened up, admitting, "Yeah, that's what I said," 'cause I had said it. No point in lying now.

How much truth I had wrapped up in that statement, I wasn't sure about.

And that I kept to myself.

Her mouth tipped up in the corner. "Then I'm not seeing what *shit* you think I'm *pullin'* here or why anything I do would have any effect on you, Jamie," she fired back. "Unless..." Tori took a step back, dropped her bag in the sand, and started shaking out her towel. "You still want it," she offered, turning her head and flashing an ear-to-ear smile.

I started breathing slower.

Shit.

Shit.

There it was. The first goddamned genuine smile she'd ever actually given me, and it was good.

No. It was damn good.

Better than the ones I took from her. The ones I *stole* from her. The ones she was always putting on others.

At Whitecaps. Hanging around at Dash's place on Sundays. To strangers or to people she knew, and her friends, the ones she really cared about.

I saw a lot of smiles from Tori Rivera. Real ones. She never faked it. Her smile lit her up. It was a beautiful fucking thing to watch. And what I felt witnessing her give that smile to other people is what kept me coming back after nine months of waiting and getting jack shit in return.

But now? Getting it put on me? *Fuck.* Yeah...it was good.

"Wow, Jamie, look at you." Tori laughed, jarring my focus. "You close to begging yet?"

I kept staring, liking the confidence growing in her voice and the way her hair looked, breeze-blown and light against her skin.

But I kept that to myself. I was winning this shit.

"You're pushin' it, babe," I told her. "Fair warning. Take it places you can handle. You don't..." I shrugged. "That's on you."

"I think I'm handling things just fine. More than fine, actually."

"Yeah?" I paused for a breath, waiting for hesitation to tighten her smile 'cause I had her pegged, and when it did, giving her a grin of my own before adding, "We'll see about that."

Handling things fine, my ass. She had no idea what I was capable of.

Legs covered her tell and rolled her eyes, uttering a quiet "whatever" before bending over and spreading out her beach towel in a spot where there wasn't much room for another beach towel considering the crowd. Didn't matter, though. She was making room 'cause she was on her little mind-fuck mission to distract me.

Whatever.

I shook my head and laughed, then turned away to watch out for this girl I was waiting on.

I had all afternoon to stare.

"Well?"

My head swiveled back around at the sound of the voice over my shoulder.

Tori was standing in front of me again with her hands on her hips, feet spread, head cocked, and brows lifted expectantly. Like she was waiting for me to do something.

Do what, exactly, I had no idea.

"Well, what?"

She smiled big, drawing my eyes down to the cute curve in her mouth. "I'm ready for my lesson," she informed me.

My eyes snapped back up to meet hers again and quickly narrowed. "Your *what*?"

"My lesson."

"What lesson?"

"I'm your three o'clock."

What the fuck?

"No, you're not."

She kept smiling at me, arguing, "Yeah, I am," as she shifted her weight from one foot to the other, swaying her hips a little.

I cocked an eyebrow, thinking she was acting weird. "Quit playin'. You ain't my three o'clock."

"Actually, *yeah*, it totally is me."

My jaw clenched. *Jesus.* I turned and squared off with her, facing her fully now and only keeping breath between us I was standing so close.

"Legs, for real, arguin' with me ain't gonna do shit," I informed her, watching that damn smile of hers keep. "You're not my three o'clock."

"*Yes*, I am your three o'clock. I swear I am. Promise."

I breathed slowly, keeping annoyance at bay and the urge to toss her hot little ass into the ocean under control while thinking back to the name printed on the sign-up sheet.

I'd checked it this morning before heading out. I knew who my lesson was with.

Then seeing that name materialize in my head, I allowed my face to relax, gave her a smile back, and shared, "Nice try, babe. Seriously. Like the effort you're putting out, too, but you want a lesson with me, you need to call the shop. My three o'clock is with a Mira." I tipped my head at her towel, ordering, "Have a seat. You can watch me with her. Know that's what you're really here for anyway. Not this bullshit about enjoying the weather."

"It's *My*-ra. Like *My* Girl," she said, tilting her head side to side for emphasis.

My brow tightened again.

"Say what?"

Tori giggled. Her hand came up and swept some stray hair out of her face, tucking the strand behind her ear.

"Aw, look at you. So confused. Myra is my middle name. Tori Myra Rivera." Her nose wrinkled in disgust. "It's terrible, I know, but I had to use it. If I would've called and told Cole the lesson was for Tori, or *Legs*, you would've known who to expect and I didn't want you expecting anything." She tipped her chin up. "You know, for the sake of the bet."

I stared down at her, blinking as everything—the timing, the location, this entire sex-shop bikini charade—started coming together in perfect fuck-me unison.

"Are you *shittin'* me? *You're* Myra?"

Tori's eyes went round as she pinched her lips together, fighting laughter.

"Straight up?" I pressed.

"What? You can't handle it?" she questioned. Her voice was pure innocence. "Is there a problem with me getting a lesson from you or something?"

I felt my chest quake with a laugh. Jesus. She was giving me a run. Good. I liked that.

"Babe, you messed up," I told her, smiling at her reaction and the lengths she'd gone to.

Her eyebrows lifted in question. She wanted to know what I meant.

Fine.

Never had a problem being up-front with Legs before when it came to what to expect out of me. Sure as fuck didn't have a problem being up-front about it now either.

There was no way I was losing this bet. So I shared.

"Not sure how Cole does it or anyone else for that matter, but the way I give lessons, I'm hands on with it. Not with everyone. Sure as fuck not with another dude lookin' to learn, but you?" I let my gaze dip down the length of her, getting an eyeful before settling on her face. "Straight up. My hands are gonna be all over you for the next hour and don't even think for one second I'm not gonna take advantage. You wave opportunity in my face, and babe, I'm takin' that opportunity, meaning you're fucked, Legs. Just bein' around me gets to you. Now you're offerin' this? You might as well throw in the towel now. Or just start moaning right here. We both know that's comin'."

When I finished speaking, I noticed she was no longer fighting laughter. In fact, she was back to looking at me the way she always looked at me—like everything I said pissed her the hell off.

And I'd be lying if I said I hadn't missed that look a little. Pissed-off Tori was sexy as shit.

"Is this part of the lesson?" she griped. "Listening to you build your ego up? 'Cause honestly? It's not worth the money I paid."

I chuckled. Fuck. I could go all day with her. And she was setting me up for it too.

"Only thing buildin' during this lesson is gonna be your need to rub one out later," I shot back. "Which, you do that, and you're callin' in the bet, meanin' I win."

"That won't be happening," she snapped. "The building part or you winning anything. You see what I'm wearing."

And there it was.

Game plan revealed.

I smiled big, confirming, "Yeah, I see it. I see a lot of bikinis doin'
what I do. And I get your play here, Legs, but for real, you are out of
your fuckin' mind wearin' that to surf."

No joke. I was predicting a minute in the water before something
shifted and popped out.

"I think I'll manage," Tori argued, reaching around her neck to
loosen the strings of her top.

She pulled them tight and went about reinforcing the tie, thinking she was making things more secure but really only causing her
tits to bounce and push up higher.

I watched this happen. I had to.

Jesus.

Guys typically had a preference when it came to size. Big. Small.
Not me, though. Tits were tits. I liked them big. I liked them small.
I liked them spilling out of my hands and fitting into my mouth.
Whatever. But seeing Tori's tits in the getup she was wearing? Get-
ting the view I was getting right now? Yeah...now I had a fucking
preference.

Hers.

I stared openly at the shadow of her cleavage until her arms
dropped to her sides, signaling she was finished, and still, I stared for
another full second before lifting my head.

Who wouldn't? She was putting shit on display for me. And on
top of that, she was making her shit bounce.

Besides, looking wasn't begging. I could look all I wanted.

"Well?" She pulled her sunglasses off and tossed them on her
towel. "You ready?"

I looked her straight in the eyes. *Fuck yeah, I was ready. Was she?*

"Don't say I didn't warn you," I reminded her, stepping back and
holding my arm out.

She walked past me toward my board, grinning like a winner,
swaying her hips and checking over her shoulder to make sure I was
watching.

I was.

Tori didn't just have the tits. She had the ass, too. And I was looking my fill.

Then I moved to stand on the opposite side of her, putting the board between us, and went about going over some basics.

Everything was protocol. I started off the same way as every lesson. Except instead of telling Tori where to put her body, I put her body in the positions I wanted her to be in, explaining my steps as I went along and adjusting her even when she really didn't need adjusting.

I was playing the game. And I was taking opportunity.

"Bend your knees more. Drop lower," I said, standing behind her and pressing close, cock to ass, running my hand down the back of her thigh and pushing it out while my other hand fit around her waist and flattened on her stomach.

She was low enough on the board. There was no need for what I was doing.

Except there was extreme need for what I was doing. She felt so damn good against me.

"That line on the board, keep it centered on your body when you're paddlin'. Right here," I told her, indicating midline by brushing my fingertips down her throat to between her collarbone and farther down, stopping just at the top of her cleavage.

Way unnecessary. Who didn't know where the center of their body was? Even a kid could point to their fucking belly button.

But again, taking opportunity. I'd be a damn fool not to at this point.

Her breathing hitched, too quiet to hear over the noise around us, but I felt it shudder and pause against the pads of my fingers.

That was her only tell. She was determined.

Didn't step out of my arms. Didn't tell me to stop. She wouldn't give an indication that this was affecting her. No fucking way.

Tori was here to win and was bringing her game just as hard.

"Like this?"

"Is this right?"

"Jamie, I ... can you help me?"

She'd ask, in this sweet bedroom voice that made blood run hot in my veins.

Smiling. Bending low. Popping her ass out. Grabbing on to me and acting like she was losing balance when she wasn't. Taking the band out of her hair and letting all that soft blond down, allowing it to blow in the breeze like she was on location for a damn swimsuit calendar shoot.

Straight up. I'd buy enough of them to wallpaper my fucking house. She was looking that good.

After I had her practice popping up on the board more times than needed, which should've been for her benefit, but considering what she was wearing, it was for mine, I told her to hop off and picked my board up off the sand.

"Come on. Let's get you out," I said, walking toward the water.

"What?"

I turned my head and looked back at Tori. She hadn't moved.

"Let's go," I urged, starting to walk again but halting when she didn't follow. "Legs . . ."

"Why?" she asked, suddenly looking unsure and unsettled, her fingers knotting together at her stomach.

"*Why?*" I echoed. "What do you mean, *why?* You're surfin', right?"

"Yeah, but why go out?" She gestured at the sand. "It's my first lesson. Shouldn't we just do everything out of the water? You know, to make sure I'm *ready* to surf? I feel like that's the right way to go about things."

"Yeah? You suddenly a pro?"

"I'm just making a suggestion."

"Well, your suggestion sucks," I shot back. "Ain't gonna be ready if you don't get in. You won't learn until you're out there."

She caught her bottom lip between her teeth and shook her head.

"Babe, for real, if you're worried I won't be touching you like I've been doing for the past twenty minutes just 'cause you'll be in the water, don't be." I smiled at her. "There's a lot I can do in that ocean."

Her eyes narrowed. She released her bottom lip and started moving toward me with purpose.

"Just make sure when you start begging, you do it with your head above a wave. I don't wanna miss it," she said when she reached my side.

Water splashed under her feet.

I chuckled, and we both continued out. She was moving slow, staying a foot behind me, but I figured it was because of her suit and her not wanting anything to shift.

Figured that was the reason for her hesitation going out initially, too.

I dropped the board in the water when we got in waist deep, keeping hold of it. "Go ahead and get on. I'm gonna let you ride a few in on your stomach first before we get you poppin' up," I instructed, looking down the board at her.

Tori had her arms pulled in close to her chest and was watching the water, eyes darting left and right, body shaking, letting the waves move her instead of bracing and keeping herself steady.

Jesus. She was really worried about flashing people in that thing.

"Legs."

Her head jerked up and those pale blues connected, then she grabbed on to the board like she needed it for safety and slid her grip down, moving deeper into the water and getting closer to me.

"You ready?" I asked, watching her do these weird, jerking movements every time a wave rolled under us.

She nodded quickly. "What do I do?"

"Just get on. I'll push you in." Looking out, I saw a bigger wave coming at us. I gripped the board to keep hold of it and instructed, "Wait. Watch this wave," then I ducked under the water while keeping my grip on the board so I wouldn't lose it, not counting on Legs to keep hold of it and figuring she'd be relying on me to do it and worrying about herself.

The wave rolled above my head.

I popped up, wiped the water out of my eyes, brushed my hair back, and braced for her to climb on.

But she wasn't there.

"Legs."

I looked left and then right, thinking maybe she'd drifted a little. I studied the crowd. All the people around me. There were a lot. I didn't see her.

"Legs!" I yelled out, searching harder.

Nothing. My chest got tight.

"TORI!"

I let go of my board and moved around, peering behind groups who were wading together and looking for blond hair.

The water was crowded. And when you're panicked and looking for someone, you don't look as well as you should.

You skim for features. You don't linger. You try and cover as much area as you can.

That was why I didn't see her until I did, which was a good five seconds after my heart crawled into my throat.

Relief flooded me as I focused on her. I let out a breath.

Tori was hunched over in knee-deep water a good twenty feet away, facing the ocean, crouched low and curled in on herself like she was shivering and trying to stay warm.

I rushed over to her, forgetting about my board. "Jesus. Are you okay?" I asked. "You scared the shit outta me. I couldn't see you."

Staying in that wrapped-up position, Tori shook her head in answer, keeping her chin tucked.

She was a little rattled by the wave. I understood that. And I figured the least I could do would be to offer up some comfort to help settle her down.

"That happens to everybody," I said, speaking nothing but honesty. "Some of these waves are brutal. Come on. You're all right." I reached to help her up, but she jerked away and hunched over even farther, nearly folding in half. "Legs."

"My top," she said, voice lowered and anxious. She tipped her head back, and I saw her gaze was wild with panic. "I lost it. I—I...I'm naked. I lost my top."

My eyes went wide.

I looked at the way her arms were crossed over her chest, making an X. Her hands were curled into fists and tucked against her neck.

"Oh, shit," I laughed.

Tori gaped at me.

"Sorry. It's just"—I rubbed at my jaw—"I told you that suit was a bad idea."

"Would you help me, *please*?" she cried. "I don't know what to do."

"All right. Relax."

I stepped in front of her and bent down, getting close. Waves crashed on my back.

"Feelin' the need to say a little prayer for this. Might suck for you, but honest to God, this might be the best day of my life," I joked, wanting to lighten up the mood a little for her since she was still looking shaken up from the wave.

Her lip was trembling. I watched drops of water run down her cheek and felt my brow tighten.

Was she crying? Shit.

She was seriously worked up.

"Come on," I said, holding my arms out. "Climb on up."

She blinked. "W-what?"

"Gonna carry you in. Just wrap around me and stay pressing close. Nobody'll see shit. Come on."

She looked at me, at my arms being offered out, going back and forth between the two and then blinking up at my face.

I dropped to a knee and moved closer. "Swear it. I won't let anybody see anything. Okay?" I promised, looking into her eyes and reading her hesitation. "Just climb on, babe. I got you."

"What about your board?"

"Fuck my board. I'll get it later."

Tori wavered, still watching me. Studying me. Wanting to read my honesty and feel it for herself. Then, keeping her elbows tucked close, she slowly reached out before fully committing to the decision, and once that was done a second later, she went for it, launching herself out of the water and climbing onto me, arms circling my neck and legs locking tight around my waist.

Her heart was pounding and her limbs were shivering.

Standing, I held on to her, gripping the bottoms of her thighs and hitching her higher before I started walking us in.

"Can't say I'm hatin' this," I shared, turning my head so my mouth was against her ear.

"Are people looking?" she asked.

I leaned away and saw her eyes were pinched shut.

"Yeah, they're lookin'," I told her, smiling and watching ahead. "They can't see shit, but they're lookin'."

She gripped me harder. Her tight nipples brushed against my chest.

"Jesus," I murmured.

"What?"

"You feel so fuckin' good like this."

I felt her head move against the side of mine. "I hate you," she whispered.

I smiled again, reaching her towel and the bag she'd dropped next to it. "You got somethin' in there to cover up with?" I asked.

Still trembling in my arms, Tori shook her head.

"Jesus, babe. You need to relax," I told her, not understanding the way her body was still tensing up. I headed toward my setup. "Got you out without no one seein' anything and I'm gonna continue makin' sure no one sees anything. You can wear my shirt. Problem solved. And straight up, plenty of people get knocked down by waves. Even me. So just let that shit roll right off you. It ain't a big deal."

"You don't know anything," she said.

"No?" I asked gruffly. "How 'bout you enlighten me then. What don't I know?"

I slid one arm up her back, keeping the other under her ass for support, then I bent over and snatched up my shirt I'd discarded, returning that hand back under her ass as I straightened up and kept us moving until I reached a sand dune that could provide the cover she was wanting right now.

It had tall brush overgrowing on the top of it and down the sides, stood above my head, and butted up against a fence that also had high, unkempt brush growing all around it, meaning no one could stand behind that fence and get an eyeful of Tori while she was changing.

"Well?" I urged when I got us back there.

She sighed. "Forget it."

"Don't do that. I fuckin' hate that shit," I bit out, then I started pulling her away from me. "Go ahead. Hop down."

She stiffened in my arms.

I stopped pulling, laughed when she scrambled close again, and explained, "Got you back here where no one can see you. You're good."

Tori slowly leaned away enough to look at our surroundings but not enough so I could see anything when I glanced down the front of her, then she met my eyes, catching me trying to get a glimpse, and warned, "You don't get to look."

I cocked a brow. "Felt 'em. Considerin' you gave me that, I'll give you this."

"How sweet."

"You want sweet?"

"I want to get dressed."

She wiggled, trying to slide down.

I locked my arms into a tighter hold, got a glare from her, and smiled. "Sorta missed that," I said, talking about her sass. I put her on her feet and handed over my shirt when she reached for it with one hand.

She kept her other arm pressed against her tits. Then after taking the shirt, she wiped at her face, sniffed, and quickly turned away to get covered up.

I shook my head, smiling. "Jesus, Legs. I always thought you had ice in your veins," I said, crossing my arms over my chest. "Alls it takes is a little wave to knock you over and you get all soft on me. What's up with that?"

"I can't swim."

My mouth tightened. Then my gaze narrowed in on the back of her head as blond popped through the hole in my shirt.

The fuck did she just say?

"You wanna repeat that?" I asked.

She slid her arms through the sleeves, tugged the hem down her body, and turned her head. "I can't swim. I'm not a good swimmer," she said on a shrug. "That wave really scared me."

I lowered my arms and stepped closer, jaw clenching so tight it started to ache. "Are you bein' straight with me right now?" I growled. "You can't fuckin' swim? For real?"

She turned around, saw my expression, and sighed, letting her eyes fall to the sand between us.

"Look at me," I ordered. Her eyes lifted, and when I had them, I stepped even closer, getting up in her face. "Asked you a question, and honest to God, Legs, know we joke around and everything, but right now, I am not fuckin' jokin' around. Tell me you know how to swim."

"I know how to swim," she quickly answered.

I released a breath. Then I inhaled another one sharply when she went on to add, "Sort of."

Motherfucker.

"Sort of? What the fuck is *sort of*? What's that mean?"

"Like, I know the basics. I'm just not a strong swimmer," she explained, still speaking fast. "I haven't really ever been out in the ocean before. That was my first time."

I pinched my eyes shut. "Jesus," I mumbled.

"And I typically stay in the shallow end of the pool."

I shook my head.

"Also, I sort of nearly drowned when I was four."

My eyes slowly creaked open, staying narrowed. "*Say again?*"

"I nearly drowned when I was four."

I stared at her, nostrils flaring, jaw tightening, and gaze so intense she slowly leaned away to get some distance from it.

"Sorry," she whispered.

Sorry?

I bridged the distance she'd just put between us and crowded her against the fence, keeping my arms on either side of her. She had nowhere to go.

"Jamie—"

"You came here wantin' a lesson from me, a motherfuckin' *surf lesson*, which is a water sport, babe, requires water, lots of it, and didn't think to mention the fact that you've never been in the ocean before, might be a little unsure about it, and fuck, I don't know, also possibly straight up freaked the fuck out about the entire experience since you nearly died drowning when you were little? You didn't feel like that information was important enough to share?"

"I honestly didn't think you were going to take me out in the water."

"We're surfin', Legs. What the fuck do you think we're gonna do?"

"I don't know. Practice on land?"

I glared at her.

"I should've said something," she whispered.

"No fuckin' shit!" I barked, causing her to flinch and suck in a breath.

"God. Why are you yelling at me?"

Her eyes searched my face. She was breathing heavy.

"*Why?*" I straightened up and jabbed a finger at my chest. "Because I'm over here having the time of my life, smiling like a fuckin' idiot 'cause I got your tits pressed up against me after forcin' you out in the water when you were scared. *That's* why."

Her eyes flicked wider.

"I saw your hesitation goin' out," I continued. "I read you, but since you didn't feel the need to share your fuckin' fears with me, I wasn't worried about it. Figured you were just nervous 'cause of that suit you were wearin'. Not 'cause you nearly died when you were a kid. Jesus Christ. What the fuck's wrong with you?"

Tori blinked several times. Her mouth tightened. "I'm sorry, okay? It was that stupid bet! I was just trying—"

"Fuck the bet! Something could've happened to you!"

She sucked in a breath and pressed her fingers to her lips, looking on the verge of tears.

"Shit," I muttered, stepping back and scrubbing at my face roughly with my hands. My chest was heaving. My muscles were locking tight.

What the fuck? I was losing it. I needed to chill out.

She wasn't hurt.

But she could've been. *Shit.*

"I'm sorry." Her voice was quiet. Barely above a whisper.

I dropped my hands and looked at her.

"I should've told you," she added once our eyes met. "I should've said something. I know that now. I'm sorry." She stepped closer. "Seriously, Jamie, I...I'm *really sorry.*"

"Yeah, you said that."

She blinked at me, fingers twisting in my shirt at her sides, chewing on the inside of her cheek and looking out of words, but also looking like she could break down at any second and fall apart in tears.

I was pissed, but I didn't want her crying.

I exhaled a breath and rolled my shoulders, eyes on the sand, trying to ease the tension pulling across my back and low in my neck.

It didn't work.

Fuck this. I had a better idea.

"Stay here," I ordered, pointing at her face.

It was tight with worry and regret. She blinked and nodded, letting me know she was gonna listen.

Good. Wasn't in the mood to track her ass down.

I stalked out from behind the dune, finding my board washed up on the beach. After propping it up against the lifeguard stand, getting permission to leave it there 'cause I was cool with the guy, I grabbed all of her shit and mine, which included my towel, a pack of smokes, and my lighter, then I went back around behind the dune, seeing Tori still standing where I left her, in the same position I left her in, with that same bothered look on her face.

"Let's go," I said, handing over her stuff. "You owe me a drink."

She blinked up at me and sniffled. "Excuse me?"

"A drink. We're drinkin'. Let's go." I moved to lead us to the tiki bar down the beach.

"I don't want to drink."

Halting, I turned my head, then I hit her with a scowl. "Worried the shit outta me. Got me hatin' my reaction to feelin' your perfect tits. And you were fuckin' scared." I grabbed her hand and tugged. "We're drinkin'. Both of us."

Eyes wide, Tori went with me. She didn't put up a fight. Not with her mouth or her body.

We were drinking.

Both of us.

Chapter Five

TORI

Jamie was pulling me down the beach. He had my hand wrapped in his and he was gripping it tightly.

And I was letting him.

Typically, I wouldn't be allowing any parts of Jamie to be touching any parts of me. Ever. No way. I knew what touching led to. But considering I'd already latched on to him like a monkey climbing a tree today, doing this half-naked no less, and also considering how terrible I was feeling about not telling him my past or my fears, I was letting Jamie do his thing and I wasn't fighting it.

I owed him that much.

Honestly, I probably owed him more than he was asking of me right now.

He was pissed. And he had the right to be pissed.

I should've said something.

It wasn't that I was scared of the ocean. Like I told Jamie, I knew the basics when it came to swimming. I *could* swim. I was just a little nervous when it came to large, unpredictable bodies of water, that's all.

Plus, there was the whole worry that I'd drown and have it be fatal this time. That might've been weighing heavy on my mind when I was hesitating walking out toward him.

Again, something I should've shared.

But no. I was playing dirty and too busy focused on hearing those sweet begging words to bother with sharing phobias. And now look at me.

Shaken up. Embarrassed. Letting this loser touch me. Missing half of the most expensive bikini I'd ever purchased and forced to cover up in a T-shirt that unfortunately didn't smell terrible, at all. In fact, it smelled amazing, and while I was being dragged down the beach, I was battling the urge to bury my face in it and inhale deep lungfuls of arrogant surfer boy.

So apparently, I was also out of my mind. All because I let some stupid bet get to me.

The tiki bar Jamie was leading us to was more like a mini restaurant right on the beach. It had the standard wooden bar top and stools for patrons to sit, torches burning, and calypso music pumping through the speakers. It also had a large seating area with tables and chairs shaded by umbrellas and a stage for a band to perform on, I was guessing. There was no one on it at the moment.

Once Jamie reached the tables, he released my hand. Then he headed straight for the bar, pulled out a stool for himself, pulled out one for me, caught my eye, and then gave me a look indicating I needed to sit in the stool he was offering or we'd be having words. Heated ones, most likely.

Again, I owed him.

He took his seat after I took mine.

I threw my bag up on the bar and kept the towel in my lap, then having free hands, I fixed my hair into a bun so it looked intentionally messy, not like I'd just gotten tossed around by a wave.

Hair situation under control, I was now halfway presentable and blending into the crowd nicely, considering everyone was wearing bathing suits or skimpy cover-ups.

"My man! What's goin' on, brother?" the bartender greeted Jamie, holding his hand out and then doing that thing guys do when they embrace by mixing a handshake with a one-armed hug.

The guy was shirtless, tanned, had long dark hair pulled back into a ponytail, and wore five different shell necklaces around his neck.

Jamie grew taller on his stool and reciprocated, leaning over the bar to do it and slapping the guy's back. Then he settled in his seat and tapped a cigarette out of the pack. "Not much, man. You? How ya been?"

"Good. Good. Same shit, ya know?"

Jamie lit up a cigarette, nodding his reply, flipped the lighter closed, took a drag, and then blew the smoke out above him.

I'd seen Jamie with cigarettes tucked behind his ear all the time, but I'd never witnessed him actually smoking before.

This was what prompted me to butt into their conversation and inquire.

"How come I've never seen you smoke?" I asked.

Jamie gave me a sideways look, barely turning his head. "'Cause I'm tryin' to quit," he answered, then he jerked his chin at the bartender. "Two Coronas. No lime for me. Give her one."

"I'm fine, thanks," I said, causing the man to pause midstep and bounce his gaze between the two of us, questioning what he should do.

"She's not," Jamie argued. "Get her a drink."

"I'm not thirsty."

"She is."

"No, really, I'm—"

Jamie turned his head.

His jaw was twitching, his eyes were hard, and he looked ready to debate my need for a beverage until one of us passed out from exhaustion, most likely me.

I sighed, remembering my poor judgment and the reason I was missing a top, then I gave the bartender a weak smile. "A Corona with lime sounds perfect. Thanks."

"Right on," he replied, stepping away to grab our drinks.

Jamie took another drag of his cigarette. He kept his eyes fixated behind the bar.

"So why are you smoking now if you're trying to quit?" I asked, watching him blow a perfect smoke ring out of his mouth. My brow furrowed. "And how long have you been trying to quit? Every time I see you, you have a cigarette stashed behind your ear. But you never smell like smoke. It doesn't make sense. Why would you have your lighter with you if you're trying to quit? Are you *really* trying to quit?" I tilted my head, studying him.

"Jesus Christ," he laughed, turning his head to look at me. "How many questions are you gonna ask me in one breath? You sound like Sunshine."

I shrugged. "What? That was like, two breaths, at least. I paused."

"Did you?" He raised his brows. "Must've missed it."

The bartender stepped in front of us again and sat our bottles down on the bar. He slid a plate next to mine that had a lime wedge on it.

"So when's your next meet?" he asked Jamie, leaning his weight on the wooden surface.

"Couple weeks."

"Nice. I need to get back out there. Knee's feelin' good now, so just need to find the time, ya know?"

Jamie nodded. "I hear that."

"I'm sorry," I interrupted, gaining attention from both of them but only giving it to the bartender. "Hi." I smiled.

He smiled back. "'Sup, babe?"

"Um, can you just give us a minute? I had a couple of questions I was really hoping to get answers to."

The bartender cocked an eyebrow.

Jamie threw his head back and laughed like he'd just heard the funniest thing imaginable.

I kept my gaze steady on the man behind the bar, thinking my request was understandable considering how curious I was feeling at the moment, and not at all amusing.

"For real?" The bartender looked at Jamie. He jerked his chin at me, asking, "This one yours?"

"Um, no. I am no one's," I answered firmly, grabbing my beer and popping the lime wedge in. "Definitely not his."

"She's obsessed with me," Jamie told the man, his amusement leveling out to a few quiet chuckles quaking in his chest.

"What?" I choked on a breath.

The bartender looked between the two of us and he did it nodding, as if he believed this nonsense.

Give me a break.

"Look at her. Shit's serious." Jamie tapped the ash off his cigarette into a nearby receptacle. "Can't keep her outta my shirts."

What?

WHAT?

I grew taller on my stool. "He's obsessed with *me*," I informed the bartender, and Jamie, since he'd apparently forgotten. "He practically stalks my entire life. And he offered me his shirt. He wanted me in it."

"Not gonna argue that," Jamie shot back, doing this while looking prideful.

My mouth was open and ready to dispute his rebuttal since I knew it was coming, but hearing that, it clamped shut. I slouched in my stool.

And I did this not thinking *anything* of Jamie wanting me in his shirt. Because there was absolutely nothing *to* think about it.

Nothing at all.

"See?" I glared at the bartender.

Smiling, he held his hands up in surrender and took a step back. "Leave you guys to it then," he said, then he looked at Jamie. "Good seein' you, man."

"Same," Jamie replied.

I watched the man move down the bar, then shifted my attention onto the lying loser's profile.

"So?" I asked.

Jamie turned his head. He brushed some wet hair out of his eyes, saying nothing.

Seriously?

"Are you going to answer my question?" I further probed when he didn't follow my lead.

"Which one? You asked me about thirty," he replied, giving attitude with his response.

I scowled. He was way off, but whatever. I decided on repeating the first question, and the one I was most curious about.

"Why are you smoking now if you're trying to quit?" I asked.

Jamie studied me for a breath and then looked away, focusing behind the bar again as he informed me, "Think you can figure that one out yourself."

I stared at his profile and thought back to his reason for dragging me here, hearing his words ring out to me in my head.

"I scared you," I offered.

His eyes slid to mine as he took another drag.

Swallowing, I nodded. *Right.* Stress was the trigger. That was understandable. People smoked and drank when they were stressed out.

And Jamie was stressed and smoking because of the stunt I'd pulled.

Damn.

I drank my beer, not liking the unsettling feeling washing over me as I took ownership of being the cause of his stress, and then I pushed those feelings aside because I had more questions I wanted answers to.

"So how long have you been trying to quit?"

Jamie blew the smoke out above him while stubbing out his cigarette, then grabbed his bottle and chugged a good bit of it.

"My turn," he said after swallowing, instead of answering me. He turned his head and read my confusion. "You got shit you wanna ask me and I got shit I wanna ask you. Just answered one of yours. Now it's my turn. That's how this is gonna go."

"Technically, I answered for you," I reminded him.

"And *technically*, you should've told me you were fuckin' scared, but you didn't," he bit out.

"I wasn't scared. I was just nervous."

His eyes hardened.

I pressed my lips together.

We were getting off track, and I wanted to stay on track, considering the questions I wanted to ask him. "Fine," I said, waving my hand. "Your turn. Go."

"How'd you almost drown?"

"It was at a birthday party. My mom thought my dad was watching me and he thought she was keeping an eye out." I shrugged when I saw emotion shadow his face. "I don't really remember it," I continued, studying the bottle I was holding in my lap. "Apparently, I got into the deep end of the pool by myself and someone saw me at the bottom."

"Jesus," Jamie mumbled.

"When they got me out, I started throwing up water. I didn't need CPR or anything, but my parents felt terrible. My mom still talks about it." I looked up at him. "I didn't get back in the pool again until I was nine."

Jamie shook his head, then looked away, uttering a "fuck" under his breath. His jaw started twitching above the sharp angle in it, like he was gritting his teeth, and his nostrils were flaring with the forceful breaths he was taking in.

I didn't understand why he was looking the way he was, like he wanted to punch my parents in the mouth for letting that incident happen in the first place, which was absurd. He couldn't be feeling emotions that deep. It wasn't possible. Why would Jamie care about something like that? About *me* like that?

No. I must've been reading him wrong. He didn't care. I was sure of it. So I swallowed a mouthful of beer and moved us on to the next point.

"How long have you been trying to quit?"

Laughter rattled in his chest as he looked at the bottle he was gripping. "Wasn't really tryin' anymore. I gave it up two months ago."

I felt my forehead tighten. "What?" I asked, leaning to the side so I could see more of his face. "What do you mean? You always have cigarettes with you."

He shrugged. "Like a challenge. Keepin' the stuff with me makes it harder to resist. Puts that need right in my face. I can't avoid it." Then he turned his head, keeping his body facing the bar and his elbows resting on the wood, and looked at me, not just at my eyes but at my whole face. My lips and the hair tickling my ear and my eyebrows. He looked at everything.

I straightened on my stool and started breathing slower. He should've stopped talking after that. Thinking back, I wished he would've.

Unfortunately, he had more to say.

"Harder it is to get somethin' you want, the better it feels when you finally get it," he added, letting his eyes settle somewhere between my chin and my cheek.

Was he...Did he mean...

No. He didn't.

Jamie was talking about wanting to quit smoking real bad and feeling good about it when it finally happened. That's what he meant. I was sure of it.

Only I wasn't.

Not with the way he was suddenly staring at me. Intently, like he was conveying something else entirely.

I stared back while a funny sensation started fluttering in my stomach.

This was not good.

There were other factors contributing to this feeling and making it stick. Factors I was paying more attention to all of a sudden or giving attention to for the first time.

We were sitting close. I was wearing Jamie's shirt. And he'd promised no one would see me when I was feeling vulnerable and made good on that promise.

Like he was protecting me. Like he actually cared.

A stupid person would think these factors meant something. That they were worthy of funny fluttering sensations and the attention I was giving them.

I was not a stupid person. And I wouldn't let myself think like one. I couldn't.

Only I was totally thinking like one. Which was why I didn't just take a sip of my beer when I brought the bottle to my lips. I downed most of it.

"So," I began after I'd finished swallowing, taking a few deep breaths and feeling the effects of the alcohol hitting hard. I looked at Jamie. "You quit smoking two months ago, and because of what happened with me, now you're smoking again?"

My stomach tensed. I didn't like being the reason for his slipup. I didn't want to feel guilty when it came to Jamie.

I didn't want to feel *anything*.

And knowing him, he'd hold this over my head until the day I was being lowered into the ground, making sure I felt it forever.

Jamie smirked, watching me take another generous drink. "Wouldn't say I'm takin' up the habit again," he clarified. "Needed a smoke after that shit, so I had one. It is what it is."

"And you're not going to have another?" I asked, bringing the bottle back to my lap.

"I don't know, Legs. You plannin' on pissing me off any more today?"

I narrowed my eyes.

"That a yes?" he questioned after I didn't respond, his full lips twisting into a smile.

"I just think it would be a shame to throw away the progress you've made. It's impressive." When his smile started growing, I quickly added, "And something a lot of people accomplish on a daily basis. Relax."

"Right," he mumbled, mouth still stretching wide.

He was enjoying this.

"Tons of people quit smoking, Jamie."

"Sure they do."

"You're nothing special."

"Think my mom will disagree with you on that."

I rolled my eyes.

Jamie laughed with his bottle to his lips, tipped it back, and finished it, then gestured for two more after noticing how low I was getting on mine.

"The house," he said after acknowledging the bartender with a jerk of his head and getting his new beer.

I finished off my Corona and swapped it out for the fresh one. "Huh?" I asked, not understanding his remark. "What house?"

"Got a pretty sick setup where you're at, and you're pullin' in waitress pay," he clarified.

I frowned. "Oh."

"I know what a house like that is worth, so I'm just wondering how it's even possible you're livin' there. What's the deal? You livin' off Daddy's money or something?"

My mouth grew tight. *Asshole.* "Hey. Screw you," I hissed. "That's such a crap thing to say, you know that? And if that's really what you think, then I don't need to be sitting here with you either, shooting the shit or whatever the hell this is. I'm gone."

I set my beer down, stood up, and reached for my bag, but before

I could grab it, I was being spun around and directed back onto my stool with a firm hand on my hip.

"Sit," Jamie ordered.

"No," I snapped, wiggling and managing to get to my feet again. "Get your hands off me. I'm leaving."

"You ain't leavin'. Sit."

He urged me onto the stool again, and this time, he did it with two hands, one on each hip, making my attempts at fighting back useless considering his strength versus mine. Then he kept his hands there, gripping me tightly as he leaned closer and put his face an inch away.

"You got a reason for what I just said pissin' you off, and you're gonna share that reason," he informed me, his tone nonnegotiable. "Made an assumption and it's one anyone would make considerin' what you do for a living, babe, so quit with the tantrum. You know I dig your attitude but only when I'm askin' for it. Now is not one of those times. And don't fuckin' forget why we're sittin' here in the first place, shootin' the shit, as you so put it."

"You shouldn't have said that," I whispered.

"Based on your reaction, I figured as much," he countered, letting his own voice dip lower, not as soft as mine but still quiet. "Now share."

I watched Jamie lean away, taking his hands off me and centering himself on his stool again. Only this time he kept his body facing me instead of the bar, propping one arm up on the wooden surface and keeping his other arm resting on his leg, where he went about cracking his knuckles, one finger at a time.

His eyes were unforgiving. Persistent bastard that he was, I knew Jamie wouldn't let this go.

He never let anything go. Not even me.

Sighing, I shook my head. "What do you want to know?" I asked. "How I got my house? You think I didn't pay for it? Because I did. And I'm still paying for it. Yes, my parents helped me with the down payment as part of my graduation gift, which is something a lot of parents do, not just well-off ones, but it's my name on the mortgage and it's my money keeping me living there. I do not take handouts from my family. All the money I have in my bank account is mine. I earned it. Waitressing and doing other things."

"What other things?"

"Pageants."

He cocked an eyebrow. "Like, Miss America shit?" he asked.

"I didn't enter that one. I quit when I was fourteen and you're not eligible for that one until you're seventeen," I informed him.

"How many . . . what'd you call them?"

"Pageants."

"Yeah. How many'd you do?"

"A lot."

"How many'd you win?"

"All of them."

A look of fascination passed over his face. "No shit," he murmured, smiling softly and moving his eyes up and down the length of me. "Looks of a fuckin' beauty queen and you actually got the rep to back it up. Nice."

I glanced down at what I was wearing, thinking I wasn't living up to that title much right about now. I wasn't even wearing pants.

"Thanks," I grumbled, tugging at the hem of his tee. I met his eyes. "So to answer your question, that's how I can afford the *sick setup* I'm living in while working as a waitress. My parents opened an account when I was little and all the prize money I earned winning those pageants went into it. Then when I turned eighteen, I got that money."

"What about your family?"

"What about them?"

"Said they were well off. What do they do?"

I gave him a look, not understanding why this question was being asked. "Uh, my last name is Rivera," I reminded him.

He stared at me for several beats, then asked, "That supposed to mean somethin' to me?"

"Well, yeah, it should be obvious."

"It ain't."

"Really?" I blinked at him. "Have you never been inside a grocery store? My head is all over the frozen food section."

He squinted in thought. "Say what?"

"Rivera Frozen Foods. Hello."

Jamie kept staring. He had no idea what I was talking about.

"Do you not eat vegetables?" I asked. "Or fruit? We do frozen fruit, too. And rice. Do you eat rice?"

"What do you mean, your head is all over the frozen food section?" he asked, ignoring my questions.

"My face is on the bags," I answered.

His eyebrows lifted.

"Well, my face when I was six. Pigtails. Freckles. I'm going like this." I curled my hands into fists and stuck them under my chin, smiling big. "Ringing any bells yet?"

He stared at me, then his chest moved with a laugh. "Honestly? No. But I typically go for fresh stuff if I'm wantin' it. Can't say I'm in that aisle a lot." He took a swig of his beer, never taking his eyes off me. "No shit, though? Your family owns a frozen food company?"

I nodded. "Yep."

"And you're a waitress?"

I knew what Jamie was getting at. And even though I could've let his question and the implication he was making by asking it anger me, I didn't.

I still kinda felt like I owed him. He smoked because of me. Also, he seemed to just be asking out of curiosity.

"I worked at the corporate office for two months after I graduated," I informed him, keeping my attitude out of it. "It wasn't working out, so I quit and moved here."

"It wasn't working out." He stated this in disbelief.

"Yeah, that's what I said."

"Explain that."

"Explain what?"

"Why you chose shitty tips over working with your family."

I shook my head, then I looked behind the bar. He wasn't getting that. I'd shared enough.

"Legs."

I turned my head and met his eyes, and instead of telling him what he wanted to hear, I shared what he needed to hear.

"I'm a waitress because I want to be a waitress, and there is absolutely nothing wrong with wanting that," I started. "I like my job. No. I love my job. I love every part of it. The people, both coming in to eat and the ones I work with. The location. The hours. The *shitty tips*, which are never shitty because I'm good at what I do, just so you know. I even love rolling silverware and filling salt shakers. I'm *that* crazy about it. Yes, I'm not gonna lie, it started out as something temporary and I wasn't planning on falling in love with Whitecaps the way I did, but it happened. And when I fell in love with it, I stopped looking at that job as temporary and started looking at it as something I could see myself doing for years, as long as I stayed happy. And that's what I am. I am happy, Jamie. Happier than I've ever been at any other job, including the one I had with my family, and I think being happy is more important than a lot of things. In fact, it might be the most important. I'm choosing to be happy. And I would appreciate it if you didn't talk *shit* about something that means a great deal to me."

"Wasn't talkin' shit," he immediately shot back. "Just curious why you were doin' what you were doin', babe, when you got opportunities elsewhere. Relax. I get you wantin' to be happy. And I get you wantin' to stay somewhere that makes you happy. Who wouldn't?"

I inhaled slowly through my nose, letting my nerves settle and tipping my chin up. "Good," I said. "I'm glad you get that."

The next breath I pulled in was sharp because Jamie leaned in and he did it quickly, letting his arm slide down the bar and crowding me on my stool. He looked deep into my eyes, lowered his voice, and continued on to say, "And whatever your reason for not stayin' on with your family and movin' to Dogwood, I'm gonna get that, too, just so you know, when you give it up."

"I'm not giving it up," I shared.

"You'll give it up."

"That's never happening, Jamie."

"It's happening, babe."

"No." I moved in, putting us even closer. "It isn't," I snapped. "That's mine. And you're not getting it."

"I'm gettin' it."

My lips curled against my teeth.

God, he was seriously annoying.

Jamie smiled, watching this happen, then he leaned away and reached for his beer, telling me, "Just like the bet. You'll give it up, Legs. Watch."

The bet.

Damn it.

My scowl was starting to form and it was going to be a scary one, until I remembered what I was capable of, what I was wearing, and more specifically, what I wasn't wearing underneath.

The bet.

Hell yeah. I had this in the bag.

I stood and I did it quickly, needing to play up the effect I was going for and figuring a little dizziness would help.

I was right.

"Whoa," I moaned, wincing. I held on to the bar and blinked Jamie into focus. "Can you help me to the bathroom? I'm feeling wobbly."

I was lying. Big-time. But Jamie didn't know that.

"You serious?" he asked, watching the display I was putting on.

I swayed and grabbed my head. This was all an act, too.

"Jesus, Legs. You barely made a dent in your second beer," he said, coming to his feet. He slid his arm around my waist, gripping me and taking my weight when I leaned into him, playing the part, then he started walking me toward the bathrooms, which were tucked back in this small, narrow hallway next to the stage, away from the crowd.

Away from everyone.

No one was about to see what I had planned, which was the reason I was going through with this.

The hallway was dark and concealed, and when Jamie stopped at the door decorated with a bikini top, *fitting*, indicating the women's room, he muttered a "there you go" under his breath and released me so I could enter.

Only, I didn't enter. Going to the bathroom wasn't part of the plan.

I righted myself, allowing my tipsy façade to fade away. Then I took a step back, turned, and blocked Jamie's path out of this perfectly hidden hallway. I looked him square in the eyes, gave myself a second to enjoy the baffled look in his, which I enjoyed immensely, he really did look confused, before telling him, "You're not the only one who never loses."

I was referring to my pageant days.

And then, I flashed him.

I *totally* flashed him.

Never before in my life had I done anything like this, but a bet was a bet. And I was winning this one.

Jamie's eyes lowered and he immediately started staring.

I was expecting shock. I was expecting desire, considering this was Jamie and I knew how he felt about me.

I got both.

I also got a groan.

Jamie McCade actually *groaned* looking at my bare breasts. That had never happened to me before.

This was the best plan *ever*. I was totally going to win.

Then he looked me in the eyes after I lowered his shirt, gaze burning, and promised, "You're gonna pay for that."

I didn't know if he meant now or later and I wasn't sticking around to find out.

Spinning around, I bolted to the bar, grabbed my things, and got the hell out of there.

And I did it grinning.

* * *

Later that night I was sitting on my couch, dressed comfortably in leggings and a baggy WildFox tee, and I was shifting my attention between the episode of *Mob Wives* I had cued up and the notepad I was doodling on, when I heard the sound of motorcycle pipes drawing closer and closer to my house.

I paused, pen stilling on the "e" I was tracing and head turning toward the window. My eyes narrowed.

He wouldn't...

The sound kept coming, growing louder until I knew without a doubt it was emanating from my driveway. Then the engine cut off.

He would.

"Bastard," I uttered, tossing the pad and pen on the coffee table and coming to my feet.

I marched to the door, unlocked it, swung the door open, and readied my greeting, which was going to be something along the lines of threatening castration if Jamie didn't step off my property immediately, I'd had enough of this, but no one was there. My porch was empty.

What the...

"Hello?" I called out, sticking my head outside and getting a look at Jamie's bike parked next to my car.

Weird. Where was he?

"Jamie?" I tried again, hollering a little louder this time.

"What's up, babe?"

Gasping, I spun around and clutched at my chest.

Jamie was standing in my living room, looking a little too pleased with himself based on the smirk he was wearing, and holding what appeared to be a take-out bag full of food in one hand and a six-pack of Cherry Coke in the other.

I blinked at him, feeling my heart pounding against my palm.

"What are you doing in here?" I asked, darting my eyes around my living space. "How did you even get in?"

"Back door. Figured you'd try and keep me out this time so I got creative," he answered, flashing me a smile when I looked into his face. He lifted his hand holding the bag of food. "Hope you like Chinese. Was gonna call, but I didn't want you expectin' anything. Sound familiar?"

I glowered.

"Got us an assortment," he added, then he started moving toward the couch.

"Excuse me?"

"Dinner," he clarified, even though I knew what he meant and exactly what this was.

It was happening again. Jamie was getting comfortable.

In my house. On my couch. With some seriously delicious-smelling food.

I shut my door, putting force behind it.

I was angry at him for showing up uninvited, again. I was especially angry at him for his honed skills in breaking and entering, a talent I was certain he'd put to use whenever the situation called for it, meaning every time he showed up at my house like this.

I'd never be able to keep him out.

And I was *really angry* because Jamie brought food I was suddenly craving and that craving was taking precedence over everything else at the moment, including my desire to get rid of him.

Fine. One last time.

"The only reason I'm allowing this to happen tonight and tonight only is because I'm starving and that food is smelling a lot better than the bowl of cereal I was planning on making myself, so don't think this is going to become a habit because it's not," I declared, walking over to the couch and taking a seat on the far end. "Also, I will be putting new locks on all my doors come morning, and they're going to be military grade."

Jamie breathed a laugh as he started unloading container after container, spreading them out on the coffee table.

"Go ahead and test my skills, babe. Just know..." He paused, turning his head to look at me. "If you're in this fuckin' house, I'm gettin' in."

I looked into his eyes, reading his seriousness. "You sound crazy, you know that?" I shared.

"Not crazy if deep down you're really wantin' me in here."

"Oh no. He's onto me," I joked, feigning alarm with an overplayed gasp and a hand to my chest.

Jamie stared at me for a breath, letting his eyes wander over my features, then he smiled, shook his head, and turned away.

"What're you feelin'?" he asked. "Got a little bit of everything. Chicken. Pork..."

A phone beeped, breaking up his rundown of what he'd brought. I knew it wasn't mine since I had mine plugged in and charging upstairs, doing that after I took a shower and got dressed. So I started peeking at the food.

While I did that, Jamie dropped the container he was holding, leaned back, and reached into his pocket, pulling out his device. He read the text.

"Shit. Figures this would happen now," he mumbled, coming to his feet. "Come on. We gotta go."

I looked up from the container of shrimp fried rice I was staring longingly into.

"Excuse me?"

He reached down and took the container I was holding, siting it on the coffee table among the others.

"We'll eat when we get back. I need to go pick up my sister, and you're tagging along. Come on. Up." He grabbed on to the underside of my arm and started pulling me off the couch.

"What—"

"Need you to come with me," he repeated, cutting me off. His voice vibrated with meaning.

I spun around, which pulled me out of his hold, flattened my hand on his chest, and pressed firm, halting him. Then I stared up into his eyes and saw they were also conveying a sudden urgency, matching his voice.

I didn't understand any of it.

"Why do I need to go with you?" I asked, needing to know a reason before I went anywhere, especially anywhere with *him*.

Jamie's jaw clenched.

I wondered if he was craving another cigarette, looking as stressed as he was looking, and that prompted me to say my next words.

"I'll go," I assured him. "I just wanna know why you need me. And I think it's a fair question. I don't know your sister."

Jamie exhaled a breath, nodding once.

"Right," he began. "She's at a bar gettin' hit on by a bunch of shit-heads she don't wanna be gettin' hit on by, considerin' they're dudes and she ain't into dudes, expressed that to them, and they're still hit-tin' on her and bein' persistent about it. She's had one too many and can't drive home. Needs me. Thinkin' if I walk in there and see what

I'm expectin' to see, I might lay a few motherfuckers out in front of people who could catch it on camera or call the cops, and that can't happen. I got sponsors I can't lose. They see me fightin' or doin' shit they don't like, they drop me. This is where you come in."

I wet my lips, letting all of that information sink in, which took me a few seconds considering the amount of information he'd shared.

"Okay," I started when I was finished processing. "But I'm still not seeing what that has to do with me."

"You're there? I'm gonna be less inclined to spend a night in jail, considerin' that option leaves you alone for them to feed on next," he explained.

I blinked at him.

Oh.

Huh.

I wasn't quite sure how to respond to that, or how to feel hearing it. I mean, it was kind of sweet and protective, him wanting to get to his sister and also his strange reasoning for including me in this plan, and Jamie wasn't those things.

I was sure of it.

So I said the only thing I could think of in that moment without acknowledging other feelings.

"Jail's bad," I whispered.

Jamie's eyes flickered wider after I spoke. His brows lifted. Then his mouth started twitching.

My mouth started twitching, too. I couldn't explain that, but I let it happen.

"Get your keys," he ordered. "We're takin' your car."

Chapter Six

JAMIE

Legs was glaring at me.

My eyes were on the road, but I could feel that glare aimed directly at my profile, and although I hadn't looked to confirm, I knew she was giving me her best shit and putting everything she had into that glare.

She was pissed. Maybe more pissed than usual, if that was even possible.

This was because instead of arguing with her over who was driving us to pick up my sister—an argument she was pushing for by not handing over the keys to her Volvo when we stepped outside and handing over her attitude instead, doing this while keeping the keys held behind her back—I charged at her and picked her ass up, locking her arms behind her so she couldn't fight me and leaving her vulnerable. Then I opened her hand with one of mine and pried the keys easily away from her while she ran off at the mouth.

That was the first thing that set her off.

After getting what I wanted, I carried her squirming body over to the passenger side of the car, not trusting her to get there herself anymore considering what all had just gone down and her reaction to it, swung the door open while keeping hold of her with one arm, and then deposited her into the seat, where she was currently sulking.

I was pretty certain that sequence of events pushed her over the edge.

That was ten minutes ago.

Now she was giving me the silent treatment while most likely plotting my death.

I didn't give a shit about the death plotting, but the silent treatment was starting to piss me off. I'd tried initiating conversation three times now and each time was met with nothing.

"You wanna listen to somethin'?" I'd asked, adjusting the volume on the radio and filling the car with some whiny chick shit I didn't recognize but knew I could handle about five seconds of before tuning it to something else.

Turned out, I wouldn't need the five seconds.

Tori didn't answer me. Instead, she crossed her arms under her chest and stared out the window. I cut the radio off.

"Goin' to Hammerjacks. That's where Quinn is. You ever been?"

I turned my head when I was greeted with silence and watched Tori cross her one leg over the other and start toeing the air with vigor and deep concentration, like she was harnessing all her energy into that one movement so she wouldn't lunge out of her seat and attack me.

I ignored her fit and looked back to the road.

"I'm in the mood to watch a movie while we eat. You feelin' that?"

This final question came after waiting a couple of minutes to see if she'd cooled off enough to have a conversation with me.

She hadn't.

Legs ignored me for a third time. This was when the glaring started.

We were almost at our destination and there was no way in hell I was letting her keep this bullshit up and carry over back at her place.

I'd had enough.

"You gonna speak to me the rest of the night, or are you just gonna continue actin' pissy?" I asked, cutting her a hard look.

Tori narrowed her gaze further. That was all she was giving up.

"Babe, get the fuck over it," I ordered, watching her eyes flicker wider. I put my attention back on the road. "If we're goin' someplace together, I'm drivin'. Don't matter whose car it is. We got someplace to go? I'll get us there. So quit with the attitude and just enjoy my

fuckin' company. It ain't like I took your ride and left you back at
the house. Straight up, though, kinda wishing I would've just done
that."

Her silent treatment was seriously getting to me. I didn't like it.
Legs typically had a lot to say when she was in a mood, and that was
the way I preferred her.

"Okay, first of all," she began, voice cutting sharp with edge.

I felt my mouth twitch. *Fuck yeah. There you are.*

"Don't tell me what to do, Jamie. If I wanna sit here and act *pissy*
about the way I was just manhandled, I'm in my right to do that.
You stole my keys and then put me in the car like some child."

"You tellin' me you would've gotten in yourself had I waited
you out?" I questioned, already knowing the answer to that one. I
glanced over again and watched Tori press her lips together. "Yeah.
Didn't think so," I said, turning away.

"I probably would've gotten in eventually, considering I wouldn't
want you taking my car anywhere without me, but I wasn't given a
choice, was I?"

"On a bit of a time crunch here, Legs," I reminded her.

She sighed, no doubt realizing I was right in rushing her and hating that fact.

I watched her turn away. "Keep goin'," I prompted.

She looked at me again. A crease in her brow was forming. "Excuse me?"

"You said 'first of all,' like you had more than one point to make,"
I said, putting my eyes back on the road. "Go ahead and make it."

Tori let out a quiet laugh. "You're not gonna like point two," she
warned.

"Comes outta your mouth, there's a good chance I'm gonna like it
no matter what it is."

That was unfortunately the truth. Never in my life had I enjoyed
getting lip from a woman before. But with Legs? I couldn't seem to
get enough.

The madder she got, the harder I got.

Those two things went hand in hand.

"Fine." She twisted in her seat and angled her body toward me. "I was going to say this was a one-time thing and that we will never have places to go together, meaning you'll never be driving us anywhere ever again, and the fact that you're implying differently as if this is going to become a habit is ridiculous. I don't even like you. That was my second point."

"You like me," I argued.

"Really, I don't."

"Really, babe, you do."

"Seriously, Jamie, I'm being honest."

"You'll start bein' honest when you admit to liking me," I told her, turning into the parking lot surrounding Hammerjacks and searching for a spot. "Right now, you ain't bein' honest. You're bein' in denial. Don't wanna feel certain things, so you're just blocking them out and lyin' to yourself and anyone who asks you. Lyin' to me most of all 'cause you don't want me knowin' how you truly feel about me. But I already know, Legs, so we can go ahead and move past this if you're finished wastin' both of our times. And straight up, bet aside, you admit to liking me and I won't act like a dick about it. So if that's your worry, you can get the fuck over that, too. Swear it. It won't go down like that."

I wasn't sure if that was one of her reasons for circling this issue the way she was doing, but I felt the need to clear the air, just in case it was.

Honestly? I didn't know what her deal was. Only thing I knew for certain was that Tori was lying and covering that lie with layers of bullshit I was gonna have to wade through to get to what I wanted.

I pulled us into a spot along the side of the building, threw the gear into Park, and turned to look at her.

She wasn't glaring at me anymore and her foot wasn't swinging in edginess, but her arms were still crossed.

"You really don't believe me when I say I don't like you?" she asked, her blue eyes daring me to say differently. She leaned forward, declaring, "Well, I *really* don't believe you when you say, 'Swear it.' I don't believe a lot of things you say, Jamie. I don't trust you."

"Said it before and made good on it," I reminded her, speaking of earlier down at the beach.

"You would've said anything to get me to climb on you the way I did."

"Probably," I replied. My lip curled up.

Hers grew tight.

"Tell me the truth," I said, throwing my arm up on the wheel and facing her fully. "Test me. Go ahead."

She sat back in her seat and tilted her head, staring at me across the small space, as if she was waiting for something and not keeping responses to herself.

I didn't understand that look. I was the one expecting. Not her.

"Waitin', Legs," I probed.

"I already told you," she shot back, holding my gaze steady.

I cocked an eyebrow. "Gave me a lie. Where's your truth?" I asked.

Tori unbuckled her seat belt, then she looked away and reached for the handle on the door. "I gave you both," she said quietly, pushing it open and stepping out.

The door shut behind her.

She gave me both?

What the fuck? When?

Only thing I heard was a bunch of lying from her, meaning she didn't give me both. Tori gave me what she was always giving me. Bullshit. I was still waiting on a truth.

Jesus.

I shook my head.

Wanting this girl was the biggest fucking headache of my life. If it weren't for the glimpses I'd gotten of what she was hiding underneath, I wouldn't think it was worth it.

I turned off the car and stepped out, tucking the keys into the pocket of my shorts after locking up. I met Tori up on the pavement.

"Let me do all the talkin' in here," I told her. "Just stay with me. Don't go wanderin' off."

Last thing I needed was her disappearing on me.

She rolled her eyes and started walking toward the door, leaving me standing where I was.

Jesus. Here we fucking go.

"Legs, swear to God, if I have to go lookin' for you, we're gonna have a problem," I warned at her back. My longs strides got me to her quickly, and when I reached her side, I added, "Pissed me off enough today. Don't push it."

Tori let out a dry laugh. "*I'll* be doing all the talking in here. Trust me. That's how this is going to work," she said, finality in her voice. She stopped in front of the door and reached for the handle.

She was doing all the talking? That's how this was going to work?

I slammed my hand on the door and prevented her from entering.

"Say again?" I growled, meeting her eyes when she stopped pulling and whipped her head around to hit me with attitude.

"What?" she asked, looking confused. "That's the plan."

"That ain't the plan," I assured her. "I'm talking. You're standing there, not wanderin' off. *That's* the plan."

"Didn't you say your sister isn't into boys?"

"Yeah."

Tori stared up at me. She grabbed on to her hips and cocked her head to the side, lifting her brows expectantly.

"What about it?" I asked when she wouldn't elaborate or give me anything else besides looks and sass.

"She isn't into boys," Tori stated again.

My jaw clenched. I was losing patience. "We covered that," I bit out.

"Boys are currently hitting on her and not taking the hint that she isn't interested."

"Why we're here, babe. You feelin' like sharin' somethin' I don't know?"

Tori smiled big. "That's where I come in."

"What is?"

"Them not taking the hint."

I lowered my hand from the door and stood taller. "Not following you," I shared.

"I'm the hint," she said.

My eyebrows rose. I was understanding her meaning now.

Couldn't fucking believe it, but I was understanding it.

"No shit," I murmured, feeling appreciation for what she was willing to do.

"Oh, and just so you know, while I'm handling this, if you wander off, I will not go looking for you," Tori added. "Keep that in mind."

I smirked hearing that, saying, "Another lie. You're rackin' them up today, Legs."

"Not lying," she pledged. "Please, test me on it, because I would love to leave you here, Jamie. Nothing would bring me more pleasure."

"I'd rather keep close, considerin' those fuckin' pants you're wearing."

My eyes lowered. I started staring at everything she had going on from the waist down.

Fuck.

Her pants were like a second skin. Highlighting her toned legs perfectly and showing their shape.

Sex pants.

Probably purchased them at the same time as that fucking bikini.

I lifted my eyes and watched Tori blink hers rapidly before looking down at herself. "I'm wearing leggings," she stated, face pinching tight with confusion when she lifted her head again.

She wasn't understanding why I was digging what she had on.

I stuck my hands into my pockets and shrugged. "Just like the uniform, Legs. On anybody else? Those pants aren't sexy. Probably wouldn't catch my attention unless the chick wearin' them was takin' them off. On you? Different story. That combination makes my dick hard."

Her eyes went round.

I smirked, liking her reaction to hearing that, and told her, "I got proof to back up my argument if you're wantin' to see it."

Wide-eyed and blushing hot, Tori spun around, yanked the door open, and rushed inside.

I followed behind, laughing. Shit was too easy sometimes.

Hammerjacks was dimly lit and packed with bodies, some dancing together and others crowding the bar, waiting to get served. I started scanning the room as I came up beside Tori, who was doing the same even though she had no idea who she was looking for.

I saw Quinn almost instantly. She wasn't hard to spot.

The bright pink spiked-out hair helped with that.

"There," I said, pointing in the direction of the bar where my sister was sitting on a stool, head turned away from the group of shit-heads swarming her.

She was alone. That pissed me off.

She was here, in town visiting, and she was looking for ass. That pissed me off, too.

Not much I could do about the second thing, I understood it, but she was gonna hear my feelings toward the other whether she wanted to hear them or not.

"What's her name again?" Tori asked as we made our way over.

"Quinn," I said.

She nodded, face serious. Then she tucked stray pieces of hair behind her ears and smoothed out the rest of her pony, pulled one sleeve of her shirt down so it exposed her shoulder and bra strap, straightened her spine, tipped her chin up, and put on a smile before rushing ahead.

"Hey, sweetie. Sorry I'm late," Tori chirped, squeezing in between my sister and the shitheads as if they weren't standing there. She grabbed Quinn's face, bent down, and kissed her cheek. "I missed you. Did you miss me?" she asked, bringing both hands to Quinn's neck and holding there while standing between her bent knees.

Tori was smiling and playing the part, leaning close and making it seem like they were really together, or at least really feeling each other.

My sister was blinking up at Tori, looking baffled but also looking like she was wanting to buy everything Legs was selling.

I wasn't surprised. Quinn shared my taste in women. And I definitely had a taste for Legs.

"Whoa, are you two...*damn*. Is this your girl?" one of the shitheads asked from behind Tori, pointing at the back of her.

"Jesus," another one chimed in, looking his fill. "What are the chances of me watchin' you two go at it? This is fuckin' hot."

I stepped up then, not liking the tone of this guy and the shit coming out of his mouth, and wanting to make my presence known.

He saw me approach and shot me a hard look, asking, "You gotta problem?"

"Jamie."

Teeth clenched and fists forming, I looked to Quinn, not taking the bait he was throwing out.

She was watching me, eyes serious and mouth tight, subtly shaking her head in warning 'cause she knew I couldn't be fighting or doing anything that could draw negative attention. Then she turned her attention onto Tori when she twisted and slid into Quinn's lap.

"Fishing in the wrong pond, boys," Tori informed them, sweeping her gaze over the three while putting her arm around Quinn's shoulders and pressing close. "Get lost. We're not interested." Then she turned all of her attention onto my sister and amped up her game, giggling as she kept her face close to hers and running her fingers through her hair, smiling, whispering, *really* flirting and looking into it, all while blocking the view of the shitheads so they couldn't watch.

And everything Legs was doing, my sister was eating up.

Wrapping her arms around Tori and holding on to her, smiling back, laughing, looking like she was falling in love and thinking this was real and something sustainable.

I was starting to regret incorporating Tori into this plan. She was a little too good at her game. Straight up. Maybe the best at it.

I was also starting to get mildly jealous watching my sister getting attention from the one woman who was hell-bent on ignoring my ass.

"Man, whatever," the one guy said, grabbing his beer and looking to his friends. "Come on. I'm not wastin' my time on lesbian pussy."

His friends murmured their agreement, mentioned something about hitting up Roy's, a bar down the street, then grabbed their beers and stepped away.

When they were out of earshot, I shifted my eyes to Legs, telling her, "Think you sold it. You can get off my sister now."

Tori smiled proudly, lifting her shoulders with a little dance. Then she looked to Quinn, keeping the smile, and said, "Hey, I'm Tori. Your brother dragged me here, so I figured I'd offer my assistance instead of letting him handle it, since he can't fight and all."

"Can fight, just shouldn't," I corrected her. I jerked my chin. "Hop off."

Quinn moved her hands up Tori's back and licked her lips. "Wicked plan," my sister told her. "I was totally into that."

"I think it got the point across," Tori replied. "I really like your hair, by the way." She ran her fingers through it again. "The color looks great on you."

"Really?"

"Absolutely. It really makes your eyes pop."

"I was thinking about going purple..."

"Have you tried bleaching the roots and just painting the color on the ends? I think that would look *amazing* with purple."

Jesus.

"Legs," I barked.

Both of their heads whipped around and faced my direction.

"You feelin' like gettin' up so we can get the fuck outta here?" I asked, thinking only about the food back at her place I was wanting to eat and not about how comfortable my sister's hands looked gripping on to Tori's body.

"She's fine," Quinn offered, keeping her hands locked around Legs. "Really. She doesn't have to move."

I shot a glare at Quinn, communicating how I felt about that suggestion, then shifted that glare to Tori.

"I was getting up. Relax. We were just talking," she huffed, moving off Quinn's lap and coming to stand beside me. "You're welcome, by the way," she murmured.

I ignored her mouth, for now, and watched Quinn come to her feet.

She was seven years younger than me, putting her at twenty-one, tall and thin, with the muscles of a track runner filling out her legs and giving her some meat, kept her hair short and her eyes green thanks to contacts, and ever since she was a kid, refused to wear anything besides all black.

Right now, she was wearing tight black jeans, black motorcycle boots, and a black tank. Solid. No design.

Quinn kept the color to her hair.

"Hey, big brother," she said with a smile, while fixing the pieces of hair around her face and making them spike out again. Dimples caved in her cheeks. "Thanks for coming to get me. I totally owe you one."

"Let's go," I ordered, skipping pleasantries.

I'd tell her how good it was to see her when we weren't in a fucking bar.

Quinn pulled her lips between her teeth after hearing me, blinked through wide eyes, and then quickly moved forward. She knew I wasn't playing around.

"What the fuck are you doin' here by yourself? Aren't you stayin' with Chante?" I asked when we made it outside. She always crashed with Chante, her ex, when she came to town.

"She's working," Quinn replied from next to me. "And I wanted to get a drink."

"You couldn't wait 'til she got off?"

"Jesus, Jamie. Ease up a little," Tori said from behind me. "She just wanted to go out and get a drink."

I stopped sharp on the pavement, causing Tori to bump into my back.

"What—"

"Not that this matters, 'cause either way I'd have a problem with it, but she ain't here to get a drink. She's here lookin' to get laid," I argued after twisting around.

Tori shifted her eyes between Quinn and myself.

"Jamie," she whispered, sounding appalled as she looked up at me. "Why would you say that?"

"'Cause it's true."

"It's *rude* is what it is."

"Oh, it's okay. He's right," Quinn informed her. "I *was* drinking but I was also hoping to pick someone up. I'm on vacation. Gotta live a little."

"Oh." Tori blinked, then she shifted her eyes between the two of us again, settling on me. "Well, it was still a rude thing to say," she mumbled under her breath.

"Do I look like I give a fuck?"

Her eyes hardened. "That's pretty rude, too. I'm beginning to see a pattern."

Jesus. Always with the attitude. I didn't need this shit right now.

"Babe, appreciate what you did in there, straight up, but you need to stay outta this," I told her. "She's my sister. If I gotta problem with somethin' she does, I'm expressin' that problem. I'm not gonna sugarcoat shit to spare feelings. That's not how I operate."

"What's wrong with her going out to meet someone?"

"Nothin', as long as she's got eyes on her in case shit goes south, which is the whole fuckin' reason why we're here. You forgettin' that?"

Her lips pressed together. I watched her agitation slip away.

Tori had forgotten why I'd dragged her out here in the first place, but she was appearing to remember now and maybe even understanding my reaction.

Seeing that and not feeling the need to argue further, I turned to Quinn.

"You shouldn't be coming to places like this by yourself lookin' for ass. Bring a wingman next time," I ordered.

Quinn chuckled. "I don't have a wingman." She leaned back to peer around me and flashed a smile. "Can I have yours?"

My eyes narrowed. Quinn saw it.

"Or not," she quickly added on a shrug, straightening up.

"I'm not his," Tori threw out, not wasting time squashing that remark.

I sliced my eyes to hers.

Her brow furrowed. "What? I'm not," she stated, as if it was crazy for anyone to assume any different.

"I'm thinking he's in disagreement with you on that," Quinn offered, laughing a little. "Wait. What does he call you again?"

"Legs."

"Huh." She paused. "Wait a minute. *Legs.*" Quinn glanced at me and then looked back at Tori, raising her finger to point. "Aren't you the girl who ran him over?"

Tori's face burned hot and contorted with rage.

Shit.

Forgot I told Quinn about that when she called and said she was coming to visit. Legs was now back to looking pissy.

I didn't want that. Especially since I planned on sharing a meal with her when we got back to her place and wasn't in the mood to fight my way inside.

Time to clear the air.

"I may have been exaggerating when I said that," I confessed, looking at Quinn and watching her shake her head disapprovingly while fighting a smile. I met Tori's eyes again. "Though contact was made. You did hit me."

"Barely," she snapped, bringing her hands to her hips. "And I apologized immediately for it. God, what else do you want?"

A smile pulled across my lips.

Tori's eyes lowered to my mouth, then quickly cut away. "Forget I asked," she mumbled.

I wouldn't. I *couldn't*.

Tugging the car keys out of my pocket, I directed my sister toward the Volvo and hung back to walk with Legs.

"Didn't say shit to anyone else about it," I informed her, reading her mind and figuring she'd think that.

Tori gave me a sideways glance. "Fine," she replied. Her voice was unbothered, but I knew better.

Layers of bullshit. This was just another layer.

We reached the car and piled in.

Quinn talked up Tori the entire ride to Chante's house, asking her questions and handing over information Tori didn't ask for, just giving it because Quinn liked her and thought she was cool for putting on that performance back at Hammerjacks. She was talking fast and easy, oversharing a little, which Tori didn't seem to mind. Legs paid attention, glancing in the back frequently, and commented when Quinn would take a second to breathe.

She even agreed to come out to celebrate Quinn's birthday when it was insisted by my sister she show up. That surprised me considering the venue. Didn't think Legs was into that shit.

"Nine o'clock! Wednesday. Don't forget, okay? And wear something hot, like those pants you got on!" Quinn hollered out as she was climbing from the backseat.

The door shut behind her.

I watched Tori tilt her head down. "Really? They're just leggings," she argued to herself.

"Babe, ain't nothin' on you ever gonna be *just* anything. When you gonna learn that?"

She blinked, then her eyes slowly lifted to the dash.

"Later, Jamie!"

I looked through the windshield and brought my hand off the wheel, letting Quinn see it after she called out.

She spun around and ran up the driveway, climbing the porch. When she got inside the house, she stuck her hand out the door and waved once more.

"She's sweet," Tori stated as I was backing us out of the driveway. "Is her birthday party *really* going to be at a strip club, though? Was she serious?"

Laughing, I started down the road. That was the only response I gave her.

When we got back to her place, Tori didn't say shit to me about not coming inside or getting gone and not wanting me there. She didn't even seem to mind when I took it upon myself to get us set up with a movie to watch while we ate, choosing a free one On Demand after plopping down on the couch and grabbing the container of chicken and broccoli, minus the broccoli.

Tori didn't say a damn thing to me about what I was doing.

It was weird. A good weird, but still... weird.

She sat on her end of the couch, knees bent and bare feet propped up on the coffee table after kicking her flip-flops off, shrimp fried rice and mango chicken containers in her lap, still warm, so we didn't bother reheating them, and watched *Mad Max* with me while alternating bites of food between the two meals and sipping on the Cherry Coke I gave her.

She didn't talk. She ate.

I was liking this side of her, the non-bitching-at-me side and the one who seemed to not only tolerate my presence, but possibly enjoy it, so I didn't talk either and chowed down.

And I was absolutely enjoying it. Every fucking second.

When Legs was finished eating, she put the half-empty containers next to the other ones on the coffee table, grabbed the tattered green quilt off the back of the couch, wrapped it around her shoulders, tucked her knees up against her chest, and continued watching the movie.

She didn't dismiss me. She didn't get up and sprint upstairs again since I was hanging around, finished eating myself.

Tori sat there, not saying a word, and gave me more of her time.

I thought that was weird, too, really fucking weird, but I wasn't about to shed light on this side of her she was showing me, figuring if I did that, she'd pile on more layers for me to peel back and become more aware, putting up a stronger guard in response.

I couldn't have that. I was liking this version of her too much.

I liked the other version, too. The mouthy, giving as good as she gets version, but I wanted it without the bullshit.

And I was gonna get it.

A bet was a bet. And last I checked, we were still playing.

When the movie was over, I made it look like I was leaving, heading out with the leftovers she didn't want while she used the bathroom down the hall.

I stood in the entryway and told her I'd see her tomorrow.

She called out, "Please don't," from behind the bathroom door.

I smiled.

Then I pulled my dick out and waited.

Chapter Seven

TORI

"I'm out, babe. See ya tomorrow," Jamie hollered from somewhere inside my house.

He was leaving. Good.

"Please don't!" I hollered back, head turning toward the bathroom door I was behind as I washed my hands in the sink.

I really needed him to leave. And I really needed to go a day without seeing him.

Things were starting to feel a little too familiar.

And when things started feeling familiar, stupid people started letting things happen, like sharing meals and watching movies together after going on a family rescue mission like some cozy duo.

I had no business meeting his family, ever, because Jamie and I weren't a duo or cozy in any way.

But I had gone with him. And I didn't just meet his sister. I liked her. She was sweet, easygoing, and talked my ear off like we'd been best friends for years.

Not many girls were that friendly off that bat.

Then Jamie and I came back here, shared a meal, and watched a movie together while sitting on the same piece of furniture. Looking like a duo. And looking cozy, considering I hadn't smashed myself up against the armrest again to put as much distance between Jamie and myself as possible.

I sat on one cushion. Comfortably.

He sat on one-and-a-half cushions, stretching his body and taking up more room than I was doing, even without stretching out his body. Jamie was absurdly fit but he was still a big guy. Tall. Broad shoulders. He took up space.

Leaving us with just a half a cushion between us.

Not enough. Not *nearly* enough.

But I had let it happen, meaning I was acting like a stupid person. Thought like one the other day at the tiki bar when I was putting meaning into what he was saying and now I was taking it a step further.

This was not good. I needed him to leave.

And I *seriously* needed to win this bet already so I could stop putting myself around him and showing him my goods.

After turning off the water and drying my hands on the towel, I flipped the light off, opened the bathroom door, and stepped back out into my living room with a plan in mind.

Lock up. Head upstairs. Get ready for bed. Maybe redo my toenail polish if I didn't start yawning once I was up there, allowing for sufficient drying time. Check my phone for any missed messages since I'd left it here to ride with Jamie to rescue his sister. Then crash.

It was a good plan, and one I was looking forward to.

But that plan went right out the window when I saw Jamie was still here and standing in my entryway. I froze. Then my gaze lowered.

And kept lowering...Holy...*shit*.

My hand flew up to my mouth. My eyes widened, then widened further when I saw a shiny metal barbell.

I gasped against my fingertips.

Jamie chuckled like the devil himself, but I didn't react. I couldn't focus on clever comebacks or even the little concentration needed to lift my head and deliver a scowl.

I was startled, rightfully so; I wasn't expecting him to still be here, but my shock and paralyzing fascination weren't deriving from Jamie's mere presence in my house when I'd trusted him to be gone.

Shorts unbuttoned and opened at the zipper, Jamie had his hand wrapped around the base of his dick.

This was what had me startled.

This was what had me paralyzed with fascination.

And *this* was what I had been dreading since the day Jamie McCade stepped foot inside Whitecaps.

He wasn't hard, not fully anyway, but God, he didn't need to be. Honestly, I was grateful he wasn't.

Two of my greatest fears were being realized without the influence of a full erection.

The first fear being that Jamie had the goods to back up his arrogance, which he clearly did, *bastard*, and the second being I'd somehow, even with all the hard work and dedication I was putting into avoiding seeing this evidence for myself, come to learn this to be true.

Well, I'd learned all right. And there was no unlearning this.

Stomach clenching and skin tingling, I stared at his beauty. At all of it. Transfixed. Awestruck. You name it. I probably looked mad.

He was long. He was thick. Perfectly formed. Manscaped nicely but not overly done. Adorned in jewelry that looked both intimidating and oddly fascinating.

So fascinating I wanted to get a closer look, but I wouldn't.

I *couldn't*.

I could, however, continue to stare from my safe distance away. I could also tilt my head in further captivation when tempted to do so, this happening when Jamie slid his thumb over the one barbell at the top of his piercing.

God...

I wondered how that felt when he—

"Jesus, babe. Knew you were hungry for it, but didn't realize you were this fuckin' starved. Shit. Look at you," Jamie said, interrupting my train of thought and finally speaking after God knows how many minutes had passed since I'd first stepped out of the bathroom. His voice dripped amusement and victorious payback.

Awareness flooded me.

Payback...

The tiki bar. The flashing.

That stupid bet.

I lowered my hand and met his eyes. My cheeks were burning. His were dimpled and lifted with his knockout smile. *Seriously wish his face didn't look like that.*

"Know what you're thinking," Jamie stated.

I swallowed, then I shook my head. "You don't."

"Wonderin' how it'll feel when it's movin' inside you," he continued, not missing a beat.

My toes curled against the hardwood floor. *Crap. He did know.* "No," I vowed.

My voice was firm. Resolute. But my body was my tell-all, and Jamie wasn't missing the signs I was showing. I had hungry eyes apparently.

Ain't that just terrific.

Jamie's smile relaxed into a smirk after hearing my lie. Then, to my surprise and possible disappointment, though I'd never admit to that either, he tucked his award-winning dick back into his shorts, drew up the zipper, and shared as he was fastening the button closure, "Know that beg is sittin' right on the tip of your tongue, Legs, and straight up, I want that, can't fuckin' wait to hear it, but I think I wanna make you ache a little first, so save it for me. Keep that lie goin', babe."

I blinked, bringing my hands to my hips. "Excuse me?"

I was in no way close to begging. He was absolutely wrong about that.

The aching part? Spot on. And it was only getting worse.

Jamie put his back to me to grab the bag of leftovers off my console table, then he took the step separating him and the front door, saying as he went, "Don't know how often you take care of the needs you got, but I'm bettin' those urges just doubled."

"They absolutely did not just double," I shot back.

My urges were fine. He was wrong about that, too.

Jamie opened the door, but he didn't step through it, keeping his hand on the knob instead. He looked back at me over his shoulder.

"That thing you were wonderin' about," he began, and I felt my insides turn into liquid.

Oh, no . . .

Please don't...

He smiled, promising, "You're gonna fuckin' love it."

My tell-all body reacted again, this time with my lips parting. It was a subtle reaction. One that could go unnoticed.

Too bad it didn't.

Jamie's gaze lowered to my lips the second they parted. "Take that back. Thinkin' those urges just tripled," he guessed with all the confidence in the world.

I narrowed my eyes.

His sparkled like moonlight on the water.

Then he looked ahead and stepped out of my house with his delicious bag of leftovers, calling out before the door closed, "Later, babe. Have fun dreamin' about my dick."

I stared, mouth agape, at my door for a solid minute. And then I went to bed, where I absolutely did not have fun dreaming about his dick.

Not for one second.

I also did not have fun thinking about it the following day when I avoided any chance of contact with Jamie by spending my day off at my parents' house. And when I finally got home close to one a.m., that not-so-fun feeling only continued throughout the night and carried over into today, bringing us to right now.

I was standing at the kitchen window at Whitecaps, fingers curving under the edges of two plates that were ready to be taken to the tables waiting for their food, but instead of delivering those plates, I was staring at the curved barbell in Stitch's bottom lip.

Never gave it a second glance before.

Now? You'd think I was witnessing a unicorn being born or something with the way I was engrossed by it.

"You got a problem?"

Stitch's hard, grating voice jolted me into consciousness.

I blinked up at him, saw he was paused in his vegetable chopping and glaring at me like I'd personally done him wrong, then decided I didn't much care for his growing attitude today and went ahead and shared that feeling.

"Catch more flies with honey. Ever hear that?" I asked, sliding the plates off the metal lip of the window and holding them in front of me. "Sure she'd forgive you a lot sooner if you started acting a little nicer."

I was referring to Shay and the grudge she was holding against Stitch for blowing off their first official date a while back, and I knew Stitch was following me.

The wrinkle between his eyebrows deepened. Stitch was scary looking without the added hostility. Tall and built in the shoulders, wide chest, limbs covered in ink. Intimidating swagger.

Total badass biker vibe.

"You and Red need to stay the fuck out of it," he bit out. "Ain't your business."

Red was Syd apparently.

It fit her. She did have wild red hair.

"I'm gonna let you think that since we're slammed and I don't have time to argue it," I told him, turning sideways and leaning closer to the window. "Just know, you chose the wrong profession if you want to keep personal stuff personal. You work with a bunch of women, Stitch. We get high off gossip."

Stitch had gone back to chopping up the vegetables, but when I informed him of this, he stopped again.

"Leave it alone," he ordered, eyes coming up.

"Ask nicely and maybe I will."

"This *is* me askin' nicely," he growled.

I straightened up, hearing the seriousness in his voice and the threat of an even angrier Stitch, something I couldn't imagine, so I decided to let him think I'd be leaving this alone for the sake of Whitecaps. Pissing off the cook could lead to him up and quitting, and I really didn't want that. So I nodded once and let Stitch see it, knowing he'd read that as my surrender, then I turned and walked away with my hot plates of food and delivered them to table eight.

"I hate being this busy, but I kinda love it, too," Shay said, meeting me at the hostess podium, where we were both putting menus away. "Keeps my mind off things." She gave me a weak smile.

I put my hand on her arm and gave it a squeeze. "He's an idiot."

"I know." Her eyes moved over my shoulder toward the kitchen. She sighed. "I just wish he'd realize that and fix it. I miss talking to him."

I started immediately regretting backing down and faking surrender with Stitch. But I couldn't do anything about that now, for two reasons. One, it was lunch rush and I had a billion tables. And two, my phone started ringing from the back pocket of my shorts.

Normally, I wouldn't take calls during work hours because it was unprofessional, but seeing as my tables were all happy at the moment and not needing anything from me, and also considering it was my mother calling, I decided to make an exception.

Typically, her calls were short. And this one should be extra short. I'd just spent all day with her yesterday.

"Two seconds," I told Shay, not wanting her to feel like I was ducking out of our conversation.

She waved me off, shaking her head and conveying what we were discussing wasn't important. But it was. And we'd be getting back to it.

I heard the door chime from behind me as I made my way toward the employee lounge, phone pressing to my ear.

More customers. I really needed to make this quick.

"Hey, I'm at work. What's up?" I answered.

"Would you *please* call your father and tell him he needs to make an appointment with his doctor? He's refusing to listen to me."

My mother sounded at the end of her rope. Her voice was tight and high-pitched.

She'd been arguing with my father about this last night, too, while I was there.

"Is he still having heartburn?" I asked, pushing the door open and stepping inside the lounge.

"If that's what it even is, and I'm not convinced. He hasn't been eating anything spicy." she replied. "I'm thinking he'll listen to you, pumpkin. Just try for me, will you? He worries me."

"Okay. I'll call him now. I'll let you know how it goes."

"Thanks, baby girl."

"Sure, Mom. Love you."

"Love you, too."

I disconnected the call and dialed my father's cell, knowing he was probably out in the factory right now and not at his desk, considering he hated being cooped up in that office.

It was newly renovated, came equipped with its own private gym, and had a spectacular view of downtown Raleigh.

I could see why he hated it.

"Your mother called you, didn't she?" he answered with a smile in his voice.

I laughed. "Can't blame her for getting creative. You know how she is." I looked at the clock on the wall. "What's going on, Daddy? You're still not feeling good?"

"Feeling fine, princess. Just a little heartburn. Nothing a few Tums can't knock out."

"You sure that's all it is? Maybe you should go see the doctor just in case—"

"No need," he cut me off short.

My father hated going to the doctor. He hadn't been to one in over twenty years.

"They're just gonna run some tests that aren't necessary and give me pills I don't even need. I know how they operate," he argued. "No thank you. I'll stick with my Tums."

The door to the lounge swung open.

I turned my head and watched Jamie stride into the room, looking like he'd just stepped out of the water and off the beach.

Hair saltwater damp and board shorts on. Thank Christ he was wearing a shirt.

And the board shorts. I did not need my memory jogged.

I gave him a look after the door closed behind him, signifying he wasn't allowed back here.

He gave me a look back, signifying he didn't give a fuck about where he was or wasn't allowed. Then he leaned his shoulder against a locker and pulled out his phone, looking down and messing with it.

Apparently he was waiting me out. *Terrific.*

I went back to my phone call.

"They aren't a cure-all, Daddy. And it might not even be heartburn that's giving you chest pain. Did you think about that?"

"It's heartburn," my father argued. "I know what it feels like. Been dealing with it for years."

"I think you need to go see a doctor to rule out anything more serious."

Jamie's eyes came up then. He looked at the phone I was holding.

"Love you, princess, but I'm gonna tell you what I told your mother. Doctors are for sick people, and I'm not sick."

"But you *could* be sick." My hand came up and started gesturing. I was getting impatient. "You could have, I don't know, heart issues or something. You don't know!"

"If the Tums stop working, I'll look into making an appointment. Until then, quit worrying about your old man. I'm as healthy as a horse."

I inhaled a deep breath, nodding. He was right. He *was* healthy. Had a little extra weight on him, but that didn't seem to slow him down.

Aside from the heartburn bringing this conversation on, my father never had anything wrong with him, which was one of the reasons he hadn't been to the doctor in so many years. There was no need for it.

"All right," I sighed, looking back to the clock on the wall and checking the time. "I'd really feel better if you got this looked at, but if you promise you'll go see someone if the Tums stop working, I guess that's good, too."

"Have my word, princess. I'll take care of it."

"Okay, Daddy."

"Gotta get back to work."

"Me, too."

"Love you, princess."

I smiled. "Love you, too."

Jamie straightened from the locker as I slipped my phone away. He jerked his chin at me, asking, "Your dad sick?"

He sounded genuinely concerned. As if he actually knew my father himself.

"Uh." I blinked. *This was weird.* "No. Not really. He's just having a lot of heartburn."

"Won't go get it checked out?"

"My father doesn't do doctors."

Jamie smiled a little. "I see where you get your stubbornness," he said.

I grabbed my hips, telling him, "I hope you're not expecting to get a table anytime soon. We're slammed, if you didn't notice."

"Not stayin'. Got work shit to do."

I blinked. "Oh."

I wanted to sound surprised. Pleased. Elated. Jamie wasn't staying. This was *great* for me. But my "Oh" came out sounding disappointed.

The hell?

Jamie's smile grew hearing this disappointment.

Shit.

"Well, good," I quickly added, wanting to shut down that smile. "What are you doing here then?"

He shrugged, slipping his phone away. "Wanted to stop in and see how you were doin' with that situation I left you in the other night. Came in yesterday, but you weren't here. Gave me the slip last night, too." His eyes lowered to my shorts. "How's the ache?"

"I need to get back to work."

"Figured it was bad last night for you to stay gone. I'm thinkin' you're on the fuckin' edge now."

"How's it for *you*?" I asked, tipping forward.

He wasn't the only one still playing this game.

Jamie mouth lifted in the corner. He stared at me, not answering as seconds ticked by. He looked like he held a thousand words on his tongue, but he wasn't giving me any.

I rocked back onto my heels. I was starting to regret even asking.

Then he smiled a little bigger and brighter, and jerked his chin, promising, "You give me the slip tonight and I will come lookin' for you."

My fingers lost their grip and slid down.

Tonight. Quinn's party.

Crap.

Jamie would be there. Of course he would. It was his sister's birthday. And it was at a strip club.

"I'm going, but only for your sister," I informed him, tipping my chin up. "She's sweet and I like her."

"She thinks you're sweet, too," he said.

My heart warmed hearing that.

"You wearin' those sex pants?" Jamie asked, eyebrow lifting.

Oh, my God. What was up with him and these pants?

"Not that it's any of your business, but I'll most likely be wearing this, since I'll be leaving right from here," I shot back. "Not *sex anything*. Sorry to disappoint you."

"Ain't disappointing me," he said. "Know how I feel about that uniform, Legs."

"Yeah. You shared that."

"Also know what's underneath," he added with a smirk.

I scowled.

I was going to regret that game plan until the day I died.

Jamie's phone beeped. He glanced at it and then tucked it away again, saying, "Gotta go, babe. I'll see ya tonight."

"Fine. Whatever," I sighed.

There was no point in fighting it. It would just take up more time, and I had work to do.

I made for the door, expecting Jamie to open it so we could both get back to our jobs, but instead of doing that, he blocked it with his shoulder the second I reached it.

We collided, my hands flying up to his chest and pushing away, but I met resistance when he wrapped his arm around my waist and yanked me closer.

"What are you doing?" I asked, voice tight and startled, looking up at him while putting pressure on his hand at my back.

"Thought I'd get a kiss before I go," he said casually, as if this were a normal thing between us and we shared kisses regularly.

I sucked in a breath. "What?" I whispered.

"A kiss, Legs. I want one."

"But we don't do that."

"Feels like a good time to start."

His face slowly moved in, drawing closer and closer as his gaze focused on my lips.

My heart was beating like crazy and my stomach was clenching tight, not in fear or disgust, but in anticipation.

I *wanted* Jamie to kiss me. I wanted to feel it again. His mouth and his need. I wanted it.

I could go back to hating him after we were finished. *Immediately* after we were finished.

Body trembling, I closed my eyes.

I was going to do it. I was going to kiss Jamie McCade.

"How's that ache now?" he whispered against my ear.

My eyes flashed open. That was when I heard his deep, amused chuckle.

Mother—

"You are such a jerk!" I hissed, shoving hard against his chest.

Jamie staggered backward, still laughing. Then he opened the door and flashed me one of the biggest grins I'd ever seen him wear before sauntering back out into the dining area.

And I got back to work and back to hating him immediately, as if I never even stopped.

* * *

I'd never been to a strip club before. Male or female varieties. And they were both in Dogwood Beach. So I didn't really know what to expect of The Dollhouse.

After showing my ID to the bouncer at the door, I paid the cover and stepped inside.

The room was cast in a pink glow, keeping it dark except for the two stages. They had additional lights above them to shine down on the dancers. A bar ran the length of one wall, and in the corner on a raised platform was a DJ booth, pumping tunes into the air. Fabric hung from the ceiling and separated the back VIP area, I was guessing. There was a very large man standing guard there and only letting certain people pass. Chairs were pushed up close to the stages for prime viewing seats, and behind them there were small round tables with stools pulled up so that people could sit together.

That was where I spotted Quinn and her group.

"Tori!" She jumped up and waved me over, then pulled me into a hug when I reached the table. "Thank you so much for coming!"

I hugged her back. "Anytime, babe."

Quinn leaned away and smiled, flashing dimples that matched her brother's. She was wearing a black bodysuit with sleeves down to her elbows, see-through stockings, and black combat boots, had her eyeliner winged out and her hair extra spiky. She faced the other three women sitting with her and went about with introductions while keeping her hand on my back.

"Guys, this is Tori. She's the kick-ass chick I told you about. Knows Jamie. He's totally staking claim, but she's not hearing that. And if she starts playing with your hair, let her. It feels *amazing*."

I turned my head and gaped at her.

Not because I disagreed with what she'd just said—she was spot on with the Jamie thing—but because that had to be the strangest introduction I'd ever received.

Quinn shrugged, catching my reaction, then started pointing around the table. "This is Chante, Jen, and Andrea."

"Hey," I greeted each of them, lifting my hand in a wave.

They were all in short, tight dresses and, by the looks of them, spent ample time on makeup and hair. The three were young like Quinn and seemed to be just as friendly by the way they were smiling at me.

"What's up?" Chante said.

"Nice to meet you," Jen offered.

"Hey," Andrea threw out last. "That was really cool what you did for Quinn. Thanks for looking out for her."

"Of course." I gave Andrea a smile, then slid it to Quinn. "Here. I didn't know what you liked, so I just got you an Amazon gift card. You can pretty much buy anything from there," I told her, pulling the small card out of my pocket and handing it over. "Happy birthday."

"Oh, my God! You didn't have to do that!" She threw her arms around me again and squeezed me tight. "Thank you. You're so cool," she whispered next to my ear.

I hugged her back and wore an even brighter smile when she pulled away, letting her see it. I really liked Quinn.

She did a little dance with her gift card before reclaiming her seat.

I glanced around the room and smoothed out the ends of my hair, not looking for anyone in particular.

"Jamie not here yet?" I asked.

I was surprised he hadn't greeted me out in the parking lot. Figured he'd be watching out.

"Oh, he's here." Quinn laughed, drawing my head around. She waved her hand in the air dismissively. "I paid for him to get a private lap dance just before you walked in. He was killing the vibe."

"He was taking all the attention away from you, you mean?" Chante asked playfully, knocking her shoulder into Quinn's.

"*Yeah.* Like I said. *Killing the vibe*," Quinn returned.

The girls kept up the banter, Jen and Andrea joining in, as I looked behind me in the direction of the VIP area and the big scary man guarding it.

A private lap dance, huh?

I smiled. *Perfect.*

Then I turned back to the girls and declared, "I'll be back. I think the birthday girl needs some attention."

Quinn's eyes started shining bright.

"Oh, Lord," Jen laughed.

"Yes, she absolutely needs some attention," Quinn said, wiggling in her seat. "*All* the attention!"

"You already have it," Andrea claimed. "What's new?"

I dug some cash out of my wallet and then sat my purse on the table, asking, "Watch this for me?"

The girls nodded.

Then I spun around and padded across the room, stepping up to the big scary VIP guard.

"Hey," I said, smiling. "My husband is back there and he's got three kids at home and one baking in the oven. Do you mind if I go remind him of that?"

The bouncer's mouth slowly stretched into a grin, revealing a gold tooth among the rest.

"You need help escortin' him out, let me know," he said before stepping aside.

"Thank you. I'll do that."

Lifting back the curtain, I moved into a separate hallway that had private rooms on either side. Each door had a small window on it to see in, a security feature, I was guessing, and I peered in those windows as I searched for Jamie.

Men were sitting on long, black benches while topless women danced in their laps. I was willing to bet Jamie wasn't far into his private show. If he got back here right before I arrived, his was probably just starting.

I was at my fourth door when movement caught my eye and turned my head.

A woman wearing a sequined bikini and spiked see-through heels was walking down the hallway in my direction. She stopped in front of a door, looked in the window, and reached to turn the knob.

"Wait," I whispered, waving my hands and grabbing her attention. I ran up to her and peeked in the window.

Jamie was sitting on a bench seat with his arms over the back, stretched out and waiting.

Yes!

I turned to the woman. "Hi," I said, keeping my voice down in case he could hear. "How much do you get paid for these private shows?"

She popped her hot pink gum.

"Three hundred."

"You already get paid?"

"Honey, of course." She laughed a little and waved her hand in the air. "I don't trust some of these guys to buy the cow after getting the milk."

I tilted my head. *Huh.* Not sure that was how that expression was supposed to be used, but okay.

"I'll pay you five on top of the three you already got to let me go in there instead. How's that sound?" I held out the bills I was offering.

Her eyes jumped between my face and the money, then stayed on the money when she grabbed it.

"Sounds like he's all yours," she said, balling the cash up in her hand.

"Oh, and there is a table of girls out there, one of them has short, spiky pink hair." I handed her another hundred. "Give her some love, will you? It's her birthday."

The women flashed me a smile as she tucked the bills into her bra, saying, "You got it, honey." Then she stepped away and headed back out into the main area, her heels clicking on the linoleum floor.

I turned my head after she disappeared and looked at Jamie through the window again.

His head was tipped back and his eyes were cast at the ceiling while his fingers tapped the back of the booth. He looked bored.

I smiled. *Relax, Loser. The show is just about to start.*

Chapter Eight

JAMIE

The door to the room I was in made a clicking noise, indicating it was opening.

Finally. What the fuck?

I tipped my head down to get a look at this chick I'd been waiting on for a fucking *minute*, eyes already set in a glare 'cause I was bored and wondering where Tori was, if she was here and if she was wondering the same about me, when the object of my attention stepped inside the room and pulled the door shut behind her.

Pressure built in my chest. My back stiffened.

We locked eyes.

The fuck?

"Hey," Tori whispered, then gave a shaky laugh and looked down, drawing all of her hair over one shoulder. "Uh, right, so I hope you weren't expecting some big-breasted bimbo wearing pasties and an edible thong. I always found those to be uncomfortable."

I cocked an eyebrow.

She started moving closer, still in her uniform and still making that shit work for her like she always did.

White shirt, tight across her tits. Shorts showing all that skin I wanted wrapped around me.

"The fuck is this?" I asked, frowning, looking between Tori's face and the door behind her. "Did Quinn do this?" I met her eyes. "Are you mine?"

Tori froze a foot away, blinking at me. She didn't speak. If she had a reason for coming in here, it looked like that reason just left her. She seemed lost.

"Legs," I probed, when she kept with the staring and not speaking routine.

"Mm?"

"What are you doin' in here, babe?"

I had no fucking idea what was going on, but unless Tori wanted to watch some chick grind all over me, she needed to get what she came for and step out.

She wet her lips. I watched her neck work with a swallow.

"You showed me your dick," she stated.

I felt my mouth twitch. *Fuck yeah.* Breathing a laugh, I relaxed back onto the bench, arms spread behind me and hands gripping the black leather cushion. I tipped my head to the side. "See that impression is stickin'," I said. "What's that got to do with this?"

"You showed me your dick after I flashed you. That was your move."

"Yeah." I nodded. *What the fuck was she getting at?*

Tori smiled. Her sin-colored lips stretching slow. "This is mine," she said, lifting her shoulders as if this shit she was declaring wasn't a big deal, which it sure as fuck was.

This is hers... *Oh, fuck me.*

Fuck. Me.

Tori moved closer. Whatever smirk I was wearing pulled from my mouth. That pressure built again, in my chest and lower. I shifted on the bench.

"Legs," I warned, my voice vibrating in my throat as I watched her walk toward me. "What'd I say about takin' this shit places you can handle? Did you think this through?"

I was willing to bet she didn't. If she had and knew how this could play out, with her bent over and me buried deep, she wouldn't be back here.

"Shh." Tori stopped in front of my knees. "If we talk, I won't go through with this," she admitted, sounding anxious. "And I doubt you'd be chattin' up the girl who was supposed to be in here, so quit it. Just sit there. Shut up. And keep your hands to yourself."

"You know what you're doin'?" I asked, looking up at her. "'Cause in this room I'm allowed to touch, babe. Rules are out there." I tipped my chin at the door, keeping her gaze. "Not in here. In *here*, I'm participatin'. You don't like that deal, you better quit now and think of another move, 'cause the second you start takin' shit off, Legs, I'm on you."

"Then I guess I don't need to worry," Tori shot back, speaking with confidence and smiling again.

The fuck did that mean? My brow tightened. "Say again?"

"I don't need to worry 'cause I'm not taking anything off, meaning you won't be *on me*. I'm just dancing."

I stared at her for a beat. Then a laugh rumbled in my chest as I thought about how fucked she was.

"What?" she asked, tilting her head all cute. "This is a really good move."

"I know it is. I ain't laughing 'cause of that."

"Then why are you laughing?" She brought her hands to her hips and studied me, looking on the verge of an attitude. Her eyes narrowed. "If you think I need to take my clothes off to win this bet, then you are mistaken, Jamie McCade. I know how you feel about me in this uniform. This is gonna kill you."

"Legs, hate to tell you this, but you're wrong, babe. You gotta worry."

"And why's that?"

I dropped my arms and sat forward, elbows resting on my thighs. "You start dancin' on me and I'm touching you," I promised, watching her blink. "You start dancin' anywhere in this room and I'm touching you. You don't gotta strip, babe. I just threw that out there 'cause that's where I thought this was headed. Telling me you're makin' a move and you're makin' it in a strip club, I figured you'd be taking shit off, but honest to God, it don't matter. Like I said before, rules are out there. Not in here. Only way I'm keeping my hands to myself is if I'm fuckin' dead."

"These are *my rules*," Tori countered, bending down to get closer. "And unless you want me to holler out for my new friend with the gold tooth who looks like he eats narcissistic assholes for breakfast, I suggest you follow them, Jamie."

I chuckled, knowing who she was talking about. Dude made sure I was clear on a few things before letting me back in here.

Something I wasn't sharing with Legs.

"And what are these rules, babe?" I asked.

She straightened and snapped, "I already told you. Sit there and shut up." Tori put her hand on my shoulder and shoved, pushing me back until I was pressing against the bench again. Then keeping her grip there, she swung her knee up, braced it on the leather, and lowered herself onto my lap, lifting her other knee and boxing me in with it.

I pulled in breath through my nose and curled my hands into fists on the cushion. "And the touching?" I asked, voice strained as I stared at the shape of her tits.

They grew closer as she leaned forward, her hands shifting to hold on behind me, and my gaze snapped up to meet hers when her face got an inch away.

"Beg for it," she whispered.

My eyes flickered wider. Hers brightened with impending victory. No shit.

Tori was gonna let me touch, but I had to call it. I had to let her win.

I had to *fucking beg*.

Jesus.

Why'd she have to be so good at this shit?

I steadied my gaze, telling her as my head tilted back, "Think I'll just enjoy the ride."

I wasn't lying. I *was* going to enjoy this, every second of it, and I didn't mind sharing that. But what I wasn't sharing was how hard it was going to be swallowing down the words I was wanting to say.

Tori laughed as if she wasn't buying my assurance. Then she gave me a halfhearted "good luck" before she slid up against me, shoved her tits in my face, pressed her stomach and ribs flush against mine, and sank down.

If we were naked, she would've slid right onto my dick. Right... the fuck... onto it.

Bad move.

Not for me. That shit was fucking awesome.

It was bad for her and she found that out quick, gasping and going rigid the second she felt the tip of my cock between her legs.

I was rock fucking hard on account of what she was doing, what she was wearing, her just being here and looking the way she did, and the fact that I hadn't jerked off since we started this bet. Hadn't fucked anyone either. Didn't even want to. Not unless it was Tori.

The second I locked her into this shit between us, that was it.

And since we weren't fucking yet and she wasn't offering hand jobs, I was overdue. My balls basically hated me.

Expecting her reaction, I gripped her hips and kept her from hopping off, figuring Legs wouldn't be able to fight this shit between us anymore and end up begging me to fuck her, realize this, and then freak.

And I would totally fuck her. Already had it planned out in my head.

Bend her over first with her ass in the air so I could spank the shit out of her for fighting this for so long, then taking her with those legs thrown over my shoulders like I'd pictured a thousand fucking times.

Fuck yeah. It would be good. And I'd drag that shit out for as long as possible.

But Tori wasn't reacting how I had anticipated her to react. She wasn't freaking. She was feeling. Me.

Yeah, she startled with a gasp and went rigid, but the second my hands found her hips, that sweet body of hers went soft and melted above me, sinking lower as her eyes rolled closed and her head fell back.

She moaned, low in her throat, as she started rocking her hips. Gentle at first, then with urgency. Moving on my dick and getting off on it.

"*Fuck*," I groaned, watching her, feeling her.

Thank Christ I was wearing shorts and not jeans.

Tori froze after I spoke. Her head snapped down and our eyes met. That was when she tried hopping off. As predicted.

And no fucking way was I allowing it now.

I grabbed the back of her neck with one hand and kept my other fastened on her hip, gripping her tighter there so she couldn't move and then pulling until her face was a breath away from mine.

Her mouth was right there, so close I could lick her fat, cherry lip, but I didn't.

She was staring into my eyes, looking panicked and turned on, breathing heavy, possibly on the verge of hollering out.

I was staring back, feeling all kinds of shit right along with her and she was reading that, loud and fucking clear.

Tori blinked, looked at my mouth, and then looked back into my eyes. Her breaths started coming out faster. She wasn't resisting.

She was waiting. Waiting for me, and I was not about to make her wait for shit right now.

Hell, I was done waiting.

I'd waited too damn long for this already.

I kept her close, my fingers staying wrapped around her neck and keeping pressure. And with my hand on her hip, I started shifting her, grinding her against my shit so hard I thought she might bruise.

Tori made a noise and shuddered like she wanted that, like she wanted this to hurt, then she brought one hand to my neck and gripped me there so she could hold on and hurt me, too.

Her lips parted. Her fingers curled around and cut into my skin.

Fuck yeah.

I groaned, grit my teeth, and started pumping my hips up, giving her more and urging her to move, to go faster, pressing her down so that there wasn't a part of me she wasn't getting.

She met my desire. She matched it.

It wasn't me moving her after a while.

Tori took over. She rolled her hips and jerked in my lap like we were fucking. Tits bouncing behind white stretched cotton. Ass slapping against my thighs. Limbs tensing. And she knew, *fuck*, she knew without me having to say when I needed faster and when I wanted her to slow down.

Drag this out. Build this with me. Please, *fuck*.

She knew what I wanted. I didn't speak. Neither of us did.

I could taste her breath as we got off like we were both thirteen. I stared at her mouth and the way she moaned through it. I wanted to kiss her.

I wanted to fuck her.

I wanted to tell her she was the hottest fucking thing I'd ever seen in my life, and the way she was getting off on me was topping actual sex I'd had with women who wore a helluva lot less.

Crazy shit. Shit I shouldn't want out in the open and known, but I didn't care.

This felt too good. She felt too good, and I wasn't even inside her.

Then her breath hitched. Her limbs started trembling and her eyes rolled closed. And instead of telling her anything or confessing shit I maybe needed to keep locked in, I yanked her closer and took her mouth.

My tongue assaulted her, pushing past her parted lips, and this time instead of being too startled or too scared or whatever the fuck it was that's always got her running, she kissed me back.

Fucking kissed . . . me . . . back.

Lips and tongue and breath, Tori gave it all. And she gave it good. Really fucking good.

Her body was still rigid with pleasure as I thrust my hips three more times, groaned into her mouth, and shot off my release.

Right in my fucking shorts.

Still . . .

My thoughts on this experience hadn't changed one damn bit. Hands down, this was in my top five. Top two maybe.

Damn. *What the fuck?*

I slumped back, keeping hold of Tori's neck after we stopped kissing and pulling her with me. Her head hit my shoulder. She was panting. I was panting.

Then my grip on her neck slid around to the front of her throat when she leaned away to look at me.

"I didn't beg," she said quickly, chest heaving and cheeks flushed.

I looked at her messy hair and heavy eyes. I saw red smeared below her bottom lip.

"Neither did I," I told her, taking my thumb and wiping away the evidence of our kiss.

Her body went rigid with a gasp. I showed her my thumb. Seeing it, she quickly rubbed below her mouth when my hand fell away, narrowed her eyes at me, then leaned in and with the tips of her fingers cleaned off my mouth, doing this while speaking fast, "This doesn't count. It was a freebie. Just... pretend it didn't happen." She dropped her hand when she was finished.

"Gonna have trouble pretendin' the load I just blew in my shorts ain't there," I told her.

Her eyes went round, fell between us, and then lifted again.

"Right, um, let me just..." She pushed off from my lap and stood, raising a finger. "Hold on. I'll get you something." Then she spun around and hurried out of the room, pulling the door shut behind her.

I dropped my head back and pulled in a deep breath, relasing it slowly.

What the fuck were we doing? Pretend this shit didn't happen? Fuck that. Was she serious?

The door clicked open. I watched Tori hurry inside with a hand full of brown paper towels.

"Here. Sorry. This isn't the type of place to stock Bounty. These are kinda rough." She stepped in front of me and held them out. "Better than nothing, I guess."

I took them, jerking my chin in appreciation. "Yeah. Thanks."

"No problem," she replied, clearing her throat and spinning around when I started working at my shorts.

I shook my head, thinking her reaction to possibly seeing my dick now was funny considering she's seen it already and I just made her come with it. Then remembering how I felt about her suggesting we forget about what just happened, I got the urge to share my feelings while I cleaned myself up.

"Look, Legs—"

"I'm gonna go, I think," she interrupted.

My head snapped up.

Tori was still facing the door, only I could see one hand was raised. She had her fingers pressing to her lips.

Could she still feel me?

"I just, I'm tired, so I think I'm gonna go home and get some sleep," she continued.

I narrowed my eyes. *Bullshit. She wasn't tired. If anything I just woke her ass up.*

Tori turned her head to the side so I could see her profile. "So bet's still on. This didn't mean anything."

"Right," I mumbled, looking down and finishing up.

"I'll tell your sister bye."

I balled up the paper towels and tossed them on the bench, huffing out breath as I did it.

"Jamie?"

"What?" I barked, tucking my shit away and then standing, zipping up as I met her eyes.

Tori was turned sideways now. She pushed some hair behind her ear and stared at me, looking timid. "Bet's still on, right?" she asked in a quiet voice.

"Yep," I answered curtly, tucking my hands into my pockets. "Why the fuck wouldn't it be?"

She nodded. "Right. I figured since, you know, this didn't count."

"Already forgot it happened."

Her eyes seemed to focus in. She pinched her lips together, then she turned away and looked down. "Okay, so I guess I'll see ya later then?"

I didn't say anything. I couldn't. Because I knew if I opened my mouth, I'd say shit I shouldn't be saying, like how I'd just lied and how I wasn't going to forget. How I didn't want to. Or worse, how I didn't want *her* to.

And admitting that shit would be just like begging.

Tori looked back at me when I didn't speak, furrowed her brows as if she was thinking hard, and then turned away, shaking her head through an exhale that sounded as exhausted with this bullshit as I was.

She swung the door open again and walked out.

I watched her leave, standing there feeling all kinds of weird shit I didn't want to be feeling, except for the anger. That I didn't mind. I understood that. The other shit? No.

Fuck no. I didn't get any of it.

I waited until I knew Tori would be cleared out and gone before I stepped out myself. I said my good-byes and paid for another round of lap dances to keep Quinn from bitching at me for leaving. Then I strode outside, got to my bike, and took off.

Not heading in Tori's direction.

Chapter Nine

TORI

I'd lied to Jamie.

Had to. I needed to get out of there.

After dry humping against him like some sex-starved preteen and getting off, *really* getting off, kissing him, too, which was just as good as I remembered only better since I'd actually participated this time, I knew I couldn't head back out to the table where Quinn and her friends were sitting and hang there the rest of the night. Jamie would be hanging out.

He had plans on staying, I was sure of it. It was his sister's birthday. Plus, strip club. Hello. Why would he leave?

And him hanging out meant sharing a table, sitting a foot away from each other, if not inches, and I didn't think I could handle being that close to Jamie after what we'd just did and how I still felt.

I stood in that room, facing away, while he cleaned himself up, but it was as if I hadn't moved at all. I could still feel his fingers on my neck and his desperate pressure on my hip. I could hear his growls and smell his skin and his hair still tickled my forehead, his thighs beneath me and the way they tensed, I felt them too, and his mouth.

Touching my lips, he was there. Still.

Jamie was all over me.

I couldn't stay and have Jamie look at me while I tasted him in my mouth and felt his dick throbbing between my legs, because I would look back. I know I would.

And I would wonder... *Do you still feel me, too?*

So I lied about being tired, then rushed home and showered under water too hot for my skin because I wanted to feel *that* long after I was finished instead of everything else.

Skin flushed and warm and muscles loose, I dried off and dressed. It hadn't worked. I still felt him. His fingerprints and his fevered kisses. The scratch of his stubble. His pounding heart.

They were mine to keep.

But I didn't want them. Or at least, I *shouldn't* want them. Wanting them was terrifying and thoughtless. It was stupid. And I didn't want to be that girl. Ever. Or at least, not again. I was stupid with Wes. I didn't see sign after obvious sign of what he was keeping from me—his wife and kid. I was too caught up. And I wouldn't get caught up with Jamie. I wouldn't lead myself toward heartbreak again. I didn't mean for this to happen. Honest.

Jamie McCade wasn't anything good or right or safe. I was sure of it. He didn't respect relationships, meaning he was the worst kind of man to build hopes and dreams on because he would look at those hopes and dreams and laugh at you for building them. So I wouldn't be that girl. I wouldn't want him.

Only... I totally wanted him.

A little, if I was lying. A lot, if I was being honest.

So okay, I would *try* not to want him. I could fight it. I was getting good at fighting it. These feelings I had would go away. The echo of tonight would go quiet, and I'd forget how his body felt beneath me.

Another hour and I wouldn't feel anything. Another two and I'd forget tonight ever happened. The idea seemed promising enough. I was hopeful.

And my house was quiet. Quiet enough to hear the slightest noise coming from outside as I sat knees bent and legs tucked underneath me on the couch with my notepad resting on my thigh and my pen in my hand. I was darkening the "m" on my doodle with a heavy outline when a car door shut, too close to be a neighbor's or someone parking along the street.

My hand stilled. My eyes lifted, head following a second later. I stared at my bay window.

A knock sounded at the door. My stomach fluttered and warmed all over.

Jamie.

I stood and dropped the notepad and pen on the couch, and my mind, that was left there, too, along with any sense I had in me, then I tucked overgrown bangs behind my ears as I crossed the room with quick, anxious steps.

"Jamie," I whispered, hand reaching for the knob.

He was here. And I was going to let him in. I wasn't fighting. I wasn't thinking.

Clearly...

There was no other explanation for what I was about to do.

Pulse racing, I opened the door and my mouth to greet him, but my "hey" got stuck in my throat and swelled until I choked on it.

I coughed, hand to my chest and eyes wide and watering. The man who took my heart and squeezed the life out of it smiled and braced his forearm on the door frame, angling closer. His deep brown lying eyes did a slow, meaningful appraisal.

"*Goddamn*, sugar, I've missed you," Wes said, his voice carrying that thick Southern drawl I used to find sweet and endearing as he looked me over.

He was still in his work clothes, meaning he most likely hadn't gone home yet to his beautiful wife and adorable-looking daughter, who I was now *very* much aware of thanks to our shocking introduction at the mall a couple of months back.

I had been shaking, on the verge of tears or my first panic attack as my boyfriend smiled at his wife and introduced me as an old friend from school. She tried to take my hand, but I couldn't offer it.

I wanted to die. He had made me the other woman.

I hadn't seen or talked to Wes since and I had zero plans on doing either one ever again. I hated him. He made me sick.

He broke my heart.

"What are you doing here?" I half questioned, half cried in his face as I stepped closer so he wouldn't enter. "Get off of my property," I hissed. "You aren't welcome here, Wes."

"Calm down, Tor. I get why you're upset. I do," he replied, sounding sincere as he straightened. He rubbed at the back of his neck. "I really didn't want it to go down like that. Honest. That sucked for me."

"*Excuse me?*" I snapped. "It sucked for *you*?"

What a dick!

"Yeah, so I get why you're pissed right now," he returned.

"You get *nothing*."

Wes stepped closer, trying to move inside, and when I didn't step back or away to give him room, he sighed and cocked his head. "You have no idea what I've been dealing with. Kim was suspicious before. Then meeting you like that? Come on. Why do you think I've been staying away? She's been all over my shit."

"You have a *wife*, Wes. She should be all over your shit. It's *hers*!"

"Don't be like that," he said, looking almost apologetic. "I've missed you, sugar. It's been hell. You know how bad I've been wanting to come over here or call? She was even checking my phone. I couldn't do shit."

"Don't call me sugar or anything else you might call your *wife*," I snapped, sliding my hand up the side of the door and readying to slam it. "I never would've gotten involved with you if I had known you were married. I cannot believe you kept that from me."

"Fucked you on our second date. If I told you I was married after that, knowing how good that was, would it have mattered?" he questioned.

I flinched, unprepared for that accusation.

"Of course it would've mattered," I shot back. "You're *married*. I never would've let it happen again. I would've ended it."

"After the sex we had? The way I worked you? Come on." He tilted his head and breathed a laugh as his arms crossed over his chest. "I took your ass and had you coming so hard you nearly passed out. You told me you'd never been fucked like that before. Is that still true?" His eyebrows lifted.

I pinched my lips together and felt my face burn hot.

"It is, ain't it?" he asked, smiling darkly. "Probably had plenty of opportunity since I've been away but you didn't take it. Why?"

"Get off of my property," I snarled, tipping forward.

"You didn't take it 'cause you're wanting it from me," he said, ignoring my command. "No one else. It doesn't matter I'm married or not, you want it."

"Leave, Wes." My voice shook. I felt my lip tremble. "I mean it. You need to leave."

Wes moved closer, stepping up so he was filling the doorway and our bodies were grazing each other's. "You want to fuck," he growled, looking down at me. "That's what you really want, and you're in luck, sugar, 'cause that's exactly what I'm here to do."

I felt his hand on my hip, squeezing the same spot Jamie had been gripping, and something snapped inside me, breaking me open and bleeding me out.

"LEAVE!" I screamed with tears wetting my cheeks, fists flying and connecting with his chest as I pounded on it and pushed, putting all of my weight behind me. "I hate you, you fucking asshole! Get out! Get out! GET OUT!"

"Jesus. What the fuck?" Wes jerked back onto the porch. "Tori—"

I slammed the door shut and locked it, yelling, "GO! Don't ever come back here! I don't ever wanna see you again, you sick fuck!"

"Don't be like this," he pleaded, twisting the knob. "Come on, Tor. Seriously."

"GET OUT OF HERE!"

"Hey. There a problem?"

I heard a man's voice. It sounded like Tom, my neighbor from next door. He liked to sit on his porch at night and smoke cigars. The smell always bothered his wife.

"No, man. No problem here," Wes answered, his voice growing softer as if he were stepping away.

"Lotta yelling going on. You sure?"

"Yeah. All good."

I dropped the side of my head against the door and held my stomach. My throat was burning and my chest was quaking with the breaths I couldn't seem to hold on to.

A car started, then a door closed. Wes pulled away from my house. I heard the unmistakable sound of his engine revving as he made his way down the street.

He had come here for sex. He was still married and he was still wanting me, and worse, he thought I'd still be wanting him. He thought I was that type of woman.

And he had touched me.

I still felt his hand on my hip. I started feeling Wes everywhere. *Everywhere.*

I was no longer feeling Jamie.

Hand to my mouth and stomach rolling, I hurried to the kitchen, where I had dumped my purse before taking a shower. I grabbed it and pulled out my keys, slid the strap up my arm to my shoulder, and made for the door, barefoot. I didn't even bother with shoes.

Tom called out a greeting when I stepped off the porch. He asked if everything was all right.

I lied, saying it was, and waved. I hid my face behind my hair.

I was crying when I got to my car, started it, and backed out of my driveway, but I was sobbing by the time I reached the highway. I couldn't control it.

I couldn't feel Jamie. I couldn't taste him or smell the sun on his skin. I couldn't remember how he shook.

I felt Wes.

Behind me and beneath me. Between my legs and inside my chest where I'd thought I had pushed him out. But I didn't. He was still there.

I wanted him out. I wanted to forget.

I would beg to feel anything but him.

My tears stopped when I saw Jamie's bike and a light on in one of the windows. He was home. He was awake.

I wiped at my face after I parked in the driveway, collecting myself as best as I could before I got out, leaving my purse and tucking my keys into my pocket. I hurried to the door and beat my knuckles on the wood. I wasn't gentle.

My hand stung, but my hip burned. I could still hear Wes's voice. *"You want to fuck."*

I closed my eyes and bit the tremble in my lip.

The light above me came on. I heard locks being turned and I lowered my hand and opened my eyes a second before the door was swinging open and Jamie was filling it.

He had on blue mesh shorts that hung low and loose, no shirt, had hair that was wet and curling below his ears and eyes that were heavy, like he was tired but couldn't sleep.

If he had showered, he didn't shave. His jaw and neck and the skin above his lip were still shadowed. He looked rough.

He looked like sex and secrets.

This was bad. And I needed it.

I stared at his collarbone, his chest, and the muscles indenting beneath it. The patch of hair running from his navel to his waistband and lower. I just stared.

"You want somethin'?" Jamie rasped, elbow bent and anchoring on the frame.

My eyes snapped up. I wet my lips and watched his eyes follow my tongue. They flashed with heat. His nostrils flared.

I lunged at him and he caught me, dragging me up his body and into the house.

"Please," I begged against his mouth.

He cursed, saying *God* and *Fuck* and hauling me closer.

Our tongues met and slid past, dipping and tasting. We kissed hard and wet. We were sloppy. We didn't care.

Jamie kicked the door closed and slammed me against it. Hard. He was untamed.

I cried out and begged inside our kiss. *Please. Please. Please. Please.*

He growled and moaned, *Yeah, baby*, and *Want this*, and *Need this. Keep beggin'.*

Tears filled my eyes. I curled my fingers in his damp hair and pulled until he growled. I dragged my nails up his back and sank them between his ribs.

I wanted this to hurt.

I wanted his touch tattooed on my skin. I wanted to leave marks and bear his desperation tomorrow.

And the next day. And the next...

Jamie dipped his head and sucked on my neck as his hands kneaded my ass. Fingers pinching. Flesh bruising. He caught my skin between his teeth and clamped down.

My breath hitched. I tasted my tears as I opened my mouth and begged.

"*Please.*"

His hand slid between us and into my shorts. He pushed two fingers inside me and told me this was his.

"*Please.*"

My voice broke.

I closed my eyes and began to sob.

Jamie tensed with his entire body. "Hey." His voice was soft and soothing as he leaned away and whispered, "Tori." His fingers left me, then I felt his hand push strands of hair out of my face. "Babe. What the fuck?" he asked, holding my cheek.

"Don't," I choked, shaking my head and blinking away tears. "Don't stop. Please. Please just, I—I want this. Please keep going."

"You're crying."

"I'm *begging*!" I screamed, lifting my chin and locking on to his eyes.

Ocean boy blues filled with confusion and concern stared back.

I couldn't take it.

I tried pulling him closer with my hands on his neck and back, wailing, "I'm begging, okay? You won! This is what you wanted! You wanted me to beg and I'm *begging*. Please!" I dropped my head and tried leaning into him. I wept harder. "Please don't stop. Please. Please, Jamie. *Please.*"

"Tori, fuck! Stop!" he growled, fighting my hold while pressing closer at the same time, but not closer like I wanted him.

His fingers on my face were gentle. Not burning and moving over my body. I wanted to hide.

"*Please,*" I sobbed.

My body broke. My hands went limp and I buckled, falling into him. Strong arms caught me and held me up. They wrapped around me and felt like a promise.

I nestled closer, lifting my head off his chest and burying my face in his neck. "Please. I don't want to feel him," I cried with tears on my lips. "I don't want to feel him anymore, Jamie."

"Baby, who?" he asked, cupping the back of my head and dropping his mouth beside my temple. "Who don't you wanna feel?"

"Wes."

His arm around my back tightened, squeezing me.

"What the fuck? He do something to you?" Jamie's voice vibrated through his body like thunder rolling. I felt it shake my bones. "Did he?"

I closed my eyes and whimpered. "He came over. I—I thought he was you."

"*Shit*," he mumbled, sounding fury-filled and something else. Regretful maybe. I wasn't sure.

"He wanted to come in," I continued. "He wanted to fuck. He thought I did, too. He…he said I didn't care he was married. That I wanted it too much. He was wanting to pick back up where we left off." I shook my head against his jaw and wrapped my hand around Jamie's ribs. "I would never do that. I wouldn't."

"*Motherfucker*," he snarled from above me. "He's dead."

"I felt you and then I felt him, and I—"

Jamie shoved me back, lifted my chin, and stared deep into my eyes, questioning with a low, grating, scary voice, "He touch you?"

I blinked, studying his hardened face. I'd never seen Jamie look like this before. He looked like rage. He looked a little crazy.

And he looked absolutely beautiful.

"Babe," he pressed, when I kept on studying and forgot his question. "Mm?"

He dipped closer, punctuating each word he spoke. "Did. He. Touch. You?"

I swallowed, staring back at blue eyes burning. "Not really. Just…" I slid my hand down his side and grabbed his smooth hip. "Like this. Where you did."

His jaw clenched. He exhaled through his nostrils, flaring them. "He do anythin' else?" he asked, staying close and keeping his fingers on my face.

"Just said those things," I replied, my bottom lip trembling and my eyes filling up fast. "Those awful things that are not true. They're not. I would never want him knowing he was married. I wouldn't." I started crying again. "I'm not like that. I swear I'm not. Even though I loved him, I wouldn't. I never would've let him in. *Never.*" I dropped my head to his chest and sobbed, "I thought it was you. That's why I answered."

Jamie's body stiffened and snapped straight. He made a noise deep in his throat like he was in as much pain as I was, then he bent down, slid one arm around my waist and the other under my knees, and lifted, cradling me against his chest.

"Should've been me," he mumbled against the top of my head, turning us and then walking across the room.

We started ascending the stairs.

I held his neck with one hand and cried with my face tucked under his chin. My eyes were swollen closed. I felt exhausted. Heart and body. I had shed my weight in tears.

Jamie carried me as if that were true.

When we reached the top, Jamie took me six more steps and then he kicked a door open.

The room was dark. He didn't turn on the light.

My lashes fluttered when I felt soft satin beneath me. It felt cool against the back of my calves.

I was in Jamie's bed.

I turned my head on the pillow and smelled sunlight and water. I watched through half-opened eyes. I was crying much softer now.

Jamie pulled back the covers, dropped his knee to the bed, and then leaned closer to peel the sheets down underneath me, wiggling them under my bottom and flipping them up and over my feet. Then he climbed in and lay on his side, facing me, tucked his arm under the pillow he was using and with his other pulled and rolled me away from him, putting us back to front.

He pulled the covers over us both.

It felt familiar, lying with him like this, even though we had never done this before. But I was too tired to question it or fight. And maybe I felt safe, cared for, protected, so I didn't want to fight it. I had been fighting it enough. And this felt nice.

Jamie kept his arm over me after he was settled and wrapped his hand around my wrist. He pressed his lips to the skin between my neck and shoulder.

"Sleep, Legs," he ordered.

"'Kay," I replied, blinking the darkness into view.

I pictured Wes standing on my porch. I felt his hand press to my hip.

"He won't be botherin' you again," Jamie promised.

I stopped blinking. The images in my mind evaporated and the only thing I felt was Jamie's body. His mouth next to my ear and his fingers holding gentle pressure on my arm.

He was steady at my back. He was strong. He was holding me like this mattered and meant something.

And he was promising again.

Knowing the history of Jamie's promises to me and how he carried them through, each and every one, I closed my eyes and drifted with a clear head.

I'd start thinking again tomorrow.

Chapter Ten

JAMIE

Need you to swing by this morning before heading in. Bring Sunshine.

What's up?

Got her girl here.

She all right?

Will be.

Shit. This serious? Syd will want to know.

Nothing I can't handle. Just need to get some info from her.

What's this got to do with?

You asking for you or your girl?

It's involving Syd. I'm asking for me.

Tori's ex showed up at her place last night. Upset her. She came to me.

Fuck.

Yeah.

Know what all went down with them. Be there by 8.

I set my phone on the kitchen island after reading Dash's last text, then I walked over to the couch and snatched the towel off the back of it, rubbing it across my head and drying off as I made for the stairs.

I didn't want to get out of bed this morning. Not with the way Tori was pressing close and letting me hold her, doing that all night and not fighting it, just feeling. Rolling into me a few times with her hand on my chest or wrapping around my ribs, legs tangled with mine, head tucked under my chin and her breath on my neck. Or staying turned away but keeping a grip on my arm that was draped over her, locking us together.

Not running. Not lying. But taking and giving it back. No layers. Just her.

Tori Rivera.

Fucking Tori Rivera. Jesus.

Thought about how good that would be more times than I could remember. Nine months of fantasies building expectation she might not meet, building obsession, too, 'cause I wanted her hot ass in my bed and she was making that shit a challenge, then I get her there and Tori doesn't just live up to what I've been pining for, but proves I've been underestimating her this entire fucking time.

Shit wasn't just good. It was *really* fucking good, even without the sex.

She held on. Fucking *held on* to me. Legs was giving it back.

Fuck. So good.

And I wanted to stay there. I wanted to keep her like that, pressing close and open, but I was edgy. Alive with anger. I couldn't stop seeing her crying. I couldn't stop hearing her begging words while she broke apart.

I wanted to find that prick and knock his teeth down his throat. I wanted to kill him. Rip him apart for what he did to her. It felt like a fever was running through me. My hands clenched around soft skin that burrowed against my side. I couldn't stay in that bed. I needed to move.

I needed to burn it out.

Being on the water did that. It calmed my mind and cleared my head. There was nothing like it. So I texted Dash and made him aware, then I grabbed my board and paddled out.

The water under me. The power of it. Feeling the air. Hearing the break of the waves. Fucking heaven.

I got some time in and I felt better. Not much. I still wanted to beat the shit out of this asshole, but there was a chance now I might not kill him. Slim, but it was there.

After changing out of my board shorts and finding Tori still asleep, rolled on her side as if I was still behind her, I left her there, wanting her to get as much rest as possible after what all went down last night. I figured she needed it. Then I went downstairs, got the coffee brewed, and poured myself a cup.

I stood at the island, drinking my coffee and flipping through a magazine while I waited. Noise of the front door opening lifted my head, and I watched Syd walk into the room wearing her blue hospital scrubs, her quick steps bringing her in fast and her anxious eyes scanning.

She stopped halfway into the room. Dash followed in behind her.

"Where is she?" Syd asked when she didn't find Tori standing in the kitchen with me or sitting in the living room. "Is she okay? What happened? Did he do something to her? I'm gonna tear him apart and then light him on fire. I *swear* to God..." She curled her hands into fists and held them in front of her chest. Her face burned red.

"Babe, take a breath." Dash came to a stop next to her, looking at his girl. "Jamie's got her. If she wasn't okay, he would've called and had us coming over a lot sooner. You know that."

Syd lowered her hands and looked at me, face soft, asking, "She's okay?"

"She's asleep," I told her. "Crashed in my bed last night."

Syd's eyes brightened, then her mouth twitched the slightest bit. She was upset and worrying for her friend but she liked hearing that.

Liked it so much she gave that quirky look she was wearing to Dash and let him see it.

He shook his head and mumbled something under his breath.

I went on elaborating. "Slept good all night, but that cocksucker made her cry. She was pretty torn up when she got here," I shared, not keeping the truth from Syd 'cause this was her girl and she deserved to know. I braced my hands on the island on either side of the magazine and leaned forward, keeping her eyes. "Showed up at her place sayin' some shit about Tori wantin' to keep what they had going even though she knew he was married. Like that didn't matter to her."

"Jesus," Dash mumbled at the same time as Syd flinched.

"He said that?" she whispered.

I jerked my chin and watched her shoulders pull back.

"On second thought," she began, raising her voice and lifting a finger to gesture. "I'm gonna light him on fire *before* I rip him apart. I want him feeling those flames."

"You can do whatever the fuck you wanna do with him. But that first shot?" I jabbed a finger at my chest. "That's mine, babe. First person he's seein' is *me*."

Syd blinked, lowering her hand. She looked on the verge of tears. "You're gonna defend her honor again," she stated softly, not as a question but as if she already knew. "Just like you did when you messed up his car. You're going for her soft."

"I'm goin' for her *what*?" I asked, brow furrowing as I lowered my hand to cool granite.

"Her soft. You want to hit it again."

"What the fuck is her soft?"

"Her heart, Jamie."

I stared at Syd, seeing she was serious. Then I shook my head, laughing under my breath and looking to Dash to watch him give his girl the same reaction I was giving her. I looked back to Syd and shared, "Sunshine, like what you're tellin' me, appreciate it, too. I'm glad I've hit that spot in her. Means I got a shot at hittin' it again. Straight up, that's good to know. But right now, the only thing I'm thinkin' about hittin' belongs to one dead motherfucker."

"I understand that," Syd replied. "I just want to make sure you're aware of what this might mean to her since, you know, she might not tell you."

Syd knew her girl. That was for damn sure.

I smiled. "I'm aware, babe. Thanks."

"Good." Syd smiled back. "Now, Trouble said you needed some information from me. What do you need to know?"

Syd always called Dash Trouble.

"Everything you know about this piece of shit. Startin' with where he lives," I said.

Her shoulders dropped. "I don't know that," she replied, sounding disheartened. "I never met him. I don't even know what he looks like."

"Don't know what he sounds like either," Dash added.

Syd smiled at him.

That was how they got together; she called Wes to tear him a new one for hurting her girl and ended up dialing Dash instead.

"Best mistake ever," I heard Syd reply.

Didn't see it, though. My eyes were pinched shut and I was gritting my teeth. I was hoping to get everything I needed from Sunshine. I didn't want to involve Tori, but it looked like I might not have a choice.

Fuck.

"You know anything about him?" Dash asked his girl, drawing my attention. "Last name? Where he works?"

Syd nodded quickly, looking from Dash to me with brighter eyes. "His last name is Asher. And I know he sells cars. I don't know where, though."

Dash looked at me, and at the same time we both said, "Asher Automotives."

"*Motherfucker*," I grated. My hands curled into fists on the counter.

"Shit. We might actually know this guy," Dash stated, verbalizing my thoughts.

"Really?" Syd asked, looking between us.

"Got our Jeeps from there," he shared. "Jamie special ordered his. He worked with a guy for a few days getting that set up." Dash jerked his chin at me. "You remember his name?"

I shook my head and straightened, bringing my arms across my chest. "Nah, but he had to be pushing sixty. He was old."

No fucking way was that dude Wes. Unless Tori was into dating men old enough to be her dad.

"I think Wes is in his thirties," Syd shared.

"Younger guy helped me. Could've been him," Dash said, lifting his shoulders.

I looked at my phone on the counter, then I snatched it up, checking the time. It was too early to call and see if that asshole was working today. After dealing with them when I was buying my car, I knew they didn't open until nine.

"What are you thinking?"

Dash's voice lifted my head.

I rubbed at my mouth and along my jaw, shrugging. "Call 'em up in an hour and check if he's workin'," I said, dropping my hand. "He is, I'll be takin' my lunch there."

Dash lifted his chin, hearing me, then he looked at Syd and told her, "Can't meet up with you today, babe. I gotta handle this with him."

Syd was nodding before he finished speaking. She turned into him and touched his arm. "Sweet of you," she said.

Dash bent down and kissed the top of her head.

I heard water running upstairs, meaning Tori was up, and hearing that, I remembered the other thing I needed Syd for.

"Her parents, you know where they live?" I asked her.

Syd turned her head and then tilted it, looking confused. "Yeah, they live in Raleigh," she replied, eyes searching for understanding.

"You know the address?"

"Why?"

I took that as a yes and rounded the counter with my phone, pulling up my notes app.

"Here." I held it out for her to take when I stopped in front of her. "Put it in there for me. I might need it."

Syd blinked up at me. She looked ready to throw a shit-ton of questions my way that I didn't have time for and didn't feel like answering, but that look slowly evaporated into one I'd seen on her a handful of times.

Typically stuff involving Dash, but she gave it to me the day I asked what type of flowers Legs was into.

"This has to do with Tori's soft again, doesn't it?" Syd asked, taking the phone and fighting a smile.

I wasn't going to answer that. Planned on ignoring Sunshine and her probing, but it turned out I didn't need to.

Footsteps on the stairs lifted my head and turned hers. I watched Tori move through the entryway.

Her hair was pulled back now and messy at the top of her head. Strands of yellow fell into her eye. She tried tucking them behind her ear as she stepped into the room, flushed face and bright eyes bouncing between the three of us. They settled on me.

I straightened and pulled in a breath, chest expanding as I looked at her where she stood.

Had all that beauty in my arms last night.

Jesus. Why the fuck did I ever get out of bed?

"Here," Syd whispered. She pressed the phone against my chest and then turned, moving toward her girl. "Sweetie, are you okay?" she asked, wrapping her arms around her. "Jamie told us what happened. I can't believe that jerk did that to you. *God*, I want to kill him."

Tori was hugging Syd back but she was keeping her eyes on me.

"Gonna give them a minute and then head out," Dash said, his voice lowered as Tori leaned away and talked quietly with her girl. Syd's hands cupped her face. "You know how you're gonna handle this today if he's working?"

I turned my head and looked at him. "Just gonna talk," I answered.

"Yeah?" he asked, brows lifting. He didn't seem convinced. "You hit him and he presses charges, you know what'll happen."

Dash was referring to my sponsors dropping me. He knew the risks I was taking confronting this asshole.

I knew them, too.

"Good thing I'm just goin' to talk then," I returned, tucking my phone into my back pocket.

That was the plan. I wasn't bullshitting Dash. How this would happen to play out, I didn't know.

If I thought Wes was hearing me, we'd only be talking.

If I didn't...

"Shit," he muttered, shaking his head as if he could read my mind. He turned and looked at the girls. "Kinda wanna knock his ass out myself for working Syd up."

"Anyone hits him, it's me," I shared, voice unforgiving.

"Figured that. Just saying. It's not like I have shit to lose."

"Just gonna talk to him," I repeated.

Dash turned his head, meeting my eyes when I did the same. "She came to you crying?" he asked.

I nodded. My jaw flexed.

"Right," he uttered, looking away.

He knew. There was a chance we wouldn't just be talking.

"Babe, you ready? Gonna be late if we don't leave now," he said, moving to get to Syd.

She took his warning and gave Tori another hug, whispering with her before pulling away. Then she glanced back at me and shot me a look full of appreciation.

That should've felt good. Under different circumstances, it probably would've. But I was still picturing Tori crying. Shaking in my arms. Her tears against my neck.

Nothing was feeling good right now.

Dash said something to Tori that had her nodding and smiling softly, then he threw his arm around Syd and called out a "Later" before leading her out of the room.

The front door closed behind them.

My eyes sliced to Tori again and I took her in. She was standing there in yellow silk shorts and a shirt too big for her. It hung off one shoulder and hid her shape, but she still looked good. She always looked good. Tori could make anything work for that body.

Bottom lip caught between her teeth and chest rising and falling slowly, she stared at me.

"Come here," I ordered. I wanted to touch her. Kiss her. I needed to make sure she was okay.

Tori released her lip. Her hand came up and tucked those strands of yellow behind her ear again. "I'm sorry about last night," she said, keeping her distance.

I ignored her apology and repeated, "Babe, come here."

"I must've looked crazy. I don't typically cry and beg for sex." She looked down, laughing a little. "I didn't even put on shoes. What the—"

"*Legs*," I barked.

Her head snapped up, eyes following and going round.

"You don't get over here right now, I'm comin' to you," I warned.

She blinked. Then she started moving toward me, not as quickly as I would've liked but she was moving, so I didn't get on her about it. She stopped in front of me and looked up, staying inches away.

"You all right?"

Tori hesitated for a second, then she nodded. "Yeah. Just . . . a little embarrassed. I can't believe I came to you like that."

"Don't," I cautioned.

Her brow furrowed. "Don't what?"

"That's mine, babe. You're not takin' that."

Her head tilted. "I'm not taking *what*?" she questioned.

"Got upset and needed to go to someone, and out of everyone, babe, you chose me," I reminded her. "Could've gone to your girl, but you didn't. You came here. Cried in my arms. Let me hold you and you held back. Don't act like that wasn't what you wanted. Don't play that down."

"I meant the begging part."

"Yeah, that's another thing." I crossed my arms over my chest. "Bet's over, babe. I'm done playin' games with you."

She looked from my eyes to my mouth and back up, asking, "You are?"

"Yep."

"Why?"

"*Why?*" I echoed.

"Yes. Why?" Her eyes narrowed. "Because I begged?"

"'Cause you fuckin' *came to me*," I said, bending to get closer, voice dropping lower and shaking in my throat.

Tori inhaled through her nose. Her eyes danced between mine. "I came to beg," she lied, speaking fast. "That's the only reason I came here."

"Nope."

"It was, Jamie."

"That's one of the reasons," I countered. "Ain't all of them."

She rolled up onto her toes. "It's the *only reason*," she shot back, holding tight to her lie.

Fuck this. I was sick of her shit. My hands shot out, slid around her waist to her back and yanked, hauling her closer until she was flush against me. Then I bent down and took her mouth, pushing my tongue inside.

I tasted her gasp and her need. I fucking ate them.

"Admit it," I said inside our kiss.

Her fingers pushed through my hair. She tilted her head, kissed me deeper, and then pulled back to suck on my lip.

Fuck.

"No," she breathed.

I kneaded her ass until she arched up and moaned. "All these lies, babe. I want a truth."

"I came to beg."

"You came for *me*." I kissed my way to her jaw and neck. I licked up to her ear and let her feel my teeth.

She shuddered and gasped. "*Jamie.*"

"You like me. Admit it."

I felt the shake of her head and the flutter of her pulse against my tongue.

"You like me."

"I don't." She sounded breathless and breakable. She sounded weak.

I growled, lifting my head and claiming her hot breath and sweet parted lips. One hand pushing through the hair at the base of her neck and holding while the other pressed low to her back.

She whimpered against my tongue. Then she started sucking on it.

Tori fought with her words. Not her body. I quit asking and just kissed her.

And kissed her.

And kissed her.

I kissed her until seconds blurred into minutes. I kissed her hard and rowdy and rough.

She kissed me harder. Sucked harder. Bit harder. Her hands gripped my back and shoulders and pulled. She wanted me close.

Tori wasn't just taking. She was giving it back.

Again.

Fuck yeah. She liked me. She liked me a whole fucking lot.

When my lips burned and the bite from her nails stung my scalp and neck, I pulled away, panting. Hands around her waist, I dropped my forehead against hers and held her eyes.

"Bet's over," I said. My voice was hoarse.

Tori kept her fingers on my jaw. She licked me off her lips, nodding and breathing heavy. "Okay," she whispered.

"Gave me somethin' last night and I'm keepin' it. You're not takin' that."

Again, she nodded.

"*Quit fightin' me*," I growled, putting pressure on her back.

Tori closed her eyes. Her hands fell between us, pressing against my chest as her throat worked with a noisy swallow. Then she blinked up at me. Her eyes were pale blue.

"I didn't just come here to beg," she admitted, keeping her voice soft and maybe a little scared.

My mouth twitched. *Fuck me, this woman.* I could've gloated but I didn't. I didn't want anything tainting this moment she was giving me.

Tori might not give it up again.

"You gotta work today?" I asked her, leaning away but keeping my hands on her. I held her hips.

"Yeah."

"When?"

"I gotta be there by nine," she said. "I told Nate I'd help him with the schedule."

"Got time to eat then."

I directed Tori with a hand to her back toward the kitchen. She went without resistance.

"You want coffee?" I asked.

"I don't drink coffee."

"Juice? Water?"

"Juice would be good."

I moved past her and opened the cabinet to get a glass, then I went to the fridge and poured some orange juice.

"Did you get in the ocean this morning?" she asked from behind me.

"Yeah. Why?"

"You smell like it."

I turned my head and caught Tori staring at me, leaning her hip against the counter and pressing her fingers to her bottom lip.

"But I guess you always smell like it." She dropped her hand and shrugged. "Like you were born out there or something."

"Been surfing since I was four."

"Really?"

I nodded, looking away to put the bottle of orange juice back on the shelf. Then I opened the cabinet where I kept food and grabbed a pack of Pop-Tarts.

"Soon as I could walk, my parents took me out. My mom surfed," I replied, going to Tori and handing her the glass. "Started out on body boards. Loved it, so I learned fast. I was out there every day."

She took a sip of her juice, watching me over the rim.

I opened up the pack of Pop-Tarts and held one out. Tori took it, brow furrowing.

"What?" I asked, biting off a corner.

She sat her glass down on the counter next to my empty cup, then she turned her hand over, examining the breakfast I was offering. "I don't think I've eaten one of these since I was a little kid," she said on a laugh.

"I eat them all the time. They're good in a pinch."

Her eyes came up. She was smiling. "They're pure sugar, Jamie. Especially this kind with the icing. I'm surprised you still have teeth."

I stared at the curve in her lips, stained red from the color she always wore on them. My chest grew tight. I had no fucking idea what she'd just said. Didn't matter, though. I had something I needed to share.

"You told me last night you wanted to stop feelin' him," I reminded her, lifting my eyes and watching hers flicker wider.

Tori gazed at me for a beat, then she slowly brought the Pop-Tart to her mouth and took a bite.

"I don't got time to take care of that this mornin'," I said. "I gotta get to work."

"Me, too," she answered, sounding anxious around her mouthful, her hand coming up in front of her lips. "I need to go home and shower, so—"

"What time you get off?"

Her eyes went round.

"From work," I added, smirking.

Jesus.

"Oh." She swallowed, lowered her hand and licked her lips. "Ten tonight. I'm working a double."

"Right." I jerked my chin. "Be at your house by ten fifteen then."

Tori blinked.

"You won't be feelin' him tomorrow," I promised.

She blinked again. Her cheeks flushed red and she coughed a little.

I smiled, liking her reaction. "Eat, Legs. We don't got all mornin'."

Without hesitation, Tori went back to eating. She kept her eyes on me the entire time.

Her face never paled.

* * *

Back pressed against the window of a 2017 Dodge Charger, jaw set tight, arms crossed and muscles tense, I scanned the lot at Asher Automotives while Dash stood beside me.

He was scanning, too, but doing it looking less inclined to beat someone's ass.

I called as soon as the dealership opened and found out Wes was coming in at ten. Hearing that, I pushed my lessons back and took an early lunch.

It was nine fifty-five.

"There." Dash pointed at the cherry red Corvette pulling into the lot. My gaze hardened.

"See he got new tires," I observed, keeping my position as I watched Wes park near the door in one of the labeled employee parking spots. "Legs wanted to set his ride on fire that night. Kinda wishing I'd let her do it."

Dash chuckled next to me.

"That was some funny shit," he mumbled. "You remember what they were wearing?"

I nodded, thinking back to that night I saw Tori going to town on this motherfucker's car, dressed like a fucking cartoon character and still making my balls ache.

Wes climbed out, closed the driver's-side door and straightened fully. He was tall. Lean build. A little scrawny in the arms.

I wasn't worried.

"Wasn't him who sold me my car," Dash said. "Good to know I didn't make that asshole any money."

The older guy I worked with a few months back, Dave, stepped out of the office and met Wes halfway up the ramp.

I spoke to him when I got here, letting him know who we were waiting for and shooting down the impression that I was looking to give a sale to someone other than him.

He seemed understanding of my issue with Wes. Apparently the shithead stole customers out from under people all the time. Being the owner's grandson, he had job security, which sucked for everyone else. Dave also shared that the cameras pointed on the lot were on the fritz and set to get worked on next week.

I thanked him by offering up my business for life.

Wes looked across the lot after getting word on us waiting for him. The fucker grinned in our direction, most likely thinking he was getting a sale.

Dick.

"I'm gonna beat that fuckin' smile off his face," I bit out.

"Thought you were just here to talk?" Dash questioned, turning his head to look at me.

I met his eyes and then cut away.

Wes started walking over. He was still wearing that grin.

"Change of plans," I said, cracking my neck from side to side.

"*Fuck*," Dash mumbled. He exhaled a tense breath. "Do me a favor and try talking first. I get what you're feeling but you got a lot to lose, Jamie. You might be able to settle this without risking what you've worked hard for."

I was hearing Dash, I just wasn't caring for what he had to say. Still, he was right.

"Fine," I said, growing more annoyed.

"You're gonna talk?"

"Yeah. Whatever."

Wes stopped in front of us, smiling and giving it to us both. "Gentlemen, Dave says you were asking for me. What can I do you for?"

Dash stayed quiet. I didn't say shit.

Wes looked between us, brow tight when we didn't answer, then he moved closer and gestured at the car I was leaning on. "Just got this in. It's a 2017 Do—"

"Shut the fuck up and listen," I interrupted.

Wes blinked, stepping close. He looked at Dash and then back at me. "Excuse me?"

I wasn't in the mood to repeat myself so I got straight to the point. "Tori Rivera," I snapped.

His eyes slowly narrowed. That was the only tell he gave to let me know he was following me. That was enough.

"You're done, asshole. Stay the fuck away from her."

Wes laughed under his breath. He mimicked my pose, standing defensively before uttering, "I don't know what you're talking about."

He was lying. Probably because he was married and didn't need anyone else knowing he was running around on his wife.

I kept at him. "Don't call. Don't show up. I hear you're even thinkin' about her, and we're gonna have a major fuckin' problem. You get me?"

"Dude, seriously, think you got the wrong guy."

Now he was just starting to piss me off. I pushed off from the car and got in his face. Dash was at my back, bracing.

"Held her last night," I shared, eye to eye with this prick. "All fucking night, had that beauty in my arms."

His jaw clenched and his nostrils started flaring.

"I see that bothers you. Funny, since I got the wrong guy."

Wes pushed against me, stepping up. "What I got with her doesn't concern you."

"You got *dick*, motherfucker. She's mine."

"Yeah?" He leaned closer. "What, was my bitch banging you, too?"

"What the fuck did you just call her?"

"Dude, shut the fuck up," Dash warned, coming to stand on my left so he could face Wes.

"Stay away from her," I repeated when I had his eyes. "Not gonna tell you again."

He grinned and licked his bottom lip, "You taste her yet? She melts like sugar, doesn't she?"

Rage burned like a fire in my veins.

"You fuckin' idiot," Dash uttered a second before I threw a right hook and connected with Wes's jaw, dropping him. Then I bent down, fisted his shirt, and yanked his whining ass up until we were nose to nose.

"Next time you see my face, cocksucker, you better run," I warned, baring my teeth. "I hear you're botherin' my woman again and I will *fuckin'* kill you."

Wes blinked. He flexed his jaw.

"*You hear me?*" I snarled.

He nodded stiffly, breathing heavily through his nose before ordering, "Get the fuck off me."

I released his shirt, dropping him onto the asphalt, where he continued to moan and hold his face. Then I turned and stalked away with Dash keeping strides next to me.

"Think he'll go to the cops?" he asked.

I flexed my hand. "He does, I'll deal with it."

"Probably just raise questions. His wife will want to know why you hit him."

Dash was right. I didn't think Wes was wanting to risk that. He wouldn't say shit.

"Surprised you talked," Dash offered up with humor in his voice.

"See? That right there." I fake glared at him. "Where's the faith, brother?"

He grinned.

I gave him one back. Then I looked away, laughing.

Chapter Eleven

TORI

I was showered. Shaved. My skin was moisturized and smelling like warm vanilla sugar. I had a clean face, no makeup, though my cheeks were pink and looking like I was wearing something on them. That was due to a combination of the water temperature I used and my nerves getting to me. My breath was minty and fresh. My hair was down and partially dried, looking extra wavy since I didn't blow it out. And my fingernails were still a little tacky from the top coat I applied a few minutes ago, doing this because the black and pink polish I had on them was starting to look drab.

Why I thought my nails had to be on point for what I was about to do, I had no idea. It had to be my nerves. I was overpreparing. I doubt Jamie would notice my shiny polish. And honestly, I wasn't sure I wanted him to.

If I was standing naked in front of Jamie McCade and the only thing he was focusing on was the upkeep of my manicure, I had bigger problems to worry about.

We were about to have sex. A lot of it, I was guessing. And although my body was ready for this thanks to the measures I'd just taken, I wasn't sure about the rest of me.

My mind was going a mile a minute. My heart was beating so fast I felt like I was on something. I was terrified. I was turned on. I was worried this was a mistake.

But I knew once we got started, I'd stop thinking and overthinking. Jamie would kiss me and I'd do what I always seemed to do when I felt his lips against mine and his grip on my skin.

I'd kiss him back. I'd grip him harder. I'd match his desperation with my own and give in to the feelings overwhelming me.

I'd let myself like him.

The second Jamie touched me, my brain would shut off and stop giving me the biggest freak-out of my life.

But until that happened, I'd continue doing what I was doing, which included standing in the bathroom wearing nothing but a white fluffy towel cinched under my arms, staring at my reflection in the mirror and the signs of my anxiety, all while running through positions, topics of conversation to use during moments of silence, if we had any, and the hundred reasons why having sex with Jamie McCade was a terrible idea.

Position-wise, I really had no idea what to expect.

He was fit, appeared to be limber, and had years of experience, I was certain.

Jamie didn't look like sweet, simple missionary sex. Not even when he smiled. Those dimples were a ploy he used as bait. He was mischief. He was late-night sneaking around when you had a curfew and a father with a shotgun.

He didn't care. Jamie took what he wanted. He didn't say please, he said now. And worse, he knew whatever he was asking for, *you* wanted just as bad as he did.

No. Jamie wasn't staring into your eyes while he took you soft and lovingly.

He was down and dirty doggy-style or up against a wall in a public bathroom. Hand-muffled screams and toys in his closet.

He was dark desires. He was what you thought of late at night while you lie in bed next to someone else.

So, position-wise, I was completely unprepared.

Awesome.

That wasn't really helping with my nerves.

In terms of conversation, I was primed to hit him with a range of topics. Anything from the weather to the ingredients I used in my chili recipe.

Silent moments with Jamie led to my mind going into hyper-overdrive. I was prepared to shut that shit down, even if I sounded crazy rattling off lists of my favorite things or naming objects in the room.

Lamp.

Chaise recliner.

Pierced dick under the blanket.

My stomach clenched.

I blinked at my wide-eyed reflection as reason number one hundred and one why this was a terrible idea hit me like a ton of bricks.

I had zero experience with dick piercings.

I didn't know how they felt. If they hurt or enhanced pleasure for women, and if that was the case, just how much pleasure they were capable of delivering. Would it be *too good*, ruining me for normal, undecorated cock for the rest of my life and turning me into some Craigslist creepster who trolled for boys with naughty jewelry, or would I hate it and call this entire thing off the second he pushed in? I had no idea.

And considering how unprepared I was for the type of sex Jamie was into, was there a risk of injury? Or if the mood hit me, was there a chance I might chip a tooth on this thing?

Shit. How hard was that metal?

I snatched my phone off the bathroom counter and clicked on my Safari app. Then I typed in "prince albert piercings" with the intentions of doing some thorough research.

Unfortunately, instead of scrolling down the page, I accidentally clicked on Images.

"Oh, God!" I gasped, hand flying to my mouth as the page loaded and my eyes were assaulted. I went to look away but found myself narrowing in on the third image instead, bringing the device closer to my face as I quietly remarked, "Oh, no, you didn't. *Why?* Why would you bring attention to that? You can't even really." I tilted my head. "Oh, there it is."

The bathroom door swung open.

Gasping again, this time somehow even more dramatic because I was about to get caught staring at a screen full of dicks, I smashed the phone against my chest and pivoted around.

Jamie stood in the doorway, brow furrowed and eyes searching the small room. "What the fuck?" he asked, looking into my face. "What happened? Why'd you scream?"

"Uh." I slid my thumb along the front of the phone, found the Home button, and clicked it. "Nothing. I . . . I thought I saw a spider, or something. It scurried down the drain. It was gross. And hairy."

His brows lifted.

I swallowed, feeling nerves constrict my throat. Then, even though I was seriously trying hard to stay quiet, those nerves got the best of me and my mouth just kept right on going at an even faster rate.

"You know, like, so much hair you can't even see what all they got. They don't groom themselves or anything. Not even to attract the opposite sex." I shook my head through a laugh. "Like, take the time, you know? Put a little effort in. It won't kill ya."

Jamie stared at me. His brows were still lifted.

I was totally talking about the penis I just saw. *Terrific.*

"Anyway." I cleared my throat and slid my phone back onto the counter, then I grabbed on to the top of my towel and held it in place while Jamie's presence in my house tripped my awareness. I stared back at him, eyes narrowing. "You know, just because you can break into my house doesn't mean you should. It's rude and, honestly, a little disturbing. There's a doorbell outside for a reason."

"You know what time it is?" he asked, reaching up and gripping on to the door frame with both hands, causing the off-white tee he was wearing to rise up and show tanned, hard abs and the trail of hair below his navel.

I glanced at what he was showing me, briefly, then I looked back into his eyes and remembered his question. "No. I've been in the shower. But what's that got to do with you picking locks instead of waiting for me to greet you?"

"Did wait," he replied. "Got here at ten fifteen, like I said I would, knocked and rang the fuckin' bell. Gave you two minutes to get your ass to that door and let me in yourself. You didn't."

I motioned at the front of me with the hand not clutching my towel. "I was showering. Hello. I would've greeted you when I was finished."

"Meaning I would've been standing on your porch for thirty fuckin' minutes, Legs."

"Excuse me?"

"It's quarter of eleven, babe."

I blinked.

Was it?

"Yeah," Jamie answered, reading my mind as he tipped forward and flexed his arms. "Waited the two minutes, got pissed at you for not answerin' the door when you knew damn well I'd be here at that exact time, let myself in with plans on gettin' on your case about it, and heard you showerin'. Hearin' that, I knew you were in here gettin' yourself ready for me so I quit bein' pissed at you. But straight up, babe, told you before and I'll say it again, you're in this house, I'm gettin' in. If I give you time to answer and you don't, that's on you."

I listened to Jamie's reasoning, and although I liked parts of it, him using the doorbell and knocking like a civilized person for one, there were parts of it I didn't like. I focused on one part in particular.

"Are you saying there will be occasions where you *don't* give me time to answer?" I asked, moving my hand to my hip and keeping the other on the towel.

"Yep."

"Like when?"

Jamie smiled.

"*Like. When*," I repeated, doing so with more sass when he didn't answer me.

"Middle of the night and I'm horny as fuck." He shrugged, keeping the smile. "Probably won't bother knocking then, seeing as you'll be asleep and won't hear it."

My nostrils flared. I tipped forward, the hand around my towel gripping tighter into a fist as I questioned, "Are you implying that I'm some sort of *booty call* to you? That you're gonna come here whenever you want a piece of ass and use me for it?"

Jamie lost his smile. Instantly. His face wiped clean of amusement. He didn't look angry, but he looked...something. Disturbed or disappointed. Maybe a little saddened. I couldn't tell.

And why did I suddenly feel sorry for calling him out on his suggestion?

Really?

He was the one suggesting it!

"Didn't mean it like that," Jamie said, voice steady and assuring.

I straightened up, stared at him for a beat, and read his honesty. Then getting that, I informed him without sass this time, "Fine, but that's how it sounded."

"Yeah. I'm gettin' that." He dropped his arms and exhaled heavily, still holding that look I couldn't read. Then he took a step back out into the hallway and turned sideways, facing my room. "We doin' this?" he asked.

This would've been the moment to change my mind. To let my hundred and one reasons rule my decision. To stay not-knowing and stay away from never-forgetting.

This was it.

But instead of opening my mouth or shaking my head, I kept hold of my towel and moved forward. I stepped out into the hallway. I wasn't going to look at Jamie. I was going to turn and walk to my bedroom and wait.

But a hand on my stomach stopped me, and because I wasn't expecting that hand, I turned my head, tipped it back, and looked at him.

Jamie didn't need to say a word. And thinking back, I almost wished he hadn't.

Staring into his eyes, I heard his promise to me before he even shared it.

"Wouldn't be like that with you," he said, and I felt his hand press deeper with the breath I pulled in. "Had that with women before. Made it known that was all it was and made it known up front. If there's an expectation there, I squash it or I move on. Messed up not to and shit just causes drama I don't fuckin' need."

He stared down at me after he was done speaking, keeping that look.

"Okay," I replied, not really understanding why he was sharing past women with me, and feeling the need to question his motives. "Why are you telling me this?"

Jamie bent down. His fingers tensed on my stomach.

"'Cause I'm tellin' you to have an expectation, babe," he shared, voice like a hot touch moving over me and breaking my body out in chills.

I blinked. Air caught in my throat. Lord...

I had no idea how to respond to that, and before I opened my mouth and said something stupid, like "okay" or "are you sure" or "I'm expecting you not to hurt me," I turned my head and my body and moved toward my bedroom. I did not look back.

God. My heartbeat was nothing before.

I stepped inside the room and looked around. The light was already on and the corner of the comforter was wrinkled.

Jamie had been in here. This was where he'd been waiting.

I moved to the side of the bed and spun around when he entered in behind me. Both hands clutched at the fold in my towel.

"Get on the bed," Jamie ordered. His tone was severe.

My toes curled against the carpet. I didn't move.

I watched Jamie reach over his shoulder and grip his shirt. He pulled it off and tossed it on the chaise recliner next to the window, met my eyes when he turned his head, and again ordered, "Get on the bed."

I trapped my lip between my teeth, staring at his broad chest and hard muscles. I didn't move.

Jamie unbuttoned and unzipped his gray, loose-fit cargo shorts. He pushed them to the floor, standing in black boxer briefs that *clung*. He was already hard.

"Tori."

My eyes snapped up at the sound of my name.

"You never call me Tori," I said, feeling the need to remind him of that.

He bent down, picked up his shorts, and pulled a sleeve of condoms out of his pocket. "About to get off on you. You're gonna be hearin' your name a lot," he pledged, keeping hold of the condoms and tossing his shorts on the recliner to join his shirt.

I huffed out a breath, draining the air from my lungs.

Wow. That was honest.

Then, because I knew he was going to order me to do it again and also because I wasn't sure my legs could hold me up much longer, I let my towel fall to the floor and quickly climbed onto the center of the bed.

Head on the pillow. Body stretched long. Thighs pinching tight. I looked down at my nakedness, at my breasts rising and falling rapidly, the tops of my knees and my hot-pink toes, then I lifted my eyes and saw Jamie was looking, too.

"Jesus," he mumbled, bringing a knee to the bed and putting weight on it as he stared, eyes trailing up and down and lingering in certain areas. He blindly tossed the condoms next to my hip, then he gripped my ankle, pushed back, and opened me up.

I gasped and pulled the soft duvet between my fingers.

"You've got the hottest fuckin' pussy I've ever seen," he said, climbing onto the mattress between my legs and staring there now, too.

My stomach clenched.

I wanted to roll away or cover up. I wanted to die.

And in the same breath, I didn't. I wanted *this* more.

Jamie lifted his eyes to me. "You wax?"

I nodded.

"Always keep it bare?"

I swallowed thickly, then nodded again.

"Like that, babe," he said, eyes darkening as he shifted closer, hands sliding up my shins, over my knees to my thighs.

I started shaking.

"Jamie," I whispered.

He leaned over me, bracing his hands beside my shoulders and lowering, letting me feel the weight of his body. The pressure of him moved in waves, starting at my hips, stomach, chest, the tops of my shoulders, until he covered me completely.

It was comfortable and it wasn't.

I wasn't a small woman. I was average height, five foot six, and the rest of me was average, too. I wasn't super skinny. I had meat on my bones and extra meat in certain areas. My butt filled out my jeans and I had to buy large tops on occasion because of my breasts, even though I was built for mediums.

I wasn't pint-sized and petite. I wasn't skinny by any means, but beneath Jamie, I felt tiny. Delicate.

He was huge and I was under him, wondering how long it would take him to break me.

When he dropped his head and kissed my shoulder, I stopped wondering and worrying and clutched at him instead, holding on to skin that felt like sunlight and smelled familiar. I gripped at the muscles in his back. I trailed my fingers up the line of his spine and curled them around his narrow hips.

Jamie rocked forward and pressed into me, leaning away and then bending to take my mouth and the moan I was giving him.

"You ready?" he asked, hot against my lips.

I nodded and whispered, "Yes." Then I braced myself. Because if Jamie asked whether or not I was ready, I *knew* that meant he was done being slow and accommodating.

He was ready to take. He was ready to push my face into the mattress and make my skin flush under his hand.

He was ready to fuck.

So when Jamie leaned back and ducked his head beside me, kissing my other shoulder and moving down my arm with his mouth, my body stiffened. I was confused.

He wasn't rushing to grab a condom and flip me over. He wasn't making me cry out while he made me forget.

He kissed my biceps and the bend in my elbow. The back of my forearm and the inside of my wrist. He opened my hand and pressed a kissed to my palm, and when he moved over each of my fingers, sliding his own between them, I had to ask.

"What are you doing?"

Head turned, I watched Jamie draw my thumb into his mouth and suck. I clenched my thighs around him.

"He touch you here?" he asked, kissing the back of my hand and moving higher, lips tickling every inch of my skin. Sometimes just his breath.

I couldn't answer Jamie because I knew what he was doing. And I couldn't *believe* he was doing it.

Every part of me that touched Wes or had been touched by him, Jamie was touching. He kissed and he felt and he let his tongue taste. My other arm. Behind my ears. Over the curve in my ribs and the dip in my stomach.

"Here?"

My hipbones, he dragged his teeth as if he knew that was where Wes held me tight. Down my legs. The tops of my ankles. My feet.

"Here?"

On my stomach, I felt his hot tongue lick up my spine. He kissed the backs of my knees. He squeezed my ass and pressed his mouth there.

Jamie was erasing fingerprints and memories. He was replacing them with his own.

My breath hitched when he flipped me over again, palmed my breasts, and then bit them. I cried out.

My soft voice begged. *Do it* and *again* and *again, Jamie, please*.

He sucked on my nipples. He twisted them between his fingers and buried his face in my cleavage, cursing, "*Fuck*, baby," as his hands shook.

I reached for him and whimpered when he sat back. I wanted more. His fingers in my hair and his teeth on my neck. "Please," I whispered, arm outstretched and fingertips seeking.

Jamie held my gaze and moved his hand between my legs.

My eyes rolled closed.

"That motherfucker lick you here?"

My eyes flew open and I looked at Jamie after he spoke. I squirmed when he slid a finger inside me.

"Yes," I whispered, in answer and in response to what he was doing.

He sank down.

I bent my knees up.

Every muscle in my body tensed.

Putting your mouth on a woman *there*, in my opinion, was a much more intimate act than sex. There was something profoundly personal about it. Hell, not all men even did it.

And Jamie was looking to get intimate with me.

On his stomach and hanging partially off the bed, Jamie dropped his head between my legs and swiped his hot tongue through my pussy.

"Oh, *shit*," I moaned, back arching and hands reaching down to grab handfuls of ocean-kissed hair.

Jamie had his hands wrapped around my thighs and was yanking me closer to his mouth. He started to work me.

Lips parted to moan and pant and beg if he asked, I looked between my legs, watching in wonder and studying, learning the way he ate out a woman.

There was technique. There was skill and practiced moves.

He didn't start slow. He wasn't savoring.

Jamie was ravenous. Greedy. He spoke against my flesh, saying *hottest pussy* and *so wet* and *so fuckin' good* and *this was never his*. He wasn't just erasing and replacing memories. Jamie wasn't simply licking and tasting to see if he liked it. He was eating and consuming, knowing he wanted it all. Hard, hungry lips and a tongue that felt like fire. He was rough.

He was unforgettable.

Jamie was making it so his mouth was the only mouth I was ever going to remember, no matter who came after him.

He was cocky here, too. And he had right to be.

I was breathing heavy before I knew it and on the edge even quicker than that.

"Jamie." My legs shook against his ears. They were trembling uncontrollably, like part of my body was having a seizure.

That had never happened to me before.

"Ja…mie, oh, *God*," I cried, tugging so hard on his hair he growled between my legs.

My violence didn't stop him. If anything, it spurred him on and drove him a little crazy.

Jamie kept on at me, sucking on my clit and speaking words against my flesh that sounded dirty even though I couldn't understand him as my head slammed back onto the pillow and my back arched.

I came hard.

He dug his fingers into my ass and told me to ride his face like it was his cock, and I did, lifting my hips in quick jerks as the wave of euphoria rolled through me.

I collapsed onto the mattress, panting and seeing stars and feeling a little drugged. My entire body felt like it was humming. And when Jamie lifted his head and my hands in turn, since they were still holding fistfuls of his hair, I looked down and met his eyes, letting go of him finally.

"So fuckin' hot the way you go off," he told me, chin and lips wet and tongue licking to savor. "The way it builds in you and you let it take. Fuck me, babe. I ain't never seen fire like that."

"Um." I swallowed. *Wow. What to say...* "Thank you."

Yeah. I settled on *thank you*.

Genius.

Hands flat on my stomach, I watched Jamie push to a standing position at the foot of the bed.

He chuckled and wiped at his mouth with the back of his hand. Then he shoved his briefs down, and although I had already seen Jamie's penis and was well aware of how fortunate he was in that department, I had never seen him fully hard, meaning I was *not* well aware of how fortunate he was in that department.

My earlier worries resurfaced. I sat up quickly and drew my knees to my chest.

"I have questions," I informed him.

Kneeling beside me, Jamie reached for the sleeve of condoms. He tore a packet off and ripped it open with his teeth, saying "Shoot" while he spit out the wrapper.

So casual. As if a pierced dick was nothing out of the ordinary.

I watched him roll the condom down his shaft. He was quick about it and maybe not as careful as I thought he should've been.

I felt inclined to bring this to his attention.

"Shouldn't you go slow and make sure it doesn't rip over that thing?" I asked, pointing at the ball that curved at the top.

"Done this enough. I think I know what I'm doin'."

My eyes narrowed when he lifted his head.

Jamie smirked.

I knew he was thinking I was looking pissy because he thought I was jealous, which I wasn't, that was absurd, so I quickly went back to looking at him with normal-sized eyes.

His smirk twisted into a smile.

"Anyway." I cleared my throat and hugged my knees. "Um, so, that won't break, will it? With the piercing..."

"Shouldn't," he answered.

"And it won't hurt?"

Jamie stared at me, his expression growing more serious the longer he stared. Then he reached down and pulled the condom off his dick, tossing it aside, and just as I was opening my mouth to question what he was doing in a way I knew would sound panicked, since he totally looked like he had changed his mind and we weren't about to have sex, Jamie grabbed my wrist and pulled my hand to him.

"What—"

"Touch me," he ordered.

I jerked back. Weakly...but there was resistance.

"Um."

"Lookin' scared of it, babe, and that's not really workin' for me. Come on." He forced my hand to wrap around him, releasing his grip on me when my own took hold.

"Oh," I whispered, sounding breathless as I leaned closer, putting weight on my knees.

He was heavy in my hand and warm. So warm. Every part of him reminded me of summer.

I studied and squeezed.

"*Fuck*," Jamie moaned, breathing heavier now. The muscles in his stomach tensing. "You got a minute before I'm takin' you."

My eyes bounced between his dick in my hand and his gaze, still serious. *A minute?* That was hardly enough time.

I slid my hand up his shaft and touched the cold metal ball at the top with my thumb, asking, "Did it hurt?"

"Pinched a little. Not bad."

"Is this the piercing you always keep in?"

"Yeah."

I studied the part of the barbell that was exposed. I felt that, too. Then I rubbed the ball on the underside.

"This isn't going to come lose and get lost inside me, is it?" I questioned, lifting my gaze to watch him answer.

Jamie cocked an eyebrow.

"This your way of tellin' me you want it bare?" he asked.

I blinked. My hand slid higher. "What?" I whispered.

He reached down and stopped my movement, jaw set tight and nostrils flaring as he did it. Then he pulled my hand away, sharing, "It's not gonna come loose. If it did, it'd end up in the condom I plan on wearin'."

"Oh." I let my hand fall to the mattress. *Duh, Tori.* "Right."

"Yeah," he replied, smirking as he picked up the sleeve of five, ripping one free and tearing into the package again with his teeth while he looked at me. "Kinda felt like you were implyin' I didn't need to bother."

My eyes widened. *Didn't need to bother? Was he crazy?*

"I was not implying anything," I countered with a quick voice, scooting back and away. "I was simply curious and not thinking about my question before I spoke it." I fell back and settled, huffing out a breath. My head turned on the pillow.

"Relax, Legs," Jamie chuckled, looking all too pleased with himself. "I came prepared, babe."

"I am relaxed," I murmured, watching as he spread the condom down his length.

I felt his touch on my body while he readied himself. I was certain he had left fingerprints on my thighs.

"What you did," I started as he dropped his hands to the mattress and crawled over and on top of me, settling between my legs with elbows bracing his weight. I brushed my fingers over his neck and lower, mouth opening to finish giving him my gratitude.

"Not done," he said, halting my speech as his hand pushed hair out of my face. He bent down and kissed me. "Brace, baby. I'm takin' that pussy now."

My stomach fluttered. "Okay," I said.

"You ready?"

"Yes."

"You like me?"

I smiled. "No."

He smiled back, lips curling beautifully, I could feel it. "Liar," he murmured. He kissed the corner of my mouth as his hand slid between us, positioning his swollen head against my lips, and then he pushed in.

"Jamie," I whimpered over the sound of his strangled groan. I gasped as he stretched me. *"Oh, my God."*

I felt a pressure moving with him inside me. It was pinpoint. I'd never felt anything like it.

He kept pushing in. Slowly...

Even though he shook and growled like he wanted to fuck, and even though I pulled, hands gripping his ass, Jamie took his time sinking deep.

He let me feel every inch. Every exquisite stress of his piercing. He didn't rush it.

This, entering me, taking those first moments, *this* he savored.

But when he buried himself to the hilt, Jamie stopped being civilized.

He reared back and started thrusting, hard, cock slamming deep as his mouth pressed to my ear where he asked, "You feelin' him now?" all smug and self-righteous.

God...

I bit my lip and moaned, feeling myself growing wetter and tighter around him. It turned me on, his arrogance. How good he knew he was at everything.

At this. *Amazing.* The best, maybe.

Jamie leaned down and fucked me harder. He growled through a laugh, watching me writhe and beg beneath him. "You feelin' him now?" he asked, smiling and snarling, looking both crazy and beautiful.

"God," I moaned.

I couldn't answer. That piercing. Holy...*shit*.

Pleasure wrapped about me and gripped on.

Jamie crawled closer as he continued to take me, pushing my thighs against my chest and turning savage.

I held on and took what he gave. I gave it back.

I bit his shoulder when he told me how tight I was. I dug my nails into his hips when he moaned and murmured *fuck* and *Tori* like this was killing him. I kissed him and I begged. I said I needed it.

It felt like I did.

"Want you feelin' me," Jamie panted, leaning back and pushing to his knees so he could fuck me and watch. "Nine fuckin' months been waitin'. Wantin' you." He slammed in, pulled out, grabbed my shins, and held me open. He pumped his hips and stared where he entered me. "Motherfuckin' good, baby. *Fuck.*"

"*Jamie*," I whimpered. Legs shaking. Body locking up tight.

He was hitting that spot, again and again, building it in me fast. Fucking me harder.

"Oh, God, Jamie . . . fuck, I . . ."

Taking . . .

Taking . . .

He dropped down and took my mouth, asking, "Who you feelin', baby?" all soft against my lips.

I gasped, closing my eyes and moaning, "*You.*"

He growled and powered back and forth. "Fuckin' right me," Jamie said through a smirk I could feel twisting across his lips. "Been dreamin' about this sweet pussy. Now you're givin' it." He groaned inside my mouth, slamming deep. Out, then back in. "You're givin' it," he rasped. "Means it's mine. Can't take this back, Legs. You hear me?"

I heard him, I just couldn't answer.

My limbs tightened around him and my pussy started clenching in pulses I felt all the way in my toes. That fire was spreading through me, and I wanted it.

I wanted to burn.

I'd come hard against Jamie's mouth but this, what he was building, this was breathtaking.

Eyes still closed, I felt him lean away as I started coming. Slow, and then it took me. The flames spread. My body arched off the mattress. My nails cut into skin. I breathed fast and heavy, whispering *yes* and *oh, God* and *oh, fuck, yes please.*

"Fuck. Look at you," Jamie panted from above me. He grasped at my breasts. He squeezed them roughly, fucking me through it, keeping it up long after the flames burned out.

"Tori," Jamie groaned, seconds later, or minutes. I had no idea.

I was staring at Jamie's chest and his unbelievably sexy collarbone I wanted to bite when I heard my name. My eyes came up and met his.

I saw his want. His need. Eyes wide and wild. He looked wrecked. He was close.

"Can you . . . " I pressed my fingers into the indents of his stomach, watching him focus on my breasts as they bounced. "Can you come on me?" I asked softly.

His gaze lifted and met mine. He stopped thrusting.

I spoke fast, quickly explaining my request. "He did. Sometimes he would. And I just, I don't want him here."

His eyes flashed and heated like hellfire as he stared down at me. He looked murderous. "Where?" he growled.

I dropped my hand between us and showed him.

Jamie looked down, his nostrils flared, then he started powering into me again, back and forth, harder, faster, growling *fuck fuck fuck*. One last time he rammed deep, then he pulled out, tore the condom off, leaned over me, and shot his load onto my stomach as he stroked his cock.

I leaned up onto my elbows and watched, whimpering when he took his hand and rubbed himself into my skin, hip to hip and up to my breasts.

"Jamie."

He leaned down, careful of what he just did, slid his other hand to my cheek, and kissed me hard and wet as he breathed heavy. Then he pushed back and stood from the bed, grabbing the condom off the floor. He disappeared down the hallway to discard it, and when he returned, he was holding a hand towel.

I lay still, watching as Jamie cleaned me off. When he was finished, he tossed the towel to join my other one on the floor.

"Get on your knees. We're not done," he said when he straightened and turned, hand moving over his cock and stroking as he stood beside the bed and stared at my body.

I blinked and bit my lip, staring back as everything, *everything*, below my waist clenched and warmed with desire.

We're not done.

I did as I was told and got into position, facing the headboard. I heard a condom wrapper tearing open and dropped my head between my arms. I started panting.

We're not done.

The bed dipped behind me, and seconds later Jamie's hands held my hips and his mouth pressed hot, hungry kisses to my back, trailing down my spine. His finger teased between my legs. He got it wet, then he slid out of me and moved higher, gently pressing against my ass.

I opened my mouth and moaned.

"He take you here, babe?" Jamie asked, slowly moving his finger in and out.

Shyly, I dropped my head.

He had. And Jamie knew. I didn't need to answer.

"Last place you're feelin' him." I felt his breath against my flesh. He bit my ass and spread my cheeks with his hands, promising, "Never feelin' him again," before he wiggled his tongue inside me.

I came two more times that night while every memory of Wes was burned away from my body. And I was right.

Jamie did fuck dirty.

He left marks. Teeth and bruises from sucking.

I stared down at them while I lay in bed and Jamie cleaned up in the bathroom. Circles and half-moons decorated my breasts, and when I closed my eyes and drew the covers up, no longer seeing the evidence that they were there, I could still feel them.

I could still feel *him*. Jamie. I no longer felt anyone else.

Just like he'd promised.

I smiled against the cool sheet.

Then the bed dipped and my eyes flashed open, covers sliding down to my neck as I turned my head and gaped, watching Jamie as he got into bed beside me.

What the...

Chapter Twelve

JAMIE

Tori pushed up onto her elbows in bed, head turned and eyes round with alarm as I stretched out on my side.

"What are you doing?" she asked, sounding confused but looking so fucking hot, all that blond hair, big and messy, falling down her back and over her shoulder. Cheeks flushed, lips swollen and parted, and those full perfect tits peeking out from the sheet sliding down her body.

Fuck me, she was beautiful. Looking like a goddamn angel I'd just dirtied up and sent back to heaven.

"Settlin' in," I answered, the need to touch her building inside me the longer I stared. I reached under the covers until I curled a hand around her hip, then I pulled, forcing her to flop back.

"Hey!"

I smashed her against my chest, keeping tight pressure with my arm across her stomach when she squirmed and tensed up. "Relax, babe."

She kept trying to wiggle free.

I gave her a squeeze and dropped my head beside hers, lips to her ear, where I harshly ordered, "*Relax.*"

Tori huffed out a breath. Her body went slack against the sheet as she stared up at the ceiling, drawing the covers to her neck. "Um, why are you settling in? You did what you came here for."

I chuckled.

Her head turned. She looked up into my eyes where I was lying on the pillow, voice soft when she asked, "What?"

"We ain't done, babe."

She blinked. "We're not?"

"Fuck no."

"But..." Her brow furrowed, eyes dropping to my mouth and then rising again. "I don't feel him anymore."

"So?"

"*So*...I'm good. You did what you came here for."

"You don't know shit," I told her, leaning in to add, "And you sure as fuck are not good."

She searched my eyes, jumping between the two. "What are you talking about?"

"We ain't done."

"Yeah, you said that," she returned, voice growing louder with edge. "What I'm asking for is clarification since we're obviously in disagreement on this."

"Careful, Legs," I warned. "You get my dick hard, you're dealin' with it."

Tori jerked back, blinking. "Excuse me?"

"Not that it ain't bound to happen with the way I got you naked and pressing close, but just sayin', I'm tryin' to recharge a little. Figured our next round wouldn't be for an hour. Maybe two, dependin'. You start throwing attitude at me and it'll be happenin' a lot sooner than that."

I watched her eyes widen. Her throat work with a swallow. "Dependin'?" she echoed, voice quiet and minus any trace of attitude.

I smiled, liking how she focused on that, and shared, "We fall asleep and your tits wind up in my face, I'm done rechargin'."

Tori pulled her lips between her teeth, seemingly thinking on that as she breathed once, twice, then she parted that sweet fucking mouth and replied, "Well, that just brings me back to wanting clarification, since we shouldn't be falling asleep together, meaning my tits shouldn't be winding up anywhere near *your face*, since you did what you came here for."

My eyes narrowed. I lost the smile. "Goddamn it. Would you quit with that shit?" I bit out. "What'd I say?"

"I'll quit when you explain this whole *we ain't done* business," she returned, staring at me and looking like she really didn't know what the fuck this was or what I was talking about, which pissed me off even more.

I propped my weight on my elbow and loomed over her. "Unless your mouthy ass is walking out the front door with me and hopping on the back of my bike, I did not, *babe*, get what I came here for."

Tori blinked. "What?" she whispered.

"You need to get used to this."

"Get used to *what*?"

"Us fuckin' and puttin' in time together after."

She stared up at me. "Huh?"

"Jesus. *This*." I squeezed her side, then feeling the need to elaborate 'cause I knew more questions were coming, I went on explaining, "'Cause unless I got work or shit I can't put off until later, I'm hangin' around, babe. Might just be to get some shut-eye with you. Might be to talk. Will absolutely be to fuck again, no question there. Only way this becomes a fuck and run is if one of us has commitments to get to. Also if we're out somewhere and we both need to get it in. Straight up, not tryin' to linger with you in some shitty bathroom or wherever the fuck. We can put the time in later."

When I was done explaining how this was going to work, Tori stared up at me, somehow looking even more confused than she did a minute ago.

"Babe," I prompted when she kept staring.

She blinked, snapping out of her staring haze. "Why?" she questioned softly.

"*Why?*"

"Yes. Why?"

I bent down, which caused Tori to smash her head against the pillow further, and still I kept moving in, only stopping when our noses almost touched.

"'Cause we both want it. We're good together. And like I told you earlier today after you got finished fucking my mouth with your tongue, I'm done playin' games with you," I said, watching her eyes flicker wider. "Gave me your pussy, babe. Ate it. Fucked it. That's been claimed. And yeah, I was helpin' you out and doin' what you asked, but no way was that the only reason for what we just did. Wasn't for me and sure as fuck wasn't for you. Now I gotta taste. I want more. Know you want more so don't even try and lie your way outta this one. Bet's over and we're both hard up. *That's* why."

Tori pinched her lips together and inhaled a sharp breath. "Do you have any idea how crude you just sounded?" she asked, face hard.

"Sure you hated every second of it," I shot back, sarcasm heavy as I leaned back to loom over her again.

She relaxed and those cheeks that were already still flushed heated more.

I smiled.

Tori's eyes lowered to my mouth, then quickly rose again. "I never said I wanted more of what we just did," she said, voice quiet and quick.

"Didn't need to. Can still feel you goin' tight around my cock, babe."

Jesus. That was the fucking truth. Never felt anything like that.

Tori's stomach tensed under my arm, which was still draped over her. Then she exhaled slowly and closed her eyes.

I watched this happen, assuming she was just thinking of something to say back to me, more bullshit, and doing this through a heavy blink, but seconds passed and she never reopened them.

"Babe."

"Mm?"

"What're you doin'?"

"Sleeping."

My brow tightened. I waited for her to say more, to smile or to fucking look at me 'cause she must've been joking.

I kept waiting. Nothing.

"What the fuck?"

Tori tipped up her chin, keeping her eyes closed. "I'm done talking to you," she said. "You're not listening to me anyway, and everything you're saying is either making me confused, uncomfortable, or not knowing what to think."

"Uncomfortable?"

"Embarrassed," she clarified, eyes opening and turning soft. "I know how I reacted to what you did to me. I was there, Jamie. You don't need to rub it in my face."

"Not rubbing it in your face, Legs. Just wantin' you to admit you liked it as much as I did."

"I liked it," she shot out quickly. "Okay? Obviously. I came. And I appreciate you doing what you did for me. But it's done. Meaning, we don't need to keep doing it."

"We absolutely need to keep doin' it," I returned.

"I'm sorry, but I don't agree with you."

"Yeah?"

"I really don't."

"You sayin' if I show up here again tomorrow night, the next night, and the next, wantin' more, you wouldn't be down, and not only that, you'd tell me to fuck off?"

Tori swallowed. "If?" she asked quietly, sounding anxious.

My brow furrowed.

Seeing that happen, she nodded sharply and added with a flat tone, "That's exactly what I'm saying."

"You're full of shit," I laughed.

Her eyes flashed with anger and narrowed. "No, I'm not," she hissed. "If you show up here again, *ever*, I'm telling you exactly that."

"Right."

"I'm serious, Jamie."

"You're seriously full of shit, Legs."

She pushed to her elbows and got in my face. "And you're *seriously* delusional if you think I'm believing anything you're saying to me right now."

My brows lifted.

Tori read that as a question and went on, keeping close to explain, "You say you want to put in time with me. That I'm safe to have expectations. What do you think, I'm stupid? I know *exactly* what this was to you, Jamie. And I will not be that girl waiting around and expecting things. Not from you. I will *not* be stupid."

I listened to Tori, staring back and reading the seriousness in her eyes while seeing the fear she was trying to keep hidden. And I remembered her "if" from seconds ago and the worry she had in her voice, thinking I wouldn't be showing up here again.

Reason hit me like a punch to the gut.

All her bullshit. The lies. The layers. Why she was always fighting me.

It wasn't that Tori didn't want me here. It wasn't that she would tell me to fuck off if I showed.

She was scared this was it. That I wouldn't come back, or that when I did and this shit built between us, becoming something real and on the regular, I'd stop showing and blindside her.

She was scared of getting hurt.

"Jesus, babe," I mumbled, staring at her as I started sliding my arm up her body to cup her face, then deciding that wasn't enough.

Hand on her side, I pushed her back.

She gasped as she fell. "What are you doing?"

I leaned into her, body sliding over to pin her down and keep her flat on the mattress, elbows planted on either side and hands holding gently to her cheeks. I ran my thumb over the flush in her skin.

She pressed her fingers to my chest, gently pushing as she blinked up at me. "Jamie, I—"

"You said what you needed to say. Now it's my turn," I told her.

She shook her head. "But—"

"Legs, shut up."

Her lips pinched together tightly. I heard her breath as it escaped her, coming out in heavy pants.

"Told you this wasn't about a piece of ass I was lookin' to score," I began, pushing strands of hair out of her face and curling my fingers behind her head. "Also told you I've had that with women, they were aware and wantin' the same thing, so you know if this was about that, I wouldn't have a problem lettin' you know up front. Last I checked, I did not give any indication I was just lookin' to get a few fucks outta my system with you. Unless I'm forgettin' I said it. Did you hear those words from me?"

She shook her head again. "No, but—"

"Shut up, Legs."

Her eyes narrowed. Looking ready to argue, she shocked me by actually following orders.

Seeing that, I continued, "Not gonna lie. Saw you that first day at Whitecaps and, first reaction, wanted to fuck."

Somehow, Tori's eyes narrowed further. Still, she didn't speak.

"Months went by. Still feelin' that. Then the more I got to know shit about you, the longer I looked and saw the way you are with people you care about, the more time we spent together after Dash and Syd hooked up, shit started changin'. Still wanted to fuck. Pretty sure the only way that urge is going away is if I'm six feet under, but bein' around you, babe, watchin' you and the way you are with Dash, how you smile at him 'cause of the way he treats your girl, *fuck*, I wanted that. Drove me crazy you weren't givin' it to me."

Tori's eyes went back to their normal, oval-shaped size. Her mouth relaxed.

I ran my thumb below her bottom lip, watching that movement as I went on.

"Came to me last night, upset, crying, wanting someone to make that shit better for you. Needin' someone." I looked into her eyes. "You got people you smile at, babe. People you take in and let live with you. And you came to *my* door. You gave me that." I breathed a laugh and cupped her cheek. "Still don't think you know what that meant to me."

Tori inhaled sharply, blinking and looking to be fighting tears.

I moved in, getting closer. "You give it up, Legs, don't matter what it is and I'm keepin' it. Know what it means to you and want you knowin' you ain't alone in that. I feel it, too, babe."

Her breath hitched.

"Trusted me to take care of shit before," I reminded her, bending lower and speaking slowly against her lips. "Gonna need you to trust me on this, too."

"I don't know," she whispered.

"Quit thinkin'."

"I have to think. I have to, Jamie. If I don't—"

I cut her off, tilting my head and kissing her. It was slow and wet, and *fuck*, she kissed back. Not fighting it. The second she felt my tongue push inside, Tori started giving it just as good.

She stopped thinking.

Her fingers moved to my jaw and she lifted up, pressing firmer against my mouth, going deeper with her tongue and telling me what I needed to know when she was too afraid to say it.

"We doin' this?" I asked.

She kissed me harder.

"You likin' me yet?"

She pulled my bottom lip into her mouth and sucked until I groaned.

"Fuck, babe," I panted, breaking away and rolling with her, pulling her body against and partially on top of mine. One hand behind her back and curling around her waist and the other reaching down, hitching her leg up and draping it over me. I turned my head and pressed my mouth against her hair. "We're doin' this," I said.

Tori didn't say anything back, but her hand moved over my chest and she squeezed her leg around me. She was holding on.

Fuck yeah. I took that as her agreeing.

"Need to recharge. Give me an hour."

"Or two, depending," she offered cutely.

I smiled, my arm tightening around her, then I shut my eyes, keeping hold of all that beauty. "Get some sleep," I ordered.

"'Kay."

Seconds went by, then I felt her fingers curl around my ribs. "Jamie?"

"Mm."

"I'm planning on getting to bed early tomorrow," she informed me. "I open the next morning and I'm pulling another double."

Eyes remaining closed, I smiled again, not sure if she was seeing it or not. "Guess I'll be pickin' the lock then," I shared.

"There's a spare key in the cabinet by the fridge."

My eyes flashed open and my arm around her tensed. I knew she felt that. Looking down, I saw the top of her head move a little as she pressed closer, bringing more of her body on top of me.

"Night," she whispered.

A tightness gathered in my chest. I dropped my head back onto the pillow and stared at the ceiling.

I knew the exact moment Tori fell asleep. Her breathing steadied and her hold on me relaxed.

An hour later I was waking her with my mouth between her legs.

I never slept.

* * *

"Oh, God! Jamie, oh, my God!"

"*Fuck*," I growled, teeth clenching, sweat dripping off me, off her, as I squeezed Tori's thighs and bucked up into her wildly.

She was coming again. Right on the heels of her last orgasm, riding my shit so goddamn hard while I fucked her standing in the middle of her bedroom.

So good.

Fuck me, her pussy was so good.

Had intentions on taking her in her bed. Her legs thrown over my shoulders while she stared up at me, then turning her to her side so I could spank her and watch her tits bounce, but the second I stepped inside her bedroom after using the spare key to get in the house, those plans changed.

Tori sat up in bed, looking wide awake and like she was waiting for me, not sleeping like she said she would be. She pushed the covers down and ripped her shirt off to show me her tits, and as I was undressing, making quick work of it so I could get inside her before I lost my fucking mind, she scrambled off the bed, climbed up my body as I was rolling the condom on my dick, slid her hand between us to position me, and sank down.

Swear to Christ, took every ounce of strength in me not to lose it the second I stretched her.

I closed my eyes and started counting as she shifted her hips against me and begged against my mouth, making it to seven before I slowed down enough I could start working her.

Then I hooked her legs over my forearms, gripped her ass, and bounced her on my dick, watching her face as she took me.

Lips parted. Eyes half-closed. Heat creeping across her face. Head thrown back when I started thrusting up.

All beauty.

Her ass slapped against my thighs. I bounced her faster, building it in her while I told her how fucking hot she looked taking my dick.

Then we were kissing and she was digging her nails into my neck and moaning my name against my tongue, looking so crazy into me, into this, driving me to slam her down, harder, harder, until she was crying out and going off.

And here she was again, the hottest fuck of my life, leaning away and grinding her hips, whimpering, skin flushed and slicked with sweat, milking her orgasm while pulling mine to the surface, no matter how hard I was fighting to hold off.

Her pussy clamped down on my dick. She whispered "harder" as a bead of sweat or a tear rolled down her cheek, I didn't know.

Fuck it. 'Cause unless I became deaf, blind, and numb from the waist down at this very second, I was losing this battle.

"God…fuck, baby, *fuck*," I groaned, pulling her close, burying my face in her neck and driving up into her hard, harder like she asked, staying deep on the third thrust and then emptying inside the condom.

"Oh, my God," Tori whispered, fingers moving in my hair as I breathed heavily against her skin. "I, uh, *was* tired. When I first laid down. Promise."

Laughing, I leaned back to look at her. She gave me a shy smile before dropping her head on my shoulder.

"Gotta get cleaned up," I said, lips to her hair.

Tori loosened her hold on me and let me lower her to the carpet. I kissed her, soft and quick, and then went to the bathroom to dispose of the condom.

I could smell her skin on me. Sweet vanilla. My mouth tasted like her toothpaste.

My dick started growing hard again as I was washing it off.

When I got back to the bedroom, Tori was sitting in the middle of the bed on her knees, facing the door, with her hands flat on her thighs. Her tits were moving rapidly with the breaths she was taking in and expelling.

Heavy, needy breaths.

She was still as worked up as I was, wanting me just as bad. Not fighting it. Not holding it in, but letting it be known. Letting me see it.

Fuck. So good.

Her eyes lowered to my dick when I started to stroke it. Lip caught between her teeth, she moved her hand to the bed and blindly picked up a condom.

It was one of mine. Tori must've been digging through my shorts.

"Gonna spank you while I fuck you this time," I told her, thinking back to my earlier desires before she mounted me and shot that plan to shit. I climbed on the bed and watched her lick her lips, nodding quickly. She wanted that, too. Then I pushed her back and hovered over her, hand beside her head while the other palmed her tit.

She gasped and arched into me.

"You're gonna be tired tomorrow," I promised, bending to take her mouth.

"'Kay," Tori whispered.

"Probably sore, too."

She smiled against my lips. I felt the foil wrapper of the condom press to my chest.

"'Kay," she whispered again, this time sounding happy as shit about that possibility.

Hearing that, I didn't smile. I fucking grinned.

Then I got back to kissing her and got started on making good on those promises.

* * *

I realized quick that having any set plans in my head about how Tori and I were going to spend our time fucking was a goddamned waste.

Not that we wouldn't end up possibly doing what I was anticipating, but right off the bat? The second we saw each other?

Fuck no.

Sex with Tori Rivera wasn't thought out and predicated. It wasn't routine.

It was chaos.

It was colliding bodies and clothes tearing. It was knocking shit over just to get to each other and then fucking on top of that same shit you just knocked over, 'cause you needed it now. Desperate. You couldn't get it fast enough. It was barely getting through the door and furniture breaking.

It was dirty and rowdy and the kind of crazy that drove a person mad 'cause they wanted it like that. They needed it. They couldn't wait.

And that was just after the third night I showed.

After getting the kind of welcome I'd gotten on Friday, I wasn't sure what to expect showing up at Tori's on Saturday.

It was after ten, so she might've been asleep. I might need to wake her if she wasn't waiting up like before.

But when I swung my leg off my bike after cutting the engine and looked up, primed to start walking up the driveway, I saw that wasn't going to be the case. Tori was standing in the doorway waiting for me. Her body wrapped in that green Christmas quilt. Her shoulders bare, giving indication she was naked underneath.

I couldn't get to her fast enough.

And when I did, I did not fuck her with her tits pressing against the glass shower door, like I was anticipating. We didn't make it upstairs.

Tori dropped the quilt the second I stepped inside, proving I was right, she was naked, then after attacking each other like kissing was something that felt just as good as fucking, spending minutes just doing that, nothing else, I took her hard and fast against the small table she had in her entryway.

Had because we broke that shit. And that was good quality wood, too. Sturdy.

Tori thought it was funny the table broke. She wasn't mad.

And I eventually got her tits pressing up against the glass shower door, but not until after I took her on the stairs.

That juicy ass in my face. It was inevitable.

Sunday I couldn't get to her until late again, considering Tori was working and I was spending time saying good-bye to my sister, not knowing when she was coming back around. After finishing up with Quinn, I spent the rest of the afternoon and well into the evening tracking down a replacement table. I had to skip out on family dinner since it took me so long. I ended up not finding shit in Dogwood and had to venture out to neighboring towns.

It was after eight when I finally showed. I used my key to get inside and was just finishing putting the table in place, arranging the picture frames on it the way she had before, when I heard a soft gasp from behind me.

I turned my head and saw Tori looking at the table, and when she lifted her eyes and gave up a smile that made all kinds of shit warm up inside me, tighten, twist, and do other weird shit I couldn't explain, I went at her.

I fucking rushed at that woman like getting to her was a necessity greater than breathing.

And she rushed at me.

Knocked over the four brown bags of clothes she had sitting in the middle of the floor, which I later found out she had packed up and was looking to take out to her car for a trip to Goodwill, and since I rushed before Tori did, I got to her first, meaning when she knocked over those bags, we ended up fucking on top of them and ripping them open.

Clothes were everywhere by the time we finished an hour later. The ones she packed up and the ones we were wearing, which now had tears in them from our frantic removal.

Tori laughed at that, too, and offered one of her Goodwill sleeping tees for me to wear home.

It had *No Pants Are the Best Pants* on the front and smelled like her skin.

I wore it home.

Now it was Monday and I was getting to Tori's without any anticipations for tonight. The only thing guaranteed was the sex, however we'd end up having it, and the eating we'd be doing since I was providing dinner.

Thai.

Tori had five business card magnets from Bangkok Orchid on the side of her fridge. I figured there was a good chance of her liking their food.

I entered with my key again, not knocking, stepped inside, and kicked the door closed, then I started crossing the room with the bags in my hands, hollering out, "Legs. Where you at?"

She came around the corner from the direction of the kitchen, not speaking but drawing my attention anyway.

I froze a foot away from the couch, head turned and eyes lowered, focused on her tits. She was topless.

Fuck.

I stared for a breath, then my eyes kept lowering, being drawn down there, too, skimming over her belly to just below. I stopped on tight, black material clinging.

Fuck.

"Hey," Tori said in the softest, sweetest voice I'd ever heard her use.

I glanced up into her face then immediately looked back down, chest heaving, nostrils flaring, and dick growing hard against my zipper.

"Sex pants," I murmured.

Sweet fucking Christ. She was gonna kill me.

Tori started moving closer, made it two steps, and then she stopped.

"You went to Bangkok Orchid?"

I blinked up at her after she spoke, brow furrowing. "What?"

Bangkok what? What the fuck was she talking about? And why was she even talking? We should be fucking already. She was wearing those goddamn pants.

Her hands flattened on her stomach, her eyes widened, focused on the bags, then she started moving toward me again, faster now. "*Oh, my God*, I love their food. Please tell me you got the pineapple fried rice," she begged excitedly.

I looked down at the two bags in my hand.

"I'm starving. I haven't eaten yet," she added, reaching me and reaching out, looking to take a bag and start eating.

Before she could grab it, I dropped the one bag onto the floor, not giving a shit about food, eating, breathing, nothing else that wasn't involving us fucking, then I turned to face her, snatched her hand out of the air that was inches away, and forced it against the front of my shorts.

Tori gasped when she felt my dick.

It was hard. It was throbbing. And she needed to get on it immediately.

In case that message wasn't coming through clear enough, I spelled it out for her.

"We're fuckin' first. Right here. Couch or floor, but I'd prefer couch since you're gonna be ridin' me. Still got rug burn on my back from yesterday and don't feel like adding to it. Shit's hot, but it sucks in the shower. Those tits are gonna be in my face the entire fuckin' time, and I don't know how it's gonna be possible but you're keepin' those pants on. Rip 'em to get me inside. Pull 'em down a little. Whatever. I'll let you figure it out. Then after we both get off, we'll get to the food I brought, which includes the pineapple fried rice. Shit looked good so I got two orders of it. But you ain't touchin' the food, babe, until after we fuck. I'm firm on that. You got me?"

She blinked. Her hand tensed around my zipper, putting pressure there I took as a yes.

The other bag of food hit the floor. My back hit the couch after grabbing a condom out of my shorts. Tori's pants were ripped down the middle seam at her pussy, and a second later, I discovered she was bare underneath when she sank down, putting me inside.

Chapter Thirteen

TORI

"Oh, God. I'm so close," I moaned, back arched, head thrown back, hands gripping strong, powerful thighs beneath me and hips jerking frantically, chasing that miraculous feeling that was building and building fast thanks to Jamie's cock and that piercing I wanted to dedicate my nightly prayers to. Also, the filthy words coming out of Jamie's mouth. Those were helping in a big, big way.

"Yeah... look at you. Taking my dick like you were made for it. So fuckin' hot, Tori."

"God, your tits. Shake em'. Fuck yeah. Wanna stare at these all fuckin' day."

"Nothin' like it. Jesus. Ain't nothin' like your cunt. Nothin' feels this good, baby."

He always talked during sex. Jamie was never quiet, but God, it seemed like the more we did it, the hotter his words became.

Plus, his smell. *Amazing*. That was working me up, too. Like a dirty surfer boy bottled up. And the way I knew his hair looked right now, fallen in his eyes and messy from my fingers. The pressure of his hands on my hips. The way he was staring up at me, also something I knew he was still doing even though I had my eyes closed. The way he could still feel commanding and controlling beneath me. Oh, and his noises. *God*, he made the best noises.

Okay, so basically everything attached to Jamie and everything he was doing.

"*Fuck yeah*," he growled. "Get down here, babe. Want those tits."

I kept my eyes closed. My head tipped back. Body arched and hands gripping as I moved faster and faster on top of him.

I wasn't going anywhere. This felt too good, Jamie's cock and the angle I was taking it. His piercing, right there, rubbing inside me in that same spot, over and over, and if I bent forward, he'd move. I'd lose that.

So, no way. Sorry. Not happening.

"Tori."

The heat was spreading between my hips. I put my weight on my shins and bounced up and down instead of grinding and oh, *oh*, that was even better.

"*Yes*," I panted, sliding up and down his cock. "Oh, God, yes."

"Legs." Jamie's fingers tensed on my hips. "Tits, babe. Now."

"Shut up. I'm close."

I bounced faster, only slamming down on Jamie two more times before I was being jerked forward, my nipple was getting sucked, my arms were being pinned behind my back and held there in a death grip with one of his, and my pussy was getting his cock slamming deep as he drove up and into me repeatedly.

I was proved wrong. Moving did not mean I'd lose that fabulous piercing rubbing in that same spot over and over and the delicious angle I was taking it. Moving meant that fabulous piercing would go from merely rubbing that spot to rubbing while hitting it at a deeper angle, a better angle, adding extra friction and giving it at a faster, more promising, better than anything I'd ever felt, rate.

"Jamie!" I cried out, growing wetter as I took what he was giving, not having much of a choice and, *God*, not really wanting one either.

This was *amazing*. The time before this, *amazing*. And the time before that. Each time getting better.

Meaning, this wasn't amazing. This was something greater than amazing. I just didn't think a word had been invented to describe it yet.

"I tell you to give me your tits, you fuckin' give 'em, babe," Jamie growled between my breasts as they dangled, jerked, and bounced in his face. His hand connected with my ass. It stung through the thin material of my leggings.

"Ah!"

His hips kept powering up, faster, harder, while his hand on my ass slid down, gripped the edge of the seam I'd ripped in my pants, and yanked it back so it opened wider and tore.

The sound of them shredding made my pussy tighten. I loved it.

This was Jamie. That's what this was. A word greater than amazing.

"Oh, my God," I moaned, feeling so unbelievably turned on with what he was doing, how he was restraining me and making me take him.

The cool air of the living room assaulted my ass. For a moment I wished he'd let go so I could look behind me and see myself.

Jamie slapped my right cheek again and sucked my nipple hard into his mouth.

That was all it took for me to stop wishing. I wouldn't change a damn thing about how this was playing out.

Eyes watering and limbs locking up, I arched my neck and came as a thousand fires lit underneath my skin. "I'm—"

"Ah, *fuck*. I'm comin', baby," Jamie groaned, burying his face in my breasts where he growled my name and *fuck fuck fuck*.

He pumped into me through our orgasms, keeping pace and brutality. He never let up.

Only after my pussy stopped clenching around him and his cock ceased throbbing did Jamie let go of my wrists and allow my arms to drop.

I slumped down and back when he stretched his legs out, collapsing on top of him, head hitting his shoulder and hand slowly coming up and pressing to his chest while the other gripped the edge of the couch.

His arms curled around me.

We lay there, both of us catching our breath and me concentrating on the feel of him still inside me.

Amazing. No . . .

Jamie. Better than amazing.

"I really like your cock," I murmured seconds later, staring across his chest at his collarbone as my fingers danced on his skin. "It's perfect. Perfect and pierced."

Jamie's body shook with a laugh.

"You sayin' you like me then?" he asked, a smile in his voice.

I tipped my chin up and pressed my face to his neck. I didn't want him seeing me.

His arms around me tensed as he breathed deep. I felt his head turn and his breath against my ear. "*My cock*, babe," he pointed out, his voice low and husky sounding. "Gotta like the man it belongs to somewhat if you're admittin' what I give you is perfect."

"I don't think so," I argued.

"Admit it, Legs."

"Nothing to admit."

"Babe, who you foolin'?" he questioned. "You like me, my cock, and the way I give it to you, this back and forth shit we do fuckin' daily, which, straight up, serves as foreplay most of the time so I'm down with it, the minutes we spend together before and after I get you off, and you sayin' you don't like me. I think you like that the most."

"I like your cock," I stressed. "What you do with it, how it looks, and our foreplay, however that plays out, whether that be our back and forth *shit* or you doing stuff to me. But that's *all* I like. I'm serious."

His chest shook again.

I was smiling so big I had to wet my lips to keep them from splitting open.

"All right, Legs. You like my cock and anything that leads to us fuckin'. That's where it ends for you," Jamie said, sounding amused as his hand slid up my back and held with gentle pressure on my neck, his other hand still holding tight to my rear.

I nodded. "That's exactly where it ends for me."

"Right," he murmured. "You shared. Guess I'll share, too. Only fair," he started, and my entire body tensed as his hand around my neck squeezed.

I didn't try and pull back, but I knew if I did, Jamie wouldn't let me. He was keeping me close and making sure I was going to hear every word of what he was about to say.

I wasn't sure I wanted to hear it. I wasn't sure I'd hate myself or not if I missed it either.

"Like your legs. Pretty sure you know that," he began. "Your ass is fuckin' phenomenal. I like 'em big and you got a big one, babe. Love hearin' the way it slaps against my thighs when we're doin' it. Shit's hot."

"Hey." My face tightened. "My ass is not big."

"It is and it's fuckin' hot."

I pinched my eyes shut, moaning, "Oh, my God." *I had a big ass?*

"Stare at it enough. Take you on your knees every chance I get." I felt his shoulder lift with a shrug. "Thought it was obvious."

"You could pick a better descriptive term for it. Big is terrible. I'd prefer...meaty. Or peach-shaped."

"Peach-shaped?"

"Juicy. Plump."

"Jesus," he chuckled. "Fine. I like your *meaty ass*."

My nose scrunched up and I opened my eyes. That sounded worse somehow. "Actually..."

"Shut up, Legs," Jamie ordered, his fingers on my big ass tensing. "Got a lot to get through."

I sighed, smiling a little again. "Fine. You like my big ass. Please proceed."

Little chest quakes vibrated beneath me.

"Your tits. There's no likin' there. Been obsessed with 'em ever since you flashed me that day. Like how your hair smells and whatever that shit is you put on your skin. Smellin' like you took sugar and rubbed it all over yourself, wantin' me to lick it off. Pretty sure I do that every time we're together. You got the hottest, tightest pussy I've ever fucked. Sweetest, too. Like how you take me and how you watch me while I'm givin' it, lookin' like you can't believe this shit could feel this good, but it does. Every damn time. And it ain't just 'cause we're fuckin' but 'cause it's *us fuckin'*, you and me. Like how you quit thinkin' on occasion and give me shit you don't realize you're givin'. I like your smile. Like when I gotta work for it and when I don't. Like the way you look at me, even when you're pissy and mad at me for somethin' 'cause you're still lookin', babe, and havin' your attention when you could be givin' it to some other guy makes me feel like a fucking king. *Fuck.*" He exhaled heavily. "I could keep goin', Legs. Could keep it up for hours. Fact is, I like you. I like you a whole fuckin' lot. You wanna give me the hours to list, I'll do that. You feel like what I just gave you is enough to go by for now, we'll stop and get to eatin', but either way, I need to hit Pause so I can go get cleaned up. This shit is startin' to leak out and I'm thinkin' a jizz stain isn't somethin' you're gonna like, even though my cock is perfect and you're feelin' that."

Jamie pulled back gently on my neck when he finished speaking.

My entire body tensed and I pressed down, pushing my weight into him and keeping my face buried.

I felt his head turn. His hand slid down to my back, pressing between my shoulder blades. "Babe," he prompted.

"Just give me a second," I requested, keeping my voice quiet so he couldn't hear how scared I sounded, but I was sure he could hear the frenzied beating of my heart. I was certain he could feel it, too.

My heart was always honest, even when I wasn't.

Jamie breathed deep. His hand on my bottom slid to the small of my back and the one between my shoulder blades moved higher, cupping the back of my head this time.

"Like this, too, babe," he shared, his voice almost sweet.

I closed my eyes. *God.* What was more dangerous? The heartbreaker or the breath-stealer. Player Jamie or the man who let me touch him like he was mine.

I didn't know.

Mind heavy, I inhaled the September sun that kissed his neck, filling my lungs with it. We stayed like that for another thirty seconds, maybe a minute, then I pushed up and slid off Jamie while he kept hold of the condom, taking longer than usual to dismount since my pants were now partially hanging off me and causing awkward, wooden movements.

"I'm gonna go put on something," I said, looking down at myself after getting to my feet.

I looked like a crime scene.

"Usin' the bathroom down here. I'll heat up the food." Jamie bent and pressed a kiss to the top of my head before he moved past me, heading for the powder room below the stairs with his shorts hanging low on his hips and his shirt still off.

It hung on the back of my couch.

To prevent any tripping catastrophes, I shimmied out of my ripped leggings where I stood, balling them up in my hand, then I took to the stairs naked, tossing my pants into the bathroom garbage before using the toilet.

I hummed song lyrics while tapping my knees, and while I washed my hands and finger-combed my hair, breaking up the tangles in the ends, I kept my mind busy by mentally organizing my red lipstick collection, starting with most used to special occasion/costume looks.

Basically, I was avoiding all thoughts of what Jamie had just confessed.

After finishing up, I went to my bedroom and dressed in a muddied blue T-shirt tunic with a stretched neckline. I kept it color-coordinated and stuck with blue hipster briefs, no bra. And after I was finished dressing, I spun around and studied my ass over my shoulder in the mirror above my dresser.

I shimmied my hips. I bounced on my heels.

My mind was on that sweet old lady I served today the entire time I was dressing and checking my big ass out in the mirror. I wondered if she ever finished the cross-stitch she was working on while eating her tuna salad on wheat.

That seemed to keep Jamie's words from circling in my head and threatening to wrap tight around my heart.

It was a danger I had to stay constantly aware of lately. And the more time we spent together, the more trouble I was having staying constantly aware.

As I descended the stairs, the amazing aroma of freshly heated Bangkok Orchid filled my living space, and the only thing I started thinking about was eating and possible negotiation tactics if Jamie decided he liked the pineapple fried rice and wanted the second container for himself.

"You get drinks?" I called out when I finished descending, readying to turn toward the kitchen since I was figuring he had himself covered but I was going to need to grab something.

Sitting on the couch and facing forward, Jamie held up a bottle of the Extra Sweet Pure Leaf Tea I typically kept my fridge stocked with but was currently out of, meaning he must've noticed I was running low yesterday and came prepared just in case.

Huh. That was nice. And thoughtful. And kind of sweet.

And by kind of, I meant *really* sweet.

Shit.

I focused on the smell of the food again and how hungry I was instead of letting meaningful gestures take root inside me. I had to stay smart about this.

"You got somethin' in mind you wanna watch while we eat?" Jamie asked as I moved around the couch and took my seat on the cushion I typically sat on, keeping space between us since he was sitting on the other end.

"Something with a lot of action. Like a war documentary." I twisted the cap off my sweet tea and took a sip. "News would be good, too."

No romantic storylines there.

Jamie chuckled. "Not really feelin' either of those, but there's a game on. Yankees are playin' the Royals."

"Perfect."

Sports. *Yes.* That was a safe choice.

I sat on the edge of the couch and peered into the open containers littering my coffee table while Jamie cued up the TV.

"I think you got one of everything," I observed, pulling back the flap on the ginger and mushroom.

"Didn't know what you liked. Figured I'd cover my bases."

"Oo, spring rolls." I licked my lips and started untwisting the end of the bag containing one of my favorite appetizers from Bangkok Orchid.

Jamie was chuckling again beside me. It sounded warm and beautiful somehow, though I wasn't sure how a laugh could sound beautiful; still, it did, and I thought about how good he probably looked laughing the way he was, so I turned my head, tucked my hair behind my ear, and gazed in his direction, really looking at him for the first time since I came down the stairs.

I was too busy eyeing the food when I took my seat on the couch to do any looking in his direction, and boy, did I miss a spectacular sight.

Jamie was sitting with his elbows on his knees and body angled forward, still shirtless, meaning all his tanned, glorious muscles were showing and flexed since he was bracing weight. And although that in itself was an eyeful one would have serious difficulty looking away from, that was only part of the package I was labeling as spectacular.

Jamie had great hair. *Amazing* hair. Chin-length layers and wavy with pieces curling lower and reaching those big muscles at the tops of his shoulders. It looked great wet. It looked great partially wet when most hair would look frizzy unless you put some product in it. It looked great even though I was certain he always let it air-dry.

I could pull off that look but only with the help of products, and again, I didn't think Jamie used any on his hair.

He always wore it down. And if pieces fell in his face, he'd tuck them behind his ear or leave them as is, looking like he didn't give a shit, and somehow, even *that* he could pull off better than anybody else. I was sure of it.

When he arrived here, it was down, as usual, and when we were finished going at it on the couch, it was looking wavier, messier, and shockingly, even more amazing.

But now it was partially pulled back. Everything above his ear was secured in a hair tie at the back of his skull, keeping the top half out of his face and leaving the rest to curl against his golden delicious neck.

I stared at Jamie and he stared back at me, smiling, and yes, I was correct in assuming how beautiful he looked in his amusement, but I was unprepared for the degree of beauty a hair tie could provide.

I could see each and every one of his sharp features without any obstructions. His hairline, which was fantastic. He had the slightest widow's peak. And he just looked *good* with his hair pulled back. Sexy. A little scrappy.

Like he was ready to pick a fight or pop the hood of my car and check the oil.

Sheesh.

That was a nice visual. Jamie all grease-stained or with his knuckles wrapped up.

My phone started ringing just as Jamie was asking, "You all right there, babe?"

I blinked, focusing on his eyes and not his hair, hairline, sun-kissed skin, or anything else I was seeing for the first time without obstructions.

"I'm great. Starved and ready to put away some of this food," I answered. Then I looked toward the table, where the ringing was coming from.

I wasn't lying. I was just leaving out a few details.

Leaning forward, I exchanged my spring roll for my cell, which was hiding behind the container of chicken with red curry, saw my mom's name flashing on the screen, and informed Jamie as he was muting the game, "It's my mom. She'll be quick."

"No rush. Don't really need sound," he returned, setting the remote down.

I settled back against the cushion, knees bent and feet tucked partially under my hip, and pressed the phone to my ear after hitting Accept.

"Hey, Mom," I greeted her, eyes on the TV and the game Jamie had kept muted.

"Pumpkin, I've about *had* it with your father," she snapped. "Do you know what he did today? Because that man is so stubborn, I made an appointment for him to see Dr. Kennedy *myself*, and he never showed! Never called. *Nothing*. Just stood the man up. Can you believe him?"

"Is he still having heartburn?" I asked, feeling my stomach tighten with worry.

"He's still having *something*. Complains of his chest feeling tight. I don't like it. And he's popping those damn Tums like they're M&M's. Those things aren't doing him a bit of good."

I exhaled heavily, feeling the couch dip beside me as Jamie stood and moved around the coffee table. "I don't think it's heartburn," I murmured into the phone, turning my head and watching him disappear into the kitchen.

"I don't either. And that could've been confirmed *today* if he would've just kept his appointment with Dr. Kennedy, but you know how he is."

"Yeah, I know. Wait." I felt my forehead wrinkle as I turned back around. "Isn't Dr. Kennedy your plastic surgeon?"

"He's still a doctor, Tori. He went to med school."

Oh, yeah. Right. I was sure he at least knew how to use a stethoscope.

"Well, I don't know what to do, Mom. You can't make Daddy go to the doctor. Not unless you drug him and get him there while he's unconscious."

"That might be my next move."

"Do you want me to talk to him again?"

"Not right now. I've put him in a bit of a mood. He's smoking a cigar outside and shootin' his gun," she said, her voice exhausted. "Maybe try tomorrow?"

"Okay." I bit my cheek and nodded. "I'll give him a call after work."

"Thanks, pumpkin. I don't know what else to do here."

"We'll figure it out. I'm sure it's nothing."

That was a lie. I wasn't sure. *I* wasn't even considering heartburn anymore. There was a strong possibility this was something else, but I wouldn't worry my mom.

"Okay." She sighed. "Talk soon. Let me know how it goes."

"Okay, Mom."

"Bye, pumpkin."

I disconnected the call and dropped the phone onto the cushion beside me, my head tipping back and eyes closing as I struggled to keep my thoughts from drifting to worst possible scenarios and terrible worries.

I didn't know what to do. I had a good idea how the conversation with my dad was going to go tomorrow. And I was serious. I really didn't think he'd ever go see a doctor unless he was passed out cold and forced to go against his knowledge or will.

But he promised me. He promised if the Tums stopped working, he would take care of this. Was I just supposed to wait him out?

I felt Jamie's hand on my forehead, brushing my overgrown bangs to the side.

"Take it your dad is still sick and not gettin' checked out?"

I opened my eyes and looked up at him. "He's stubborn and insisting it's heartburn," I said.

"Maybe it is."

"Maybe it's something more serious and the dangers of him not getting it checked out are only making matters worse," I shot back. "Maybe it's nothing. But he won't know that unless he goes to the doctor and gets checked out. And I can't drag his body to a vehicle and hoist him up into it when he's knocked out and nothing but deadweight. I have zero upper body strength." My eyes slid to Jamie's thick, muscled shoulder. "You don't seem to have that problem."

Jamie was smiling softly when I looked back up into his face. "Maybe you give it another day. See how he is tomorrow night."

"I doubt it'll make much difference."

"Might."

"Slim chance."

"Babe."

"Mm?"

"Give it another day," he repeated, not requesting this time but telling me that was what I needed to do, and there was something in Jamie's voice I was hearing. Something comforting, like he *knew* I just needed another day, he was sure, and things would be better.

He was promising it. I didn't understand how Jamie could do that, but I knew that's what he was doing.

I let myself believe him. I wanted to.

Swallowing, I whispered a "'kay," as I looked up into his face again, unobstructed by those sandy waves he had. "I really like your hair like that," I shared.

He smiled; no teeth, just full lips stretching slow and dimples popping out.

I really liked his dimples, too. But I'd shared enough.

"That's two," Jamie replied, looking pleased.

My brows pulled together.

"Wearin' you down, babe. First my cock. Now you're diggin' my hair. Pretty soon you'll be admittin' to likin' it all. To likin' *me*."

"Never," I returned, poker face engaged.

"It'll happen."

"Nope."

"I'm wearin' you down."

"You're letting our food get cold. That's about the *only thing* you're doing right now."

Jamie threw his head back and roared with laughter, and from the angle I was sitting to him, I had full view of his neck, which was golden, had thick cords running down each side and muscles there, too, plus a predominant Adam's apple, which was moving with his enjoyment.

I really liked his neck. Maybe more than his dimples.

He had a really good laugh, too.

When Jamie was finished finding what I said funny, he looked down at me again. He was grinning. Bright white teeth. Dimples. The whole shebang.

Nope. I liked his laugh and his neck, but his dimples were holding top rank.

"Better quit listenin' to you list what all you like about me, then," he said, humor still heavy in his voice. "Don't know how good this food will be heated up twice." He rounded the couch and the coffee table, looking to reclaim his seat.

"No threat there," I replied, sounding sassy as I reached for my spring roll. "I just named the only other thing I like about you."

Jamie didn't sit at the far end of the couch this time, where he typically sat. No, he picked up my phone and placed it on the coffee table, then he sat on the cushion next to me, turning his head and looking over after he settled.

I didn't know if he was looking at me waiting for me to protest or to question why he'd just chosen the middle cushion, which was the spot nobody chose unless they had to—it wasn't as broken in and you didn't have an armrest—but I didn't do either.

Keeping his eyes, I bit into my spring roll, sharing around my mouthful, "Still warm. You're lucky."

Jamie's gaze lowered to my mouth, his lips twitched, then his eyes met mine again. "Fuckin' right I am," he replied.

My cheeks heated. I knew he was not referring to being lucky in terms of the food. And before I reacted any more to hearing that, I broke eye contact and shoved as much spring roll into my mouth as possible.

We ate our dinner with the game muted, talking about random things. His sister, where she lived, and if she'd be visiting again soon. He didn't know the answer to that last one, but she lived four hours away in the same town as his parents. Jamie told me about his lessons that day, and I told him about the staring match Stitch and Shay competed in when she took an order back that was wrong and was forced to speak to the man she was hell-bent on ignoring.

After we were finished eating and the leftovers were put away, we watched the rest of the game unmuted. I fell asleep sometime after the seventh inning stretch, my head starting out on Jamie's shoulder and then getting moved to his chest when he pulled me down and stretched out on the couch, putting me between him and the back cushion and situating me so I was partially lying on top of him.

Belly full of food and horizontal with a good-smelling man under me, I couldn't fight it. I dozed pretty quickly after that.

My eyes fluttered open when I felt cool satin underneath my legs and a sheet being pulled up my body. I was in my bed. I turned my head on the pillow and watched Jamie move toward the door.

"You're leaving?" I asked, sitting up and gripping the covers to my chest. I swore I didn't sound panicked. I was just curious. And maybe a little surprised.

But when Jamie turned his head to look at me, I knew he was hearing emotions in my voice I was sure weren't there. He didn't speak. Looking away, he closed the door instead of walking through it, and then he started removing his clothing.

"It's fine. I was just asking," I said, watching Jamie step out of his shorts and lay them across the bottom of the bed where his shirt was, having already discarded that.

He walked around the bed and climbed in beside me, wearing only his briefs.

"Really, Jamie. I'm not asking you to stay."

"You want me here. I'm stayin'."

His hand reached out. I felt it curl around my hip, then I was being pulled closer and turned so I was facing away, his arm wrapping around my waist and his legs pushing mine to bend.

"I never said—"

"Babe, shut up," he interrupted. I felt his lips press down the line of my neck to my shoulder. He drew in a slow, deep breath. "Be leavin' you early in the mornin'. I had to move my lessons up 'cause of shit I got goin' on, so if you wake up and I'm not here, that's why."

"Is that why you were heading out?" I asked, blinking into the darkness of my bedroom.

"Yeah."

"What sort of . . . *shit* do you have going on?"

Jamie's breath burst against my shoulder.

"What? That's what you called it," I said, knowing he was laughing at me for repeating his term for the obligations he had.

"Sweet when you say it, though," he told me, then his arm gave me a squeeze as my lip curled up.

I was totally blushing. Thank God I was facing away.

"I got an interview with *Rail Magazine* after lunch," Jamie informed me. His tone casual. "Last year that shit took all afternoon and I had to cancel on people. I'm not tryin' to have that happen again, so I'm gettin' started early."

I caught the last bit of his statement looking into the shadow of his face, which was peering above my shoulder, seeing as my neck was craned and I'd turned my head as far as I could comfortably turn it.

"You're being interviewed by a magazine?" I asked. I could hear the wonder in my voice. *Wow. How cool was that?*

"Yeah," he answered, still just as casual. "It ain't a big deal."

"Like, a *real* magazine?"

"Pretty fuckin' legit, yeah. You surf or follow the sport, you know *Rail*. They've been around since the fifties."

I blinked, thinking on that. *Huh.*

I really needed to start checking out the other magazine sections at Barnes & Noble. I typically stuck to Women's Interest when I browsed.

"I think that's really cool," I told Jamie. His shoulder jerked. He was playing it off. "I'm serious. I do."

"I get that, babe. And I appreciate you thinking somethin' I'm doin' is cool, but really, it ain't a big deal," he repeated. "I've done a bunch of these, and half the time they always end up pissing me the fuck off 'cause they ask questions that don't got shit to do with surfing. That's what I'm there to talk about. Hell, that's what I'd rather be doin' instead of some stupid interview. I just do 'em to bring business to Wax. Plus, my sponsors like it. Keeps them happy."

"Well, I still think it's cool. And I'm *really* looking forward to reading it," I said with enthusiasm as I looked into the shadow of his face.

Maybe he'd mention me in the article...

I pinched my eyes shut. *Really, Tori? Really?* Then I quickly uncraned my neck and plopped my cheek against the pillow again.

I sighed. *Do not even go there.*

Jamie chuckled. His chest shook against my back. Then he kissed my neck before dropping back on the pillow behind me and, with his arm already tight around my body, gave me another squeeze.

My body instantly relaxed.

"Night, babe," he murmured.

"Night," I murmured back. I closed my eyes with Jamie McCade in my bed, and although this wasn't the first time he was sleeping over, not even the second, it definitely felt like it was.

* * *

It was the next day, the lunch rush was starting to pick up, and I was having the best time working alongside my best girl.

We didn't get many shifts together now that Syd worked full-time at the hospital, so when we did, I cherished them.

No way was anything getting me down today.

"So Sunday dinner is canceled this week," Syd informed me, coming to stand behind the bar, where I was currently pouring drinks.

I set the pitcher of water on the counter, turned my head to look at her, and frowned. Well, okay, maybe there were some things that could get me down today. I loved Sunday dinner.

"Why?" I asked. "Do you need to cover a shift?"

Syd shook her head. "My mom wants to meet Brian." Her eyes widened and she laughed lightly. "Crazy, right? I wasn't expecting it either."

I turned to face Syd, giving her my full attention. This was huge.

"She does? What happened to her not being supportive and a massive bitch about the whole thing?" I asked.

Syd's mom completely shut her out after she found out her daughter was living with Brian and moving on from Marcus, her ex-husband, who she was separated from. Didn't have any interest in meeting the man who made her daughter the happiest she'd ever been and made that known.

I hated watching Syd go through that.

"Apparently she saw Marcus out with my replacement and let him have it right in the middle of a Sonic parking lot," Syd replied.

A laugh erupted in my chest. "What? Really?"

She nodded, smiling a little. "Yep. When she got home afterward, she called and said she saw Marcus eating hot dogs and looking happy about burning in hell for his sins."

"Oh, good Lord. Your mother."

"I know."

We both started laughing.

Syd shrugged. "Anyway, she said she'd like to meet Brian, and I thought we'd go up Saturday and maybe spend the night and come home late on Sunday. I want to show Brian where I grew up."

She sounded disappointed, even though I knew she was bursting with joy inside about her mother coming around and possibly wanting to rebuild their relationship.

I reached out and took her hand, giving it a squeeze. "This is way more important than dinner, hon."

Syd smiled. "I'm glad you think that," she replied softly. "I think so, too."

"We'll skip a week. No biggie," I assured, releasing her and grabbing the glasses I'd just filled. "Or maybe I'll host it. That could be fun."

"I'm sure Jamie would think so."

I turned my head and looked at Syd, keeping a straight face while she offered up a gleaming smile and bright, knowing eyes.

"You need to spill the beans," she added, stepping closer and pressing her fingertips to her mouth. Her voice raced with excitement.

"None to spill, hon. And I got tables."

Syd narrowed her eyes. Her hands fell, revealing the smile she was still wearing. She held her hip with one hand and lifted her other to point at me. "You had a sleepover with Jamie McCade. I know you did. And you've been mysteriously quiet the past few days, which leads to me thinking you've now had *several* sleepovers with him." She tipped forward, hand flattening on the bar and voice lowering when she added, "You have so many beans to spill, they are practically coming out of your eyeballs."

"I don't know what you're talking about," I returned, playing dumb as I stepped out from behind the bar.

I glanced at her as I walked past. She wasn't smiling anymore. She was grinning. Big-time. *Typical.* Team Jamie all the way.

Shaking my head, I left her goofy grinning ass standing there and carried the drinks to the customers waiting on them. As I was checking on another table, giving them more napkins before they had the chance to request any, movement at the front of the restaurant caught my eye and I looked up.

Jamie walked up to the hostess podium and greeted Kali, who was standing there. Then his eyes met mine and held while he continued speaking.

My heart became one of those cartoon drawings with the arms and legs, waving at Jamie while it jumped up and down fanatically.

He was wearing a bright yellow O'Neill tee and cargo shorts. Typically, when Jamie came in here for lunch, he'd be wearing a pair of board shorts, either getting ready to give a lesson or coming from one. But I knew he had that interview this afternoon so I was figuring that was the reason for the shorts he was wearing. And even though he'd finished with his lessons for the day, his hair was definitely still damp. It had extra curl and looked darker at the roots.

I knew he smelled like sunscreen and the summer breeze, but a huge, pressing part of me wanted confirmation on that. My face buried in his neck would provide that confirmation.

After Jamie claimed a vacant booth in my section, I walked over, pen and ticket book at the ready.

"You know what you want?" I asked, skipping introductions and now beating Syd out on goofy grins, I was sure of it. I had to be taking the cake on the one I was currently wearing.

Jamie grinned back, head tilting to the side and arm coming up to lay across the back of the booth. "Yep," he replied.

"What?"

"That sweet fuckin' mouth."

I scrunched my nose up and shook my head, telling him, "Ah sorry. I think Nate took kissing off the menu last week."

"Yeah? It ain't a special today?"

Lips pressing together, fighting yet another goofy grin, I slowly shook my head.

"Right." Jamie kept his grin. He didn't fight it. "I'll take two spectacular tits in my face and a handful of that ass, babe."

My eyes widened and a giggle caught in my throat. He was completely serious. I just knew he was.

Face burning, my stomach fluttering, and my heart reaching out, no longer waving but wanting to touch, I asked him, "How about I just surprise you with something?"

"Fine by me," he replied. "Not really here for the food today anyway, so it don't matter."

I held his eyes for a breath, wondering if I'd ever seen a pair so blue, then scribbled down Jamie's order, which I'd decided was going to be the BBQ chicken biscuit since I knew he liked that. With extra sauce.

"I'll be back with your drink," I said, looking up.

"I'll be here," he said back, smiling, looking happy and making me want that kiss, right here, out in the open in front of everyone.

I quickly spun around before I lost all of my sense, and made for the kitchen, ticket ripped off and pinched between my fingers.

"Here you go, Stitch," I said, sliding the paper across the metal lip of the window, then once I got the head jerk, meaning he'd heard me even though I was speaking to his back, I spun around and grabbed a glass and the bottle of grenadine from beneath the bar.

"Hmm. Interesting," Syd murmured, moving to stand beside me again.

"What?" I asked. I scooped some ice into the glass and started filling it with Coke.

"Oh, nothing," she sighed. "Just that you put in the order for Jamie without adding on the Loser Special. That's all. No big deal or anything. Except it totally *is* a big deal. A huge deal."

I stopped filling up the glass with Coke and held it there, finger on the dispenser button but no longer pressing.

She was right. She was *totally* right.

I always added on the Loser Special to Jamie's orders. Always. Since that very first day. And now I wasn't. Never again.

I was done asking Stitch to mess with Jamie's food, because I was done wanting him to catch something, get sick, and never return.

I was done running away, avoiding, and trying my hardest to keep Jamie from seeing me. And I was done trying to convince myself I didn't want to see him. I wanted him coming here. I wanted him coming here for *me*.

If my heart had a mouth, it would totally be saying "I told you so" right about now.

Lips curling up, I finished dispensing the Coke into the glass. Then I spun around and reached for the bottle of grenadine, my eyes lifting to look at Jamie since I'd just had a revelation, and hell, I wanted him seeing how I felt about it.

The hand reaching for the grenadine bottle gripped it, but didn't raise it up.

I blinked. My stupid, quick-beating heart curled into a ball and sank into the pit of my stomach. And I was transported back to that night I stood in Jamie's bedroom doorway and watched him engage in a foursome with those women.

The same ones who were apparently joining him for lunch.

Chapter Fourteen

JAMIE

"Well, look who it is."

Dragging my eyes off Tori as she walked away, I turned my head and tipped it back, looking at the three faces smiling down at me and not having any fucking clue which one of them just spoke.

Not really caring either. *What the fuck were they doing here?*

"Mind if we join you?" Amy Baker asked, moving before I answered and sliding into the seat across from me.

"Yeah, I do fuckin' mind," I shot back, not sounding like too much of a dick but making it known I wasn't feeling having them join me.

Amy laughed. So did her sisters, Becca and Sue, who apparently couldn't hear for shit or were just choosing not to listen. Becca slid in next to Amy, and Sue squeezed onto the five inches of bench seat I had vacant on my end.

Didn't have much opinion of the three of them after our night together. Didn't have much opinion of any hookup, if that was all it was. And these three were definitely a hookup. Nothing more. Step-sisters wanting to pass me around and do a little sharing and not giving a fuck they were sort of related.

Knew I'd see them around again eventually, but here? I did not need to be seeing them here. And I sure as fuck didn't want to share a meal with them, which looked to be their agenda.

"You deaf?" I asked Sue, glaring at her and not scooting over to give her room, which meant she stayed pressing against my side to prevent from falling off.

She rolled her eyes, huffing, "Fine." Then she stood up and squeezed onto the bench with her sisters.

Jesus. Here we fucking go.

"We wanted to talk to you about surf lessons," Amy informed me. "We were going to call Wax but since you're here—"

"Call Wax," I interrupted. "Talk to Cole about it."

"But Cole isn't here," Becca pointed out, a smile slowly lifting her lips. "*You're* here."

"Why I said to call," I returned coldly.

Becca stopped smiling.

"Jesus, Jamie. What's crawled up your butt?" Amy griped, acting like I'd invited her ass to sit down and now all of a sudden I was giving her shit about it. "You can't answer our questions? Why? 'Cause you're off the clock or something? That's crap."

"Yeah. And bad business," Sue added.

I filled my lungs with air, releasing it slowly as I looked between the three of them. Guess I could answer their questions if that was all they were wanting. Maybe if I did, they'd get the fuck up and leave.

"What'd you wanna know?" I prompted, keeping my one arm on the back of the booth and bringing my other hand up to rest on the table, cracking my fingers one at a time.

"How much are they?" Amy inquired.

"One-fifty per lesson for private. We got package deals where you can book three to five. Those are four twenty-five and seven hundred. We offer group lessons as well."

"And how much time do we get with you?" Becca asked, resting her chin on her hand.

"None," I replied.

"What do you mean? Why not?"

I looked at Sue after she spoke. "Lesson times run about an hour. You wanna talk specifics, you can talk to the man who's gonna give them to you. That ain't me. Only other option you got is Cole and he's at the shop, which is why I said to call Wax. Don't know his schedule so talkin' to me about it is a waste of time."

"But why can't you give the lessons? You're the best," Sue asked.

"Yeah." Amy bit her lip. "The *best*."

Becca covered her mouth and giggled. Sue was smiling and Amy was practically eye-fucking me across the table.

My gaze hardened. *Jesus.* This wasn't about lessons. They were looking for a repeat.

And I had zero fucking interest in partaking in that even though I knew *exactly* what a repeat with the three of them would involve.

Wait...

I blinked, scanning their faces again while remembering what was being offered up. *Really* remembering. Yep.

Zero fucking interest.

My mouth twitched. *Motherfucker.* I'd been claimed. Tori Rivera owned my shit. And I was more than okay with that.

"Jesus," I muttered, shaking my head through a laugh.

"What?" Becca asked shyly.

"Yeah. What, Jamie?" Sue asked, leaning forward with curiosity.

Movement caught my attention, and I turned to watch Tori take the remaining steps to reach the booth, eyes holding mine, looking hard but also looking filled with hurt, lips pinched together, cheeks hot, and my glass of Cherry Coke in her hand.

"Here." She leaned down and sat my glass in front of me. "Your order's just been put in. It'll be out in ten and Syd will bring it to you," she said, voice shaking a little.

Syd will bring it to me? What the fuck? Brow furrowing, I reached for her. "Babe."

Tori straightened, stepped back so I couldn't touch her, and then turned to Sue, sticking her hand on her hip and raising a finger to point directly in her face. "You need to leave," she snapped, voice shaking for a different reason now. She was pissed.

"Excuse me?" Sue asked, looking offended.

"*Leave.* None of you are getting served," Tori continued. "And if you ever come back here, you aren't getting served, so don't bother. We keep the garbage out back. You're hungry? Go ahead and pick through it. I'm sure you'll feel right at home."

"Legs, what the hell?"

Where the fuck was this coming from?

"Hey, you can't talk to my sister like that," Amy hissed, sitting taller like she was fixing to climb over the other two to get to Tori, who when I looked at her was standing less defensively now, her one hand sliding off her hip and the other pressing flat to her stomach.

She blinked, her chest rising and falling severely. "She's your *sister*?" Tori asked quietly.

"Yeah," Amy replied, heavy on the attitude. "They both are. And you aren't going to talk to them like that."

Tori ignored Amy and turned her head to look at me instead. The hurt was back in her eyes but it was mixed with something.

Disgust.

I stared at her. I didn't understand why she was looking or acting the way she was. Wasn't like I was flirting with them or appearing the least bit interested.

"Hey, don't I know you?" Becca questioned, speaking up for the first time. "You look really familiar..."

I watched Tori slowly turn her head and glare at Becca. Her nostrils flared. They stared at each other for several breaths, then Becca snapped her fingers and pointed, waving at Legs.

"Ohhh, that's right." Becca dropped her hand to the table and nudged Sue, leaning into her to ask, "Remember I told you I saw that girl watching us the night of the party?"

My eyes sliced to Tori. Something pinched in the center of my chest.

Fuck. She saw me with them. She came looking for me that night.

"Oh, yeah," Sue replied, appearing to think back to that conversation. "That was *you*?"

I watched Tori squeeze her eyes shut and draw in a breath, then she turned her head and slowly looked at me as Amy muttered an indifferent, "Huh. Small world."

Heat burned across Tori's cheeks. She was embarrassed. And I knew why.

God-fucking-damn it.

I slid to the edge of the bench, moving to stand so I could explain and do it touching her.

"You can leave, too," Tori informed me.

I froze, held her eyes for a breath, then wiped my hand down my mouth. "Babe, look—"

"I'd like you to leave, Jamie. I'm *asking you* to leave," she repeated, her voice back to shaking again. She turned her head and glared at the Baker sisters. "Get out," she snapped. "Or I'll have Stitch remove you."

"Who is *Stitch*?" Sue asked, but Tori was already moving away, fleeing in the direction of the kitchen but she wasn't stopping there.

I knew where she was headed.

"Jeez. What was her problem?"

I looked to Amy after she spoke, eyes hard and jaw tight. "Get the fuck outta here," I ordered.

Amy blinked. Her face went slack, wiped clean of attitude, and she pushed into Becca with her shoulder, saying, "Get up," on a hurried voice.

I was standing before Sue had a chance to get up and pushing past her when she finally stood, causing her to gasp and lean back into her sisters so she wouldn't collide with me.

Smart move.

I kept walking, heading to the back of the restaurant and passing Syd, who was standing behind the bar, arms crossed over her chest and face in a scowl.

"Check that attitude, Sunshine. I'm handlin' it," I called out.

"I'll check it once it's handled, thank you very much," she returned at my back, possibly going heavier on the attitude since I was telling her to do the opposite.

Jesus. Forgot how good she was at hating on me. Between Tori and Syd, I was sure they could teach a fucking class on it.

I reached the back of the restaurant and the door to the employee lounge I saw Tori disappear behind, and pushed through it. Legs was pacing in front of the lockers but stopped when she saw me, head lifting, breath getting pulled in sharply and eyes going round with alarm.

"You are not allowed back here," she bit out, sounding and looking like she was only letting herself feel anger, but I knew there was something else there. "Get out. Right now, Jamie. I mean it."

I pushed the door shut and reached up, sliding the lock in place. When I looked back at Tori, her eyes had grown even rounder and her face was heating.

"No." She shook her head quickly. "I don't want you in here. I don't want to see you right now. You need to go."

"I ain't goin' anywhere."

She flinched, hissing, "*Get out*," between her teeth after pulling in another breath.

"You went lookin' for me," I said, knowing the truth now but still needing her to admit it. "Came to that party wantin' me, babe. Only reason you were there."

Eyes closing through a heavy blink, she shook her head, laughing under her breath. "Fine." Her eyes flashed open. "Is that what you need to hear so you'll leave? *Yes.* Okay? I *did* come to that party for you. And I did go looking for you, after I waited thirty fucking minutes in a bedroom I *thought* was yours. Had a bunch of surfboards in it and trophies. All of which had your name on them. I checked. I waited in that room thinking you'd come find me, but you didn't, did you? Because you're not that guy, Jamie."

My brows lifted. "Say again?"

"You're not that guy," she repeated. "You're the guy who gets the chance to fuck three girls at once and takes that over going to find the one girl who's waiting for you. It's all about how much pussy you can score. You're *that guy*. And now what, you're having lunch with them? Chatting and looking all cozy. I can't believe you'd ask them to come here."

"Babe, you don't know shit," I told her, arms crossing over my chest.

Her mouth dropped open again. She blinked. "*Excuse me?*"

"Didn't invite them here. Didn't know they'd show up. And when they did, told them I didn't want them sittin' with me."

"Well, unless I'm imagining things, I'm pretty sure that's where they were sitting," she shot back. "And it didn't look like you were dragging them away either. In fact, you were smiling at them. I saw it."

Hearing that, I couldn't help it. I laughed. "Jesus, Legs."

And seeing me laugh and interpreting that wrong, Tori started moving at me, eyes flashing and lips curling against her teeth.

"Get out," she snarled. "I don't want to see you right now. I'm getting back to work and you're leaving." She stopped, jerking back before crashing into me since I hadn't stepped aside. Chin tipping up and fists clenching at her sides, she glared at me. "Move, Jamie."

"Wanna know why I was smilin'?" I asked, still not moving.

"I don't give a damn. Now *move*."

I bent down, getting closer to her. "You give a damn, babe," I said harshly, watching her eyes blink and dilate. "Probably more than you'd like right now considerin' what you're lettin' yourself believe, but you're wrong, Legs. Everything you're thinkin' right now. Didn't ask them here and sure as *fuck* wasn't smilin' 'cause of them."

"I don't believe you," she replied, voice quiet.

"Can't say that surprises me," I returned.

Her eyes narrowed. She rolled up on her toes to get closer, ordering, "Move."

"No."

"*Move*, Jamie."

I shook my head.

Tori rocked back, looking on the verge of tears. "Please move," she whispered.

"No, babe. You're gonna hear me out," I said, standing firm. "Got a lot to say and you're not gettin' out of here until I say it."

"There is *nothing* you could tell me right now that could make me stay in here another second with you. I'm getting back to work," she countered, looking behind me at the door and then back up into my face. "As soon as you move."

"Not movin'."

She started panting through her nostrils, shaking her head, lip trembling and tears filling her eyes. "I swear to God, Jamie, if you don't move—"

"You're gonna hear me out," I repeated, interrupting her as I dropped my head even lower, our noses almost touching. "Gonna stand there and hear what I got to tell you. Every fuckin' word, babe, and you're gonna do it not arguin'. Said what you had to say. I took it, keepin' my mouth shut even though it was bullshit. *All of it.* Now it's my turn. You interrupt me or try and debate and I'm startin' over. I'll move when this is done."

She gasped when I dropped my arms, ripped her apron off, and tugged at her uniform shorts, popping the button.

"Jamie—"

I stepped closer, pushing her until she was flat against the lockers. "Startin' now, only thing I wanna hear comin' out of your mouth is my name, babe. That or those hot as fuck noises you give." Hands on her shorts, I yanked them down along with her panties, lifting her foot to step out as I dropped to my knees in front of her.

Tori's breaths were coming out fast. Her body was stiff, hands flat against the lockers, but when I hooked her left leg over my shoulder and stared at her pussy, she whimpered and reached down, pushing her fingers gently through my hair.

"You think I want anyone else when I got this?" I asked, leaning forward and pressing my mouth there, lightly kissing her as I spoke. "You think I'm even *lookin'* anywhere else? Fuck, babe. If it ain't you, I'm blind. You gotta know that." I bent lower and started licking her.

Tori gasped, "*Jamie,*" then her moans started coming, low and raw in her throat.

"Night of that party, I didn't know what I had when you showed up," I admitted against her flesh. "I didn't know what you were givin' me. Might sound harsh, Legs, but it is what it is. Lookin' to fuck that night. You showed and I thought maybe you were down, and then you disappeared and I figured you changed your mind. We weren't anythin' to each other then, babe. I don't gotta apologize for hooking up when I didn't think I had you."

Her nails dug into my scalp. I sucked on her clit and she relaxed, breath catching and then moving heavy again as she tugged me closer.

I kept sucking, buried my nose there and then licked her lower where she was growing wettest.

"I don't gotta apologize for that," I repeated, hooking my arm around her thigh and using my fingers to hold her open, then lifting my head to look at her.

Tears were streaming down her face. Her chest was shaking.

"But what I am gonna apologize for is for you seein' it," I continued, keeping her eyes. "Knowin' now what you just shared, hearin' you were waitin' for me, that's messin' me up, babe. And that's somethin' I'm gonna feel for a while. Straight up. I wanted you for more than just a fuck, Tori. I always did."

She shook her head. Fresh tears building, from what I just confessed or for the pain she was feeling reliving that night, I wasn't sure.

I leaned in and swiped my tongue through her pussy, watching her head drop back and her lips part as she tugged on my hair, whimpering, "*Please*," like this was killing her or like it would if I stopped.

For seconds I ate her slowly, just concentrating on that and the feel of her muscles tensing against my head and under my hand as I pressed against her stomach. I was kissing her like I kissed her mouth after we fucked, desperately, like I was asking if I could have this and *can I keep you?* and *do you feel this, too?*

Going down on a woman had never felt so intense. It had never felt like much of anything, just a prelude to sex and sometimes the path to get us there more quickly, but that wasn't what this was. I wasn't even thinking about getting off.

I was on my knees for someone I would stay there for. If she asked or if she couldn't, it didn't matter. I knew that.

And that's when it happened.

I stopped asking. There was no question. It was *this is mine* and *I know you feel this* and *I'm never letting you go*. I became rough and wild. I took her there, to the very edge where she was shaking and begging and so close to coming I barely had to touch her, then I leaned away and looked up, breathing heavy against her pussy because I was panting, too.

"Smilin' at them 'cause they were offerin' another go and I wasn't feelin' it. Not even a little," I shared, watching her lips part. "I sat there knowin' I belonged to you and I was fuckin' happy knowin' that. Only thing that would've made that moment better is if you were claimin' me, babe. Too bad you couldn't do that."

Tori's breath was hitching in little gasps as she stared, listening, those tears still flowing down her cheeks, possibly from what I was admitting or from regretting the opportunity she had and didn't take, or maybe she was just so far gone and suspended there she was breaking down, I wasn't sure.

I wasn't asking.

I leaned in and watched her eyes roll closed and her neck arch, head dropping back and hitting the lockers.

I latched on to her clit and sucked it hard.

Her leg on my shoulder tensed, her body pressed down against my mouth, hips grinding, fingers pulling my hair, and moans escaping her sweetly.

I closed my eyes as her taste flooded my mouth. Hands gripping her hips and urging her to keep moving, then feeling her come down, her body melting and softening against me and her fingers in my hair moving slowly, not gripping.

I looked up, meeting eyes that were heavy-lidded. Her face was flushed and her hair was sticking to her cheeks, which were wet from her tears. I pressed my mouth to her thigh and lowered her leg from my shoulder, then I stood, leaning in and looming over her, arm bracing on the locker above her head and other hand pushing the hair from her face, tucking it behind her ear and then gripping her neck.

"I hate that you saw me with them," I said, bending down and getting even closer. "Hate that I had you in my old room, probably sittin' on my old bed, touchin' my shit, lookin' at stuff that means somethin' to me and I wasn't there watchin' you do that. Fact that I missed out on that fuckin' sucks. Fact that you saw me with them is gonna eat at me, babe. Straight up. But ain't nothin' I can do to change that. Ain't nothin' you can do to change it either. I fucked up by not lookin' for you longer than I did. But you"—my fingers on her neck squeezed—"you fucked up, too, Legs."

She blinked. Her breath hitched. "I—"

"You wanna act like a jealous girlfriend, then you can fuckin' admit that's what you are to me," I interrupted, watching her trembling lips press together. "*Claim me*, babe, otherwise you got no reason to be throwin' attitude and tellin' me to leave. I didn't do shit, and you thinkin' I did and not trustin' I'm with you, even though you ain't admittin' that's where you want me to be is fucked up. Same as gettin' mad at me for shit we both let happen. I'll feel that, babe, but you're feelin' it, too."

"Jamie—"

I slammed my mouth down on hers and kissed her then, hard and hurried, shoving my tongue inside and expecting protests, her hands pushing away or her head turning, body twisting out of my arms, but getting none of that.

And when Tori started kissing me back, which happened a whole two seconds after I let her suck the taste of her pussy off my tongue, I ripped it away from her.

I jerked back and stepped away, leaving her panting against the lockers, half dressed, her shorts and panties around one ankle, her pussy bared and glistening from my mouth, blue eyes blazing hot and still spilling tears. Her face wet, her lips parted and trembling, and her hands pressing flat to her stomach.

She looked worked up again and on the verge of collapsing. She looked like she wanted me to catch her.

I would. She just needed to ask.

And knowing Tori wasn't there yet, reading that shit on her face like I'd been reading it, knowing her, *fuck it*, I turned and walked to the door, slid the lock over, and walked out.

Chapter Fifteen

TORI

In my opinion, there were two types of girls.

The ones who acted first and thought later, going after what they wanted, getting it, and then taking a moment to pause after the fact, wondering if they had made the right decision and risking regret because they didn't wonder this sooner. These were the girls who did things on impulse, like dying their hair a radical color without having a consultation first with their stylist or getting a tattoo of a boy's name somewhere on their body, or even just getting a tattoo in general after liking butterflies a whole five seconds.

That was the first type.

And then there were the ones who think and overthink and then rethink what they were originally thinking, knowing what they want but then convincing themselves maybe they don't know what they want, getting confused, second-guessing their own hearts or not trusting them enough to follow. The girls who could talk their way out of any decision. Who hesitated committing to a nonpermanent hair color without sitting down with a professional first. The temporary tattoo wearers. The ones who whispered words to boys who were asleep so they couldn't hear them: *Please don't hurt me* and *Please be real* and *I like you so, so much*.

The girls who watched love pull back and walk away. Who stayed silent against the lockers until they were left alone and then spoke behind their hand between heartache. Who finished out their shifts under a cloud instead of chasing after the sun.

I was that girl. Wanting something and knowing where it was but going in the opposite direction. Wanting something, but wait, maybe I didn't or I shouldn't or I couldn't.

I drove home because I was the girl who went home. I sat on my couch after washing off the best smell in the world and pretended I didn't miss it. I doodled the same name over and over and told myself I wouldn't think about him when he was the only thing I could think about.

The other girl was fearless and I was afraid. The other girl let Jamie catch her and I stood on the edge, worried he wouldn't because I didn't know which boy held out his arms: the one I met that first day who laughed at love or the one who could promise it.

I didn't know what to do. Every time I let myself move toward Jamie, I would find a reason to stop. Even getting as far as my car, I still hesitated and wondered if I was doing the right thing, and now I sat in my driveway, keys in the ignition but not turned on. Not getting that far before I started second-guessing.

I ran out of my house knowing where I wanted to go and who I wanted to be with, and now I wasn't sure.

"*Come on*," I groaned, eyes closing and head dropping back against the seat. I felt the beginnings of tears prick behind my lids.

I should've talked to Syd earlier. Maybe if I would've instead of lying to my best girl, telling her I was fine so I wouldn't have to reveal why I wasn't, I'd be able to make a damn decision. Go to him or don't. One or the other.

"*Claim me, babe.*"

God, I wanted to. And in the same breath, I was terrified.

Was Jamie McCade even claimable?

My phone started ringing.

Opening my eyes and turning my head, I looked down at my passenger seat and read the name of the caller flashing on the screen.

Shit. I completely forgot. I promised my mom I would get on my dad about going to the doctor's again. She was probably calling to remind me of that.

I hit Answer and pressed the phone to my ear.

"I am so, so sorry. I forgot to call him," I said as a greeting, expecting my mother.

"Princess, it's your father."

"Oh." I blinked. That was unexpected. "Hi, Daddy. How are you feeling?" I asked, wiping away smudged mascara from underneath my eyes.

"Expected something like this from your mother, Tori. Not from you," he replied, voice hard-edged and angry. "Told you I was fine and you can't trust me to handle things if and when I feel it's necessary."

"It wasn't heartburn, John! And now we know!" my mother hollered out in the background. "Thank God we didn't wait for you to handle things!"

I felt my brow tighten.

What in the world?

"Doc said what I was feeling mimicked the sensations of heartburn, Dee," my father argued away from the phone. "Wasn't like I was that off base."

"You were *completely* off base!" she argued back.

"What are you both talking about?" I probed, wondering why I was in the middle of a conversation the two of them seemed to be having.

The line made a clicking noise, then my dad started talking.

"That doc came by the house about an hour ago," he said, his voice insinuating I knew what he was referring to. "Now, princess, I know you're just looking out for your old man, but that was something that should've been cleared with me first. Don't like people just showing up at my house. Especially if I don't even know 'em. Hell, he was lucky I didn't shoot first and ask questions later. I was in my right."

"Oh, John. Don't be ridiculous," my mother scoffed, her voice clear now and as loud as his. She had picked up the other house phone. "You were not in your right to shoot him. My God," she added.

"Got a *No Trespassin'* sign up, Dee. I was in my right."

"I'm sorry," I cut in before my mom had a chance to keep disagreeing. "But I really have *no* idea what you're both talking about. Did a doctor come see you or something?"

"You know he did, princess. You arranged the damn thing."

I squinted out the front windshield. "What? I didn't arrange anything. Who said that?"

"Said he was doing a favor for his brother. That he insisted," Dad replied. "Mc-something. I don't know. I can't read this chicken scratch handwriting. Here, Dee."

Mc-something?

Oh, my God.

I sucked in a breath, stomach tensing as I asked, "What?" on a whisper.

"McCade. His name was McCade," my mom said. "Ooh, and he was young, wasn't he, John? I didn't know doctors could be that young."

"His name was McCade?" I asked in a quick voice, sitting forward in my seat and gripping the phone harder.

"That's another thing," Dad grumbled. "Not sure I should be taking orders from some kid. What's he know anyway?"

"I like that he's young. Means his mind is fresh on the books," Mom contended.

"Would you both quit arguing and pay attention to what I'm saying?" I shrieked, now gripping hold on the steering wheel with one hand. "You said his name was McCade? Is that what I heard?"

"Yes. Dr. McCade," my mom answered, also speaking in a way it was as if I should know this information already. "His first name is Travis."

"How'd you know that?" Dad asked, sounding flippant.

"It says so right here on the prescription. Really, if you would just wear your glasses—"

"Forget the glasses!" I interrupted. "Jamie had his brother come to your house and *treat you*? He...he really did that? Are you sure his last name was McCade?"

I couldn't believe what I was hearing.

"Pumpkin, why are you acting like you don't know anything about this?" Mom asked.

"*Because I don't know anything about this*," I informed both of them, breathing heavy now I was so worked up. "I can't believe...wait, what did he tell you? That it's not heartburn? What else?"

"Went through two bottles of Tums," Mom mumbled under her breath. "What a waste."

Dad exhaled heavily in my ear. I pictured him glaring at my mother all while holding her hand and giving it a loving squeeze.

It was how they operated.

"Said my pressure is up. Took some blood and told me to go get some tests or something," he shared. "Said the chest pain could be from my pressure, but he wanted to make sure. Also gave me a prescription for some dog scan."

"A CAT scan, John," Mom corrected.

"Same damn thing."

"And he said something about you losing weight," Mom added. "I heard him."

"Don't remember nothin' about that," Dad returned.

"He wrote it down. Again, if you'd just put on your glasses..."

"Oh, my God," I murmured as they continued to debate in my ear, and this was strictly in reaction to what I was realizing, not because of my parents and their bickering.

They bickered out of love all the time. I was pretty immune to it. I wasn't reacting to that. I was reacting to what I was thinking about—last night with Jamie and our conversation before we started eating. The one we had right after I hung up from my mom.

Travis McCade.

My hand slid off the wheel to press to my stomach at the same time as my eyes lowered and lost focus.

"He told me to give it another day. That's what he said," I muttered mostly to myself. "He...he told me to wait and see how you were doing 'cause he knew I was worrying and he didn't want me to. He was taking care of it."

He said it like a promise. *Give it another day.* He promised me.

"What's that, pumpkin?" my mom asked.

"Jamie got his brother to go check on you." I swallowed thickly, shaking my head. "I didn't ask him to do that. I—I didn't even know he *had* a brother."

Why didn't I know that? Didn't I ever ask him questions? I know he asked *me* questions.

"I didn't know doctors still made house calls," Mom said on a chuckle. "Lucky for us since your father is so stubborn."

"Still on the line, Dee," Dad pointed out.

"He had his brother go check on you," I repeated, barely above a whisper.

I closed my eyes and pressed my lips together, breathing deeply and quickly through my nose and feeling it tingle.

Jamie did this. He took care of something that meant everything to me. Didn't have to. Wasn't asked. He just did it. He was always taking care of things.

That was the kind of man he was.

"Baby girl, I missed that. I'm sorry. What did you say?" Mom asked. "Oh, and also, would you like to share how you know this McCade boy? I don't remember you ever mentioning him."

"Claim me, babe." Jamie's voice whispered in my ear and over my heart. I started breathing heavier.

"I need to go," I said instead of answering my mom or repeating. "Um, can I just..." I held the phone between my ear and shoulder and started the car while reaching for my seat belt. "Can I call you guys later? I'm really glad you got checked out, Daddy."

"Still something you could've warned me about," he grumbled. "Almost shot the man."

"Oh, for God's sakes, John, you were not even carrying," Mom reminded him.

"Okay, great!" I called out, realizing if I didn't hang up, they'd just keep at it with each other and leave me on the line as an afterthought. "Glad you didn't shoot him. Let me know how your tests go. Love you both."

I hit End and dropped my phone on the seat before backing out of my driveway.

A fifteen-minute drive was managed in ten. And this was with traffic.

I was in a bit of a hurry. I also may have run a stop sign.

I parked my car behind Jamie's Jeep and dropped my keys twice on my sprint up the driveway and onto the porch, finally succeeding in tucking them in my back jean-short pocket before I started knocking.

My hands were shaking and my heart was so happy to be here, it was leading a parade inside my chest.

I patted my thighs restlessly and stood on my toes to peer through the small rectangular window next to the door. I rang the bell and knocked again, this time using the side of my fist instead of my knuckles.

Nothing.

Hmm.

Holding on to one of the accent beams, I leaned off the porch to make sure I saw both of Jamie's vehicles in the driveway, his bike and his Jeep, confirmed that, then knocked and rang again.

Nothing.

"Okayyy."

I wasn't typically the type of person to let myself into a house where I didn't live, past or present, but I was desperate and anxious and here to claim a boy I sort of already belonged to.

Manners were being shoved aside right now.

I twisted the handle, and the door opened freely.

"Hello?" I called out, stepping inside and peering around the entryway.

The house was quiet. My voice echoed off the tall ceiling and most of the lights were off. As I leaned to the side, I caught sight of a warm glow flickering in the room behind the stairway.

"Jamie?"

I moved down the hallway and stepped inside the large living room/kitchen space.

The fireplace was on. That was the light I was seeing. Orange and yellow flames danced behind a panel of glass.

He was home. Somewhere...

He wouldn't leave the fire going.

After checking the upstairs and every room on the first floor, I pushed the slider open and stepped out onto the deck. I moved to the railing and curled my fingers around the wood, looking out at the ocean.

Jamie.

My fingers tensed on the rail. My stomach clenched. And my heart, Lord, my heart was going crazy. Jumping up and down and pointing with frantic fingers, yelling, *There he is! Go get him! Go!*

Jamie was on his board, riding a wave just under where it curled.

I knew it was him even though he had to be at least two hundred feet away, partially obstructed by the wave he was riding, and harder to see thanks to the setting sun.

But I *knew* it was him.

He looked like he was controlling the water. Every drop of it. Something so powerful moving with his will. He made it look effortless.

Only my Jamie could do that.

I crossed the deck and descended the stairs, keeping my eyes on the water and on Jamie as he paddled out again. When I hit sand, I kicked my flip-flops off so they wouldn't slow me down and took off running down the pathway that led to the beach.

Jamie was riding another wave when the sand beneath my feet became damp. I stopped and stood there, watching, so close to him now if I closed my eyes, it wouldn't be the ocean I was smelling, but him.

He whipped his board left and rode in toward the shore, and when his head came up and our eyes locked, I lifted my hand to my stomach and waved.

I waved . . .

Honestly, I didn't know what else to do. I mean, I was pretty certain my heart had decorated signs at this point and was holding them up for Jamie to read as if it was standing front row at his rock concert.

Come hold us, boy! We love the sound your heart makes!

With all that happening, I felt good about a wave.

When Jamie stuck his board under his arm and started walking in, I moved closer, staring at him and studying his expression. Eyes serious and those thick brows shadowing them. Jaw tight. No smile. Not even a hint of one as he shook the water out of his hair.

He didn't look angry. He looked tortured and frustrated and uncertain of my motives. He was gauging me as he moved, as *I* moved.

And I swore if his heart could speak like mine, it would be telling me to run to him.

Water squished beneath my feet and crashed against my ankles as the breeze off the ocean blew underneath my top. I tucked my hair behind my ear and stopped walking when I was an arm's length away.

Jamie kept moving and cut that distance in half.

He always put us closer.

"You here for somethin'?" he asked, voice even and brows lifting in question.

Head tipped back due to how close we were standing now, I blinked up at him. I had so much to say. *Ready* to say. The words danced on my tongue, but Jamie was acting like he wouldn't care if I was here for something or not. Or that he knew I wasn't because *he knew me*. He knew which girl I was.

I didn't have a tattoo on my body, and Jamie knew that.

So instead of asking the questions I needed to ask or telling him the words I only told him after I knew he was asleep, I became that other girl.

My body leapt across that tiny distance separating us, my hands wrapped around his neck, gaining purchase, and as I rolled up onto my tiptoes, I yanked Jamie down at the same time, claiming his mouth right there in the middle of a public beach.

One that just so happened to be dead at the moment, but the point I was trying to make was coming across loud and clear. I was certain of this.

Because when my lips hit Jamie's, his board hit the sand. Then immediately after that his hands snaked around my waist and started roaming and gripping as he bent farther, mouth opening and tongue touching my lip. Feeling that, I opened mine, and *that* was when we went from kissing to eating each other alive.

For a solid second.

Gasping inside our kiss, I broke away, body going rigid as I shrank back and pressed my heels into the sand. I touched my fingertips to my lips and blinked up at him.

"You smoked?" I asked Jamie, knowing already that he had.

Nicotine saturated my mouth.

I felt Jamie's hands slide to my hips and hold there. I heard his voice, deep and rich and wrapped around a chuckle, say something but I couldn't make out what it was.

Eyes lowered to the sand, the only voice I could hear was my own.

He smoked because of you. You did this. If you were that other girl, this never would've happened.

"Babe."

My head jerked up. I blinked Jamie into focus and felt tears building.

"I like you," I admitted, voice soft and trembling. "I like you so, so much. Not just your hair or the sex stuff. More than that. I lied. I've *been* lying. I am a really good liar, Jamie. It's a talent I'm not proud of and I'm sorry for it."

Mouth twitching, Jamie brought his hands to my face and bent down. "You're a shitty liar, babe," he said, catching my tears with his thumb.

"I'm not. I'm really good at it."

"Yeah? You're so good at it, how come I've known for months?"

"You didn't."

"Did," he argued.

I shook my head between his hands.

His brows pulled together. "Babe, you suck at lying. You've been feelin' me for as long as I've been feelin' you. Ain't just me seein' it either. Ask your girl."

"Not like this."

He stared at me for a breath, expression sticking, then his brows slowly lifted and his face got soft.

"I'm feeling you more than you think," I confessed, getting that out quick and continuing on before he had chance to interrupt me. "I know you've known about me liking you. Even when I denied it. And if we were having this conversation months ago, then you'd be correct in saying you know how I feel. But we're not. We're having it now and you *don't* know. You have no idea. I liked you when you slashed those tires, Jamie. That was the first day I really liked you. And it's just been building. It was slow and I could feel it, then it built really, really fast. It's more now. I doodle your name on notepads, do you know that? And in my ticket book. On napkins. I'm constantly doing it. And I say things to you when you're asleep and you can't hear me. I say so many things. And I watch you and I think about you." He started coming in to kiss me, and I pushed firm against his chest. "Wait! No, please, let me say this. I have to get this out."

"Said enough, babe," he claimed, still leaning closer.

"I didn't! There's so much. I—" I shook my head. "It's my turn. You said you liked my big ass, remember? Now it's my turn."

Jamie's mouth twitched again as he stared at me. He breathed a laugh, then he ordered, "Hurry up," and stopped pressing against my hands but stayed bent down and close, thumb sweeping across my cheek.

My eyes narrowed and my mouth grew tight. Immediately, it was as if I hadn't been emotional about any of this *at all*.

"I'm admitting things to you I've never admitted," I pointed out, my words dripping attitude. "This might take some time."

"Condense it."

"I've got a lot to say. Honestly, you might want to have a seat."

"Give me the gist of it, babe."

"I am *not* rushing this, Jamie McCade. This is too important."

"*Legs,*" he growled.

I tipped my chin up, repeating on a hurried whisper, "I'm not rushing this."

Now his eyes were the ones narrowing. "I'm two seconds away from takin' you right here, not givin' a fuck if anyone sees us or not and also not botherin' with grabbin' protection," he informed me, speaking the truth. I could hear it in his voice. "Condense it," he snarled.

"You smoked because I didn't claim you."

"And?"

"This is me claiming you."

Jamie's eyes returned to their normal size. His lips parted.

"I really want you to know what all I like," I added, sounding desperate because I was. I needed to tell him. My fingers wrapped around his ribs. "Please," I whispered. "Let me tell you my truths."

Jamie pressed his lips together and drew in a deep breath, looking like hearing that meant something big to him. Then dropping one hand to my hip, he slid the other to the back of my neck and curled his fingers there, squeezing as he dipped closer.

"Give me what you need to give me," he began. His voice was rough and heavy with meaning. "I'm talkin' what's urgent, babe, then you hold on to the rest until I'm moving inside you. I wanna feel all that beauty while you give me that. You got more to share after we're done, which straight up, is gonna be a while, you got time, 'cause ain't no fuckin' way are you leavin' me. Probably won't make it to the bed to fuck, but you'll be wakin' up there. That's for damn sure. You got all night to tell me what you need to say."

I smiled big, liking the sound of that plan better than my own.

"Maybe we get as far as in front of the fireplace?" I suggested, stepping closer so my hands wrapped around his slippery back. I leaned in and kissed his chest. "I like this," I shared, tasting saltwater on my lips. "You make me love the ocean."

Jamie's entire body tensed up, his fingers on my neck squeezing deeper now.

"Two seconds," he warned.

I tipped my head back and looked into his eyes. Shit. What was urgent? *Everything.* How could I choose? I thought about it as I sucked on my lip.

"Babe," Jamie pressed.

"I like how you take care of things that are precious to me," I rushed out, knowing that was important and at the very top of my *Things I Like About Jamie McCade* list. "My nana gave me that pie plate before she died, and I can never replace it. It's the only thing I have of hers. I love it. I won't bake a pie in anything else, and you were careful with it, Jamie. You could've thought it was silly when Syd told you what it meant to me, but you—"

"Syd didn't tell me," he interrupted.

I blinked up at him, confused. "What?"

"She didn't tell me," he repeated. "She asked me to take it to you, but she didn't say shit about the plate."

"She didn't?" I watched him shake his head while thinking back to that night. "But you said you knew it meant something to me. You acted like you knew."

Jamie shrugged lightly. "Just figured it was somethin' you cared about since it looked old as shit. My mom keeps dishes like that in this special cabinet. Know how she is with them. Thought maybe you were the same."

I inhaled sharply through my nose. It tingled. *Oh, God...*

"What?" he asked.

I blinked at him again, feeling the tears building behind my lashes and, a second later, the quivering in my lip.

I was not a crier. Not at all, but *God*, I couldn't help it. He was killing me.

Jamie watched my emotions take hold. His brow furrowed. "Babe?"

"I can't condense it!" I cried, face wet now and voice breaking again. "My God, it's impossible! I like so many things about you and each one of them is urgent! Even little things, like how you play with my hair sometimes when we're falling asleep, I like that *so much*! I even tried recording you doing it one night with my phone after your eyes were closed but my eyes were closing, too, and I basically only ended up with a video of your elbow." My shoulders dropped on an exhale. "I kept it, though. I like your elbow," I added softly.

Jamie slowly grinned.

"I can't condense it," I repeated through my tears, a little quieter this time. I reached up and held his face. "I can't choose what's most important because I know I'll think of something that's just as important and I might not think of it until an hour from now. Or in the morning. And I don't want you thinking the way you look at me isn't something I like as much as something else. It's *equally* important."

"Fuck it then. Don't condense it," he suggested, grin softening to a smile as he stepped into me. His grip slid down my body, over my ass to the backs of my thighs. Our foreheads touched. "Just start listin' what you like, Legs," Jamie said, voice dropping low and quiet. "I'll know what you say now means just as much as what you tell me when I get inside you. Same goes for what you think of and feel like sharin' tomorrow. And the next day. And next fuckin' month. That work for you?"

I nodded, liking that he was thinking about next month. "That works for me," I told him. Then I gasped when Jamie lifted me off the sand and guided my legs to wrap around his waist. I slid my hands to his neck and held on.

We started moving.

"What about your board?" I asked, speaking against his lips as we kissed softly.

"Fuck my board. I'll get it later."

I smiled. He was always saying that.

"'Kay," I mumbled.

Jamie pushed his tongue inside my mouth, pulling back to suck on my lip. "How much you like me, babe?" he asked.

"So much," I whispered.

"Yeah?"

I nodded as he took us up the stairs.

"You gonna start namin' shit then?"

I smiled again, then I pressed my lips to the corner of his mouth, his cheek, his ear. I closed my eyes. "You want a truth?" I whispered.

"Yeah."

I love you.

Chapter Sixteen

JAMIE

"You gonna give it up?" I asked Tori, moving my thumb in circles over her clit while I pumped my fingers into her pussy.

She arched off the floor and dug her nails into my thigh, moaning, "I did. I told you."

"Lies, babe."

She shook her head.

This was the game we were playing.

I knew Tori had a truth she was keeping from me and she knew I knew it, but instead of sharing whatever it was, she was insisting the bullshit she gave up on the deck was the only thing on her mind.

I knew she was lying the minute I saw her face.

"You want a truth?" she whispered.

"Yeah."

I reached the top of the deck and started crossing it to get to the slider, getting there before Tori gave up what she was offering and what I was asking for.

"You fall asleep or somethin'?" I chuckled, feeling her breath blowing slow and evenly against my ear. I paused at the door.

Tori moved her hands to my shoulders and slowly leaned away to look at me.

Her cheeks were flushed and her eyes were big and bright, looking like she'd just heard something that surprised her.

What the fuck was she thinking about?

"Legs," I prompted after several beats.

I watched her eyes close and a smile twist across her mouth, slow and shy. Then she shook her head and looked at me again, cleared her throat, tipped her chin up, and admitted, "I like that you call me Legs. I always did. I just pretended I didn't because I didn't want you thinking I did. But I do. I like it."

She smiled big.

I stared at her, looking between her smiling mouth and her eyes that were still bright but not as big as before and settling on them. My gaze narrowed.

"What's the truth you had ready to give up?" I asked.

Tori's smile wavered the slightest bit. "What do you mean?" she questioned, knowing damn well what I meant.

"Might like that I call you Legs, but that wasn't what you were thinking about a minute ago," I told her.

"Yes, it was."

"You had somethin' else on your mind and you're coverin' with this."

"I'm not covering."

"You're coverin', babe."

Her smile wiped clean from her face. "Liking that you call me Legs has been the only thing on my mind," she insisted. "Nothing else. I'm not covering."

"Liar."

"I'm not lying."

"You're lyin'."

Her eyes pinned me with a hard look.

"Coverin', too," I added, smiling at her.

Tori glared at my mouth, glaring harder the bigger I smiled.

"You wanna kiss me?" I asked.

"Nope," she answered immediately.

"Liar."

Tori's mouth twitched.

"You wanna get fucked?"

Her gaze lifted, met mine, and started heating.

"You wanna get fucked," I repeated, saying it as a statement now.

"Absolutely not. That's the last thing I want," she contended, mouth tight, no longer twitching.

This was the game.

The little shit was lying. She was lying about a lot.

Telling me she didn't want to fuck, but the second I got her inside, she started tearing at my board shorts, practically ripping them in half she couldn't get them off me fast enough. Then crawling back up my body and kissing me like there was a time limit on that shit and she was racing the clock. Kissing me after saying she didn't want to kiss me. Sloppy, wet, using her teeth, her lips, her tongue. Forgetting about breathing and just kissing for minutes until she had to break away, gasp for air, fill her lungs, and then go back in for more, giving it to me harder because she'd been deprived for a whole fucking second.

Only time Tori faltered and took on the lies she was telling, making them seem believable, was when I carried her into the kitchen and grabbed a sleeve of condoms out of a drawer I kept random shit in.

Flashlight. Batteries. Deck of cards. Condoms. Everyone had a drawer like that.

Tori stopped kissing me and pulled back, leaning to the side to look behind me as I carried her across the room, then she straightened up and looked into my face.

I made sure I wasn't running us into the couch, getting us around it first, then doing that, I looked at her.

Tori was studying me. Eyes squinted in focus. Brows pinched together. She looked curious. Maybe a little pissy since I obviously kept condoms in the kitchen for a reason, and she was guessing that reason wasn't because of her, that I had put them there a while ago and probably used them with others. Figuring this and deciding she was right in her assumptions, Tori went rigid in my arms and turned her head when I tried getting at her mouth.

I smiled against her jaw.

"Makes my dick hard when you act jealous," I shared, laughing when she turned her head even farther until she was looking behind her. "Means you don't like the idea of me touchin' anyone else, even if that shit was before you and shouldn't matter. I get that, babe."

I moved lower and licked her neck. I bit down until she gasped and her limbs trembled.

"I wanna break the hands of every motherfucker who ever touched you," I confessed.

Tori went rigid in my arms again, but it was different this time. She liked hearing that. I knew this because, along with going rigid, she whimpered and slid her fingers up the back of my neck and into my hair, gripping handfuls. Then she turned her head and let me get at her mouth again.

She was frantic before. I didn't know what the fuck this was.

We were biting and hitting teeth more than we were actually kissing. Mouths crashing together. Noses getting in the way. Acting like neither one of us knew what the fuck we were doing, just knowing that we needed it and further knowing we'd do anything to get it.

Draw blood. Break bones. Didn't matter.

She was crazy. I had lost my goddamned mind.

I got her naked, spread a blanket out in front of the fire, and tossed a pillow down, all while we kept kiss-fighting, which was the only word I knew to describe it. Once I got Tori beneath me and slid my fingers inside her, touching where she never lied, where she *couldn't lie*, I started chipping away to get to the truth.

And she kept playing the game.

Denying it. Telling me there was nothing else she was thinking about while I fingered her slowly and stroked my dick so she could watch. Now I was adding my thumb and making her breaths come quicker, building it faster, knowing she was close to giving it up. And knowing Tori. Knowing her this entire fucking time.

She was mine, and I knew *exactly* what she was hiding.

"Think you love me, babe," I offered up, tired of waiting for her to admit it.

Her eyes sliced to mine and widened in panic. I inhaled sharply through my nose when her nails cut in deeper on my thigh.

Fuck.

Tori's fingers relaxed. She bit her bottom lip.

"Yeah," I murmured, pulling my hand out from between her legs. I planted it on the floor next to her hip and crawled over her, smirking. "You fuckin' love me, don't you?" I asked, dropping to my elbows and pressing us together, trapping my hard cock between us.

Lip still caught between her teeth, Tori slowly shook her head.

"You love me," I stated.

She shook it quicker.

"Babe."

"I don't," she argued, voice quiet. "Really."

"*Really*, you do. That's your truth, Legs."

"It isn't. I like that you call me Legs."

"You like that *and* you fuckin' love me. Said it built in you and that it's more now. You said it. No denying what you said." I bent closer, hovering over her mouth that was pinching together tight. "You're way past likin' me," I murmured. "I hit your soft and I'm fuckin' stayin' there."

She pulled in a breath, blinking.

"How much do you love me, Legs?" I asked, watching her eyes jump between mine.

"There are steps between like and love. I said I *really* like you. That's the step I'm at," she debated softly.

"Skipped right over those steps. You love me."

"I didn't skip."

"You skipped."

"*No, I didn't!*" she snapped, bending her one leg next to my hip and planting her foot on the floor, then pushing off with all her strength and rolling us.

I laughed as my back hit the blanket. "Babe, just give it up," I said, tucking the pillow under my head. "We both know what you're feelin'."

"There isn't anything to give up, and I am not feeling anything other than what I just said," she argued, hands flat on my stomach as she pushed up to her knees and slid down, straddling my thighs. "I like you. I like a lot of things about you and I like those things a lot, and we can waste time arguing that it's only like and not love or you can lie there and shut your mouth for five minutes while I tell you what all I like." She huffed out a breath and pushed her breeze-blown hair out of her face, tucking it behind her ears. "Or at least some of what I like. I'll need more than five minutes to cover all of it," she added, holding my hips.

I smirked and lowered my gaze to her chest. I stared at her hard nipples, asking, "Can I tell you what *I* like?"

"I think we've covered that."

"I like your tits," I stated.

"I know."

"A lot."

"I got that."

"Wanna cum on 'em and watch you lick it up after."

Her legs tensed around mine.

I lifted my eyes to her face.

"Me, too," she said quietly, reaching back and drawing her hair over one shoulder. "I want that. I want all the stuff you want. I think I always did."

My chest tightened. I started breathing heavier.

Fuck me, this girl.

Holding my eyes, Tori leaned down and pressed her lips to my chest, kissing her way to my ribs. "I like how strong you are," she began, watching me as she spoke. "And how tall you are. We're at perfect hugging height."

I cocked an eyebrow. "Perfect hugging height?"

She blinked. "It's a thing."

"Right," I mumbled, suppressing a laugh as I tucked my hands beneath my head and boosted myself up higher. "Take your word on that. What else?"

Fuck, I felt arrogant, wanting her to list what all she liked about me while her sweet mouth moved closer to my dick. Even strange shit I didn't understand, like hugging height. I wanted to know it.

I wanted everything. Her body, her mind, her sanity. Having her break into my house or coming to my fucking work. I wanted her ruined.

I wanted Tori Rivera as fucked up and crazy about me as I was about her.

"I like how you...groom yourself," she continued to list. Her shoulders jerked. "I feel like that's important to mention."

My lips curled up. "Right back atcha, babe."

"I like how you watch me all the time. When I'm at work or if we're all hanging out at Syd's. Every time I look at you, you're already looking. It's like you're never looking at anyone else. And I like thinking that's true, even if it isn't."

I stared at her, mouth relaxing out of the smile I was holding, and Tori stared back. Not breathing. Not blinking.

She was waiting, wanting to know if what she just admitted was okay, if I liked it, too, and *fuck*, she liked how I watched her. She wanted me to do it and she wanted that shit to mean something.

It did. And I had no problem sharing.

"Go ahead and think that, babe," I ordered, watching her eyes flicker wider and feeling the breath she was holding release against my chest. "I told you, if it ain't you, I'm blind. Where the fuck else would I be lookin'?"

"It's not just that you look, it's *how* you look," she explained. "Like I'm precious to you or something. And I know that's probably just me wanting to see that, it's not really there and you're just thinking about having sex, but—"

"You got any idea what I feel when I look at you?" I interrupted, needing to shut down where her mind was going since that shit was toxic, wasn't true, and she didn't need to be thinking that.

Tori's head lifted as her hands flattened on my chest. Her breath was coming out heavier now. I could hear it.

"It's there, babe," I told her. "How you think I'm lookin' at you. For months, I've felt that."

She swallowed thickly, then licked her lips. "I like the kind of man you are," she stated, speaking a little louder and keeping her head raised and her big, round eyes focused on mine, blue orbs holding all kinds of truth and meaning in them.

My entire fucking chest got warm, like Tori had just lit a match and dropped it inside my rib cage. I closed my eyes and breathed deep.

Fuck. That felt good. And that was something I wanted to keep feeling.

"Say that again," I ordered, eyes opening to look at her.

She blinked. Her mouth lifted in the corner. "I like the kind of man you are," she repeated, speaking louder, more boldly. "And

I—wait! I'm not finished!" Tori shrieked through a giggle when I grabbed her wrists, yanked her down, and then flipped us again so she was beneath me. "Jamie!"

"Finish when I get inside you," I said, kissing my way down her soft, sweet body. Moving fast and frantic. Gripping her hard and handling her like I fucking owned what I was touching. "*Fuck*, babe, I…*what the fuck?*" I pushed her legs open, dipped my head, and gave her a long, slow lick.

"Oh," she moaned, fingers lacing through my hair. "W-what? What's wrong?"

I rocked back onto my heels between her legs and grabbed the sleeve of condoms off the floor, chest heaving, hands shaking. I felt like I was on something.

"*Fuck*," I panted, pushing a hand through my damp hair. "Telling me you like the kind of man I am and lookin' at me like you mean that shit more than anythin' you've ever said in your entire fuckin' life. Givin' me that shit after nine months of wantin' you. Wantin' nothin' *but* you. You claim me and then give me *that*. *Jesus*." I stuck the wrapper between my teeth and tore it open, spitting out the foil as I held her eyes. "Babe, you got no fuckin' clue."

I was referring to what that meant, what she just gave up, and what I was never letting her take back, and Tori was hearing that. She understood.

Sucking on her bottom lip, she nodded, letting me know she was following me. "I didn't mean what I said earlier at Whitecaps," she admitted as I got to work on the condom.

"I know."

"About you being that other type of guy, the one that only cares about scoring pussy. I—"

"Babe," I interrupted, meeting her eyes. "I know."

Tori nodded again and went back to sucking on her lip. Getting that, I went back to what I was doing.

"I love my dad," she whispered a breath later.

I paused, condom rolled halfway down my throbbing dick, and looked up at her, saying in a warning tone, "Legs," because, *what the fuck?*

She wanted to talk about him *now*?

"He's an amazing man," she continued, not heeding my warning. "Not just to his family. He's a great boss. Fair. Honest. And he's always been great with Syd. He's just, the best. The best man I've ever known."

My dick started going soft. I squeezed my eyes shut for a beat, breathing deep, then opened them to look at her again. "I get that you think that, babe," I said. "Straight up. You're feelin' appreciation for what I did and I feel that. But now is not the best time for you to be sharin' shit about your dad."

"I'm not just sharing. I'm making a point," she argued.

"Any chance you can make it without bringin' him up?"

"Probably not."

"Then save it," I told her. "My dick is out and we're about to fuck. Maybe make your point later."

She let out a breath. I watched her sit up and draw her knees to her chest. *Fuck me.* She was making her point now.

"Babe," I pleaded.

"Syd told me about you offering to help Brian after his accident," Tori began, ignoring my final attempt at shutting this shit down.

I took my hand off my dick and rubbed my face as she continued.

"That might've been the nicest gesture I've ever heard about. I didn't tell *her* that 'cause I knew she'd tell you, but I was thinking it. And I saw how you were with your sister, wanting to protect her and get her safe, and then there's just how you are with Syd. You're sweet with her. Like you care about your friend being happy and wanna show that by being good to his girl. She's my best friend. I want everyone treating her good and you treat her good. That means something to me."

I dropped my hand to my thigh and looked at Tori then, hearing in her voice what all that meant to her and wanting to see it in her face. And I didn't know what she saw when I looked, but whatever it was, it had her coming closer.

She pulled her legs to the side and slid them beneath her, then she was up on her knees and right in front of me, putting my face between her hands and breathing against my mouth. "And then there's what you did for my dad," she continued, staring deep into my eyes. "And what you've done for me. All of it. Being there for me and taking care of things and making promises. Just being *you*, Jamie. And I guess...well, the point I'm trying to make is..." She paused to swallow. Her chest started heaving, and three breaths later, she declared, "Now he's the second best."

I blinked. Everything started burning up. I tried to breathe, but I couldn't.

Tori was telling me I was the best man she'd ever known. She was giving me that.

Kerosene.

My chest was already on fire, and Tori Rivera just dumped a bucket of kerosene on the flames.

"Jamie?" she whispered, dipping closer, her eyes anxious as they searched mine.

"Changed my mind," I said, reaching between us and getting my dick ready that was so fucking hard now I could feel my heartbeat in it. "You got somethin' you wanna share with me, some point you need to make, no matter what I'm doin', what *we're* doin', if my dick is out or if we're already fuckin', you share it, babe."

Condom on, I squeezed the base of my dick.

Tori gasped when I palmed her ass hard and lifted her off her knees, getting her legs out from under her so she could wrap them around me.

Her arms slid around my neck. Her ankles linked around my back. I held her weight with one hand and moved the other between us, positioning my cock.

"Don't care what it is, I want it the second you're wantin' to give it. You hear me?"

She nodded, mouth opening and head dropping back as I slid in the first inch.

"Oh, God," she panted.

I lowered her slowly onto my cock. Another inch. Another.

God, she felt so fucking good.

Tori moaned deep in her throat and closed her eyes.

"Didn't think you could top what you already gave, then you give me that." I rammed deep, thrusting my hips and sinking all the way inside her. Tori cried out. I slid my one hand around her back, slid the other up to her neck, gripped firm and tipped her head down, forcing her to look at me.

She opened her eyes, parted her lips, and whimpered.

"You fuckin' *give me that*," I repeated, seeing understanding brighten her eyes. I pulled her closer. Our lips touched. "Nine months was nothin', babe. I would've waited *years* for you."

Tori gasped against my mouth. Her limbs tensed.

"Gonna fuck you now," I said as I tipped forward, putting her back on the floor and my hips between hers, getting her beneath me.

She was whispering *yes* and *please* as she kissed my mouth, my jaw, my neck. Her teeth found my shoulder when I dragged my hips up and sank home.

I dropped lower and kissed her, sliding my tongue along hers, and then I was pushing back and putting weight on my knees. "Gotta watch you," I said when she started whimpering and reaching out.

The sun had set now, and the glow from the fire warmed half of her face. I held her hips up and started thrusting, pulling her into me, sinking deeper.

Deeper.

Deeper.

Fuck.

She was swollen and so fucking wet, her thighs glistened. I felt her tightening. I heard her breaths growing tenser. Quicker. Her nails scratched at my stomach and sank into the backs of my thighs. And then she was coming, back arching and head falling back as my name rolled off her tongue in soft little begs. I fucked her harder. Faster. I sank deeper. I wanted her to feel this tomorrow. And next year. And if there was life after this, I wanted her feeling me in it.

Tori came down but only a little. I kept her there. Right there. I wouldn't stop building it.

I groaned, slumped forward, and held fistfuls of her hair, powering into her, our bodies slapping together, our mouths desperate, hands desperate, voices desperate.

We were fucking but we weren't. This was more. It *meant* more.

I loved her.

God...*fuck*, I loved her. I had for a while.

Tori kept clinging to me, kept pulling me closer, kept kissing and licking and biting, and I fucked her wild. I was insane for this girl. Crazy shit was coming out of my mouth, words I didn't realize I was feeling until it was too late and I was speaking them against her lips and in her ear when I took her from behind. Hand wrapped around her throat, I told her I needed this, that nothing had ever felt this good and that I wished I wasn't wearing a condom. *Forever* and *feel me* and *love me, say it*. And it was a game, me telling her *you love me* and her shaking her head and moaning in my ear, *no*, over and over when we both knew. We *knew*.

It was a game, but it was *our* game.

Tori moaned and pleaded, "Harder," and sank back against me, getting me deeper, and then she was coming again, body trembling in pleasure as my fingers rubbed her clit.

"Jamie...oh, God, Jamie!" she cried, reaching back and grasping at my hip as I kept pumping.

"Close," I groaned. My spine burned. "*Fuck*, baby, come on."

I pulled out and stood, tearing the condom off and stroking my cock as Tori spun around and knelt in front of me with her hands under her tits.

"Do it," she whispered.

I groaned and pushed her hair out of her face so I could watch her lips part and the heat in her eyes as I shot my cum all over her chest, and she wasted no fucking time dipping her head and licking it off.

And when she was finished, Tori slowly lifted her head, dragged her tongue across her bottom lip, savoring me, and smiled.

My chest was so fucking tight, I was waiting for it to split wide open.

Tori's eyes widened. She looked down and moved her hand between her cleavage, saying, "I, uh, missed some. Can you—"

"Get you a towel," I offered, watching her head lift and then drop slightly.

"Thanks," she whispered.

I bent and grabbed the condom and wrapper, disposing of those in the kitchen trash on my way to the bathroom. I washed off. I got the hand towel damp, returned with it, and handed it off to Tori so she could clean herself up. And while she was doing that, I claimed the pillow and stretched out on my back in front of the fire.

My eyes closed. I felt her warm body pressing against my side and the soft cotton of another blanket pulling across my feet.

"I'm cold," she whispered.

Eyes opening, I wrapped my arm around her, hand palming her ass and hauling her closer.

Her head hit my chest, her arm curled around my stomach and her leg bent and pressed on top of mine.

With my other hand I drew the blanket up and covered her to the tops of her shoulders.

I didn't need the blanket. She made sure of that.

Those flames were still burning.

"I heard it might just be his pressure being high," I said after my head hit the pillow, letting her know I had been updated on her dad. "Travis said he gave him a prescription to take. Told him to get some tests done."

"Does your brother make house calls a lot?" she asked softly, watching the fire.

"No."

"Ever?"

"No."

"Does he even *live* in Raleigh?" she questioned, head popping up and round eyes meeting mine.

I smiled and grabbed her arm, giving it a tug until she dropped back down, head hitting my chest again. "He lives in Durham. Doesn't make house calls, but we're close, and if I ask him for shit, he does it. Goes both ways," I explained.

"Do you have any other siblings?" she asked, blinking at the fire.

"None you haven't met already."

"I'd like to meet Travis, too, if that's okay. I want to thank him."

"Think we can arrange that."

Her head dropped in a nod. She sighed.

I closed my eyes again.

"I like your heart," Tori whispered seconds later, and my eyes shot open.

Fuck.

"Baby," I breathed.

"I would've died waiting years," she added.

The arm I had around her tightened. I lifted my head and saw Tori was watching me with blue eyes wide and focused.

"I would've," she whispered, then she snuggled closer, pressed her cheek to my chest again, gave me a squeeze with her arm around my waist, and closed her eyes.

Just like that. Denying she loved me and then she gives me *that*.

I didn't press for the truth anymore. I didn't ask Tori if she was ready to admit she loved me.

I dropped my head onto the pillow, kept my hold on her and closed my eyes. For tonight, this was enough.

It was everything.

Chapter Seventeen

TORI

Fifteen minutes later

His breaths were relaxed now. Slow-paced and sleepy.

I peeked my eyes open and blinked at the flames dancing behind the glass. I pressed my hand flat to his heart.

"Jamie," I whispered.

Nothing.

He breathed out and stayed deep inside his dream.

I shifted until my chin was resting on his ribs, then lifted up and peered into his face. Eyes closed. Lips touching, not parted. And head turned. The glow from the fire crawled up his shoulder to his neck. His face was shadowed.

"Jamie," I whispered again, watching him. Listening.

Nothing. His body didn't move aside from his chest lifting with his next breath.

I dipped my head and touched my lips to his skin, hand over his heart still and eyes focused and inspecting.

I breathed out. I breathed in.

"I love you," I whispered. Then I waited.

Nothing.

His arm around my back didn't tense. His lashes didn't flutter.

His mouth didn't smile or open to tell me *know that, babe* and then maybe, *maybe* admit the same.

Jamie didn't move. He didn't speak.

He never heard me.

Chapter Eighteen

JAMIE

I woke up alone on the floor with the blanket thrown over my waist.

The fire was out, meaning the timer either turned it off or Tori did, and the light was on in the kitchen, but when I sat up and stood, pushing my hair out of my face and looking around, the room was empty.

It was pitch black outside. The clock on the stove read 12:07.

If she fucking left . . .

"Legs," I hollered, rounding the couch and crossing the room when she didn't answer.

The laundry room was next to the kitchen, and I stopped in there and pulled on a pair of mesh running shorts before cutting through the dining room I never used as a dining room—had a pool table set up in there—getting to the front door, swinging it open, and peering outside.

The streetlamp at the end of the driveway was shining on Tori's car. It was parked behind my Jeep.

She hadn't left. *Good.*

Now where the fuck was she?

I closed and locked the door, then hit the stairs and took them two at a time. The upstairs hallway was dark, so when I reached the top, it was obvious which room Tori was in.

My old room.

Fuck yeah. I was gonna get to see her in there. Been wanting that.

I stopped in the doorway, going unnoticed, and pressed my shoulder against the frame, pulling my arms across my chest as I watched her.

Tori was dressed again, wearing the frayed jean shorts and steel blue sleeveless top she showed up in that felt like silk and billowed at her waist. Her back was to me and her hair was down—long, tangled waves that looked messy from fucking. She was barefoot and stood on her toes to peer at the trophies on the back of my old dresser. Her calves tensed. Her hands curled around the beveled lip of the wood, keeping her balanced.

I loved her barefoot in my house. I loved her clothes on my floor. I wished they were still there.

"Wow...*seven*? Really?" Tori mumbled under her breath, pausing to stretch higher on her toes, then whispering, "That's so cool."

"Seven what?" I asked.

She startled with a gasp and spun around, hand pressing to her chest as it heaved. "*God*, Jamie, you scared the life out of me." She took several deep breaths and tucked a stray curl behind her ear. "Wear a bell or something."

I smirked and pushed off from the frame, crossing the room and repeating, "Seven what?"

Tori looked from my bare chest to my face, then glanced behind her and pointed over her shoulder. "You were seven when you won that trophy. That just seems so young to me." She turned back around. "Was that the first competition you ever won?" she asked, looking up into my eyes after I reached her.

I nodded, knowing which trophy she was talking about. I didn't need to search it out and, instead, kept my gaze on her and the red glop she had smeared on her bottom lip.

It glistened near the corner of her mouth.

"How'd you know I was seven?" I asked, taking her face between my hands and bending down. Her eyes froze. She pulled in a breath a second before I drew her lip into my mouth and sucked, tasting sweet strawberry filling on my tongue. "Been eatin' my Pop-Tarts?" I teased, leaning back but keeping hold of her face.

Her mouth twitched.

"I was hungry," she admitted softly, sucking a little on her lip now, too. "And the, uh, trophy was dated."

"Doesn't explain how you know I was seven."

"I may have looked at your license. I know you're twenty-eight." She watched my brow arch, then looked back into my eyes. "Your wallet was on the counter," she explained on a quick voice. "I saw it when I was getting my snack and was curious what your middle name was." She tipped her chin up and smiled, whispering, "*Jamie Carter McCade.* I like it. I like that you're four years older than me, too."

"Yeah?" I mumbled, sliding my thumbs along her soft pink cheeks.

She nodded, then her face fell. "Is it okay that I did that?" she asked, eyes troubled as they jumped between mine. "I just looked at your license. I didn't look through the whole wallet."

I shrugged, explaining, "Lookin' 'cause you wanna know shit about me. I want you knowin', babe. You can look all you want."

Tori smiled again, liking my views on her snooping through my shit. "'Kay," she murmured.

"What else do you like?"

She smiled bigger. I felt her warm hands take hold of my hips.

"Well, just going off your license, I like that you're six-three and an organ donor," she shared, stepping closer until I felt the fabric of her shirt against my stomach. "And that you're a Scorpio. The Aries in me *really* likes that."

I slowly shook my head. "Jesus," I chuckled. "You follow that shit? You sound like Quinn."

"No," she giggled. "Not really. I just know which signs I'm compatible with and which ones to stay away from."

"Yeah?" I dipped my head until our foreheads touched. "Should've checked my wallet nine months ago, babe. Saved us the time."

"No way. Then we never would've had our bet."

"And?"

"And I liked our bet," she admitted sweetly, rubbing her hands up and down my back. "Didn't you?"

"Like what we're doin' now better."

"Yeah," she sighed. Her nose wrinkled. "This is okay."

My brows grew tight.

Tori watched this happen and laughed quietly, then she linked her hands behind my back. "You have eleven trophies in here and eight in your other room," she stated.

"Yeah."

"Plus six in that office downstairs."

I smirked. *Fuck yeah.* She'd gone around counting.

"And one in the bathroom," she continued. "Which, I really don't understand that placement but I'm assuming it's there so guests will see it."

"Piss excellence. Might as well have a trophy for it," I told her, face serious.

Tori leaned back, studying me. "You did not just say that."

"Said it. You read the plaque?" I questioned. "Says on there what I won."

Her eyes shifted away, then her head turned, her brows knitted, and she started biting the inside of her cheek. She was thinking hard. And she looked really fucking sweet doing it.

"Babe," I laughed, ready to give up the lie.

"It said, *East Coast Surf First Place Champion, 2002.*" Her head snapped back and she made a face, half smiling, half scowling. "Ha. You did *not* win that for using the bathroom. Nice try."

I stared down at her, at her smiling lips and her bright eyes and the freckles splattered on her nose, trying to breathe but fighting against an impossible weight pressing heavy on my chest.

"You know what it says," I mumbled, sliding my hands to her waist and holding tight there. "What year I won it. Twenty-six trophies, all saying different shit, and you can spit that out like it's nothin'." I turned her and started backing her up across the room, taking the four steps to reach my old bed.

Tori gripped my biceps, eyes soft and curious and smile slowly fading. "I have a good memory," she revealed. "A really good one. Just a glance and—"

"How long you been awake, babe?" I interrupted.

Her cheeks heated. "An hour."

"Yeah." I pushed her back, slid my hand around her waist, and hoisted her higher up the bed. I crawled over her body and gave her my weight, forearms on the mattress and hips between hers. "Been lookin' at 'em. Studying 'em. Wantin' to know me," I growled.

Her limbs were warm against my back and hips. She pushed her hands through my hair and held it out of my face.

"I took pictures, too," her soft voice admitted.

My brows hit my hairline.

She watched this happen, pulled in a breath, met my eyes again, and added, "And a short video, which can *totally* be deleted if you—"

Hand on her cheek, I slid my thumb over her lips and pressed, shutting her up.

"Got a meet this weekend in Cocoa Beach," I shared. "I want you comin' with me."

Tori's breaths were sharp as I moved my thumb away. I curled my fingers around her jaw.

"Um"—she wet her lips—"where is Cocoa Beach exactly? Is it close?"

"Florida ain't close unless we're flying," I answered. "Flights already booked, but if you're down and can't get one last minute, we can drive. We'll leave Friday and come back Sunday."

"I can't go," she rushed out. Her eyes heavy with sadness. "I, that's too last minute for me to get coverage. I work all weekend."

"Can't ask one of your girls to help you out?"

She shook her head. "No. They're all either working or have stuff going on," she explained. "Syd's taking Brian up to meet her mom. They're leaving Saturday. And I know Kali doesn't have a sitter on Sunday 'cause I'm covering for her." Tori's fingers tensed in my hair and gave a gentle tug. "I would love to go. Really. I wish I could."

"I'll give you enough time for the next one. It'll happen," I shared, not wanting her to feel bad for this since she couldn't help the conditions. They fucking *sucked*, but she couldn't help them.

"But you wanted me at this one," she said, speaking quietly.

"Want you at all of 'em, babe."

Tori's lips slowly parted. Eyes searching, she slid her palms to my cheeks, asking, "Why?" on a whisper that sounded fragile and hope-filled and she must've heard it, because she blinked and smiled shakily to cover her truth. "I mean, you're gonna win with or without me, right?" Her voice was confident now. "You always do. *Jamie Carter McCade* never loses."

"Never had my woman watchin' me either," I returned. "I'll give you notice and then I'm gettin' that, babe. And straight up? Pretty sure that's gonna feel better than a win."

Her shaky smile vanished. She stared deep into my eyes.

"What?" I asked.

"I'm your woman," she stated quietly, not questioning it, but as if she was repeating it for herself, hearing it for the first time and letting it settle inside her.

"Yeah, Legs," I said on a chuckle. "I thought we covered that."

"I'm your woman because you claimed me." Her voice was louder. Quicker. Nearly panicked. Her eyes were wider. "You did it months ago. You were coming to Whitecaps to see *me*. Everyone knew that. They all saw you claiming me. You did it out in public in front of everyone, Jamie. And I"—she shook her head, whispering—"I didn't do that."

"You didn't do what, babe?" I asked, brow furrowed, not understanding what the fuck she was going on about.

"Oh, my God," she whispered instead of answering me, eyes falling away. "I screwed it up. I didn't do it right. No one knows I've done it. There was no one else on that beach but us. Nobody saw me. Nobody knows."

She was breathing fast and talking even faster. Tori was straight up freaking out.

"Babe, you need to relax," I told her.

Her eyes sliced to mine again. "Are you crazy? I can't relax! I screwed it up!" she shouted.

I flinched, head jerking back. "Screwed *what* up?"

"You need to take me somewhere," she ordered, ignoring me. Her voice rough and quick and demanding as her palms pressed firmer to my cheeks. "Somewhere with people, Jamie. *Lots* of people."

"Right," I chuckled. "Get on that first thing tomorrow." *She was fucking nuts.*

Tori's head lifted off the mattress. "That won't do at all," she hissed, inches from my face. "We need to take care of this now. It's urgent."

"Middle of the night. You forgettin' that? Where we gonna—"

"It's urgent!" she cried.

"It can wait, babe. Whatever the fuck it is."

"No it can't!" Tori argued. "I need to claim you in front of people and you need to take me someplace where I can do that! I want everyone knowing, Jamie. *Everyone.* You're mine and I want them knowing!"

I blinked. That weight that was pressing on my chest threatened to crack bone and crush me beneath it. *"Fuck me,"* I muttered, staring deep into her eyes.

"See?" Her head dropped back down. "Now do you really want to wai...oh, okay. You don't."

She giggled when I pushed to my knees then to my feet off the bed, taking her with me as I stood.

"Might wanna mention when somethin's urgent, babe. Save us the back-and-forth shit," I teased as I hurried her out of the room.

* * *

Tori was tapping her foot impatiently and surveying the inside of The Seaside Diner, arms crossed over her chest, wearing a scowl and looking ready to flip the fuck out on someone.

I was standing back, also had my arms crossed over my chest, wasn't giving a fuck about anyone else in the room but her, and couldn't scowl 'cause I was too busy keeping my laughter quiet so she wouldn't hear. All bets were off if she did flip the fuck out, though. I was cracking up if I saw that.

"Unbelievable," she mumbled, lifting her hand in the air, then letting it drop to her thigh before turning her head to look at me. "There's five people here. And I'm counting the waitstaff."

"One a.m., babe," I reminded her. "What are you expectin'?"

"Enough people to fill a canoe would be nice." She sighed, shoulders sagging. "There's nowhere else we can go?" she asked.

"Head west and hit a different time zone," I suggested.

Tori stared at me for a breath, contemplating this, then shook her head and rubbed at her sleepy eyes with her knuckles. "No. That would take hours. And we'd probably end up getting somewhere at one a.m. and be stuck going to a diner with five people in it." She dropped her hand and looked at me. "I don't know. I guess this will have to do."

I smiled, liking how this was bothering her. She wanted this place packed. Tori was wanting everyone to see us together. I felt like I'd been wanting that my entire fucking life. Couldn't remember not wanting it.

"Whatever you wanna do, babe," I said. "Either way, I'm gettin' somethin' to eat."

Her brow furrowed. "What? We're not eating," she argued.

"We're eatin'."

"No, we're not. I'm claiming you and then we're going back to bed."

I shook my head, smiling.

Tori brought her hands to her hips and shot me a challenging look, head tilting and lips pursed.

"Babe, don't make me force your ass into a booth," I threatened. "Gettin' somethin' to eat since we're here, I'm hungry, and I know they got good biscuits and gravy. Good pancakes, too. Gonna sit and eat and you can claim me while we do that. Then after we're done eatin', we're getting back to bed. But I'm eatin' first. Food smells good and you ate all my Pop-Tarts." I smiled bigger when her eyes doubled in size. "You ever eat here? Biscuits made from scratch."

Tori blinked and gathered breath through her nose. "I had *one* Pop-Tart, Jamie," she snapped, tipping forward for emphasis. "And the other one is still in the pack. I left it for you."

"Sweet of you," I murmured, mouth lifting.

"Oh, I'm regretting it. *Believe you me*," she shot back, going even heavier with the attitude.

Laughing, I shifted my attention to the waitress when she walked over and stopped at the podium. "How'r ya'll doin'? Just two?" she asked, grabbing menus.

"Yep," I answered, stepping up and putting my hand on Tori's back.

I was preparing to force her ass into a booth.

"Great. Right this way."

"He's with me," Tori rushed out, halting the waitress as she was turning to lead us.

I stopped moving, stopping pushing Tori forward. My chest went motherfucking *tight*. *Fuck*.

The older woman's eyes widened in question. She kept her smile. "Pardon?" she asked, looking from me to Tori.

I looked down then, too, turning my head and meeting eyes that were shining, full of beauty for me and want for this moment. She was excited and sure and calm—this wasn't scaring her. It was like Tori had been saying this shit daily to herself and out loud for months.

"He's mine. He's with me," she repeated, voice so fucking sure. She looked back at the waitress as her arm slid around my back to my waist and held tight. "I just wanted you to know that. And everyone, so if you have an intercom system I could use? I don't want anyone missing it in the back."

"Jesus," I mumbled. I bowed my head and held my laughter inside my chest.

"Oh, well, we don't have one of those, but that's very nice, dear," the waitress replied. "You got that love inside you, it's best to share it. I don't think anyone would mind if you made a quick announcement, that is, if you're feeling inclined."

I looked at Legs again, brows lifting and face stuck in a grin. That shit was permanent.

She looked back at me, tipping her chin up and wearing the sweetest fucking smile I'd ever seen in my entire life. "I'm gonna do it," she whispered excitedly.

"Babe," I murmured, and that one word, *fuck*, that one word held so much feeling and meaning and promise—for her and for us, and she felt that.

Sucking in a breath so full it felt like she was draining all the air straight out of me, Tori turned her head to face the room, rolled up onto her toes, squeezed her fingers into my side, and did it.

My woman claimed me in front of five people at 1 a.m. in the middle of a diner, saying I was hers and everyone needed to know it, and informing those five people to spread the news around after giving out our names, which really had the waitress smiling and looking pleased to be working that night and a witness to this announcement.

Nobody else seemed to give a fuck. The two construction workers sitting at the counter or the old man sitting alone at a booth. The cook didn't seem to care either.

Didn't matter, though. That didn't stop Tori from saying it. Didn't stop me from feeling it either.

It did, however, still prove to be not enough of a crowd for her, and Tori made that known when she dug her phone out of her back pocket and sent out a mass group text after making that announcement.

"What'd you say?" I asked her after she tucked her phone back into her pocket.

"Same thing I just said. That you're mine and I'm yours and I'm claiming you. And for them to spread the word." She smiled big.

"Who'd you send it to?"

"Everyone on my contact list."

My brows lifted.

Tori got a text from Sunshine exactly one minute later. I didn't know what it said but figured it was something good since Tori was smiling reading it and replying. Shortly after that, I got a text from Dash.

She's crying her eyes out and won't go back to sleep. What the fuck?

Then he sent me another one.

Heard the news. Happy for you.

Aside from those two getting on us, the phones had been quiet.

"You're incredible," I whispered against her cheek.

With her legs thrown over one of mine, Tori leaned into me, giggling and sucking pancake syrup off the side of her thumb.

We were sitting in a booth with enough food in front of us to feed a small army.

Turned out, claiming me worked up one hell of an appetite. After skimming the menu, Tori ended up ordering more food than I did.

"I'm so awake now," she murmured, licking her lips, smacking them, and setting her fork down on her plate. "Can this be our thing?" she asked.

"What?"

"Breakfasts at midnight. Here. Always here." She turned to look at me, reaching out and taking hold of my face. "I don't ever wanna sleep again," she whispered, grinning through her sugar high.

I smiled and spread my hand across her stomach. "Told you the food was some good shit."

"It's not the food."

I stopped smiling.

Tori stared at me for a breath, then she pinched her eyes shut, swallowed, shifted closer while keeping hold of my face, and when she was practically in my lap, opened her eyes and her mouth to give me something else, something important, I could tell, but her words were halted when our waitress walked over.

"How'r we doin'?" she asked kindly.

Tori bowed her head and grumbled under her breath. Her hands fell away.

Laughing, I slid my arm around her and gave her a squeeze. I kissed the side of her head, then looked up at our waitress, answering, "We're good."

"Can I get ya'll anything else before the kitchen closes? Our cook's about to head out."

Gasping, Tori's head shot up. Her eyes were panicked as she stared into my face.

"Babe, I think we're good. You still got another stack of pancakes," I told her, thinking she was freaking out about the kitchen closing.

My woman could eat. I fucking *loved that*.

"No, um ..." She looked behind her, saying, "We're good. Thank you." Then when the waitress moved away, Tori turned her head around to look at me again. "I need to tell you something," she said, gripping on to my faded black Hurley tee.

I looked down at her holding-tight hands and then back into her face. "This serious?" I asked, brows lifting.

"It is."

"You scared to tell me?"

She nodded, swallowing before admitting softly, "I'm just worried it'll mess things up. And God, I don't want that. I don't want to go backwards."

I felt my mouth twitch. "Don't gotta worry about that," I promised.

She shook her head, letting her eyes fall away. "That's sweet, but you don't know what I've done."

What she's done?

Jesus.

Now I was starting to get worried.

"Babe, just tell me. It ain't gonna mess shit up."

Fuck it. Whatever it was, I was so fucking deep at this point, she could plot to have my ass killed and I'd give her a pass.

Tori heard me promise this, looked at me, nodded, then closed her eyes again, so tight this time it made little wrinkles pop out next to them. "Up until very recently, I've been having Stitch do stuff to your food," she admitted.

Immediately, I started grinning. Not smiling. Fucking *grinning*. And not knowing when Tori would open her eyes again, I held that grin for a breath and then wiped it clean from my face.

"I was trying to get you to stop coming to Whitecaps," she continued, eyes still pinching shut. "And I thought maybe if you got sick from the food, you'd stop coming, but then you weren't getting sick and so I just kept doing it out of spite and 'cause I liked you but I didn't *want* to like you. Same with messing up your order all the time. It was stupid and childish and I'm so, so sorry. Please don't be mad at me." She peeked one eye open, then the other. "I'm really sorry, Jamie," she repeated, shifting closer again. "I don't think he was doing anything besides dropping it on the floor for five seconds. Honest. I think that was it. I had Syd requesting it, too, but then she started liking you and wanting us to be together, and I think she stopped requesting it once that happened. But every time I waited on you, I would do it." She brought her hands up to my shoulders, my neck. She leaned her face an inch away from mine. "I know I've probably messed this up," she continued, voice trembling. "You have every right to be mad and hate me and—"

Not being able to hold it in any longer, I dropped my head back and roared with laughter.

"Um, Jamie?" Tori's hands put pressure on my chest.

"Nine months," I choked out, eyes watering so bad I had to wipe underneath one. "Nine fuckin' months I've been eatin' food that's been dropped on that dirty-ass floor and you've been arrangin' that? Are you fuckin' with me?"

Tori's brows drew together. "No," she whispered. "I'm not fucking with you. I did that. I arranged it. It was called the Loser Special. That was my idea, too."

I burst out laughing again, propping my elbow on the table and sticking my face in my hand.

The Loser Special?

This was fucking fantastic.

"Jesus," I mumbled, wiping underneath my eyes again. "Even had a name for it. Goddamn, babe."

"I don't understand how you're reacting right now," Tori said, her voice soft and worry-filled.

Hearing her and the stress in her tone, I tilted my head, lifted it, and looked into her face. She wasn't crying, but she didn't look far from it.

"Legs," I murmured through a laugh, lowering my hand to the table. "What the fuck?"

"You're laughing," she whispered. "You're laughing and you should hate me."

"Why the fuck should I hate you?"

"'Cause I was awful. I've *been* awful. I've done awful things."

"Could've found out about that months ago. *And* you could've kept doin' it. Straight up? Wouldn't have mattered. I still would've been showin' up and lickin' my *fuckin'* plate clean." I flashed her a smile, laughing still. "Jesus," I mumbled. "You think I'm gonna hate you after hearin' that? Do you know what you just gave me?"

"I just admitted to messing with your food and enlisting other people to help me do it," she replied.

"You just admitted to wantin' me so bad, you knew the only way we weren't gonna happen was if you fuckin' killed me," I returned, reaching around her, grabbing hold of her hips, and sliding her closer until her ass was pressing against my thigh again. I leaned in, getting in her face. "You're right about that, babe. I'd have to be dead."

The corner of Tori's mouth lifted. She shook her head and lowered her eyes. "I never wanted to kill you," she argued quietly. "I wasn't even fully committed to not liking you. I pretty much sucked at it." Her eyes found mine again, then she reached out and held my face between her hands. "I'm sorry," she repeated, all sorts of meaning in her voice.

"Know you are, babe," I murmured. "Don't need to be, but I feel that."

"I still think you should hate me. Even if it's just for an hour."

"I've never loved you more than I do right fuckin' now," I shared. "And that's saying a lot, 'cause ten minutes ago I was crazy about you."

Tori sucked in the quickest, quietest breath. Her eyes were wide. Her lips were pressing together. She looked stuck somewhere between crying her eyes out and putting on the biggest smile of her life.

I grinned, unable to help it. "You fuckin' love me, girl. Look at you," I murmured, wiping my thumb across her cheek.

Tori blinked and allowed her lips to curl, then she let go of my face, twisted her upper body, grabbed her silverware, forked three squares of pancakes, and shoved them into her mouth, mumbling two words around her bite.

"So much."

Chapter Nineteen

TORI

Three days later

You win yet?

I sent my message, then glanced up at Nate's office door. It was still closed, so I looked down again, keeping focus on my phone while I stood behind the bar at Whitecaps.

I had been on it all morning, more than I'd ever been on my phone before while working a shift. Just reading and sending texts, not talking, but still. It was unprofessional. I knew that. I knew it before Nate caught me and then caught me again the two times he'd stepped out of his office today.

He didn't say anything, just gave me a look indicating the level of unprofessionalism I was hitting. I read it loud and clear, tucked my phone away, and got back to work.

Then my pocket vibrated again and I was reading and smiling and typing, doing this while keeping an eye out just in case Nate needed a third refill on his black coffee.

I couldn't help the sneakiness and the risking I was doing. Really . . .

Okay, that wasn't exactly true. I *could* help it. This could absolutely be helped. I just didn't want to. I wanted other things more.

I wanted to talk to Jamie. I wanted to be there with him on the flight to Florida he took yesterday morning. I wanted to be with him in his hotel room and do hotel room things, like have sex in the bed and in the bathroom, and if there was a desk, I wanted to be bent over it or have my butt hanging off the edge and my legs spread wide, because that's what you did when you shared a hotel room with someone you were seeing. You had vacation sex, and I wanted vacation sex with Jamie.

Our everyday sex was phenomenal so I *knew* vacation sex with him had to be out of this world amazing. I was really wanting to experience that.

More importantly, though, over everything, over holding hands on flights and neighbors in the next room complaining about the noise level and middle-of-the-night wall banging, I wanted to stand on that Florida beach and watch my man take first place in his meet today.

I wanted it badly. So, *so* badly. It was killing me not being there.

But there was nothing I could do about it. I couldn't do those things. Any of them. At least not this time. I had to work a job that never really felt like a job to me, until today and a little yesterday when I was thinking about Jamie alone in his hotel room. But now, right now, it was *really* feeling like a job and one I no longer wanted.

Ridiculous. I *loved* working here. I always did.

But today and yesterday and maybe for months, I loved Jamie, too. *I loved him.*

Name doodling and spare house keys and *can this be our thing* kind of love, which was why I was being unprofessional and staying on my phone as much as I was doing. I was excited for him and sad that I wasn't there and I loved him.

I loved him. I loved him. I loved him.

And I was certain he knew it, too.

I hadn't said it yet. Not really. Not so that Jamie could hear. I said *so much* and nodded and moaned *yes yes yes* when I was coming and he was in my ear, growling *you fuckin' love me, girl*, but I never said it. That was our game. I wouldn't say it then. If I did, we wouldn't have that anymore, and I wasn't ready to give that up. I wasn't sure I'd ever be.

I loved our game almost as much as I loved Jamie.

Maybe I would say it when he got back from Florida. Maybe I would say it a month from now or in the next message I typed. I didn't know. I was waiting for it to happen as much he was.

Love was an adventure. It should be spontaneous and irresponsible and a little crazy. Not planned for. Not overthought. I had no idea when I was going to say those words to Jamie, and I liked not knowing.

I wanted impulsive *I love you*'s and reckless desires. I wanted this how it always was between us—uncontrollable. Overwhelming. And never, ever contained.

The phone vibrated in my hand as a new text appeared on the screen. I smiled reading it.

Hasn't started yet. All these assholes got their girls here to watch them lose. Sucks for them.

God, he was so damn cocky. And I totally loved that, too.

Sucks worse for me. I wanna be there.

You are here, babe.

I felt my cheeks warm.

Oh, *yes*, I liked that. Jamie was saying I was with him even when I wasn't. That was seriously sweet.

I wanted to give him something seriously sweeter. So I pulled out my ticket book and flipped to the page I'd been doodling on all morning, snapped a pic of it, and sent it through with a caption.

You're here, too.

The page had Jamie's name scribbled all over in different sizes and fonts, some darker than others, with hearts and starbursts and decorative swirls filling in the white. And in the center was a thought bubble with the word LOVE deeply bolded.

Again, I wasn't saying the words, not exactly, but kind of, *maybe* . . . I was.

My phone started vibrating with a call as I was sliding my ticket book away, and although I had been using it all morning, I hadn't been talking on it.

Texts were one thing. I could be discreet with those, like I was doing right now by keeping my phone below the lip of the counter. But taking a call was different. That would be difficult to hide if Nate walked out.

Too bad I totally didn't care if Nate walked out right now and saw me. Jamie was calling and I wanted to answer it. So I did.

I was certain I could convince Nate of this phone call's importance later if I needed to. And if I couldn't, well, I did have a nice run here.

"Hey," I answered through a smile, keeping my voice down. I turned to face the kitchen, listening to beach breeze and the rushing of waves in the background. I could hear the crowd gathering around to watch.

If I closed my eyes, I could pretend I was there watching, too.

"That from today?" Jamie asked, talking about the picture. "Fuck. Can you hear me? Hold up, I'm movin'. There's too many fuckin' people over here."

"I can hear you." I chuckled at his irritation, then followed up my laughter with an honest, "Sort of," lifting my shoulder as I said it.

The background noise grew quieter in my ear. I could tell Jamie was still outside near the water, but he was away from the crowd now, not standing among them.

"Better?" he asked.

"Better."

"And?"

"It's from today, yes."

"You got more of those?"

My mouth twitched. "Pages and pages," I answered honestly.

"*Fuck*," Jamie breathed, and I knew right then how much he thought of the picture I'd sent him.

It was totally just like saying the words.

"Wanna be here," he went on telling me, talking about the meet. "I haven't won this yet and been wantin' to win it. Got my sponsors here. Got people who came out to see me, no one else, but I'm two seconds away from saying fuck it, you know?"

I bowed my head, heart swelling and that funny, fluttering sensation warming my belly. "Yeah," I whispered. "I know how you feel. I totally hate it here."

"Yeah," Jamie replied, understanding. He knew I was crazy about this job. "I get back tomorrow," he continued. "Flights not landin' 'til late, but I wanna see those pages, babe. All of 'em."

"Okay."

"I'll come to you. Got my key so you don't gotta wait up."

"I'll be up," I told him, knowing there was no way I'd be able to sleep waiting on Jamie. I never could. Even when it had only been hours since I last saw him, I still twisted in my sheets restlessly and stared at the bedroom door.

He exhaled heavily in my ear.

"What?" I smiled. "Your fans follow you or something? Move around again."

"Years, babe," Jamie mumbled, his voice rougher and richer, carrying meaning.

He was definitely not talking about his fans.

The hand I had curling around the lip of the counter behind me curled harder. I lost my smile. Jamie was referring to how long he would've waited for me again. He was feeling that truth hundreds of miles away and making sure I knew he was feeling it.

I was. And right now, I did not need him making sure I was *feeling* anything.

"Damn it. Stop being so sweet," I scolded, looking up and checking behind me for Nate. His door was still closed so I turned back around, informing Jamie while I did that, "I'm already hating this place today. You're just making it worse."

"Makin' it worse for me just by breathin', Legs. I think you can handle me telling you somethin' I've already fuckin' said."

My mouth fell open. Oh, my God. *Seriously?*

Even when he was being a little dickish, he was *still* sweet.

"I'm gonna go before I set fire to this place and hop on the next plane," I told him, pinching the bridge of my nose. "You say anything else and I'm afraid that's what it's coming to."

Jamie laughed in my ear. I was completely serious.

I dropped my hand, grinning as I listened to that beautiful sound while turning toward the front of the restaurant. I spotted Shay tending to one of her tables, then looking near the door, I saw Kali leading Jenna, Brian's sister, and her seven-year-old twins, Oliver and Olivia, to an open booth in my section.

I'd met them a few weeks ago when Syd started having her Sunday family dinners.

Olivia jumped up and waved frantically at me when she caught my eye. Her pigtails bounced in the air. I waved back to her and Jenna. Oliver kept his attention on the game in his hand as he slid into the booth.

"Gotta go, babe. Shit's about to start," Jamie announced after he was finished sharing his amusement, but he was still grinning. I could hear it. "That okay, or are you lightin' a match?" he teased.

Yep. Totally grinning. I ignored his teasing and focused on a much more pressing topic.

"Text me after you win?"

"Call you," Jamie corrected me, letting me know a text wouldn't do. He was going to be wanting to talk to me after.

I could've argued and insisted on the text, but I didn't. Job be damned at this point. Plus I was certain I could sneak in another quick phone call somehow.

Which led to me agreeing and giving Jamie a "'Kay," instead of anything else. "Good luck," I added.

"Don't need it," he replied.

I sighed, was in the middle of an eye roll and about to tell Jamie I knew he didn't need luck, when he lit the match himself.

"Don't need it," he repeated, voice softer. "Like that you wanna give it, though, babe. Means somethin' to me. More than anyone else givin' me that."

I inhaled sharply through my nose, feeling it tingle. "Damn it," I whispered. "You suck. I'm hanging up now."

Jamie chuckled in my ear. "Later, babe."

I disconnected the call and stuffed my phone into my back pocket. Then I grabbed a short stack of napkins and three rolls of silverware from underneath the bar, moved out from behind it, and padded

across the room in the direction of the booth Jenna and her kids had
claimed.

* * *

My phone was vibrating in my pocket. Long vibrations letting me
know I was getting a call, not a text.

I immediately pictured Jamie standing on a podium, cocky smirk
in place, holding his first-place trophy in one hand while flipping off
his competition with the other.

Was he finished already?

I stopped pouring Oliver's sweet tea, glanced up, and saw Nate
was still out on the floor talking to his mother, who had stopped in
for a visit with Marley, Nate's adorable baby girl.

My boss was right there. Barely ten feet in front of me. *Crap.*
There was no sneaking a phone call now. Nate would totally bust
me. Three strikes and I was out.

Begrudgingly, and against all of my heart's desires, I ignored the
call and went back to pouring the sweet tea.

My phone stopped vibrating, then a second later it started vibrating again, and not indicating I had a voice mail waiting on me. No.
This was another call. Jamie didn't even bother with a message. He
was hitting Redial.

He was *really* wanting to talk to me. And I was *really* wanting to
talk to him. *Screw it.* I set the pitcher down, let go of the glass, and
reached for my back pocket.

Nate turned his head at that exact moment, as if he could fucking
sense my unprofessionalism from where he was standing and the
lengths I was willing to go to, and looked at me through his dark-
rimmed glasses with eyes that were hard and suspicious and calcu-
lating firing strategies.

At least, that's what I was seeing.

I flashed him a smile that was top-notch employee professional,
and resumed gripping the pitcher and the glass.

Nate looked away and resumed speaking with his mother. The
phone stopped vibrating. I closed my eyes and gathered breath in my

lungs, started to expel it slowly and calmly, hoping to embrace that feeling instead of going manic up in here, but nearly choked on my breath when my pocket started vibrating *yet again*.

My eyes flashed open, widened, and focused on Nate's profile. We were up to call number three.

Three. Three attempts wasn't just wanting to talk to me. Three attempts was *needing* to talk to me. Later wouldn't do. It had to happen now.

My heart started racing.

I spun around while digging my phone out of my pocket, bringing it in front of me after I was facing the kitchen so Nate couldn't see it. I looked at the screen, my thumb automatically sliding to unlock it so I could shoot Jamie a quick text of explanation when the name of the caller came into focus.

My thumb quit sliding. Jamie wasn't calling me right now. My mother was.

And after the final vibration cleared the screen a second later and my missed calls displayed, I saw it had been her calling me all along.

My stomach clenched. My heart was racing for an entirely different reason now. My mother never dialed me up urgently like this.

What if something was wrong? *Oh, God...*

Gripping my phone in my hand, I spun around and held it in the air, waving it and grabbing Nate's attention.

"It's my mom," I whispered, counting on his ability to read lips since my voice couldn't carry any louder right now.

Worry had its hand curled tight around my throat.

Nate nodded, then jerked his chin at the door to the employee lounge, indicating that was where I needed to take the call. I made it out from behind the bar before I was dialing her back, but I never made it to the lounge.

My mom answered on the first ring, and I heard her voice, her panic, which told me all I needed to know before she even uttered the words a breath before my phone hit the floor.

I never even bothered to pick it up. I was too focused on getting out of there and getting to my parents.

As it turned out, I did leave in the middle of a shift that day. But not to hop on a plane.

While my man was winning another title, I was driving to Raleigh Regional Hospital.

My father had suffered a heart attack.

* * *

"*Mom*," I groaned, covering my face with my hands as I stood at the foot of the hospital bed.

I had arrived minutes ago after hightailing it out of Dogwood Beach like a bat out of hell.

I shaved close to forty-five minutes off my three-hour drive time. I got cleared at reception and assigned a visitor's pass, was told my father's room number after screaming my demand for it, and ran through the ER with tears streaming down my face.

I was expecting the worst. My father hooked up to machines and possibly unconscious, or news that it was just too late, *we're sorry*, and *we did all we could do*.

My mother could've been calling to inform me of this devastation. However, I had no way of knowing since my phone was back in Dogwood Beach.

I was panicked, hysterical, and scared out of my mind.

So you can imagine my shock and alarm when I threw open the curtains to his room, darted inside, and saw the state my father was currently in. Sitting up in bed. Hooked up to machines but with nothing beeping, only monitoring. Eyes alert. Smile tugging at his mouth as he watched my mother's continuing freak-out.

That's right. The man was smiling on the day he'd possibly had a heart attack.

Possibly because I didn't know for sure if he'd had one or not. I was still trying for specifics. It was like pulling teeth at this point.

Dropping my hands to the foot rail and holding there, I frowned at my mother as she stood beside the bed, arms folded under her chest, foot tapping, and anxious eyes glued to the monitor.

My father had just revealed there was a chance he hadn't

suffered a heart attack. His exact words being, "Your mother exaggerates."

"Okay, you need to tell me *exactly* what the doctor said," I insisted, directing my words at either of them, not caring who answered, just needing *an* answer. "Was it a heart attack, or what? What are they saying?"

My mother's quietly admitted "They aren't sure" came at the exact time as my father's conceited and overly confident "Nope."

I pinched my eyes shut and shook my head. *Oh, my God. This was beyond frustrating.*

"*Mom,*" I snapped, looking to her again and waiting to continue until after her head turned and her eyes pried off the numbers flashing on the screen. "You said on the phone you were in the ambulance and they were telling you Daddy was having a heart attack."

"Well, that's what the paramedics thought," she replied, brow tightly furrowed. "He was showing symptoms of it. Chest pain. Shortness of breath. And he was sweating like crazy. They assumed that's what he was having."

"I was sweating 'cause it was so goddamn hot in that attic and I was working up there," Dad offered up, tugging at the collar of his hospital gown. "Christ. Get me my shirt. If I'm gonna be waiting around, I'm doing it in my own clothes."

"You are staying in that gown until they release you." Mom slapped his hands away, then pushed against his chest when he tried getting up. "And if you were sweating 'cause of the attic, how come you were still sweating in the ambulance? It wasn't warm in there."

Dad waved her off with a dismissive hand, looking away as he revealed, "They were poking at me and you were saying the Lord's prayer. I thought I was dying."

"Oh, so it's *my fault* you were showing symptoms? Is that what you're saying?"

Mom was leaning over the bed with her hands on her hips now. And I knew if I didn't step in soon, she'd probably throw my father into heart attack symptoms *once again*.

"So the paramedics thought it was a heart attack, but the doctor doesn't think that's what it was?" I asked, interjecting.

Holding her scowl, Mom straightened up, stared at my father for another breath, then turned to look at me. "They're waiting on some test results, but it could still be serious even if it wasn't technically a heart attack," she replied.

I breathed deep. *Stay calm,* I told myself. *If you freak, she'll freak, then freak out on him, and that can't possibly be good for his heart, attacked or not.*

"Okay." I nodded, reaching up and gathering my hair over one shoulder. I twisted the strands into a bundle so my hands stayed busy and my mother couldn't see how badly they were shaking. "Well, we just need to stay positive and wait. That's all we can do," I told them both.

Mom nodded once, agreeing with me, then reached for my father's hand and squeezed it on the bed. "That's all we can do," she repeated, softly smiling at him.

Keeping his hand, she reached back and pulled the chair closer to his side, sat it in, passed the smile she was wearing my way, then lost it when her eyes slid over my shoulder and focused behind me.

She stood out of her chair, lifting my father's hand off the bed and gripping on to it with both of hers. I spun around then and saw who my mother was reacting to. The muscles in my legs tightened and my knees locked.

My God...

It was Jamie, only older by a handful of years, I was guessing. And instead of board shorts, the man wore a white lab coat and had a stethoscope around his neck. Instead of overgrown wave-tousled hair and a permanent five o'clock shadow, he was clean-cut, close-shaven, and more *GQ* than model gone rogue.

He was Jamie G-rated. Smoke-free lungs, I was sure, and most likely had no idea how to pick a lock.

I preferred my boys dirtied up and restraining order persistent. This man probably took no for an answer. Jamie took it as a challenge.

Still, *wow*, the genes in this family were unreal. The McCade parents should've kept producing. They couldn't go wrong.

Dr. McCade stepped forward and glanced up from the paper in

his hand. "All right, so…" He paused, noticed me in the room, and lifted his brows in question.

I studied his face.

He had the same high cheekbones as Jamie. Same thin nose and ocean blue eyes. Same lean-muscled physique and summer-touched skin. *Beautiful.*

I guessed he worked out of this hospital? Durham was only twenty-five minutes away. That wasn't too long of a commute.

Damn. I wished Jamie's commute was only twenty-five minutes from here. I was dying to talk to him. And I would, as soon as I knew for sure what was going on. I didn't want to worry him if this was nothing. I needed answers first.

"This is our daughter, Tori," Mom shared, reading the question in Dr. McCade's eyes. "She just got here."

"Hi," I said, hands still twisting my hair into a tight coil.

He offered a friendly smile and a genuine, "It's nice to meet you, Tori. I've heard a lot about you."

I smiled back, giving that to him while internally hiding my amusement.

Full sentences. Polite. *Total G-rated Jamie.*

"Did you get the results back?" Mom asked. Her voice was small and stressed.

Dr. McCade nodded, looking toward the bed. "To the EKG, yes, and I'm confident in stating I do not believe this was a heart attack, Mr. Rivera."

"Oh, thank *God*!" Mom cried, bending down and pressing repeated kisses to my father's hand.

I let out an anxious breath.

"However," he went on, voice somber and drawing my head back around. "From the results here and the preliminary blood work, I do believe you are showing signs of heart disease."

The air in the room went colder. My stomach knotted up and my hands tightened around my hair. I heard the change in my mother's cries, her weeps of joy becoming distressful and doom-filled.

"What does that mean?" I asked. "What is that?"

"It's when plaque builds up in the arteries that supply blood flow to the heart," he answered, bringing his arms down in front of him and gripping on to his left forearm, his left hand holding the test results. "This is usually something that happens over time, and the symptoms, such as the chest pain, that feeling we thought was indigestion, those are all signs of it. It's something that *can be* life-threatening if it isn't treated. It can lead to more serious conditions, such as a heart attack, *but*..." He paused and directed his attention to my parents. Mainly my mother, I was guessing. "There are treatments we can do. Medications. Lifestyle changes, taking some of that weight off, Mr. Rivera, like I suggested..."

I looked at my father's large, protruding belly. It strained the material of his hospital gown.

He played Santa at the company Christmas parties every year. Kids loved him.

My mother released my father's hand and shot him a glare. "I told you he said you needed to lose weight," she hissed.

Dad scoffed, folded his arms across his chest, and looked back to the doctor, brows pinched together in irritation.

"On top of your pressure being elevated, your cholesterol is high as well. We'll need to bring that down. The weight loss will help with that, but I'm going to start you on some medication for it for now, as well as for the hypertension. That really should've been started already."

"Daddy," I scolded, turning to look at him. "You haven't been taking those?"

"I was getting to it," he returned. "Just got the prescription a few days ago, goddamn it. You and your mother need to relax. You heard him." Dad jerked his chin at Dr. McCade. "I didn't have a heart attack. I'm good to go, right? Get my meds and then I'm outta here."

I looked back to Jamie's brother, catching the shake of his head.

"You'll be here through Monday, Mr. Rivera," he informed my father. "I've ordered you a stress test. That'll let us know for sure if this is heart disease. I don't want you leaving without getting that done."

"And they can't do that *today*?" Dad gestured toward the door, face tensing even further and turning red behind his salt-and-pepper beard. "Got all these doctors and nurses here. What's everybody doin'? Get 'em in here. Let's go."

"John," Mom cautioned.

"Daddy, what's the rush?" I asked. "If you're here, they can at least keep an eye on you. That's not a bad thing."

"Princess, I don't like hospitals," he scoffed, leaning back against the pillow and folding his arms across his chest again.

"You need to fast for that test, sir," Dr. McCade advised him. "Monday will be the soonest we can do it."

"Oh, for Christ's sake." Dad shook his head, jaw clenched tight. "Well, I tell you what, if I'm gonna be here for two days, starvin' to death, I'm puttin' on my pants."

"Oh, my God," I moaned, hand coming up and covering my eyes.

That was my father's biggest worry. That his ass would show if he stood up. Not that he could have serious heart problems. *This was so embarrassing.*

Dr. McCade let out a chuckle. Hearing that, I dropped my hand and turned to look at him.

"You can put on your pants," he said, grinning at Dad and popping out those glorious McCade family dimples. *Sheesh.* "Just keep the gown on so we can access the leads on your chest."

Dad made a noise in his throat, a grunt in compliance, before shifting his attention to my mother. "You're gonna have to call Cal and let him know I'm not coming in on Monday. Give him a heads-up."

Cal was my father's second in command at the factory. He kept things running smoothly there when Daddy actually put time in at the office.

"I'll take care of it," Mom said sweetly, patting his shoulder. "You just focus on getting healthy."

"Right," he muttered, looking away as if he was irritated at her, too, but reaching up and grabbing hold of my mother's hand.

I smiled. Fighting and loving. They did it better than anyone.

Although Jamie and I seemed to be getting pretty good at that as well.

"I'll be in later to check on you," Dr. McCade said, meeting my eyes when I turned back around. He grinned at me, jerking his chin. "Legs," he said as a farewell.

My cheeks warmed. *Jamie told his entire family my nickname.*

I totally loved that he did that.

After Dr. McCade stepped out of the room, I walked over to the side of the bed, leaned down, and gave my daddy a kiss on the cheek, getting a "love you, princess" paired with an arm squeeze in return. Then rounding the other side, I received a bone-crushing hug from my mother, waiting until after she was finished before I asked if I could borrow her phone.

"Of course. Let me just make a couple calls first," she replied, spinning around and digging through her purse where it hung on the back of the chair. "Tillie and Georgette are probably going crazy through all this waiting."

Tillie and Georgette were my father's sisters, both living out West, Tillie in California and Georgette in Arizona. They adored my father more than anything in the entire world. His name wasn't John to them. It was Johnny, or Baby Brother. Baby Brother especially when they were doting on him, which happened nearly every time they came out to visit and absolutely every time they got him on the phone.

I swore they thought he was still ten years old sometimes the way they mothered him.

While my mom got to work on her calls, I claimed the other chair in the room and collapsed into it, drawing my knees against my chest. I wrapped my arms around them and dropped my chin on top.

And then I got comfortable.

Unlike her phone calls with me, my mother never kept it brief with Tillie or Georgette, but I always thought that had more to do with them and their insistence on staying on the line to gab. And in this circumstance, with my father being where he was, I knew she needed to give them their time.

So I waited.

I watched as nurses came in to check my father's vitals. I laughed at the serviceman they sent in after my father complained that the

TV wasn't working right, laughing because my father was telling the man how to do his job, then threatening to pop the leads off his chest and do it for him when he was taking too long with it.

Luckily, the man finished up before that threat was followed through with.

While my mom was waiting for Georgette to return her call, telling me I could use the phone after, I listened to my parents bicker about everything from the temperature in the room to the definition of *fasting*, which my father insisted allowed for occasional bites of food and one full meal.

After the twenty-minute call with Georgette, I finally borrowed my mother's phone, stepped out of the room, and dialed up Nate first. I told him about my dad and that I would be in tomorrow to cover my shift, then thanked him profusely when he said to handle things here and not to worry about it. He would see me on Tuesday.

Seriously? Best boss ever. I was never being unprofessional again.

Unless Jamie called or texted, then I'd just be *extra* careful about it.

I would've called Syd after speaking to Nate, and I wanted to, her voice would've been nice to hear, but I remembered just as I was dialing that she was having her mom time with Brian. That was important and something I didn't want to disturb. And since my father's situation was no longer life-threatening, or as life-threatening as we all thought it was, I figured I'd just wait and fill her in when I got back to Dogwood.

I wouldn't stress her out and take away from what she was experiencing. Never. She needed this.

Unfortunately, not calling Syd meant not getting Jamie's number from her. And since I didn't have it memorized yet and relied solely on it being programmed into my phone, I was stuck. I couldn't call him.

I couldn't ask him how his meet went. I couldn't explain why I had been silent with him for hours.

It worried me. I didn't want Jamie thinking I didn't care.

When his brother came back into the room to check on my father two hours after we last saw him, I charged at the man like a woman off her meds, gripping his lab coat and begging for Jamie's number, getting it, then letting go and calmly thanking him for everything he was doing for my dad, currently and what he'd done in the past.

I received an amused response to my insanity, McCade dimples and a billboard-worthy smile, then I snuck out of the room again and made my call.

It went straight to voice mail.

"Damn it," I whispered, listening to Jamie's recording as I dropped my head back against the wall. The line beeped. "Hey, it's me. Um, so, this is way late, I should've called you earlier, but I'm in Raleigh at the hospital with my parents. My dad sorta had a heart attack scare. He's okay. They don't think that was it. Or at least your brother doesn't. He's here." I laughed a little, looking down at the speckled tile floor. "God, you two look so much alike, it's weird. Anyway . . . " I paused to exhale a breath. The fingers on my free hand curled under my uniform shorts. "My dad'll be here until Monday so I'm gonna stay for a while. I don't have my phone on me, so when you get this, can you call this number back? I really wish you were here. Or I was there. I miss you. *God*, I miss you."

I shook my head at myself.

It had been a day. *One day.* That was it. I saw Jamie yesterday morning before his flight out and I was acting as if it had been weeks, or months. I was starting to forget what he smelled like. If I wasn't terrified of the thought, which I completely was, I'd drive straight to the ocean and stick my face in it.

Lifting my eyes when movement caught my attention, I watched Jamie's brother exit my father's room. He saw me and offered a kind smile.

I waved back, hoping he knew how grateful I was for everything he had done and was doing for my dad, and watched him move down the hallway and disappear into another room.

Then I grinned into the phone and whisper-pleaded before hanging up, "Never cut your hair, okay?"

* * *

I was at the beach.

Or at least near it. I could smell the water all around me. The salty air. The end of summer sunlight.

Dream Jamie.

God . . . So, so good.

I lifted my chin and inhaled lungfuls through my nose. My body hummed and my toes curled inside my sneakers. It was the best smell in the world. Jamie and the ocean and Jamie and sand and sunlight and *Jamie Jamie Jamie*.

I wanted his smell to fill me and stay there. I never wanted it gone. I never wanted to wake up.

I moaned softly inside my dream when the smell seemed to curl around me and tighten, drawing me nearer to it. I smiled and buried my face there. I burrowed closer, begging a quiet *please* to God to keep me under.

Dream Jamie chuckled. His laughter shook my body and warmed the skin beneath my overgrown bangs. I pictured his self-righteous smirk and sky-colored eyes. I felt his smooth, sin-speaking lips press to my forehead.

Like, really felt them. *Felt them* felt them. His laughter, too.

And his arms around me and his body beneath me and his heartbeat under my hand and *please please please* don't let me wake up.

"Baby," his soft voice whispered.

And even that felt real. Sounded real, too. Jamie's breath on my forehead. His voice seeping into my ears and into my heart. His finger under my chin, gently lifting and *wait* . . .

I peeked my eyes open, slowly because I was scared. Scared of leaving my dream and the Jamie I could feel, here, right here, right now, because I knew the second I opened my eyes, he would be gone, back to his hotel room in Florida.

And I would go back to struggling for comfort in an unforgiving hospital chair that had needed new padding a good ten years ago.

Only now even as I slowly woke up, it felt like the most comfortable place in the world. *Huh* . . .

Breath catching in my throat, my eyes fluttered, barely opening, lashes obstructing my reality, then the finger under my chin added pressure, craning my head back and I gasped the second I felt his full, perfect mouth nibble and nip at mine before pressing into a kiss.

It lasted a second, barely, and it was gentle and sweet, not dirty like Jamie always kissed me. These weren't lips that craved and needed. These were lips that cherished. That said, "Missed you," and "Fuck, so much, babe," and "Baby... Legs, look at me," and *wait* ...

Wait. *No... My God. How good was this dream?*

I pulled away from warm breath tickling my mouth and my cheek, slid my eyes fully open, and blinked at the face staring back at me.

I blinked again. And again.

Then I shot ramrod straight, peeling my body off rock-solid muscle, and slid my hands over cheeks that scratched and bit my palms. I pushed my fingers through too-long hair that was gritty from sand and salt water curled and *oh, my God oh, my God oh, my God*.

I sucked in a breath. My boy of summer smiled and made my heart dance inside my chest.

He was here.

"Oh, my God," I whispered into the dark room, quiet except for the beeping of the monitors and the sleepy sounds coming from my parents. "*Oh, my God*," I repeated, staring into surprising eyes, still whispering but sounding more urgent now. "What time is it? How did you get here? How did you..." I glanced over Jamie's shoulder and squinted through the window blinds, focusing in on the streetlights illuminating the parking lot. Then sliding my eyes back to his face and my hands to the tops of his shoulders, I leaned closer and asked, "Have I been asleep for *days*? How are you even here right now?"

I felt delirious and drugged from my dream.

Was it Sunday already?

Jamie laughed inside his chest. His smile lifted his cheeks.

"Travis," he stated, wrapping his arm tighter around my back and giving me a squeeze. "He called when he got word on your dad being here. I took the first flight out I could get. Fuckin' airline." Jamie's mouth hardened in irritation. His fingers tensed on my hip.

"Would've been here sooner if we hadn't gotten delayed on the tarmac waitin' on a gate to free up. I tried callin' you."

"I left my phone at work," I explained, frowning.

"Know that," he replied. "Got your message when we landed. I think your mom's phone is either off or dead. My call went straight to voice mail."

It was dead. I knew the second it happened, too, considering how glued to it I had been.

"She doesn't have her charger with her." I pouted. "I gave her a nice long lecture about the importance of always keeping an extra in the car in case of emergencies like this."

Jamie smirked. His arm around my back and his hand on my hip tugged me closer. "You fuckin' missed me, girl," he murmured in that teasing way he always did, running his nose along my cheek.

I closed my eyes, smiling and softly admitting, "Yeah," as my hands slid around his warm neck. "Like crazy. I've decided I can't handle you going to competitions without me. I need to be there, too. *Oh*"—my eyes flashed open and I leaned back—"do you have your trophy with you?" I asked him, then tilting on his lap, I looked on the floor beside the chair, spotting the black duffle bag he had packed for his trip. "I want to see it," I added.

Jamie said nothing. Righting myself, I watched his smirk melt into something softer.

"What?" I asked, not understanding why he was looking at me the way he was doing.

"Got the call from Travis right before it was time for my run." His shoulders lifted. "Couldn't do it. Knew I needed to be here, so I left. I dropped out."

"You *left*?" My eyes widened as I shifted closer. "You didn't compete?"

Jamie shook his head.

"But..." I stared into his eyes, trying to comprehend. "You said you were always wanting to win that one. That your sponsors were there. They didn't mind you leaving?"

"Don't know since I didn't ask what they fuckin' thought about it. I just left," he replied, not sounding remorseful about that decision one bit. "And yeah, I wanted to win that one. It would've been a nice title to claim, but I wanted to be here more than that. I didn't know how serious this was gonna be with your dad. I didn't want you havin' to go through this alone even if it wasn't serious, which, spoke to Travis and got the update. Glad to hear your dad's gonna be straight, babe. That's good. But honest? I got that update before I even boarded the fuckin' plane to come here and I still boarded it. I wanted you more than that win. Wouldn't be surprised if I felt that shit at every meet either, so don't be shocked if this is a recurring thing. I like that you wanna come with me, Legs, but I know that ain't gonna always be doable. You got a life here. A job you can't be skipping out on. I leave and come back a day later or, fuck, hours later without a trophy, you know why." He smiled, adding, "Ain't 'cause some asshole beat me out. That ain't ever gonna be the case."

I blinked. My chest starting rising and falling rapidly.

My God. Did he just say all that?

"Babe," Jamie prompted when I remained silent. His hand left my hip and cupped my face.

"I skipped so many steps," I whispered, scooting closer as my fingers spread along the back of his neck.

Jamie's eyes searched mine for meaning. For understanding. "Steps?" he asked.

I nodded. "To get here with you. How I feel..."

His face relaxed. Jamie knew what I was saying. He was following me. "Yeah," he murmured, sliding his thumb along my cheek and smiling softly. "Think we skipped 'em all, babe."

Oh, God. *We?* He was going to kill me.

"I am so happy I hit you with my car," I confessed, watching his brows lift and disappear behind his hair. "But not really, you know? Just..." I inhaled a shaky breath. "It started everything. It got us going. That bet."

Jamie's mouth lifted in the corner then. He understood.

Still, I kept going. I had so much more to say.

"I have no idea how long it would've taken me to quit fighting you and what I was feeling if it wouldn't have happened and I don't like thinking about it," I continued sharing, getting the rest of this out quickly. "I don't like thinking about the past few weeks without you, Jamie. I don't. I hate it. My only regret besides hitting you with my car and almost hurting you is that I didn't do it sooner."

His eyes went round.

"I had so many opportunities to run you over. I should've jumped on those," I explained. "Moving day at Brian and Syd's when you refused to get on your bike and allow me to back out of the driveway, I could've done it then. I should've. *God*, I could've been skipping steps *months* ago. Can you imagine where we'd be right now?"

Jamie's eyes were shining so bright they were lighting up that hospital room.

"You sayin' you wanna skip more steps with me?" he asked, beautiful grin stretching across his mouth as his hand slid to the back of my neck and curled there.

"I'm saying I just wanna keep going how we're going, no matter how crazy it feels or too fast or whatever, I love what we're doing," I replied. "I love every part of it, Jamie, and I don't wanna slow down. I feel like I have months to catch us up on and I'm gonna do that. It's my fault we aren't further along. Not yours. I'll get us there."

"Babe," he murmured, sounding ready to argue.

"I'll get us there. I promise," I urged, holding firm to my plan, moving closer until our foreheads kissed and whispering, "I'll give you all of my truths, I will. Just don't hurt me, okay?"

I felt a rush of air leave Jamie's body. His fingers on my neck squeezed, and I could read in his eyes what he was wanting to say, that I was crazy for thinking he *could* hurt me. That he ever would. But he didn't say those words.

He slanted his head, leaned in, and pressed his lips against mine, murmuring three words inside our kiss.

"Get us there."

And I knew he was talking about me telling him all of my truths while moving us further along to our catching-up point.

But I also knew that was Jamie's way of promising me he'd be participating in that. *Fully* participating.

Dream Jamie was amazing but he had nothing on the real thing. Absolutely nothing.

I slid my hand to his cheek and kissed him back, soft and slow, then I shifted in his lap so I was turned sideways again, both of my legs thrown over his and my head ducking underneath his chin. "Can you sleep?" I asked. "What time is it?"

He inhaled deeply, curling his arms around me tighter. "Late," he said. "I didn't get here 'til after eleven."

"Are you tired?"

I felt the shake of his head against mine. "Gonna stay up awhile. I'm sure your parents are gonna wanna know who the fuck I am. Guy they don't know holding their daughter..."

"Oh, they know who you are," I told him. "I had to explain that group text I sent out the other night. Both of them got it."

Jamie's chest rumbled with a laugh.

"Probably seemed strange," he said.

"Nah." I smiled, hiding my face so he couldn't see. "I mean, my dad didn't have much opinion about it, except that he wasn't too happy getting a text like that. That was understandable, though. He doesn't think anybody's good enough for me, but my mom got it. She understood the importance of claiming a man in the name of love. Women just get that stuff."

Jamie's arms around me tensed. I smiled bigger, flattening my hand to his chest.

"Night," I whispered.

His head shook against the top of mine. "Always dropping shit like that and then passing out on me," he murmured, and I could hear he was smiling, too. "What the fuck, Legs?"

"Shh." I snuggled closer.

He grunted deep in his throat.

After that, I fell asleep and slept soundly in Jamie's arms, only waking hours later when my father woke up and made that fact known to the entire room.

"I suggest you take your hands off my daughter before you lose 'em both," he ordered, voice threatening and louder than I'd ever heard. "I might look bedridden, son, but I assure you, I am not."

Introductions were a little tense after that, needless to say. But once I informed my father of Jamie's apparent love for firearms, something I found out when I was snooping around his house after our lovemaking by the fire—he had a gun cabinet in his office among the trophies—it was as if Dad hadn't caught Jamie passed out with his hand clutching my ass.

They got to talking about hunting and gun ranges and forgot my mother and I even existed, which was fine since we were busy whispering about the McCade family genes and how incredible their bone structure was.

Chapter Twenty

JAMIE

Five days later

"Legs!" I hollered, kicking the front door closed and tossing my keys on the entryway table.

I fished the piece of paper out of my back pocket and was already crossing the living room and searching for Tori when she called out from the kitchen.

"In here! I'm ..." She paused, eyes lifting from the bowl she was stirring when I entered the room. "Oh, hey." She smiled, red lips stretching wide. "I'm just getting these potatoes coated and ready to roast in the oven. Then I'll cut out the biscuits. Give me fifteen. We'll be ready to eat."

She went back to stirring.

Tori was cooking us dinner, something she hadn't done yet but felt was long overdue, this feeling coming over her last night while we were shacked up on the couch, watching TV and scarfing down the half-everything, half-just-pepperoni pizza I'd brought over.

Nearly finished with her second slice of pepperoni, she set her plate down on the coffee table and turned to look at me, stating, "I'm making you a home-cooked meal tomorrow. So don't be coming over with food. I got it covered."

Reading the look on her face as this being something important to her, that it was gonna mean something when she gave it and wanting her to tell me that, I'd asked why.

I was a fucking moron thinking she'd tell me the real reason.

Tori shrugged, picked up her pizza, took a bite, and answered around her mouthful, "Eating in is cheaper and better for you. I'm getting a belly."

She wasn't getting a belly. The little bulge she showed me after I called her out on it wasn't no fucking belly either, and truth be told, even if it was, I'd still be hard up. Tori could have a belly and *two* fantastic asses and I'd be wanting her nonstop like I was doing now. I told her that, too.

That led to us eating cold pizza and missing the rest of the Yankees game. Except I didn't miss nothing. Neither did she.

Now here she was, cooking something that smelled delicious. Any other night, I'd want to let her continue but not right now.

"That shit can wait," I told her, stepping up to the island and standing across from where she was working.

Tori stopped stirring, lifted her head, and narrowed her eyes on me. I started smiling. She had a dusting of flour on her cheek, a swipe on her forehead, and even more covering the apron she was wearing. Plus, she looked pissed, and Legs looking pissed dressed as Betty Crocker while looking like a fucking beauty queen was hard not to smile at.

"I have never in my life made biscuits that were *shit*, Jamie," Tori shared, heavy on the attitude. "I follow my late nana's recipe each and every time. The day I start making *shit biscuits* is the day I move out of the South."

"Babe," I started, but she kept right on going and cut me off.

"And no, shit or not, they can't wait. None of what I'm doing can wait." She gestured at the stove behind me with her hand not curled around the spoon. "I got everything timed perfectly with the pork chops, except the green beans, which have been cooking all day. They're ready whenever. But the rest? I mean, seriously. Do you want to eat cold meat and warm sides, because I sure don't."

Not waiting for an answer, Tori went back to stirring again, doing it more vigorously now and causing her overgrown bangs to fall into her eyes. The rest of her hair was pulled back into a ponytail, looked messy, and had flour sprinkled throughout it.

I slapped the paper I was holding down on the counter, rephrasing and repeating, "Legs, trust me, it can fuckin' wait."

Tori's hand stopped moving again. She shook her head to clear her hair from her eyes, then leaned over to look at the paper I was keeping flat. By the time her eyes reached mine, they'd gone soft. "Is that..." Her voice, free of attitude now, trailed off when I jerked my chin.

She pulled her lips between her teeth, released the spoon, and slid the bowl aside. Then she wiped her hands off on her apron and padded quickly to the fridge, where she pulled down a paper secured by magnets. Tori came around the counter to stand beside me and laid her paper next to mine.

Her throat worked with a swallow before she looked up, hands tucking the fallen pieces of hair behind her ears and then knotting together at her stomach. She looked uneasy all over again.

After everything that had gone down Monday, were we now back to this?

We were pulled off the road at a rest stop, getting five miles from the hospital before Tori was jerking me off through my shorts and forcing me to take us off the highway before I wrecked her car.

Didn't know what it was that had her wound up and needy like this. Straight up, it could've been several things.

I'd been gone one night, got Tori off over the phone, which didn't relieve her, just worked her up even further and had her missing the real thing twice as hard.

We were finally alone after the two days with her parents in that hospital room, not having privacy to do more than kiss and not really getting time for that either.

Or it could've been the news of her dad's condition after the test he had done that morning. Moods were high after that.

He had heart disease. Not typical good news, but it was good compared to what they'd been fearing. The fact that it was manageable had Tori and her mom breathing easy. That paired with Travis doing me a solid and saying he was gonna stay on top of her dad and routinely check in on him had Legs in high spirits.

I barely got us parked at the back of lot and concealed by a tractor trailer rig before she was climbing over the console, throwing my seat back, and straddling me.

Thought she was looking to give me a hand job. She wasn't, which was fucking great, but I wasn't prepared for what she was wanting right now.

"Babe," I murmured against her hot, hungry mouth. I groaned when her hand slid into my shorts and wrapped around me. "Fuck."

"I know," she whispered excitedly. Her hand felt like the warmest, tightest glove. Form-fitting to my flesh. "Someone could see us having sex, but I don't care. I don't care, Jamie. Let them see us. You stayed. You stayed for me."

I stayed.

Oh yeah. Right. Forgot about that. The other reason this was going down right now.

Tori figured I was leaving sometime yesterday to head back to Dogwood Beach. Made that known when we were getting coffees and looked ready to ride my shit right then when I told her I'd already called Dash, told him to cancel my lessons and that I wouldn't be in until her dad was released and she was leaving with me.

That could've been driving her. Or maybe it was a combination of everything that was motivating her to raise my hand job to a fuck. Whatever. She was feeling this and needing it to happen.

I was feeling it, too, needing it to happen probably more than she did, but like a dumbass, I wasn't prepared. And we hadn't been here before.

"Legs," I murmured, gripping tight to her hips as she stroked me.

Her skin smelled like the hospital soap she'd used this morning during her shower. Antiseptic. I missed the sweet sugared lotion she typically wore.

"I'll keep my top on. No one will see." Tori released me, leaned back on my thighs, and popped the button on her shorts. "Can you help me take these off?" she asked. "I need help."

I watched her fingers glide the zipper down.

I knew she was naked under those shorts. Tori made sure I knew it.

Her panties she'd been wearing before her shower were currently in my pocket. She'd stuffed them in there. Ten feet away from her parents, the little shit.

"I don't have a condom," I announced before this went any further, watching her head slowly come up and her focus leave her zipper.

"You don't?" she asked. She looked surprised.

"No."

"Why not?"

"Why the fuck would I?" I returned. "Didn't need 'em."

She tilted her head.

I read her question and answered it. "You weren't in Florida, Legs. No reason to pack condoms if the only woman I'm fuckin' is back home."

Her mouth twitched the slightest bit. Tori liked hearing that. But it didn't last, and remembering the reason we were paused right now, she started frowning again. "Well, um," She bit her lip, released it, then shifted on my lap. "This sucks. I guess we'll just have to wait the three hours then."

I smirked. Her disappointment was cute as fuck. It also wasn't needed.

I dropped my head back against the seat. "Babe."

"Mm?" She was dragging her teeth across her lip again and staring at my shirt.

"Knew this talk was coming considerin' how things are movin' with us, though straight up, wasn't expecting to have it on the side of the road at some dirty-ass rest stop," I began, keeping hold of her hips.

Tori's eyes lifted. Her thighs squeezed mine and her plum-painted fingertips dug into my stomach. She was tense. And I didn't want her nervous.

"Fact that you want me at some dirty-ass rest stop is hot, babe. Fact that we're havin' this talk 'cause of you wanting me and not bein' able to wait three hours is even hotter. Don't think it isn't."

She shook her head and lowered her eyes to my chest. "I wasn't thinking that. I just—"

"I've always fucked with a condom," I interrupted, getting her attention again. "Never had any close calls. Never did any of that just feelin' shit to see what it was like. Got tested once when I was paranoid and heard this chick had something, but other than that, I don't have reason to be worried. I know I'm good."

Tori's chest was heaving now. Her breathing was filling the car.

"Nothin' needs to happen now," I told her, reading her apprehension. "I'm just sayin' so you know, I'm good if you want that."

"I know," she replied.

"Because I want that."

She stopped breathing.

"Never had this talk before," I quickly added, watching her eyes grow bigger. "Not just 'cause I was screwin' around either. Had girls I was seein' for a while. Long enough you'd have this talk and still didn't want it. I want it with you."

"Jamie," Tori whispered. She looked uneasy.

"Babe, I just don't want you thinkin' I've been here with anyone, 'cause I haven't."

"I have," she revealed, worry tight in her voice.

I stared at her. Tori's apprehension. Her reserve. It hit me like a swift blow to the gut. My jaw clenched.

That motherfucker.

"Legs," I murmured, sitting up and taking her face between my hands, lifting it when she tried letting it drop in shame.

"I—I didn't know," Tori whispered, talking about that worthless piece of shit being married. "I didn't know, Jamie."

"I know, baby."

"I never would've given him that if I'd known. I swear."

"Shh," I said, pulling her against me and wrapping my arms around her.

Murderous, rip-his-fucking-throat-out rage filled me. It burned in my veins and watered my mouth. I wanted to tear Wes apart. And not just 'cause he'd had Tori the way I was wanting to have her. Yeah, that was part of it. No fucking way could I ignore that right now. But the biggest thing driving me—what I was fighting the urge to hunt his ass down for—was hurting her the way he did. For the pain she was feeling now.

And that feeling had absolutely nothing to do with me. Not a fucking thing.

Tori stayed quiet for a few minutes, just letting me hold her, then her soft, broken voice uttered, "I'm so sorry," into the hollow dip in my throat.

What was worse than pulling someone's limbs off and letting them feel it?

Whatever it was, I was there. Sign me up for that.

"Babe." Hand sliding to her hip, I drew Tori back to look at her. I cupped her jaw. "You don't need to be sorry for shit that's got to do with him," I said. "None of it. Not fuckin' ever. You hear me?"

"I have to get tested," she said brokenly. "I've never had to do that. I—I don't even know how to go about doing that. God, I . . ." She shook her head. She tried lowering it, fighting against my hand. "I'm so embarrassed right now."

"Baby—"

"I didn't love him like this."

I inhaled sharply through my nose. Jesus. That . . .

Fuck it. I was going to jail for murder.

"I'll get tested," I told her, getting her eyes again. "We'll both do it. It ain't a big deal."

Tori stopped trying to drop her chin. "What?" she asked, blinking at me. "But why? You don't need it."

"You gettin' it done?"

"I have to."

"Makin' sure I'm only gettin' you when we do this. You're givin' me that?"

Tori nodded gently.

I leaned in, fingers tensing on her jaw. "I want you knowin' you're only gettin' me," *I rasped.* "Nothin' else. No doubts. No wonderin' or feelin' shame for you havin' to do it. None of that shit. Nothin' but me, babe."

Tori pulled in a breath through her nose. She blinked. "Really?" *she whispered, bottom lip trembling.*

"Yeah." *I swiped her cheek with my thumb.* "Shit's settled. I'll get it done."

Whimpering soft in her throat, Tori leaned in until our foreheads touched, held my face with her hands, closed her eyes, and breathed deep.

But more importantly, she breathed easy.

Past couple of days with her, she'd been fine. Even three days ago when she went to the doctor, she was smiling and cracking jokes with me later that night. She wasn't back to looking like this.

"Babe, you don't need to be embarrassed," I reminded her, rubbing my hands up and down her arms. "It wasn't a big deal. Pissed in a cup. Nothin' to it."

"No, I . . ." She licked her lips, eyes slicing to the oven and then meeting mine again. "We only have twelve minutes now until the pork chops are ready."

I stared at her, brows lifting. "And?"

"And that's hardly enough time for everything I'm wanting to do."

I looked between Tori's anxious eyes and her fidgeting fingers. My hands stilled at her elbows. My nostrils flared as I pulled in a breath.

Oh fuck yeah.

She wasn't embarrassed. She wasn't thinking about that cock-

sucker and what he'd put her through. Tori was weighing her options: dinner she'd prepared, eating it hot and ready, or blowing off
all her hard work and spending the rest of the night fucking bare,
nothing between us.

Nothing ever between us again.

I didn't see the dilemma. Easiest fucking decision I'd ever made.

"We're fuckin' right here. Timer goes off and you gotta take shit
outta the oven so it doesn't burn, you do that," I told her, watching
her eyes flicker wider and a flush burn across her cheeks. "Got a microwave for a reason. We'll use it when we're ready to eat."

Tori thought about this plan and she took all of a second to do
that, which was lucky for her since that was all the time I was giving
her to use.

"Okay, but I gotta put the biscuits and the potatoes in," she said,
moving to turn away.

I grabbed her hips and kept her facing me. "Put 'em in later," I
countered.

She shook her head, arguing, "It'll just take a minute."

"That's a minute I wanna use." I yanked her against me. "*Later*," I
repeated, voice firmer this time.

Tori's mouth twitched. She slid her hands around my neck, turned
her head, and checked the oven again. "Ten minutes," she said, looking up at me, eyes heating and that hot little tongue peeking out.

Jesus.

Fuck those ten minutes.

Cursing, I spun around, prowled to the stove, cut the oven temperature in half, and doubled the time.

"Jamie," Tori giggled from behind me, watching me do this.

I turned my head and saw her hand covering her mouth and her
cheeks lifting and pinked in color. Then I turned fully, back to the
stove so I could face her. I reached behind my shoulder and stripped
my shirt off, tossing it next to the sink.

Tori quit giggling. Quit smiling. Her eyes lowered to my chest,
heated. Her hand lowered and stroked down her throat. She started
panting.

Fuck. Yeah.

I wasn't sure who moved first after that, her or me. Whose mouth took possession first or whose hands were stripping what the fuck off, but then Tori was naked with her ass perched on the edge of the counter, legs open and feet hooking behind my thighs, and I had my shorts down, bunched at my ankles, my hand wrapped around the base of my dick.

I played with her pussy. I pressed the metal of my piercing against her clit and slid lower, wetting my shaft. I felt her smooth walls pull me in and *fuck fuck fuck*.

"Look at me," I said, just the head of my dick inside.

Tori had her eyes glued between her legs but lifted them when I spoke. Her hair was messy from my fingers. Her lips were open. Her breaths were coming out in short little pants.

"He never fuckin' had you," I said, pushing in, watching her mouth open wider.

"Jamie," Tori moaned, face blissed out. She tried hurrying me. Her hand on my neck pulled and her fingers around my shoulder dug in deep.

"No, baby. Let me take this," I said, keeping pace.

"Please," she begged.

I bent down and took her mouth, giving her my tongue and letting her work that while I took my time.

My thighs burned. My chest burned. The need to fuck scratched under my skin. I moved slowly, fighting urge. I wanted to pound into her and get us there. I wanted to finish inside her so I could know what it was like.

She was so wet. So warm. Perfect. So fucking perfect. And mine.

This was mine. Mine mine mine mine.

"God, *fuck*," I groaned, seating fully inside now. Chest heaving. Legs shaking. "Nothin'…Jesus, *nothin'*, babe, has ever…" I panted, losing my breath and my mind, that shit was fucking gone. "I'd do crazy shit for this," I told her, staring deep into her eyes as my fingers curled around her neck. "I'd burn the whole fuckin' world down for you, you know that?"

That was the truth. I wasn't lying. I wasn't just saying shit 'cause my dick was inside her either.

I loved her. She knew that. But this was bigger. It *felt* bigger.

And Tori understood that. She bit her lip and nodded, looking like my words were hitting that soft she kept hidden, but no longer hidden from me. She gave it freely now. Trusted me with it. Just like she was doing with this.

"Please," she whispered. Her feet slid up to my ass and her heels dug in.

She was needing it.

"You're fuckin' beautiful," I said, cupping her face as I started moving inside her, hips thrusting as my other hand held her thigh. Her mouth right there. "Fuckin' mine. All this beauty. I'm takin' it, babe, and you're givin' it."

"Yes," she moaned. I felt her hot breath on my tongue.

"Givin' me somethin' you never gave, aren't you?"

"Yes, Jamie."

"Never gave this." My hips pumped harder. Tori's legs spread wider and her breath caught. "He never fuckin' had this," I growled. "Never touched it. Never came close to what I'm touchin'."

"Yes!" she cried out. Her fingers dug into my neck. "Oh, God, Jamie!"

I took my hand off her thigh and slid it up her stomach, grabbing her breast. I thumbed her nipple. I pinched and twisted it.

She moaned, tipped her chin up, and crashed her mouth against mine. Her tongue slid past my lips, dipped into my mouth, and tasted while I fucked her.

My hips were pounding. I was jarring her body so hard Tori was falling back, spreading her arms wide, and knocking shit off the counter.

Bowls. Sheet trays. Food. Didn't matter. She didn't care and neither did I.

I kept it up, fucking her deep every time. Sinking home again and again. Staring at her tits as they bounced. Her small, pink nipples. Her lips, parted and wet. Her stomach as it clenched beneath my fingers and the curve of her waist. Never wanting to stop. Never wanting to forget what this felt like and how she was looking at me, so fucking hot, so turned on, but with mad, crazy, fucked-in-the-head love. Love for me. Only me.

Never gave him that. Never came close to giving it.

This was mine.

I yanked her up so I could suck on her nipples, wetting her entire breast and dragging my tongue between them, pulling away and then getting jerked back again with her fingers in my hair. She rubbed her tits in my face.

I growled and fucked her harder.

Tori giggled through a moan. Her hips started jerking on the edge of the counter, lifting up and grinding down.

My groin throbbed.

I was going to come.

"Jamie," Tori whimpered. Her legs tightened. I felt her back arch away from my hand and her mouth open on my cheek. "Oh, God. Please don't stop. Please. Please..." She started shaking.

Her warm, slick pussy clenched around my dick as she moaned *yes yes yes*.

I forgot how to breathe. Hips thrusting, my orgasm raced after hers. I felt desperate. I couldn't stop.

"Fuck," I panted, pumping two...four...five times and then, "Ah, God, *fuck*, I'm comin'. I'm comin'."

A jagged groan escaped my mouth as I yanked her close, buried deep, and finished inside her. The muscles in my legs and arms twitched. I felt Tori's warm breath tickle my neck and her fingers stroke up and down my spine.

She wouldn't let go of me.

"Babe," I rasped, hearing the alarm on the oven.

No fucking idea how long that had been going off.

Tori collapsed back, not caring about it, and pulled me down on top of her. And I went. I sure as fuck didn't care about anything else but this right now.

Her. Us.

I was never letting go either.

She held me close, limbs circling my back as our chests matched with racing breaths. Her fingers in my hair. Her lips moving over my ear.

"This feels like forever," she whispered.

I closed my eyes, thinking the same. The alarm kept sounding.

Pizza was ordered an hour later and eaten with her sides—roasted potatoes, all-day green beans, and biscuits.

We tossed the burnt-up pork chops in the trash.

Chapter Twenty-one

TORI

I blinked at my bedroom ceiling as Jamie dozed beside me, his breath warm and sleep-heavy on my neck. His arm across my chest and the other under my pillow, elbow bent and fingers curled into my hair.

This feels like forever.

I exhaled a breath. Knees bending, I tug my toes into the mattress and fought the urge to squirm.

Yep. That was me. I'd said that. Those words *totally* crossed my lips.

Not that I didn't mean them, because I did. It wasn't just the afterglow of fantastic kitchen sex speaking. I really, *truly*, felt this thing with Jamie becoming something bigger. Outlasting and enduring. This love overwhelmed me.

I could see it next month. And deep into the winter. I could picture Jamie a year older at twenty-nine with his hair longer and messy on my pillow. I could see next summer's sun on his skin and feel the heat of it beneath my palms.

This feels like forever.

It did. So I said it.

And he said nothing. Nada. Zip.

At least not right away anyway. And definitely not in response to the honesty pouring out of my heart.

He said *get you cleaned up* and *pork chops are burnt—what're we orde-*

rin'. He told me I looked sweet after I changed into the well-worn shirt of his I stole. He pulled me on top of him and held me while we watched the Orioles spank the Yankees, easy conversation flowing like it typically did.

And then Jamie passed out after murmuring *Night, babe* into my hair and throwing his limbs around me.

But forever? There was no talk of forever. No *baby* paired with some meaningful, heart-heavy look. No *feelin' it, too*. None of that.

My stomach was knotted tight. I couldn't close my eyes. I felt restless.

Crap.

This was seriously bothering me.

Carefully, so I wouldn't wake Jamie, I slid out from underneath his arm and out of bed, then I tiptoed out of the bedroom, padded down the hallway, took the stairs, and headed for the kitchen.

Peering into the fridge, I grabbed a Pure Leaf off the shelf and a baggie of cut-up veggies. I nudged the door closed with my hip and moved to stand at the island, then I snapped into a carrot while blank-staring at the countertop.

My thoughts spiraled farther and farther into freak-out central as I chewed. I never should've said it. I never should've said anything about forever.

I should've just told Jamie I loved him, or *that was amazing*, or *you're right, I never gave him that*. I had options. Great options. *Fantastic* options. Options that could've and should've prompted a response that had absolutely *nothing* to do with food or the aftermath of sex.

Instead I chose to skip a thousand steps ahead and leave Jamie behind.

My little cartoon heart curled in on itself and pouted. Then a frightening thought entered my head. What if he never caught up to me? What if Jamie stayed at the *I love you now* step while I waited waited *waited* for him, and he never wanted to move?

What if he was forever happy at his step? *Oh, God...*

I shoved the rest of the carrot into my mouth and twisted off the cap of my sweet tea.

I never should've said it. You, Tori, are a giant, freaking—

"What's on your mind, Legs?"

Jamie's voice lifted my head and my eyes off the counter. I turned to look at him.

He had his shoulder leaned against the wall just inside the kitchen, arms folded across his wide, bare chest and feet crossed at the ankles. He was in his boxers. Nothing else. His hair was pulled back out of his face, a face that didn't look a bit sleepy anymore. His eyes were bright. And he was wearing a smirk that read *busted*, like he'd just caught me staring at the spot on the counter I had to heavily disinfect earlier.

"Nothing," I lied around my bite, releasing my bottle and covering my mouth with my fingertips. "Just wanted a snack."

Jamie stared at me. He slowly lost the smirk. He wasn't buying what I was selling.

"Tense upstairs, babe. Felt it when I held you," he shared, pegging me dead on.

I swallowed my bite of carrot.

"Tense before that when we were chillin' on the couch, but you were hidin' it better. Probably 'cause we were eatin' and you weren't thinkin' about whatever it is that's got you down here."

"Food has got me down here," I lied again, holding up my bag of veggies. I shrugged. "And I'm not tense. I'm just not tired."

"Do I gotta fuck it outta you?"

My head jerked back. I lowered the baggie to the counter, reading the seriousness in Jamie's eyes.

Mm. Now there's an idea.

"I'm out of Lysol," I informed him.

Jamie's brows lifted. "Say again?"

"I'm out of Lysol. If we do it in here, you can't be banging me on the counter again. I don't have anything to disinfect it with."

That smirk returned, only it looked ten times as sexy now because it was merging with a smile. And smiling Jamie had to be one of my top five favorite things to look at in the entire world.

And I'd been to Paris. But the Eiffel Tower had nothing on Jamie McCade. He was beautiful when he smiled.

He was beautiful all the time, but when he smiled? Boom. Billboard beauty.

"Gotta whole house to work with, babe. I'm not limited to a counter," he informed me.

I immediately started cataloging hard surfaces on the first floor alone. My insides were tingling. I could stand here, eat, and continue lying, or I could have sex with Jamie and avoid his third degree.

He thought he could get it out of me while we did it, but he was apparently forgetting that we didn't work that way. Never had.

He'd ask questions or affirm I felt a certain way, and I denied *everything* he was suggesting. We'd both get off, normally me a time or two more than him—Jamie was hardly selfish when it came to orgasms—he'd press once more for confirmation after we were finished, wouldn't get it, and then we'd both end up dozing off or moving on to a different conversation.

Fuck it out of me? Hardly. I was a vault.

"Okay." I freed my hands up, twisted away from the island, and grabbed the hem of my night shirt. I started lifting.

"Hold up," Jamie ordered. His voice was rougher. Firmer. Meaner even.

I studied his face. He was no longer close to that smile since he was no longer smirking. His eyes were hard now. Mouth tight. He looked...*knowing*.

Crap.

That was not a good look for Jamie, solely because of how it was going to affect *me*. Not because he didn't look sexy in this state as well. He did. Maybe even sexier.

Hands frozen at belly level with my shirt bunched there, I held on to his eyes, waiting for Jamie to speak. But he didn't speak.

He straightened from the wall, moved farther into the kitchen, crossing in front of the stove, and started opening my upper cabinets and searching through them.

Seeing this, I let my hands fall and released my shirt, covering up again. "What are you doing?"

Jamie shut a cabinet door after retrieving a large mixing bowl. "Makin' pancakes," he replied.

My eyebrows shot up. *"Now?"*

Mixing bowl set aside on the counter, he slid my canisters containing flour and sugar in front of him, turned his head, and jerked his chin at the stove, saying, "I know you said it had to be at that diner, but I don't feel like goin' anywhere. We're doin' breakfast here."

I slid my eyes to the stove and saw the time, smiled, then looked back to Jamie, smiling bigger when I caught sight of the bright orange elastic band securing his hair—it was one of mine. I watched him move to my spice cabinet and take out the salt and baking powder.

He was making us breakfast at midnight. I wanted that to be our thing, one of many things, and Jamie was giving me that.

I glanced down at my baggie of cut-up veggies and pushed them aside. *Nobody wants you.*

"So I guess we're eating first, then getting to the sex?" I asked, hoisting myself up onto the counter and swinging my legs. "I'm good with that."

"Depends," he replied.

I tiled my head. *Depends?* "On ..."

Jamie pivoted around and crossed in front of me to get to the fridge, saying as he went by, "You give up why we're down here instead of upstairs sleepin' and I'll give it to you after we eat. You don't? We ain't fuckin'. I ain't stupid, Legs."

My eyes bugged. *What?*

We ain't fuckin'?

WHAT?

I watched, mouth open, as Jamie took the milk, eggs, and a stick of butter out of the fridge, nudged the door closed with his elbow, and walked back to his work area next to the stove.

"Excuse me?" I asked when he got there.

"I ain't stupid," he repeated with his back to me.

"Okay." I laughed a little and tucked my hair behind my ear. "What's that got to do with us having sex after we eat?"

After setting everything down, Jamie turned around to face me and braced his hands on either side of him, gripping on to the counter.

"I know how we fuck, Legs," he began. "You don't give up shit.

But usually that don't matter 'cause I know what you're thinkin' anyway. And straight up, I don't hate it. That's our game. Wanna keep doin' it for as long as we feel like doin' it. Difference right now is, I ain't solid on what's got us down here. I got no fuckin' clue what's goin' through your head."

"I told you, I just wanted to get a snack."

"Bullshit," he shot back, voice growing louder. "Somethin's got you tense and I wanna know what it is."

"I'm not tense," I argued.

"You're tense, babe."

"No." I tipped forward a little. "I'm not. I was just hungry."

"Tori."

"I'm not tense!"

"Jesus," he muttered, shaking his head, then tilting it when he asked, "Do I need to call Sunshine? Get her in on this? Probably catch shit from Dash but fuck it." His shoulders jerked. "If it'll get you talkin'..."

I scowled. *Damn it.* He'd do it, too. And I didn't want to disturb Syd and Brian. It was the middle of the night, and knowing Syd, she'd most likely start bawling again and keep Brian up.

"I said forever and you didn't say anything, okay? There." I huffed out a breath, twisted, and grabbed my bottle of Pure Leaf, unscrewed the lid off the rest of the way—I had only loosened it earlier—and brought the bottle to my lips.

My eyes connected with Jamie's as I sipped, which, seeing the way his eyes were looking now, his whole face for that matter—gentled, sweet, soul-touching—I got one mouthful down before I was forced to stop sipping for fear I'd suck sweet tea down the wrong pipe.

I knew that look. I'd seen it on Jamie's face a handful of times now. One of those times being that very night I showed up at his house begging for sex and he promised me I'd never be worrying about Wes again. Another time being in front of the fire before we made love when I told Jamie he was the best man I'd ever known.

I couldn't sip tea right now. Not with Jamie looking at me like that. Not when I knew the next words out of his mouth were going to hit my soft, sink in deep, and stay there.

"You couldn't sleep 'cause I didn't tell you I was with you on that," he suggested, eyes soft and voice lowered.

I wiped my hand across my mouth, then I nodded my head and lowered my eyes, staring at the label on my bottle.

"Look at me, babe."

I lifted my eyes again.

"Tense all night. Worryin' I wasn't feelin' you. That wasn't the case," Jamie began to explain. "Just came in a woman for the first time. That woman bein' you. I was processin' shit. Not three weeks ago you wanted nothin' to do with me. Now we're here, you're talkin' about forever—"

"I know," I interrupted him, sighing heavily. *See! Never should've said it.* "I was being stupid, okay? I didn't—"

"You don't know," Jamie shot back, interrupting me this time. "And you weren't bein' stupid. You were feelin' something and you shared it. That happens, no matter what it is you're tellin' me, that ain't you bein' stupid."

"Okay," I said, mouth twitching. That was nice to hear. Still, there was a problem. "But now I'm, like, twenty steps ahead of you," I pointed out.

He smiled then. *What the hell?*

"This isn't funny, Jamie," I hissed.

"It's funny, babe," he returned, reaching up and scratching his jaw. "You thinkin' you're ahead of me is fuckin' hilarious."

"No, it's not. It's embarrassing."

He smiled bigger.

"Stop smiling!" I snapped.

"Catchin' up," he muttered.

I squinted at him, head tilting slightly. "What?"

"You," he said, hand lowering back down and curling around the counter. "Catchin' up."

It hit me then, what Jamie was leading at. He'd been twenty steps ahead of me this entire time.

Breath catching, I righted my head and stopped squinting.

"You get what I'm sayin' now?" he asked, still smiling but doing it softer.

"I get what you're saying."

"Good." That smile he was wearing grew brighter again. "Now, are you gonna keep sittin' there or are you gonna come here? I wanna hold you without you bein' wound tight."

I set my tea aside and slid off the counter, then I started moving.

"It's really only been three weeks?" I asked when I reached him, thinking back to what he'd said. My hands curled around his smooth hips.

Three weeks didn't seem right.

"Just about," he answered, his arms around me, his head dipping down and his mouth pressing to my forehead.

"It feels longer than that," I said, feeling his arms tighten and give me a squeeze in response. I slid my hands around his back and pressed closer, face lifting to hide in his neck. "I know I said forever," I murmured. "And I know you said you're with me on that, but I'm good with us taking the rest of the steps as they come. Together. We can go slow. We don't have to keep skipping ahead."

"I want you movin' in with me," Jamie shared.

My back snapped straight. I leaned away and gaped at him. "I just said we don't have to keep skipping ahead," I repeated, voice rising an octave higher.

Did he not hear me?

"How the fuck is you movin' in with me skippin' ahead?" he questioned, brows drawn, his arms still keeping tight hold on me as if he was preventing my escape. "Just said forever, babe. What do you think that means? I'm not gonna shack up with you?"

My shoulders sagged. He had a point.

"Well..." I paused, wetting my lips. "I don't know. I just...why can't you move in here? My house is nice."

Jamie smirked. "Ain't as nice as mine."

My eyes narrowed as I tipped my chin up. "Your house is only nicer because you have a better view," I argued. "It's way too big, Jamie. What do you have, seven bedrooms? You don't use them. That's just space that collects dust."

"Won't be once you start poppin' out my kids. We'll fill it."

My eyes were no longer narrowed. They were taking up the majority of my face. I just knew it.

Poppin' out his kids? KIDS?

"Babe," Jamie laughed, looking down at me.

Yep. Totally taking up my face.

"I said quit skipping steps!" I cried, rolling up onto my toes to get closer.

"You're freakin' out," Jamie observed, mouth stretched wide and dimples showing.

"Of course I'm freaking out."

"Why?"

"Because you're..." I paused, staring at Jamie's smile, his dimples, his bright blue eyes.

Why was I freaking out?

"I don't know," I answered finally, voice quieter. I rocked back onto my heels. "You can't talk about that stuff unless you really mean it," I blurted out.

There it was. That was my why.

"Legs, for real, you're movin' in. What'd you think is comin' down the road, babe?" Jamie asked, laughter faded out now but the smile he had going with it still holding.

I blinked up at him as I thought on that, *down the road with Jamie*, and all that could entail, not thinking I looked a certain way while I envisioned it but apparently I did.

Jamie's smile faded even more until there wasn't a trace of it left. The brightness in his eyes dimmed. His arms were no longer holding tight to me because his hands were coming up to cup my face.

"Hey," he murmured, eyes filling with warmth. With love.

My chest tightened.

He loved me. Jamie McCade loved me and wanted *down the road* with *me*.

My God. That felt amazing.

And right. And perfect. And I no longer felt that fear holding me back.

And since it was no longer holding me back, I hurled myself forward, nothing stopping me.

I slammed Jamie against the counter he was already leaning on, causing him to grunt, drew my arms tight around his back, and crashed my full weight into his chest—which forced his hands to slide to the back of my head and palm there. Face turning, I flattened my cheek on his beating heart and closed my eyes.

I didn't say anything and neither did he.

But he did shift his hands a little, one staying on the back of my head and the other sliding lower and then curling around my waist so his arm was holding me, too. His head dipped down. I felt his breath blowing across the top of my head.

This felt right, too. And perfect. So perfect I didn't want to move.

But then my stomach made a noise like I had an animal in there and it was dying of hunger.

"Um..." I murmured.

Jamie started laughing a second before I did.

Then we separated, but only so I could watch Jamie make us homemade pancakes and staying glued to his front made that a challenge. When it was time to eat and we'd made it to the couch, I was back to pressing close. I sat on his lap, feeding him and myself from the same plate while Jamie channel surfed.

I was right. We did eat before we had sex. Only Jamie didn't fuck me like he originally implied.

We made love.

It was slow. It was sweet. It was unbelievably hot. It was a little sticky, on account of the syrup.

It was right.

It was perfect.

* * *

The wind was in my hair. The sun was beating down on my skin.

I had my arms circled around Jamie's waist, hands locked together on his stomach. My eyes were pinched shut and my face was buried in his back.

You'd think I wasn't enjoying my first ride on Jamie's bike, but I was totally enjoying it.

I was too scared to open my eyes. I was terrified of the other cars around us. But this . . . felt . . . *amazing*.

And Jamie knew I was liking it. Even though I had a death grip on him and my body was rigid and showing signs of anxiety, my laughter and squeals every time he sped up were letting him know differently. Plus, every time we stopped, I hollered out, "This is awesome!" over the rumbling of the pipes.

It *was* awesome. I could totally get used to traveling like this and hopefully open my eyes eventually.

Last night Jamie asked me to move in and expressed his desire for everything a future could hold with me, then we made love and I fell asleep with one of the biggest smiles on my face, happier than I could remember ever being.

That happiness was possibly getting trumped today.

The sun was high in the sky, on account of it being close to noon. It was a beautiful day. Jamie was taking me to work and then picking me up after, and then?

Then we were starting the process of me moving in.

Pack. Discuss what was going with me and what I could either sell or get rid of. Talk to Jamie's dad about eventually listing my house and all the details involved in that.

I wasn't scared. Not anymore. Not one bit.

Clinging to Jamie as he whipped us down the highway with what felt like lightning speed, I was terrified. Enjoying it, but terrified.

But moving in with the man I wanted *down the road* with, nope. Not at all.

Bring. It. On.

The bike slowed down and I peeked an eye open, thinking we were coming to another red light but then seeing the side of Whitecaps, its worn white wood and boat-style windows, and realizing we'd arrived.

The parking lot was nearly full, meaning we were slammed already, and there were also groups of people walking up from the beach and others heading back down the sandy path that led to it with bags in their hands.

That was typical for a Saturday when it was still warm out. People either came in to eat to get a break from the sun or took their food to go.

Either way, Whitecaps was going to make a killing today by the looks of it.

The gravel popped under the tires as Jamie pulled us into the parking lot. I sat up tall, both eyes open now, and watched heads turn and gazes follow Jamie, especially the women who were outside.

Really couldn't blame them. He looked exceptionally sexy on a bike.

All that hair blowing in the wind. Those tanned arms thick with muscle peeking out from his T-shirt. *Sexy.*

I released my arms from around him and maneuvered off after he pulled us into a space and cut the engine. Then, standing beside the bike, I threw my hands into the air and pumped my fists, yelling, "That was coolest ride of my life!"

Jamie smiled huge looking over at me. "You see any of it?" he asked, swinging his leg off, throwing the kickstand down, pivoting, and then leaning back against the bike.

"Not a thing!" I yelled, just as enthusiastically.

Arms pulled across his chest, Jamie threw his head back and laughed.

"Still. So. Freaking. Cool!" I unclipped my helmet, took it off, and handed it over. "I need to get one of these so you can wear yours," I told Jamie after he took the helmet, then I went on to say as I fixed my ponytail, "I didn't like you not wearing anything. Plus, I'm pretty sure the law says you need to."

"Better you wearin' it than me," he said, twisting and letting his helmet hang off his handlebar, then turning back to me.

I tucked my overgrown bangs behind my ears and stepped forward, getting between his legs, circled my hands around his neck, and pressed my forehead to his. "Your head is just as precious as mine. I don't want anything happening to it," I said, not sounding enthusiastic anymore but meaning my words just as much.

Jamie's hands curled around my back. He looked like he was feeling my meaning and let me know that when he agreed, stating, "We'll get you one then."

Sweet. I was getting a helmet. I smiled. "I want a pink one."

He smiled back.

"Or leopard print," I added, watching Jamie's brows lift. "And I want it to cover everything. Not just the top of my head."

"You really don't wanna see shit, do you?" he asked through a chuckle.

"If I see anything, I might not ever get back on," I replied, half-serious. I knew I'd eventually look.

"Come here," Jamie mumbled, tipping his chin up while pulling me with his hands, not giving me much of a choice.

I stepped closer, bent down, and kissed him, with just a little tongue since there were people around. Then I drew my arms around his back and gave him a hug, ducking my head beside his.

"How many lessons do you have this afternoon?" I asked as we were hugging.

Jamie drew in a breath to answer, but that breath held and his words never came because his phone started ringing.

"Hold up," he said, easing me back with his hand on my hip.

I stood between his legs, letting my arms drop to my sides.

Jamie kept his one hand on my hip and leaned so his other hand could fish the phone out of his pocket, then he hit Answer after checking the screen and brought the phone to his ear. "Yeah."

Jamie listened. He didn't speak for what had to be close to a minute. His brows drew together as his eyes stayed locked with mine. He was breathing slowly through his nose, looking like he was concentrating hard on each and every breath he was taking.

He looked tense, too, maybe. Or at least bothered by something. Jamie was no longer smiling about leopard print helmets, that was for sure.

"Yeah, I hear you," he finally said. His voice was gruff. "Nah, I wouldn't. Made your decision. What's there to talk about?"

Who is it? I mouthed, but Jamie just shook his head and kept his focus on the call.

"Right. Yeah, I'll do that," he mumbled. "Yeah, you, too." He pulled the phone away from his ear, hit End, then leaned to the side again and slid it back into his pocket.

"What's going on?" I asked him.

Jamie slid his hand to my other hip again so he was holding me with both and tugged me closer, answering, "Nothin'," as I went.

He was lying. Something was definitely going on.

"Not nothing," I argued, gripping on to his shoulders and pushing back so I was leaning away. "Tell me. Who was that?"

"Don't worry about it."

His hands kept urging. I kept resisting.

"Tell me," I insisted, putting pressure on his hands and his shoulders where I held. I wasn't letting this go. "Jamie—"

"My major sponsor just dropped me," he revealed, looking into my face, his hands no longer tugging me forward but just keeping hold.

I blinked at him, feeling my stomach drop out. "What?" I whispered.

His sponsor *dropped* him? What the hell? *Why would they do that?*

"Babe," Jamie started, head shaking as he prepared to play this down, I just knew it.

"Why would they do that? What happened?" I asked him.

"Don't matter," he replied curtly. "Made their decision. It's done."

"Yeah, but *why*?"

"Let it go. It don't matter," he told me, then he jerked his chin as his eyes moved past me. "Come on. I gotta get goin' and you're gonna be late," he said, pushing off from his bike and forcing me back a step.

I slapped my hand against his chest as he tried directing me to move, informing him, "I don't care one bit about being late, and I will not let this go. I wanna know what happened."

Jamie quit trying to direct me.

"Let it go, babe," he repeated.

"No," I said, moving my hands to my hips and pushing his off. "Tell me right now what happened. Why did they drop you?"

Jamie's jaw clenched. His nostrils flared as he pulled in a deep breath.

"Got pissed when I took off the other day and went to Raleigh to be with you," he revealed, not looking sad or angry or hurt. Just stating facts. His face was expressionless.

Something sick twisted in my gut. I thought I might vomit.

"Not just 'cause I left without telling 'em, but 'cause I was supposed to plug some new sports drink or some shit while I was down there, and considerin' I never got to run, I never got to be seen drinking that shit while holding a fuckin' trophy," he continued. "They're pissed 'cause of that and 'cause that wasn't the first time I bailed on them. Pulled the same shit when Dash had his wreck. Needed to see to him. Needed to see to you. They don't get that, they can fuckin' drop me. I don't give a fuck." He jerked his chin at Whitecaps again, keeping my gaze. "Now give me a kiss and get your ass inside. You're gonna be late."

I blinked, lifting my hand to cover my mouth.

Jamie watched this happen. His face got soft, then his hand darted out, snaked around the back of my neck, and pulled, crushing me against him.

I went easily, burying my face in his chest and gripping on to his shirt.

"I'm so sorry," I whispered, feeling responsible for this and so, so sad for him. I couldn't imagine what he was feeling right now.

Jamie's hand at my neck gave me a squeeze, then he murmured, "Pick you up after your shift," into my hair, not sounding a bit sorry for what he'd done and the consequences he was facing. He pulled back at the same time as I did, pressed a kiss to my forehead, released me, and jerked his chin one more time in the direction behind me.

"Go, babe," he ordered.

This time, I didn't argue. I went.

Chapter Twenty-two

JAMIE

"You have obligations to us. This isn't a one-way street."

"We warned you before, Jamie. If you can't commit to your part of the deal, then we can't work with you."

"I'm sorry, but this isn't working for us anymore."

I replayed that conversation in my head as I stood on the deck, body bent and tipped forward with elbows braced on the rail. I stared out at the ocean, waiting for something to hit me.

Anger. Regret. Shame. Calm for being out here 'cause that's what I always felt being this close to the water. Smelling it. Hearing the waves crash.

I closed my eyes, pulled in a breath, released it, then looked back out.

I didn't feel a motherfucking thing.

I wasn't embarrassed for getting dropped. I didn't regret what I did either. I wouldn't go back and keep myself at that meet or turn around once getting word from Travis that Tori's dad wasn't critical. I wouldn't stop myself.

I'd do it again. I'd do it all over, knowing the outcome. I'd always go to her.

I took a drag from my cigarette, holding the smoke in my lungs and letting it burn, then blowing it out above me.

Losing a sponsor was more humiliating than anything, even though I wasn't feeling that right now either. I could still surf. Could still compete. I just wouldn't have them backing me. I wouldn't have that worth they instilled on me wanting to be tied to my name. That support from them, it was gone. And everyone would know it.

This could affect Wax. I pulled in a lot of business offering lessons. Having them behind me gave me bigger clout. It drew attention. Now I wouldn't have that. And getting dropped, once word got out, there was a chance my other two sponsors could cut ties with me as well. Straight up, this could hurt us. Could hurt us to the point of Dash and me losing our dream. If shit got really bad, we'd have to sell.

Thinking on that, I waited to feel it. Remorse. Guilt. Dash and I could fucking lose everything and still . . . I would do it again.

My reputation on the line. All of my sponsors threatening to pull out. I would do it again.

Fuck it. Fuck everything that wasn't her. I told Tori I would burn the world down and I was. If choosing her meant losing everything, I'd hand it over. I loved her. Fucking *loved her*.

I took another pull of my cigarette, staring out at the water. Feeling nothing.

Nothing but that love.

Chapter Twenty-three

TORI

Jamie was in shock. I just knew he was.

He'd said four, five words, *maybe*, since he picked me up thirty minutes ago. Those words coming when I went rushing out to him from Whitecaps and hurling myself into his arms.

"I'd do it again, babe," he'd said, his arms tight around me, his breath in my hair and his hands running soothingly up and down my back. He was comforting me.

I should've been the one comforting him. I wanted to be.

I asked if he was okay and if there was anything I could do, if he needed anything. "Mm," was all he'd said. *Mm.* I typically didn't count noises as words, but that was Jamie's only response.

I didn't know what that meant. Yes—he needed me? No—he didn't need anything? My stomach was in knots.

After he brought us back to the house and I followed him inside, I asked if I could make him something to eat, figuring we could sit and talk. I wanted to talk to him. I wanted to know what this meant—Jamie losing his sponsor and how he felt about it and what was going through his head. Something. Anything. I wanted him to know what was going through mine.

But Jamie just shook his head at me, bent down, and pressed a kiss to my hair. He was acting unconcerned, unaffected, un-Jamie-like. Then he turned and made for the slider that led out to the deck.

He didn't ask me to follow. He didn't want to talk. He was stepping out.

His pack of cigarettes in his hand. One lit before he even made it outside.

He was smoking, so I knew the *Mm* and the blasé attitude were just a front. Jamie only smoked when something got to him. Stressed him out. Worried him. Pissed him off. He was definitely feeling something, maybe a lot of things. I just didn't know what.

I wanted to help him. I wanted to do something. Make this better somehow. But what could I do?

I stood inside the house watching through the slider as he lit cigarettes two and then three. I couldn't take it. I turned and prowled toward the fridge.

He said he didn't want to eat, but maybe if I didn't present Jamie with a choice, he'd sit and talk to me. I could probably whip something up in thirty minutes, depending on what was on hand. That might be enough alone time for him anyway. I might not even have to initiate conversation.

Right. Decision made. *Let's see what he had.*

I opened the fridge first, examining his leftovers and hoping for some sort of protein I could salvage. No such luck. But Jamie did have tomatoes, an onion, and a couple cloves of garlic. I could make a sauce.

Meat. I needed meat.

I supposed I could always thaw something out in the microwave if I had to. That might have to do right now, unless I made a run to the store. And I really didn't want to leave him.

Closing the fridge, I straightened up and checked the freezer next. My mouth fell open as the air cooled my face. I felt my eyes widen. It was as if Rivera Frozen Foods had purchased Jamie's freezer as an advertisement space.

It. Was. Filled.

"Oh, my God," I whispered, taking in the sight.

Top to bottom, side to side, *stuffed* with bags of vegetables, fruits, rice blends, pasta dishes. Everything we made and one of each, it seemed. My little childhood face was everywhere...in his freezer, which was kind of weird, but still, *God*, so, so sweet. There was no other brand. Just my family's. I couldn't believe it.

I started breathing faster. My heart started jumping around and going crazy inside my chest. Jamie had gone to the aisle he never ventures to and purchased enough frozen food to feed himself for an entire year.

I'd never checked Jamie's freezer before. I had no idea how long these had been in here, but I had a feeling...He went shopping after I flashed him. The day he found out about my family's business. I just knew he had.

And he didn't do it because he loved frozen vegetables or quick and ready meals. He did it because this meant something to me, it meant something to my family, and Jamie cared about anything and everything attached to his woman.

That was me. I was his woman. I was his woman even then. Right at the start of that damn bet.

And finally, *finally*, standing there and staring at that sight, at that gesture that might've been insignificant to everyone else in Dogwood Beach, in the state of North Carolina, hell, *everywhere*, just not to me. To me it was everything. And looking at it all, it clicked.

I knew what I could do to help.

My hand reached for my back pocket where I had my phone. I pulled it out.

Then I dialed up my father.

* * *

Ten minutes later, I stepped outside and found Jamie on one of the sun loungers, head tipped back with his hands interlocked behind it, eyes closed, knees bent, and feet resting on the wood on either side of the chair.

Despite his relaxed position and the fact that he was no longer smoking, I knew he was anything but relaxed. I was hoping to change that.

"Hey," I said, claiming the lounger beside him and stretching out.

The cushion was warm beneath my calves. I looked over at Jamie, sharing, "I just got off the phone with my dad."

Hearing that, Jamie's eyes slid open and his head turned. He pinned me with a look of concern, asking, "He good?"

I gave him a soft smile. *God...* All he had going on in his head, and he was thinking about my family. Ready to put everything else aside if something was wrong.

My man was amazing.

"He's good," I assured him. "Hating that he's having to eat healthier, but he's doing it. Mom's making him mind. Dad said he's already feeling a lot better."

"That's great, babe," Jamie said gently. "He needs anything, he knows to call Travis. If he can't get a hold of him, he knows to call me. I'll get a hold of him."

Jamie was wearing a look now that read he'd drive the three hours or so to Travis's doorstep and personally deliver him to my father if he had to. And I knew he meant it.

A word greater than amazing. For sure.

I sighed and dropped the side of my head against the cushion. Jamie watched me do that, then he turned his head so it was tipped toward the sky again and closed his eyes.

It was time to give him my last truth.

"After I got my MBA from Duke, I applied for a position at Rivera Frozen Foods," I began, and immediately Jamie's eyes were flashing open and he was looking back over at me. Once I had him, I went on. "I wanted something in advertising," I continued. "I had an internship where I focused on that and really liked it. I knew I could be good at it. So I checked online. There were two jobs posted. A low entry-level one and then one for senior management. I applied for the first, figuring I could work my way up. The head of marketing interviewed me—Walt. Sweet older man I've known since I was a kid. I didn't even tell my dad I interviewed for it. He had no idea I'd even applied."

"Why didn't you tell him?" Jamie asked.

I laughed a little. "'Cause I wanted to do it on my own. But looking back, it wouldn't have mattered either way."

Jamie's brow furrowed.

I turned my head and pressed it back against the cushion, staring up at the sky above the railing. "I was hired for the position in senior management, which was crazy, but given my degree and the experience I had interning, Walt was confident I was fit for the position. My dad agreed after he found out. He was really proud of me."

"I bet. That's fuckin' awesome."

"He was also pissed I didn't come to him about a job, but I didn't want that, you know?" I turned to look at Jamie again. "I didn't want anybody thinking that I used my name to get where I was. That was important to me. I wanted to earn it."

"Sounds like you did," Jamie offered. "Hired you for a reason, babe."

"Yeah, well, not everyone thought that." I looked away again and drew my knees up, staring at the tops of them while I picked at my cuticle. "I was brand-new and fresh out of business school, and all of a sudden I was a boss. I had people under me. People who had to report to me and answer to me. Who were older than me. They hated it. These women who had bachelor's degrees or who were working toward graduating, they looked at me as if I'd done terrible things to them. They *hated* me. And when women hate women, it's bad, Jamie. It's really bad."

I glanced over at movement. Jamie was sitting up and throwing one leg over the cushion and planting his feet on the wood between our chairs. Then he leaned forward and dropped his elbows to his knees.

"How bad?" he asked. His voice was sharper. Jamie was getting tense. He was growing worried and I didn't want that. He had enough on his mind.

"It wasn't like I was getting beat up or anything," I explained, hoping to quickly settle him. "They would just...talk." I shrugged. "Say things behind my back. Sometimes not behind my back. They didn't think I earned the position I had. They said I wasn't qualified."

"They were talkin' shit," he threw out.

I nodded.

Jamie leaned closer, adding, "They were cunts, babe."

I pulled in a breath. That word was like nails on a chalkboard to me. It was tough to hear.

Jamie was right, though. Those women were...*that word*, but still. Tough to hear. I couldn't help but react to it.

"Jealous 'cause you were younger, smarter, probably hotter," he continued, staying pitched forward. "Couldn't handle the fact you had all that goin' on plus everything else you got goin' on, which is a fuckin' lot, babe, so they dogged you for it."

"They dogged me all right," I echoed, laughing a little at that expression.

Jamie didn't laugh watching me. He didn't smile. He didn't lose that tense, worried look in his eyes either. If anything, it grew thicker.

"Babe," he mumbled, and I knew his next words before he even asked them. "Tell me you did not let those bitches run you out of there. That's fucked up."

"I did not let them run me out of there," I told him, watching his head jerk and his eyes lower. "Me leaving was my decision. They might've influenced it, but they did not make that choice for me. I did."

Jamie's eyes lifted again. They narrowed and his mouth got tight.

I sat up then, swinging my legs over the side of the cushion to join him in his position. Reaching out and taking one of his hands between both of mine, I planted my feet so they staggered with his and slid forward, putting our knees together.

"I am very protective of my family, Jamie," I started, holding his eyes. "I don't ever want anything touching them that could hurt them in any way. Not even if that thing is me. Those women were talking and they weren't being shy about it. The things they were saying got around and eventually got back to me, and I knew it would only be a matter of time before they spread further. I didn't want that. I didn't want anyone thinking badly about my father. I didn't want people saying he was the type of man who didn't care about his business because he was letting family work there who weren't qualified to run it into the ground. I didn't want that. I didn't want his character getting tarnished."

"Why would that happen?" Jamie questioned. "That shit wasn't true. You were qualified."

"Rumors about John Rivera's daughter being qualified and earning the position she got aren't juicy. They don't travel," I explained. "But rumors about how John Rivera's daughter got her position by begging her much older boss, *from her knees...*"

Jamie jerked back. White-hot anger flashed in his eyes. "Fuck. Are you serious? They were sayin' that about you?" he asked gruffly.

"They were saying a lot of things about me. That was one," I confirmed.

"Jesus," Jamie mumbled. He shook his head and twisted his hand inside mine, taking hold of me as he got closer. His other hand reached out and cupped my face. "Legs, straight up, they should've been fired for that," he said, staring into my eyes. "You should've taken that shit straight to your boss and let him handle it. You should not have been dealin' with that."

"I agree with you," I told him. "They deserved to be fired, but I didn't want to draw more attention to it and I really didn't want Walt knowing what all they were saying. He's the nicest man. Always close with my family. He was like my grandfather. I didn't want him hearing that ugly. Firing four women over one quitting would've drawn attention and spread it wide. I didn't want that. I didn't want him finding out. Or my dad. That could've reflected on him if people believed it."

Jamie's brows shot up. "Your dad still doesn't know?"

I shook my head, saying, "Only you," and watching Jamie's eyes get soft. "You're the only person who knows. Syd doesn't even know."

Jamie closed his eyes for a breath, feeling what I just gave him and letting it sink in deep. Then he looked at me again and moved his thumb over my cheek, whispering, "Babe," as his fingers curled around my neck.

"I quit after two months and I don't regret it," I continued. "Not only because me leaving killed those rumors, but because I didn't love that job. I liked it. It was a job. It was something I could've done until I retired and I would've been satisfied, but I wouldn't have been happy. Not really. Not like I am now."

"What'd you tell your dad?" Jamie asked.

I smiled, stating, "That I wasn't happy. He told me to go find my happiness and I did. Right here."

Jamie's mouth twitched hearing that, but not much. He was still angry at what I'd gone through.

I reached out and took his face between my hands. I scooted to the edge of the cushion.

"I am very protective of my family, Jamie," I repeated, wanting him to cling to these words and the ones that followed. To hear these over the others I'd said. "I would never let anything near them that could hurt them in any way. Or bring them shame or anything negative. I wouldn't let it happen."

"I got that, babe," he replied. "Loud and clear."

"Good." I smiled again. "Then you should get why I had no problem asking my father if Rivera Frozen Foods would like to sponsor their first world-champion surfer."

Jamie's brows shot up. I felt his jaw tick beneath my palms.

"He said yes, by the way," I added, smiling bigger because Jamie was looking shocked. "But you're going to have to talk to him because I have no idea what all he has to do and he has no idea either. They've never sponsored anybody before. But that doesn't matter. Dad said he would be honored to back a man like you."

Jamie's nostrils flared as he pulled in a deep breath.

"He also had some choice words for the sponsor who dropped you," I continued on a chuckle, remembering those words and how quick he was at letting them fly. "Dad said if people don't want to back a man who goes to his woman and chooses her over everything else, then they're a bunch of idiots—only he didn't say idiots." I chuckled again, thinking Jamie would join in this time, but he didn't.

Tilting my head, I let my eyes roam over the heavy expression he was wearing. I couldn't read him. He wasn't saying anything. Wasn't smiling. His jaw was still tight. He was still holding my face but his thumb was no longer moving.

He was a statue, only breathing and blinking.

And not knowing how Jamie felt about all of this led to me having a panicking thought.

"Do you not want to be sponsored by them?" I asked, keeping the hurt from my voice because I didn't want him hearing it. "It's okay if you don't. I know they're just a frozen food company and not some major sports retailer. If you'd rather they didn't, I can talk to my dad. It won't—"

My words were halted when Jamie slid his hand to my neck, yanked me forward, and crashed his mouth against mine in a hard, deep kiss that made my toes curl inside my shoes and the muscles in my stomach clench and every fear or worrying thought I had go quiet inside my head.

"You did that for me," Jamie panted against my lips, keeping his grip firm on my neck and bringing his other hand up to palm my cheek.

"It was nothing," I whispered, my breaths heavy. "All you've done for me..."

"It was everything," he argued back, staring into my eyes. "Givin' me your family. Trustin' me with that. After everything you just said, straight up, babe, this ain't nothin'. I know it ain't."

He was right. This was far from nothing.

"Easiest phone call I ever made," I declared, speaking that honesty straight from my soul.

It was as if someone had flipped a switch and turned off everything around us. Stilled the water. Silenced the summer wind. The world went still.

Jamie's fingers on my neck squeezed. He closed his eyes for a breath, then opened them again, brought us closer, pressed his forehead to mine, and swept his thumb over my cheek.

"I'd do it again," he said quietly, staring into my eyes. "Don't give a fuck what I'd end up losing as long as that ain't you."

I let his words circle my heart and sink inside it. I was never letting them out.

This love was mine.

Then pushing my fingers through the ends of his hair, I dipped lower so I could brush my mouth against his and whisper-teased, "You fuckin' love me, boy," just like Jamie was always doing with me.

His lip curled up, then he kissed me, slow and sweet, and told me he didn't, which meant that he did.

So, so much.

Chapter Twenty-four

JAMIE

Six weeks later

Tori was kneeling between my legs and running her tongue down the underside of my shaft. I closed my eyes and hissed when she licked my balls.

"Fuck, babe," I growled, looking down and watching her slowly work her way back up to the tip. *Too fucking slowly.* "Quit with your playin' and swallow me."

"You like it when I play," she purred, looking at me from behind her lashes. "You especially like it when I do this." Tori kept one hand firmly planted on the mattress next to my thigh and wrapped her other around my base, then she sucked the head of my dick into her mouth and pulled back until my piercing clacked against her teeth.

The muscles in my legs jumped.

"Fuck yeah, I like that. *Jesus*," I groaned.

God-fucking-damn. My woman knew how to give head.

"And this," she said before hollowing out her cheeks and sucking me so hard it felt like she was trying to pop the head of my dick off.

My hands tightened in her hair as I inhaled a breath.

She pulled her mouth away but stayed crouched forward, giggling as her hand leisurely stroked me.

I pushed her hair out of her face, watching her.

"See? I told you you like it," she said, then she gathered her hair over one shoulder and started leaning down and parting her lips, and I saw the wet flash of her tongue, readying to keep up this game.

A game I fucking loved, but right now I was over it. She'd played enough. And Tori knew I liked coming in her pussy more than anything, even her hot-ass mouth that fucking watered for it.

The little shit thought she could keep it from me. She thought wrong.

Jerking upright and gripping under her arms, I yanked Tori up my body, causing her giggle to mix with a squeal 'cause she loved teasing me but she also liked getting taken, then I was flipping her underneath me and kneeling between her hips, dragging the tip of my cock through her pussy and pressing in in in.

So wet. God, *fuck*, she was getting off on licking my dick.

Tori dropped her knees and arched off the bed, moaning *yes* and *do it* and *I wanna feel you come inside me*.

"Yeah?" I asked as I rammed in. We both moaned. "Thought you were playin', babe," I teased, dragging my cock slowly back out, then pushing in. Out. In. My hips jerking as I pushed her knees back and held them open. "Sure you don't wanna go back to that? I know your mouth wants it."

"No, don't stop," she begged, her eyes looking like she'd kill me if I stopped.

"Think I'll stop," I shared, starting to pull back again.

Tori's eyes flashed with panic, then she slid her hand between her legs and started rubbing her clit. Her lips parted. Her eyes rolled closed.

I froze, my eyes going between her hand and her face, blissed out as she built it.

Jesus fuck.

She was trying to come before I slid out of her. Tori was wanting my dick in her when she went off. Damn she was good. Better at the game than me.

No fucking way could I keep from getting there if her pussy started squeezing my dick.

I grabbed Tori's wrist that was moving over her stomach and her other that was flat on the bed, then I plowed forward and filled her.

She gasped and shook as I moaned into her neck, pressing her hands on the pillow behind her and then sliding them above her head, my fingers skimming over her palms and pushing through hers, connecting us.

I leaned back and looked into her face as I fucked her, hips trusting deeper as her heels dug into my back.

"Harder," she whispered.

I pressed my mouth to hers. "You love me?" I asked.

"You know I do."

"Say it, babe. You want harder, I wanna hear it," I said, keeping the pace I was good at keeping until we both came in an hour, or two, or tomorrow when we were both mad and wild for it.

"I love you, Jamie," Tori said against my mouth, kissing me softly. "I love that you're mine. I want everyone knowing it."

"Yeah, you fuckin' do," I murmured, rearing back and going at her harder now that she gave me that. I slammed my hips against hers and pressed her hands into the mattress.

She moaned into my mouth, dragged her legs up my back, and dug her heels in.

"I want three," Tori said between panting breaths.

I felt the sweat of her body stick to mine.

"Three what?" I asked, kissing down to her jaw.

"Kids," she gasped, then her legs tightened around me when I stopped building it in her because, *fuck me*, she was bringing this up. She never brought this up.

I brought it up. She'd agree she wanted it, too, or she'd attack me with her mouth and let me know she was feeling what I was wanting, but never, not once, had Tori broached this topic on her own.

"Jamie, please," Tori begged, her legs pulling to urge me, and I could feel her growing tighter and wetter and tighter.

Fuck. She was right there.

I lifted my head and took her mouth, and then I fucked her hard and fast, powering into her, and Tori was coming within seconds, crying out and bringing on my own orgasm with how fucking snug her pussy got around me.

I groaned once more into her mouth as I finished.

Tori shuddered and panted beneath me, trying to catch her breath.

"All boys," she added when I leaned back to look at her. "With hair like yours and skin that always smells like the ocean. I want that so bad."

I gave her hands a squeeze, pressing my fingertips into her bones as I looked at her messy hair on my pillow and flushed skin, shiny with sweat, then lowering my gaze and seeing the beauty she was giving me in the smile she had lifting her full, soft mouth.

"You wanna get cleaned up before we talk about this?" I asked her.

Tori kept her smile, pinching her lips together, and shook her head.

I smirked, knowing she'd choose that 'cause lately she was always choosing it, saying she liked messy sex with me or some shit like that, then I slowly pulled out, shifted my hips up, and trapped my wet dick between us.

Tori hummed and wiggled beneath me. She loved it when I did that.

"Can't even get you to go out in the ocean with me again," I reminded her of the one thing she was still fighting me on and kept pushing off until *another time*. "And you're wantin' a bunch of boys who live in it like I do?"

"Yep." She smacked her lips on the "p," smiling bigger.

"Want 'em to surf?"

"Yep."

"Probably gonna want their momma out there joinin' them eventually," I threw out. "You down for that?"

"I'll be ready when they are," Tori replied, looking proud of herself.

"Mm." I lowered my head and nipped at her lip. "Five," I said.

Tori blinked. Her head pressed farther against the pillow so she could see me better. "Five? You want *five kids*? Really?" she asked, blue eyes growing wider.

"Yep," I echoed her, letting my lips smack on the "p."

Her mouth twitched.

"Got seven bedrooms. We're in one. Five for them," I started explaining. "That leaves a game room or a place we can store our trophies, mine and theirs, 'cause they sure as fuck will be collectin' 'em like I do. Talent's in the genes, babe. And there ain't no point in stoppin' at three when we got room for more."

"Yeah but, *five*? I don't know about five," she murmured. "Three was sounding really good to me. Perfect actually."

"Five. I'm firm on that."

Her eyes narrowed and her mouth grew tight.

"Three," she shot back.

"Five."

"Four," she countered, adding sass to her offer.

I smirked and pressed a kiss to her mouth. "Knew you'd give in," I said.

"Um, I didn't. You wanted five."

"Wanted four," I revealed, leaning back again and watching her blond eyebrows pull together. "Knew you'd give me shit 'cause you like givin' me shit. That's how you work, babe. Knowin' that, I figured I'd shoot high and then ease off to get what I wanted. Wanted four. Now we're getting a trophy room and a motherfucking game room. That's badass."

Tori pulled her lips between her teeth as she stared up at me. She was fighting a smile.

"You good with four?" I asked.

She nodded slowly.

"Want a girl, too," I shared. "You get three boys outta me, I'm getting a mouthy little beauty from you. You're givin' me that."

Tori was no longer fighting a smile. Her face was going soft.

"Can you let go of my hands?" she asked quietly.

"Sure thing, babe," I replied, doing what she was asking and propping my weight on my forearms.

Once her hands were free, Tori threw her arms around my neck and drew me down, pulling my head beside hers with her hand sliding into my hair. She held me tight like she was always doing when I was hitting her soft, letting me know how she felt about what I was giving her.

I wanted this, but I was wanting her words now, too.

I breathed deep against her neck, saying, "You gonna give me that?"

"Yes," she answered, no hesitation.

I closed my eyes for a beat, then I slid my hands under her shoulders and rolled us, getting to my back and pulling her so she was lying half on my chest and half plastered to my side. I slid my hand down her back to palm her ass and hitched her leg over my hip with the other, keeping hold there.

Tori's fingers traced a pattern on my ribs as she pressed her cheek to my chest.

"I'm pretty traditional, Jamie. I'd like to get married first," she proclaimed.

I smiled at the top of her head.

"Beach wedding. Firm on that, too," I told her, curious as to what she would say to that.

I felt Tori's quiet laughter rattle in her chest and against my side. Her fingers stilled, then she turned her head and planted her chin on my chest, meeting my gaze.

"Fine," she said, surprising the shit out of me as she lifted her head to speak. "But we're sticking to a dry honeymoon. I'm talking desert conditions. And Jamie?"

My body was shaking with laugher. I stopped so I could answer her, asking through a grin, "Yeah, babe?"

Tori crawled higher up my body and got in my face, plastering her tits to my chest and touching noses with me.

"I'm firm on that," she proclaimed. "*Real* firm."

Grinning still, I tipped my chin up, watching her own mouth start lifting.

"Give me a kiss, Legs," I ordered.

She gave me a kiss.

It started slow and sweet but my hand on her ass starting gripping and then my other joined in as Tori moaned inside my mouth and *fuck it*. I pulled her thigh so she was popping up to straddle my hips, breaking away and breathing heavy. "Want you ridin' me this time," I shared. "Keep those gorgeous fuckin' tits in my face, and when I tell you, babe, get your mouth on me. I'm finishin' on your tongue."

Tori nodded as she tried getting control of her own breathing, then she put her weight on her knees and reached between us, positioning me. She slid down.

Three orgasms later, her two to my one, Tori passed out with her limbs curling around me and her face nuzzling my neck.

We never bothered cleaning up that time either.

I relished the feel of her while thinking about everything she was wanting to give, then an hour later, I finally dozed off.

I never slept better.

* * *

It was the next day, nearly noon, and I was standing inside Wax, looking at the new shipment of T-shirts we'd got in with the Rivera Frozen Foods branding on the back.

Turned out, being sponsored by Tori's family was pretty kick-ass. Her dad was cool as shit about it, coming down here a couple of times now to check out Wax and talk to me about what all I needed from them and what all they needed from me.

My other sponsors never stepped foot inside where I worked. Not once. It was more about my name and how I could benefit them. What the fuck did they care about me owning a surf shop? They weren't getting anything out of that.

Not John, though. He cared. Wasn't shy about letting me know that either.

I didn't need them to do anything for me, and I told him that. Being sponsored was never about what all I could get out of companies. I just cared about surfing. Someone wanted to back me and put my face on their products or give me shit for free? That was up to them. I never asked for it. John understood how I felt about it and said they would support me in any way I needed. He was honored to be backing me and that meant a lot.

Straight up, though, being that it was Tori's family and knowing how much this meant to her, knowing how fucking huge this was, I was the one who felt honored.

It was why I was staring at another shipment of T-shirts advertising them and why the boards I used were now detailed with their logo.

Tori got a huge fucking kick out of that.

"Can't believe how these things are selling," Cole commented, stepping up beside me after I'd opened up the boxes. "Seriously, I'm pretty sure you could put a hemorrhoid cream logo on a tee and triple their sales."

I slapped his shoulder, grinning. "Leave that one to you, man," I said. "You should reach out and see if they're looking to sponsor."

"Right," Cole chuckled. "They'd probably fucking pass. And my luck, that shit would get around. I'd never get laid again."

We shared a laugh, then the bell chimed behind us, indicating someone was stepping inside the shop. I turned my head and watched Tori walk inside.

She was wearing a sweater that dipped low in the front and showed some of her cleavage—all fucking class, though—tight faded jeans that had tears up the front of one thigh, and black knee-high boots. Her jeans were tucked into them. Her hair was half up out of her face, except for those pieces that always fell out and wouldn't stay behind her ears. Her eyes were lined black. Her lips were painted red. And she was smiling big at me as she lifted her hand to wave.

"'Sup, babe?" I greeted her, turning sideways so I could see her better. "Got the shirts in. Perfect timing."

"Oh, good!" She clapped her hands together and started walking over. "I told Dad they were set to come in this week. I wanted to grab a couple for him and Mom."

"Set you up with that," I replied.

"I'm heading out. Gonna go grab something to eat," Cole said. He turned and tipped his chin at Tori. "What's up?"

"Hey," she greeted him, smiling as he walked past.

"Later, man," I called out.

"Later," Cole replied, getting to the door. "See ya around, Tori."

"See ya," she said back, keeping her eyes on me.

Cole stepped outside.

"Hey, you," Tori said, stopping in front of me. She rolled up onto her toes and tipped her chin up. "Kiss," she requested.

I grinned at her, keeping my arms pulled across my chest and not bending down. "Fuck?" I countered.

Her head jerked back and her eyes widened. She grabbed my elbows for balance, informing me, "Syd and Brian did it on the desk in the office once."

"Shit," I muttered. "He christened the place before I did? What a dick." I bent down then and kissed her soft mouth. "You look hot."

"So do you," she said through a smile, rocking back onto her heels but keeping her hands on me.

"Yeah? Wanna fuck?"

Tori swatted my arm and made a face, letting me know she was down but trying to cover that desire.

I chuckled.

"What size you want for your folks? I got 'em up to 2XL."

She thought for a second, dropping her hands and leaning to look behind me. "I think Dad is down to an extra-large now. He's lost close to twenty-five pounds."

"That's great, babe," I replied, meaning that.

I knew how important getting his weight down was for his heart. Not just from Tori telling me, but from Travis mentioning it.

Tori looked at me again. Her mouth was lifted. "Yeah. I'm proud of him. I know it's been hard. Mom is a medium. And she wanted to send my aunts both out a shirt. I think they're larges."

I jerked my chin, then I turned around and fished her out the sizes she needed.

"Got something for your dad in the back," I said, handing her the shirts. "I'll grab it for you. You meeting up with them today?"

"Yeah," she answered. She held the shirts against her chest. "Dad has a follow-up with Travis at two and then we're going to grab something to eat. It'll be early, though, so I shouldn't be home too late."

"Take the time you need, babe. I'll be there."

"I know," she said, eyes closing when I wrapped my hand around the back of her head and kissed the top of it.

"Lemme grab what I got for your dad so you can head out."

"'Kay," she replied. "I'll browse."

I chuckled, stepping back to look at her. "You don't have enough Wax apparel?" I asked, backing away.

Every time Tori came in here, she was leaving with a bag full. Fucking *loved that*. She was wanting to support me and wasn't shy about showing it.

Tori made a gasping sound. "What? Never! I can always use more surf tees and booty shorts." She smiled big, then spun around and started moving about the shop.

Booty shorts. Jesus fucking Christ.

I shook my head, laughing inside my chest, then I turned and headed for the office.

Once in there, I grabbed the hat with the Wax logo John was eyeing up last time he was in here—we were running low so I kept one in the back. Good thing, too, since we ran out last week and the next order wasn't set to come until the end of the month.

Tori was standing at the counter when I made it back out into the shop again, head down and eyes focused on something. Her profile was tense.

"Babe."

She looked up, meeting my gaze, and I saw the hurt in her eyes. I stopped at the edge of the counter.

What the fuck?

"Why wouldn't you tell them about us?" she asked, turning to face me. "How could you not say anything, Jamie? I mean, really, you literally said *nothing*."

"What?" Confused, I glanced down at the opened magazine she was standing in front of. Tori had her hand on a page. It was my interview with *Rail*. She'd read it. Or she at least read the question I'd dodged.

"I don't answer questions like that, Legs. I told you," I reminded her, tossing her dad's hat on the counter next to the stack of shirts. "I'm there to talk about surfing. That's it. They wanna forget that and try and get personal shit out of me, they're gonna get those kind of answers."

"You 'no commented.' That's not an answer."

"It's my answer." I shrugged. "Only one they're gonna get, too."

Tori blinked, mouth falling open as she looked down at the magazine. "How many people read this?" she asked, meeting my eyes again. "Ballpark. What do you think? Thousands?"

"Probably."

"And how many times have we talked about claiming each other?"

I stared at her for a breath, seeing her seriousness and not understanding it, then I harshly wiped my hand down my face, shaking my head before gearing up to argue. "Babe, look—"

"I claimed you to my parents and to five strangers in a restaurant," she interrupted. "And to everyone on my contact list, which I haven't cleaned up in, I don't know, months, so I'm sure there's people on there I don't even talk to anymore, but it didn't matter. I wanted everyone to know, Jamie. I wanted a restaurant *full* of people. And you had opportunity to claim me in the most public way, the biggest way you could ever claim me, and you don't."

She was upset and angry, or she was at least getting there. *Over this?* What the fuck?

"Quit takin' it personal, babe," I said, hoping to squash this. "It's ain't personal. I don't answer those questions. Never have."

"*Quit taking it personal?*" she echoed, sticking her hands on her hips, cocking one and hitting me with daggers.

Jesus. She wasn't letting me squash this. Tori was going to keep going.

"Come here," I ordered, thinking if I got her in my arms, she'd let this go.

Tori shook her head, standing firm.

"Babe, come here." My voice was sharper. Firmer.

"No." Her voice shook with emotion.

I took a step toward her. She took a step back.

Jesus.

"I just don't understand why you wouldn't do it," she said, losing some of that fire in her eyes. "You're the one who's been pushing us to claim each other this entire time. That was so important to you. And I wanted that. I wanted you to claim me to *everyone*, Jamie. That's what made this real. I wasn't your little secret. You weren't hiding me like Wes did. But now, I don't know, it kinda feels like you are."

I drew my arms across my chest. "Legs, straight up, even if I did answer those questions, what the fuck would I have said?" I asked, growing irritated with this. "You wouldn't admit to shit then. We were just fuckin'. You weren't stakin' claim to me. So what the *fuck* would I have said?"

Her eyes widened. "We were just *fucking? Really?* When you did that interview, that's all we were doing? There was nothing else between us? What about that night when I came to you crying? When I could've gone to Syd, or *anybody else*, what about then? I guess that meant nothing, huh."

My brow tightened. She was blowing this way the fuck out of proportion. "Babe, ease up on the attitude. You know what I meant."

"I don't need to ease up on anything, thank you very much," she snapped, tipping forward. "You're the one saying we were just fucking and there was nothing else going on between us when, *clearly*, that wasn't the case. At least not for me. So thanks for that. Glad I finally know how you felt about it."

I felt my jaw clench. My nostrils flared as I pulled in a breath. "You know how I feel about you," I began, voice vibrating low in my throat. "I've told you. I've always told you. Never kept nothin' from you, even when the only fuckin' thing you admitted to likin' about me was my cock, babe. And still, even gettin' that was like pullin' teeth. I've been claimin' you since the fuckin' beginning, and now you're gettin' pissy over some stupid interview I did when practically every motherfucker in Dogwood Beach knows I'm in love with you? What the fuck? Are you on your period or somethin'?"

She had to be. Getting on my case over nothing? This was bullshit.

Tori inhaled sharply through her nose. She straightened up. "No, I'm not on my period," she hissed.

"You about to get it?"

Her eyes narrowed. She didn't answer.

"Take that as a yes," I murmured.

"Okay." She shook her head, looking exacerbated. "You know

what? Maybe I could have seen your point, but now you're just being really rude."

"Get over it. You're bein' emotional over shit that means absolutely nothin'."

"It means something to me, you *dick*."

"Easy, Legs," I warned. "You wanna stand there and run your mouth at me, you better have a damn good reason for it, and right now, you don't."

"Oh, is that right?" Her brows shot up. "I don't have a damn good reason right now?"

"Nope."

"I was excited to read that interview. I couldn't *wait* to read it. And yes, I was hoping and maybe expecting you to mention something about us in there because I thought for sure you would, and you didn't. And it hurt my feelings. Okay? I was hurt, Jamie. And you don't seem to care at all. You're just being an asshole about it."

"You're hurt over somethin' stupid," I affirmed. "And I'm not bein' an asshole. I'm just givin' it to you straight."

She blinked, mouth falling open. "Wow. Thanks." She shook her head. "Thanks a lot. I'm glad how I feel matters to you." Sarcasm dripped from her tongue. Legs glared at me, lips curling in disgust but also trembling, like she was on the verge of either clawing my eyes out if I got any closer or bursting into tears.

Christ. She drove me fucking crazy.

"Blowin' up over nothin'. Puttin' somethin' this stupid between us. That's fucked up," I shared, needing to make sure Tori knew she was wrong. "I don't got nothin' to apologize for. I told you how it is."

"Yeah, you did. And you know what?"

"What?"

"*Fuck you*," she hissed.

"Fuck *me*?" My brows shot up. "Fuck *me*? What the fuck? Fuck you!" I roared.

"You should care about how I feel, and you don't!" she yelled. "You should care that I'm upset about this. So *fuck you*. For that *stupid* interview, and for not knowing this is a *damn good* reason. I'm going home." Tori turned on her heel and made for the door, leaving her shirts behind.

My jaw was clenched so tight it fucking ached. She was going home. I knew what that meant—*her* home. Not mine.

This was complete bullshit.

"Legs, swear to Christ, woman, if you don't get your ass back over here and get over this shit, I'm lettin' you leave. And babe..." I met her eyes when she craned her neck around to glare at me. "You walk out that door and I ain't followin' you."

Tori paused, hand flat on the glass, looking back at me with rage burning in her eyes. She wasn't wearing that hurt anymore. She was pissed. And I knew what that meant, too.

Hurt might've kept her here. But that anger was driving her out.

I watched Tori push through that door and walk. And I didn't follow. Said I wouldn't, and I didn't.

Chest heaving, teeth clenched, and muscles locking up, I dropped my arms and turned toward the counter, bracing my hands there. I looked from the stack of shirts piled next to the register to the open copy of *Rail*.

Then I stared. Until I couldn't fucking take it anymore.

"Fuck!" I roared, sweeping my arms across the counter and clearing it. Shirts. Her dad's hat. Even the fucking register. Everything went flying. I didn't give a shit.

She walked. *And I let her.*

Chapter Twenty-five

TORI

Groaning, I closed the kitchen cabinet and dropped my head on the door with a thump. I shut my eyes.

No. I wouldn't do it. I refused to eat another Pop-Tart for lunch. I had one for breakfast. Two, actually. That was all the pathetic I could handle for one day. I still had my limits.

Padding into the living room, I collapsed onto the couch and fell sideways, tucking my knees against my chest.

For showing purposes, my house was still fully furnished. Thank God. I had taken most of my personal items to Jamie's—clothes, bathroom items, some favorite things I didn't want to leave behind, such as my Christmas quilt. And when I left, I brought all of those things back with me.

It was as if I had never moved out.

Nine days. It had been nine days of no contact with Jamie. No calls. No texts. No middle-of-the-night lock picking.

I was a miserable mess.

I wanted to stay angry. And for the first three or four days, I did. I was pissed. I didn't want to see him. I didn't want to talk to him. I couldn't believe how heartless he had been. How cold and unapologetic. Not caring how I felt about that interview. Not giving a damn how hurt I was. That didn't matter to Jamie. He wasn't sorry. In his eyes, I was overreacting and getting emotional over something stupid.

He didn't get it. He didn't get what being claimed by him meant to me.

Everything. God, it meant *everything*.

I'm not crazy. I understood his point—Jamie didn't like getting personal in those interviews. He was there to talk about surfing. That was it.

I got that.

But I really thought he would at least mention something about us, *anything* about us, when prompted, and when I saw that he hadn't, I wasn't just surprised, I was hurt. Deep in my heart, I felt that.

You can't help how you react to things. And that was my reaction. I wasn't about to keep that from Jamie. He wanted all of my truths, and I wanted him to have them. I didn't want anything between us. So I shared.

I thought he would understand. I *wanted him* to understand. To talk to me about it and not make me feel stupid for reacting the way I did. But he couldn't do that.

In his eyes, I was wrong. That's all he was seeing. He became mean. Callous. He brushed off my reaction as if it meant nothing. And that hurt me more than anything.

But I didn't show him that. I stayed angry, and I held on to that anger for as long as I could.

I worked and I slept and I avoided. Even going as far as to take my house off the market so I could keep up with this plan. I refused to see Jamie, and being in the same house would make that a challenge. I couldn't be around him. I was too angry. I refused to talk about him. I refused to think about him. For days, I kept this up. But when you care about someone as much as I cared about him, when you loved someone the way I loved Jamie, whole heart, down-the-road kind of love, it was impossible to keep that pain out.

I started missing him. A little at first. Just for a second, and then in a single breath it became all I felt. At home and at night and at work. I missed him everywhere. I cried when he didn't come in to Whitecaps to claim a booth, and later into sheets that wrapped around me and smelled like summer. I ate takeout on my couch and gave up all use of my dining room table. I doodled Jamie's name while I listened for him, the sound of his bike or his key in the lock, and it killed me on days seven and eight and now when I still didn't hear it.

My heart wanted me to go to Jamie, but it needed him to come to me. And I was over wanting a sorry from him. I just wanted *him*. Jamie wouldn't need to say a word.

Just come here, my heart begged. *Hold me. We won't make it to day ten.*

A knock on the front door sounded.

I gasped, eyes widening in hope-filled panic as my heart lifted its tear-stricken face. *Jamie.*

I pushed up and quickly stood from the couch, crossing the room in a sprint. "Please please please please," I whisper begged, reaching the door with clammy hands and pulse racing. I twisted the knob and swung it open, mouth readying to greet Jamie with a "sorry" for both of us.

The word never left me.

"Oh." I blinked, jerking back at the sight of Brian standing on my porch. I shifted my weight on my feet, looking up at him.

He was tall, built like Jamie, but you wouldn't know he was a surfer just by looking at him. He didn't have the sun on his skin the way Jamie did. His hair was buzzed short, not falling into his eyes and damp from the ocean. He wasn't summer in November.

Brian was gorgeous all the same, though. Even right now, dark eyebrows drawn together, eyes heavy with something and jaw more chiseled than usual, meaning he was clenching it.

Crap. Was he angry at me?

"Hey. What's up?" I greeted him, keeping my voice unknowing just in case I was reading him wrong, which could've been the case. I hadn't known Brian all that long. I didn't know all of his tells. "Is Syd okay?"

Brian jerked his chin, indicating she was fine. "Got a sec?" he asked.

What in the heck was this?

"Uh...sure, yeah, of course." I stepped back and held the door open for him, letting go and backing into the living room as Brian entered the house.

My heart was back to pouting, head lowered as it kicked at the ground.

I really thought it was Jamie.

I pulled my shirt down so the hem touched the front of my thighs over my leggings. My fingers curled under the well-loved material and glued there. I didn't want to fidget, but I knew if I let go, I would.

This was weird. *Really* weird. Brian never came over without Syd.

"What's going on?" I asked him.

Arms crossed over his wide chest as he stood inside my entryway, Brian stared at me. His face was serious. His eyes were hard. His chest was heaving slowly as he kept staring and not speaking for another breath, then another . . .

"Brian, you're seriously freaking me out," I told him. "What is it?"

"You and Jamie," he began gruffly, and I felt my stomach drop out.

Oh, God . . .

I should've taken that box of Pop-Tarts upstairs, crawled into bed, and hibernated for the winter.

"The two of you, that ain't my business," he went on. "Don't want it to be my business. Don't ask about it. What you got going on, that's got nothing to do with me."

"Um, okay," I replied hesitantly.

I had no idea where this was going.

"That being said, Jamie's like my brother. If he gets with his girl and he's happy, I'm happy for him. If something happens with his girl and that shit starts affecting him unlike anything I've ever seen, causing him to slip up and stop performing at the level of talent that idiot was fucking born with, I'm gonna ask about it. I asked. That's why I'm here."

"Um." I squinted, hearing his words and tilting my head. "What do you mean, *causing him to slip up*?" I asked. "What are you talking about?"

"San Diego last weekend. Did you hear how he placed?"

I shook my head.

I knew Jamie had a competition in San Diego. I was wanting to go with him, but with my dad's health and the fact that he wasn't one hundred percent out of the woods yet, I felt that this wasn't the right time to leave the state. I wanted to be close.

"He didn't," Brian informed me. "Didn't even break top ten."

I felt my eyes go round. *Jamie didn't even break top ten?* What? That couldn't be right. He always broke top ten. He was number one. He couldn't be beat.

"Yeah," Brian mumbled, seeing my reaction. His brows lifted. "That's never happened before. Even when Jamie was first starting out, he always placed. His head isn't in it."

I stared at Brian as a knot formed in my stomach. I could feel myself getting upset. Was he trying to make me feel bad? Like *I* was to blame for Jamie not placing? Why was this all *my fault*?

"So you know what happened then," I said to verify.

"Yep."

"He told you everything."

Brian shrugged. "Pretty much."

"Did he tell you he's the one who acted like he didn't care?" My voice grew louder, hiding my pain. "That when I told Jamie how I felt about that interview, about him not mentioning anything about me or us, he made *me* feel stupid for feeling that way? I was hurt, Brian. I was hurt and he didn't give a damn about it. I may have walked out, but he hasn't done anything to try and fix this. He hasn't called. He hasn't come here."

"What have you been doing?" he asked.

My lips pressed tightly together. Brian cocked his head, eyes all-knowing.

Damn it.

"He didn't claim me," I argued. My face was hot. I could feel my flush creeping down my neck. "I was upset! I've *been* upset."

"What'd he tell you about those interviews?" Brian asked. "He say anything?"

"Yeah. He said he didn't answer personal questions. And maybe that's true, but—"

"Not maybe," Brian interrupted. His voice was somber. I watched him reach into his back pocket and produce folded-up pages that looked to be torn out of a magazine. He held them out for me to take. "Here."

Brow furrowed, I hesitated briefly, letting my hand hover in the air before reaching out and taking them. I unfolded the pages and pulled them apart. There were three. Different issues of the same magazine. *Rail.* These were Jamie's interviews.

"He never said anything different, Tori," Brian said as I found the question and word-for-word answer he was referring to. The same 'no comment' answer I read nine days ago. "Jamie does those interviews 'cause he knows it'll draw attention to Wax. It's not about him. Yeah, he talks about what surfing means to him, why he loves it, but if you read those articles, Jamie is always putting emphasis on the *sport*, not him. And he name-drops Wax every chance he gets. *That's* the kinda guy he is. He could be like everybody else and talk all kinds of shit about himself, brag, do it for the attention, but he doesn't. And those dickheads at *Rail* and every other magazine that's interviewed him, they tell him, flat out, the questions are gonna be geared toward surfing. They know not to ask him personal shit. He makes that clear before he even sits down. So when they go there, every fuckin' time he gives them the only answer he can give without telling them to fuck off. He's *never* said anything different. He never will."

I look up then, lips parting, my breaths coming out short and quick.

"It's not about you and him. Not in those interviews," Brian continued, holding my gaze. "Jamie's told *you* how he feels. That's what matters to him. *You* knowin'. Your friends, your family, the people you care about. All of us. *Christ*, we all sure as fuck know. His family. Mine. Everybody in his life, babe. He's never been quiet about it. And to the people that matter, he never fuckin' will be. You just gotta decide if that's enough for you."

A dull pain shot through my chest.

It *was* enough. I was never Jamie's secret. All of the people we cared about knew. Everyone in my life and in his. Jamie's family, he'd told them all about me. His sister and his brother. He claimed me to them before I was even allowing myself to admit I wanted this as much as he did. They mattered. And Brian and Syd, my family, *they* were who mattered and *God*, I was so, so stupid.

I blinked several times as tears filled my eyes.

"He knows you were hurtin', babe," Brian shared, keeping his voice gentle now. "He wasn't gettin' it at the time, but you women gotta give us a break. We can be pretty fuckin' stupid when it comes to you."

A laugh bubbled in my throat. I brought my fingers to my lips.

"You gotta know, this is killing him. He's hurtin', too. I probably wouldn't be stepping in if it wasn't for him not placing, but Jamie's always had my back. Always will. Never need to ask him to have it, he just does. He's a good man, Tori."

"I know that," I whispered, letting my hand skim my throat as my tears started to fall.

He was the best man. The *best*. And he was mine. I had him.

"I messed up, Brian," I whispered. "I . . . I shouldn't have left him. I shouldn't have blown up like that."

"Yeah, well . . ." Brian drew his arms across his chest again. "His ass shouldn't have let you leave. And he should've been comin' over here already, but he's stubborn as shit. Swear to God, he's fuckin' miserable, though. I can't take it."

I didn't want Jamie miserable. I couldn't even imagine it. He was always smiling. Whenever I saw him, he was sweet dimples and mischief behind the smuggest, most perfect grin I'd ever seen.

And I was woman enough to admit when enough was enough. We were both at fault in this. I didn't need him to come to me. He always came to me. Maybe it was my turn . . .

"Is he home right now? Or is he at the shop?" My voice raced with a nervous energy. I pressed the torn pages against my chest and stepped closer, nearly begging, "Do you know where is?"

Brian's mouth lifted in the corner after hearing me, which I thought was a little strange but I didn't have a chance to tell him that.

"It's Sunday. Where do you think he is?" Brian asked, shoulders lifting casually. Then the other half of his mouth curled up and he gave me that before turning around and stepping outside. The door shut behind him.

I blinked, sniffled, and wiped at my face.

It was Sunday. Sunday was family dinner. I knew that. And Jamie never missed one of those, not unless he was away and Brian would have told me if he was.

My stomach tensed and warmed all over. My skin tingled. I was so close to making this right. To getting my guy back. I couldn't help it, I smiled. My first smile in nine days.

I knew it. We weren't going to make it to ten.

Realizing where I was headed, I folded those torn pages back up, set them on the table Jamie had replaced for me, and immediately got to work in the kitchen.

Never in my life would I ever show up to family dinner without a dish.

* * *

Using my elbow since my hands were full, I rang the doorbell at Brian and Syd's place and stood on the porch, waiting. The November air cooled my cheeks.

I needed that. I was nervous. Freaking out, if I was being honest. My smile was long gone. I had no idea how Jamie was going to receive me. But that didn't mean I hadn't done everything in my power to appear ready for this.

I was completely dolled up, wearing full makeup, my hair curled more than usual and styled in a twist so it was half pulled back, and one of my cutest outfits—an oversized cable knit sweater, leggings, which weren't cute but I knew how Jamie felt about them, and my brown knee-high boots that had a substantial heel.

I never dressed this fancy coming over here. It was Sunday dinner. We were all just hanging out. I'd even wear my uniform sometimes if I was coming straight from work.

But it had been nine days. *Nine. Days.*

Nine days called for fancy.

I had parked behind Jamie's Jeep, so I knew he was here, and being this close to him, this close to possibly fixing things and making things right, was causing my stomach to flip-flop and my heart to batter and the pulse point in my throat to pound.

I was fine back at the house getting ready and on the drive over here, but now, all of a sudden, standing on this porch, I was terrified. What if I couldn't fix this? What if it was too late? It had been nine days. Nine days of me not going to him. What if Jamie didn't want to hear me out now? Brian said he was miserable, but what if he was angry, too?

The door swung open just as panic soaked into my bones and settled.

Syd filled the doorway. She tilted her head with a soft smile and reached out her hand.

"Hey, sweetie. Come on in. You're just in time," She pulled me inside the house and reached around me to close the door. I looked around.

We were the only ones in the living room. Voices were coming from the kitchen. I assumed dinner had either started already or was just about to start.

Stepping closer, her fingers wrapped around my elbow. "He's going to be so happy to see you," Syd leaned in to say.

I felt my stomach clench as a lump formed in my throat. "I don't know," I whispered my worry, looking into my best girl's eyes as I felt that panic sink deeper and deeper until it folded in around my heart and saturated it. "What if he doesn't want to talk to me? What if it's too late?"

She gave my elbow a squeeze. Her eyes were gentle.

"It won't be. He loves you," she stated. "He's loved you forever."

Instantly, in that second, I broke down. My head fell forward and I began quietly sobbing, mindful of the pie in my hands.

It had been nearly a year, not forever, and I knew Jamie hadn't loved me for the whole thing, but hearing forever got me thinking about how long I'd fought him. How much time I'd wasted and how much of it I'd ruined and those nine stupid days.

Our love felt like a forever's worth. A lifetime.

And I couldn't stop overreacting and messing things up.

"Shh, Tori, it's okay," Syd tried to sooth me, moving her hand to my back and rubbing there. "That pie looks really good. Is it strawberry rhubarb?"

I nodded as my shoulders quaked, keeping my head down and my eyes shut. "I think Jamie really likes it," I whimpered. "He ate a lot of it before."

"Yeah? I think he does, too," she replied, a smile in her voice. "Right, Jamie? You like strawberry rhubarb, don't you?"

A sob caught in my throat. I trapped it there along with my breath, then I peeked my eyes open and slowly lifted my head to see everyone standing in the living room now, everyone except Shay, who had to work tonight. Our typical Sunday night crowd was here. They'd heard me and walked in from the kitchen.

Brian and Jenna and her adorable twins, Oliver and Olivia. Kali and Cole, who was holding her son, Cameron, and looking really comfortable doing that, which I wanted to ask about but couldn't think on at the moment. And Jamie. He was standing in front of me with his too-long hair and bright blue eyes and more shadow on his face than usual. He hadn't shaved in days. Maybe nine. I wasn't sure. And he was wearing dark layered Henley thermals and faded jeans, just like the first day I saw him.

They were all looking at me with concern and curiosity, all except Jamie, who held questions in his eyes and that anger I feared, it was there. I could see it. And I was standing in front of him sobbing with a pie in my hand and half of my makeup running down my face.

"Right. Let's eat before the lasagna gets cold," Brian suggested, his deep voice giving off a tone that said this wasn't a suggestion. It needed to happen.

"Momma, why is Ms. Tori crying?" Olivia asked her mother.

"Liv, now. Let's go," Brian insisted.

"She almost dropped her pie. Wouldn't that have been terrible?" Syd threw out as an answer, walking toward the group and leaving me where I stood.

Olivia's eyes bugged out. She nodded quickly while everyone else wore faces saying they knew that wasn't the reason. Everyone except

Oliver, who had his eyes on the game in his hands, and Cameron, who was too little to pick up on that kind of stuff.

"Come on. Uncle Brian is right. Let's get started." Syd held her arms out as if she was trying to herd the group. "Nobody likes re-heated lasagna."

Everyone except Jamie filed out of the room and into the kitchen. He didn't move.

Hands in his front pockets, he stood there staring at me, and I thought I saw that anger and coldness slipping away and melting to something warmer, something that said he understood why I was here and what I was feeling, but then he turned and left the room, disappearing into the kitchen with everyone else.

My lips parted on a gasp. I felt more tears build behind my lashes.

He left me. Walked right out of the room. He *left me*.

Jamie wasn't staying around to hear me out. He didn't want to. It was too late, and that could've made me angry or upset me further, but I understood it.

I walked out first. Now it was his turn.

And right then, feeling that realization hit me, I could've left. I could've given up. Cried at home in the shirt of his I stole. I was close to doing that.

But then my feet were carrying me into the kitchen and I was coming to a stop at the island, scanning the faces at the table and looking for Jamie's, then not finding it.

"Where," I started to question, but movement caught my eye and I turned my head just as Jamie came walking around the fridge.

He halted seeing me.

I carefully set my late nana's pie plate down on the counter, quickly wiped at my mess of a face, then after doing that, stuck my hand on my hip and flattened the other on the marble.

"I love you," I began, watching Jamie's brows lift and hearing the soft, emotional gasps of Syd and most likely Jenna and Kali, but knowing for sure Syd was giving one without even looking to ver-ify. "I know you're always having to ask me, and half the time I'm denying it because that's our thing, but you don't love me any more

than I love you. I love you just as much, Jamie. Whole heart. Forever. Deep in my soft. It's there. I love you. And it terrifies me."

Jamie's brows relaxed. He took a step closer.

I held my hand up, stopping him.

"I've been scared since I first saw you, because I was *seeing you*, you
know?" I lowered my hand to my side and watched his jaw twitch.
"I thought I knew the kind of guy you were when you laughed at
my relationship with Wes. I had you pegged. I didn't want anything
to do with you because I *thought* you were that guy, Jamie. But then
you would do things like slash those tires or be good to my girl or
make promises to me and keep them, and then I was scared because
I didn't know *what* guy you were. I didn't know if I could believe
what you would say to me or how you would make me feel. I didn't
want to be stupid. I didn't want to fall for this guy who acted like
I meant something to him and who would say things to me that I
would think about for hours after he left. I didn't want you to hurt
me. I was scared. That's why I fought it. Then I stopped fighting it. I
stopped because I knew who you were. My heart knew exactly which
guy you were. It still knows and *that...*" I shook my head, laughing
a little. "That scares me the most. Not because I worry you might
hurt me but because I know I will never get over it. Not after nine
days. Not after forever. I will never get over you."

Jamie inhaled a breath through his nose. His nostrils flared. Then
he took another step toward me.

"Hold on. I want to get this out," I said quietly, lifting my hand
again. "Please. I know you don't want to hear me right now. I know
you're mad at me and maybe I don't even deserve to be heard and
that's why you left me in there, but I—"

"Went to grab you some tissues," Jamie interrupted.

I blinked. My mouth snapped close and I looked down at the hand
at Jamie's side. White tissue was peeking out of his fist.

The powder room. He'd been coming from the powder room.

"What?" I questioned, looking into his eyes. "Why?"

"Got shit all over your face, babe," Jamie informed me. "Black on
your cheeks. Figured I'd help you out. I was coming back out there
but you followed."

"Can we watch the language, please?" Jenna asked.

"Shh," someone said in response, sounding like Syd again since this was something I knew she was heavily invested in, but it was a *shh* so I couldn't be sure.

"You were gonna hear me out?" I asked Jamie, ignoring everyone else.

"Yeah."

"You aren't mad at me?"

"Nope."

"But..." I tilted my head. I didn't understand. "Why?"

"*Why?*" His brows lifted.

"Yeah. Why? I walked out. I cussed at you and I left. Why aren't you angry with me?"

"Nine days, Legs. Straight up, I've been in hell," Jamie shared. "You show up here lookin' like that, all done up for me and holding a pie you didn't need to make considerin' Jenna supplied dessert this time, meanin' you made that pie for me and no one else, you do all that, I'm gonna hear you out, babe. Not just 'cause you're workin' for it, but also 'cause I messed up. Honest? This should've been me. I'm the one who should've been comin' to you. I never should've let you walk out. And I never, hear me, babe, I *never* should've made you think that what you were feelin' meant nothin'. Didn't realize that's what I was doin' at the time, but I get that now. Those nine days are on me."

I inhaled sharply through my nose. It tingled.

"I overreacted," I said firmly, needing him to know this.

"You reacted, Legs. Felt somethin' and you shared it." Jamie argued. "And I'm guessin' you understand now where I was coming from, but I should've answered that question. It's you, babe. Never had nothin' like this. Never had nothin' even close. And never will again. I know that. I should've claimed you so the whole fuckin' world knows you're mine. That's on me."

"*Jamie,*" Jenna hissed as Olivia and Oliver giggled at the profanity.

I felt the tears brimming again. He wanted to do that, I saw it in his eyes, and even though I loved Jamie for it, he didn't need to. I knew that now.

"I don't need you to do that, Jamie," I said. "This is what matters to me. You doing this here, in this room. And at the hospital in front of my parents. And to your sister outside a bar. That's what matters. I never should've walked out. I never should've screamed at you the way I did. I should have known what mattered and I didn't. I ruined this. I ruined everything."

"You're here, babe. I'm over it," he returned. The corner of his perfect mouth lifting.

It *was* perfect. *He* was perfect. And mine. Maybe...

Was he?

I shook my head, falling apart. "I messed up," I cried, wiping at my face. "And I know I'm going to mess up again. And you're going to get sick of it and get over me and I'm never gonna get over you. I won't. And then I'll turn into some stalker you can't get rid of. You're going to have to get a restraining order. And honestly, I'm not even sure that'll keep me away. I'll be showing up at Wax all the time and your house. I know I will."

I heard muffled laughter coming from the table. My head snapped in that direction and my tear-filled eyes narrowed.

"I'm serious!" I exclaimed, looking between their smiling faces, mainly the girls. Cole and Brian seemed to be focused on their food and unconcerned with the drama. "I have no problem admitting right now how psycho I'm gonna be. I love him!" I shared.

"We don't doubt that, sweetie," Syd replied, looking on the verge of laughter again.

"Legs," Jamie called, drawing my head back around. He smiled when he got me. "You wanna stalk my entire life, you go right ahead, babe. I'd welcome it. But just know, you show up at my place and I ain't there, I'm most likely staking out your place if I ain't already inside it."

My eyes flickered wider as more muted laughter came from the table. I ignored them this time.

"You're mine. And I'm yours, Jamie. And I promise, I am never getting over you," I shared again, speaking louder and clearer, needing this to stick over everything else, especially the stalking stuff.

Jamie's mouth relaxed. His eyes turned soft.

"Are you ever getting over me?" I asked him.

He grinned big. "Not a fuckin' chance."

"For God's sakes," Jenna scolded, just as more little giggles erupted from Oliver and Olivia. "No repeating that. I mean it," she added, speaking to her children, I was sure.

"I'm comin' to you," Jamie warned. "Done waitin'. You hold up your hand, I'm ignorin' it."

I smiled through my tears. No way was I holding up my hand. Not a chance.

"You ready, girl?" he asked.

"I'm ready."

Then he came to me, getting halfway before I closed the distance by leaping into the air and into his arms.

I would always give back. I was with Jamie. Now and always. We were in this together.

"I never had nothing like this either. Only you," I said against Jamie's ear as Syd, Kali, Jenna, and Olivia clapped and cheered us on while the guys focused on eating.

Jamie's arms tightened around me. I felt his head turn and his breath against my cheek.

"Packin' your shit *today*, babe. Soon as we're done eatin'," Jamie said.

"'Kay," I replied.

"Lowerin' your askin' price, too," he added. "Want that house sellin' so you can't leave me again."

I never planned on leaving Jamie again so I liked the sound of that.

"We'll call your dad tomorrow," I suggested.

"Call him tonight. Again, soon as we're done eatin'," he countered.

I buried my face in his neck and grinned. "'Kay, Jamie. We'll call him tonight."

"Good." His arms gave me another squeeze. "Love you, babe. You got no fuckin' clue how much."

I did. I had an idea. "I love you, too," I replied.

"Yeah," he murmured, breathing deep as his arms kept their hold.

And I knew that *yeah*. I knew that meant Jamie was feeling my love for him.

But I also knew it was his way of telling me he knew I did. In his heart. In his soul. Forever. Jamie knew I loved him even when I couldn't say it. And even when I wouldn't.

That was our game.

Epilogue

JAMIE

Six months later

"Legs, you got five seconds," I warned, calling out over the sounds of the waves and the seagulls above and the air whipping around me. "You don't get in, I'm puttin' you in. Let's go."

Tori quit pacing in the sand, turned to face me where I was wading waist deep in the water, and brought her hands to her hips. "I said I'd do it," she snapped, her hair blowing back behind her. "Just give me a minute! Jeez!"

"Gave you ten, babe," I reminded. "Probably closer to fifteen now."

"This is a big deal, Jamie. You know how I feel about this."

I did. I knew how Tori felt about the ocean, but I also knew she was ready.

Conquered the pool four months ago when I started taking her to the gym with me. She was a strong swimmer now. Confident. Relaxed in the water. There was no reason why she couldn't handle this.

I held my arms out, promising, "Right here. Not gonna let anything happen to you."

Tori blinked. I watched her chest rise and fall with a breath, then she dropped her arms and started nervously pacing along the shoreline again.

Jesus.

"Babe, straight up, if I gotta come get you, you ain't gettin' this ring," I threatened.

Tori stopped pacing. Her head turned and her eyes locked with mine. "What ring?" she asked.

"The ring I got in my pocket."

She stared at me for a breath. "You do not have a ring in your pocket," she stated with some attitude, sounding sure of herself, as if she took that moment to inspect my pockets.

"Sure as fuck do."

"What kind of ring?"

"One you're gonna want," I said, smiling when her eyes widened.

Tori turned to fully face me again. Her widened eyes narrowed. "I don't believe you," she shared. "You're just trying to trick me."

"You remember a few weeks ago when I said I had to meet up with your dad to talk promotional shit?"

Tori didn't say anything. She just blinked.

"We didn't talk promotional shit," I admitted. "Spoke to him. I let him know what I was wanting to do, then met up with your mom and Syd. Had an idea for a ring but wanted their opinions."

Tori still didn't say anything. She just blinked.

"Size five, right?" I asked, brow lifting.

That got her.

"Are you being serious right now?" she shrieked. "You met up with my dad and asked him if you could *marry me*?"

"Said you wanted traditional, babe. I went traditional." I smiled at her.

"You have a ring in your pocket?"

"Yeah."

"An engagement ring?"

"Jesus, *yeah*," I said. "That's if I still have it. Might be gone by now. Been waitin' a fuckin' year for you to get your ass out here."

I knew I still had it. I was just messing with her.

But Tori didn't know I was messing with her, and it was either the realization that I was being serious—I had a ring—or it was the threat that I might not have it much longer that got her moving.

Sprinting like something was chasing her, Tori entered the water

while squealing in either fear or delight, probably both, lifting her knees high to get herself up over the waves. She looked like one of those Olympic hurdlers, except her tits looked fucking awesome and I never wanted to bang an Olympic hurdler.

"If you're lying, I am never giving you road head again," Tori threatened, reaching me and taking hold of my shoulders.

"Regular head is still on the table? I'm good with that." I grinned big, gripping hold of her waist under the water. "Hey, babe."

"Hey," she giggled, smiling up at me. "God, my heart is going crazy." She panted several breaths and licked the salt water off her lips.

"Yeah," I murmured, thinking the same as I watched her. I kept one hand on her hip and used my other to dig the ring out of the Velcroed pocket on my board shorts. "You scared?"

I was talking about this, what I was about to do, and I was referring to her being out here. And Tori knew that.

"Not a bit," she answered, tipping her chin up.

"You look good out here," I said.

"Thanks."

"'Bout to look even better."

I heard Tori inhale a shaky breath. She was still smiling, though. Not nervous. My woman was ready.

"Can't really kneel out here," I informed her, reaching up and grabbing hold of her left wrist, then bringing her hand between us. "You want that, I'll take you in. Whatever you want."

"No. Here is perfect," she said, grinning so big now, you'd think I already asked the question. "Please, do it here. It's so you."

I looked down at her, at all of that beauty she was about to hand over to me for life. Trusting me with it. Forever. She was giving it. No layers. No lies. Just her.

Tori Rivera.

She was mine. Out here in my world and in hers, she was mine.

Then I did it right there.